Between Friends

Also by Debbie Macomber in Large Print:

One Night
For All My Tomorrows
A Season of Angels
Shadow Chasing
The Playboy and the Widow
16 Lighthouse Road
Fallen Angel

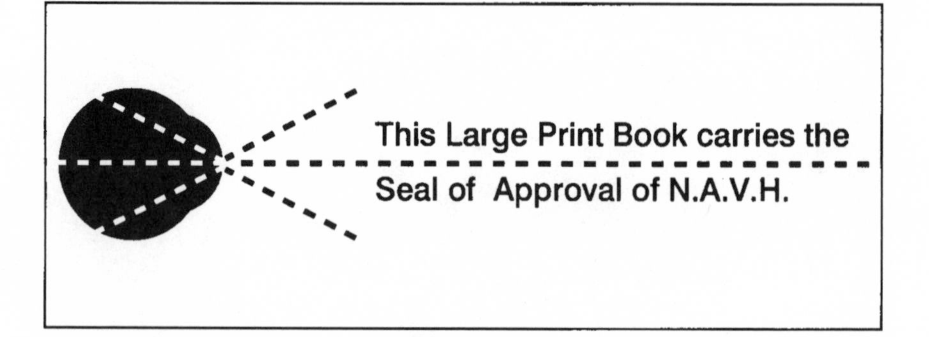

Between Friends

Debbie Macomber

All characters in this book have no existence outside the imagination of the author and have no relation whatsoever to anyone bearing the same name or names. They are not even distantly inspired by any individual known or unknown to the author, and all incidents are pure invention.

Published in 2003 by arrangement with Harlequin Books, S.A.

Wheeler Large Print Hardcover Series.

The text of this Large Print edition is unabridged.
Other aspects of the book may vary from the original edition.

Set in 16 pt. Plantin by Al Chase.

Printed in the United States on permanent paper.

Library of Congress Cataloging-in-Publication Data

Macomber, Debbie.
Between friends / Debbie Macomber.
p. cm.
ISBN 1-58724-363-6 (lg. print : hc : alk. paper)
1. Female friendship — Fiction. 2. Married women — Fiction.
3. Women lawyers — Fiction. 4. New York (N.Y.) — Fiction.
5. Washington (State) — Fiction. 6. Large type books. I. Title.
PS3563.A2364 B48 2003
813′.54—dc21
2002190760

For all the wonderful women who have graced
my life with their wisdom.

My mother — Connie Adler
My aunts — Betty Stierwalt,
Gerty Urlacher, Paula Malafouris,
Betty Zimmerman and Lois Munson
My mother-in-law — Marie Macomber

Dear Friends,

It's become tradition for me to write a letter to my readers with each book. Generally I explain where the story idea came from and add a few pertinent details. I'm not going to do that with *Between Friends.*

This story is unlike anything else I've written. The format is unique. I think the characters are perhaps the strongest and most compelling of my twenty-year writing career — and I hope you'll agree. Lesley and Jillian have been best friends their entire lives. They learn from each other, support and encourage each other. They're the best friend you had in high school and have never forgotten. They're baby boomers, like many of us — like every woman who grew up in the '50s and '60s. If that wasn't when *you* grew up, perhaps your mother did or an older sister or a friend. Whether Lesley and Jillian reflect your own experience or that of someone close to you, I think their lives and times will have meaning for you . . . as they do for me.

No project has touched me the way *Between Friends* has. You'll understand why I say that when you meet Lesley and Jillian. And so, my friends, laugh, cry . . . remember.

Debbie Macomber

P.S. I enjoy hearing from my readers. Feel free to write me at P.O. Box 1458, Port Orchard, WA 98366, or visit my Web site at www.debbiemacomber.com.

1948

Judge and Mrs. Leonard Lawton

2330 Country Club Lane

Pine Ridge, Washington

Joyfully announce the long-awaited

Birth of their daughter

Jillian Lynn Lawton

On

January 15, 1948

6 lbs, 3 oz.

19"

Pine Ridge Herald

BORN SEPTEMBER 1, 1948

Adams, Mr. & Mrs. Charles,
112 Folsom Avenue, boy
Adamski, Mr. & Mrs. Michael,
220 Railroad Avenue, girl
Burns, Mr. & Mrs. Harold,
456 North 3rd Street, boy
Franklin, Mr. & Mrs. Oscar,
33 Main Street, boy
Johnson, Mr. & Mrs. Gary,
743 Weeping Willow Lane, girl
Lamb, Mr. & Mrs. Dolphus,
809 South 8th Avenue, boy

❖

September 10, 1948

220 Railroad Avenue
Pine Ridge, Washington

Dearest Momma,

I thought you should know Mike and I had a baby girl on September first. I realize Daddy said I wasn't to contact either of you ever again, but I felt you'd want to know you had a granddaughter.

We named her Lesley Louise and she weighed 8 pounds. Lesley because it seems like such a pretty name and Louise after you, Momma.

Mike wasn't home to take me to the hospital, so Gertie Burkhart, who lives next door, drove me. My labor took almost twenty hours. I thought I was going to die, but all that pain was worth it the first time I got to hold my daughter. She's a beautiful baby, Momma. She has your nose and Mike's forehead, with soft wisps of blond hair. I think her eyes are going to be blue, but the nurse told me we won't be able to tell until Lesley is six weeks old.

I wonder what the future holds for my baby girl. Will she grow up to be smart and pretty? Will she have a chance to finish high school? Dare I dream that one day she'll go to college the way I always hoped I would? Mike says asking questions like that is a waste of time. Still, I can't help wondering if those were the same questions you had when I was born, Momma. Did you love me as much as I love my baby? I'm sure you did and I can't believe you no longer love me now.

Mike and I are doing all right. We live in Washington State — it seems so far away from Mississippi. We're renting a two-storey house and Mike's uncle got him a job at the lumber mill. He's working lots of hours and I've been putting a little bit aside every week for when the mill shuts down, which it seems to do on a regular basis. Unfortunately, Mike was so excited the night Lesley was born that he got drunk and was arrested. I had to use the money I'd saved to bail him out of jail.

I miss you, Momma. I'm not any of those ugly

names Daddy called me.

If I don't hear from you, then I'll accept that you agree with Daddy and want nothing more to do with me. When I look at my baby, I don't think of the circumstances that led to her birth. What Mike and I did was a sin, but we're married now.

Lesley is a beautiful child, created in the image of God. That's what Father Gilbert said a child is, and I believe him. I hope you'll love her despite everything.

Your daughter,
Dorothy

Mrs. Leonard Lawton
2330 Country Club Lane
Pine Ridge, Washington

October 12, 1948

Dearest Aunt Jill,

I regret taking so long to answer your letter. After waiting fifteen very long years for a child, one would assume I'd be better prepared for the demands of motherhood. I had no idea an infant would take up so much of my time and energy. I'm months behind on my correspondence and can only beg your indulgence.

Jillian is truly our joy. As you know, Leonard and I had given up hope of ever having a child. We're both convinced her birth is a miracle and we are so very grateful. I know how pleased you are that we named her after you, but you've been a mother to Leonard since his own dear mother's death. Without you, he wouldn't have any memories of her.

Leonard is thrilled with his daughter. Every night he rushes home from court in order to spend time with her. She's already standing on her own and it looks as if she'll be walking soon. I'm afraid Leonard must bore everyone at the courthouse with photographs of Jillian. In his eyes she's the most brilliant precious child ever to appear in this world. She has deep blue eyes and dark brown hair and a cheerful, happy disposition. She loves listening to the radio; her favorite show is *Kukla, Fran and Ollie*. Leonard claims it's really my favorite show, and Jillian gives me the perfect excuse to listen. One show she doesn't like — I think it scares her — is *The Lone Ranger*. Every time she hears the music she buries her head in my skirt.

Thank you for recommending Eleanor Roosevelt's book *This I Remember*. I've ordered it from the library, but my reading has been severely curtailed since Jillian's arrival. I've been making an effort to read during her afternoon nap, but the problem is, I usually fall asleep myself. With her teething, I haven't slept an entire night in weeks. The poor child is having a difficult time of it, but the pediatrician assured us everything is normal.

Leonard and I are delighted that you've accepted our invitation to spend the Christmas holidays with us. Jillian will surely be walking by then — and sleeping through the nights!

I'll write again soon. Give our love to Uncle Frank and everyone.

Yours truly,

Leonard, Barbara and Jillian

1955

Mrs. Leonard Lawton
2330 Country Club Lane
Pine Ridge, Washington

January 4, 1955

Dear Sister John,

Enclosed please find the invitations to Jillian's seventh birthday party. Would you kindly distribute them to all the children in both first-grade classes? My husband has hired puppeteers to perform at the party and there will be cake and ice cream for everyone. I would consider it a big help if you could let us know how many children we should expect.

Thank you in advance for your assistance in this matter.

Sincerely,
Mrs. Leonard Lawton

Pine Ridge Mills
Pine Ridge, Washington
Lay off Notice
Effective January 7, 1955
Attn: Mike Adamski

January 10, 1955

220 Railroad Avenue
Pine Ridge, Washington

Dear Judge Lawton, Mrs. Lawton and Jillian,

Thank you very much for the invitation to Jillian's birthday party. Unfortunately we already have plans for next Saturday, and Lesley will be unable to attend.

Lesley so enjoyed the afternoon she spent with Jillian following their tap dancing class. We'll have Jillian over to visit soon.

I've had to withdraw Lesley from dance class, but we're hoping she'll be able to start back soon. Jillian's been teaching her the new steps at recess so she won't be too far behind. These two have certainly formed a fast friendship, haven't they? I'm grateful Lesley has such a good friend.

I'm sure Jillian will have a wonderful birthday. I'll get in touch with you about having Jillian visit for an afternoon.

Sincerely,
Mrs. Michael Adamski

KAKE RADIO dedicates "The *Ballad of Davey Crockett*" to birthday girl Jillian Lawton. Happy seventh birthday, Jillian, from all your friends here at KAKE RADIO.
Now everyone put on your Coonskin Cap and sing Happy Birthday for seven-year-old Jillian.

❖

Pine Ridge Library
300 Main Street
Pine Ridge, Washington

October 1, 1955

Dear Mrs. Adamski,

At your request the library is holding *Marjorie Morningstar* by Herman Wouk and *Auntie Mame* by Patrick Dennis until the end of the week.

Sincerely,
Mrs. Joan McMahon
Head Librarian

September 28, 1955

Dear Grandma and Grandpa O'Leary,

Thank you for the Betsy McCall doll. I named her Jilly after my best friend in school. I can read now.

Love,

Lesley

❖

November 14, 1955

220 Railroad Avenue
Pine Ridge, Washington

Dearest Momma and Daddy,

Lesley loves her birthday gift! She's wanted a Betsy McCall doll for months. She wrote the thank-you note herself, but then you could probably tell that. She's a smart little girl and can already sound out words. I take her to the library often and she loves books as much as I do. Even when she was two and three years old, she insisted I read her a story before she'd settle down for her nap. Now she's almost reading on her own!

Susan is eager to read, too. She starts kindergarten next year and follows her big sister everywhere. Mikey and Joe are growing big and strong like their daddy.

Mike was laid off for three months, but he's

back working at the mill again. We managed all right. I didn't tell him about the money you sent, Momma, so please don't mention it. I bought groceries and a few chickens to raise for the eggs. I bake all our bread myself, just the way you always did, Momma, but my baking powder biscuits just aren't as fluffy as yours. Luckily Mike never tasted your chicken and dumplings because mine just don't compare. I wish I'd paid more attention when you were cooking.

Momma, I should have told you sooner, but I was afraid you'd be upset with our news. I'm pregnant again and due to deliver any time now. I thought Mike and I had a complete family. Four children in six years have worn me out, but God had other plans.

If we have a baby girl, we're going to call her Lily. I don't have a boy's name picked out yet. Mike said he didn't care what I named the baby. Since Mike, Jr. was born, he told me I could call the babies anything I wish. I know Daddy was pleased when I named our Joe after him.

You asked about Mike's drinking. He does like his beer, but he doesn't get drunk as often since he returned to work. Don't worry, Momma, we're all fine.

Your daughter,
Dorothy

1959

Pine Ridge Herald
May 2, 1959
Lesley Adamski
Wins Fifth Grade
Spelling Bee

Lesley Adamski took top prize at the tenth Annual Spelling Bee sponsored by the Women's Auxiliary of the Veterans of Foreign Wars. She successfully spelled the word serum, besting runner-up Jillian Lawton, daughter of Judge and Mrs. Leonard Lawton.

As the first-place winner, Lesley Adamski was awarded a Fifty Dollar U.S. Savings Bond. Jillian Lawton received a Twenty-Five Dollar U.S. Savings Bond.

The money raised by the Annual Spelling Bee has been donated to the March of Dimes for polio research.

Six fifth-grade classes competed in the Annual Spelling Bee from schools all across the county.

May 3, 1959

I won! Jillian and I practiced and practiced, and I was sure she'd win, but I did. Jillian was happy for me. I would've been happy if she won, too. My mom took the $50.00 savings bond and put it in a safe place. Mom and Susan, Mikey, Joe and baby Lily were at the spelling bee to see me win. Dad was with his friends, but that's all right. Afterward, Mom said she was proud of me and took us all to the Dairy Queen for hot fudge sundaes. She invited the Lawtons, and Judge Lawton insisted on paying for all the ice cream we could eat. I'm so excited I can't sleep.

Mrs. Leonard Lawton
2330 Country Club Lane
Pine Ridge, Washington

June 23, 1959

Dearest Aunt Jillian and Uncle Frank,

Leonard and I are overwhelmed by your generosity to Jillian. We received the paperwork regarding the $25,000 trust fund you've set up for her college education, and it took our breath away. We don't know what to say other than to thank you both from the bottom of our hearts.

I'm so sorry to hear you won't be able to join us in Hawaii this August. Uncle Frank, take good care of yourself!

We love you both, and although Jillian is too young to fully comprehend the significance of this trust fund, Leonard and I certainly do.

All our love,
Leonard, Barbara and Jillian

Jillian Lawton/English J. M. J.

September 7, 1959

HOW I SPENT MY SUMMER VACATION

School let out on Memorial Day and Lesley Adamski and I spent three whole days together while her mother was in the hospital having her baby brother, Bruce. We got to go to the Country Club with my dad and he let us carry his golf clubs for him. After that we went swimming and got a sunburn. The best day of the summer was when Lesley and I were at the pool at the Country Club.

Then in August my parents and I flew to Hawaii. This is the third time I've been to Hawaii. I didn't get airsick on the plane. The stewardess let me hand out gum to the passengers before we took off and said I did a good job.

We were in Hawaii on August 21st when it became the fiftieth state. My father wanted to buy property, but he says no one can afford $1.25 a foot for beachfront.

I like Hawaii, but I like Pine Ridge better. Pine Ridge is home and that's where my best friend lives. I feel sorry for all the Cuban refugees who are coming to America, having to leave their homes behind. I hope they'll be able to return to their homeland soon. There really isn't anyplace better than home. That's what I learned this summer.

St. Mary Parochial School
1521 North Third Street
Pine Ridge, Washington

November 2, 1959

Dear Mr. and Mrs. Michael Adamski,

I regret to inform you that your tuition payment for Lesley, Susan and Mike is now three months past due. We trust that you will take care of this matter at your earliest convenience.

Sincerely,
Sister Philippa
Bookkeeper

Jillian's Diary

October 23, 1959

Lesley spent the night and we watched Rowdy Yates in *Rawhide* – he's so handsome!!!!! Then we watched *The Twilight Zone* and hid our eyes at the scary parts. Lesley's family hasn't bought a television yet and she said she doesn't mind, but I think she does. After Mom and Dad made us turn off the light, we lay on my bed and talked and listened to the radio. I called in and requested Bobby Darin's "Mack the Knife" and later Lesley got through and asked for Paul Anka's "Put Your Head on My Shoulder." I wanted to ask for "Kookie,

Kookie, Lend Me Your Comb," but the disc jockey said I could only request one song at a time. I think Edd Byrnes is cute. Lesley does, too.

Lesley Adamski is my best friend for life.

1962

Jillian's Diary

January 1, 1962

This is my first entry in the new diary Mom and Dad got me for Christmas. My name's engraved on the front. They got Lesley one, too, with her name engraved on it. We both plan to write in them every night all year.

My day started off bad. Mom and I had a fight about the bomb shelter. It's all finished now and takes up half the basement. Dad had it built in case of an atomic bomb. It's ugly, with bare concrete walls and shelves filled with canned food and emergency supplies. I told Mom that if Russia dropped a bomb on us I'd rather die with the rest of my friends. Mom said Dad built it because of me and I should be grateful. She also said she won't have me talk about dying when there's a perfectly safe place for us in our own home.

I went to my room and closed the door. Well, actually I slammed it. I used to be able to talk to my mom about anything. I still can with my dad. He's older than a lot of my friends' dads, but he understands what it's like to be almost fourteen. Sometimes on Saturday mornings he takes me to breakfast and I sit with all his attorney friends. Dad includes me in the conversation and that makes me feel important. We talk about me going to law school one day, and I think I will. I like listening to my dad and I'm proud that he's a judge. People respect him and like him. I bet there isn't anything he doesn't know about the law.

Lesley phoned in the afternoon and I told her about Mr. Hanson kissing me at midnight. (I know him from breakfast on Saturdays with my dad.) It wasn't a real kiss, but it was close. He kissed my cheek and told me I was going to grow up to be a beauty. I hope he's right. I don't feel beautiful with a mouthful of metal braces.

The New Year's party was really cool except Mom kept insisting everyone go downstairs to take a peek at the bomb shelter. She thinks Dad was prudent by having it built. She insists he was the one who wanted it, but I know Mom put the idea in his head. She mentioned it first and then found the plans and talked to the contractor. The concrete was poured while we were in Hawaii this summer.

I had a good time at the party, and I'm glad Mom and Dad finally realized that I'm old enough to participate. I'm not a child, although Mom treats me like one. Jerry Lee Lewis married his cousin and she's younger than I am!

Lesley told me about her New Year's Eve. We

talked for half an hour, but she's on a party line and we kept getting interrupted. She spent New Year's Eve baby-sitting for the Randalls. She said it was the easiest $3.00 she ever earned.

Lesley hasn't been kissed for real, either. I don't understand why because she's super pretty and smart, too. She's pretty enough to be a high school cheerleader if she wanted. I told her she should try out next year but she can't because her mother needs her to help at home. She has five brothers and sisters now. I wish Lesley was my sister. Her mother hasn't been feeling very well since Bruce was born and her father doesn't always have a job. But Lesley never complains. In all the years we've been best friends, I've only stayed the night at her house once and then we camped outside. I don't mind, though. I think Mom and Dad prefer that she comes here, and they don't need to tell me why, either. (Mr. Adamski drinks too much. Sometimes when I call Lesley, I can hear him yelling in the background.)

Larry Martin phoned after dinner and asked if I'd be at the boys' basketball game next Saturday. I told him I would.

Mom and Dad have already told me they want me to attend Holy Name Academy next year. I don't think I'm going to like attending an all-girls school, but it'll be all right as long as Lesley is there, too.

No one else phoned and I lay on my bed and

listened to music for the rest of the afternoon. I like Roy Orbison and the Supremes the best. Mostly I thought about next year and high school and wondered if I'd ever be kissed for real and by whom. Lesley says I probably will be soon. Maybe Larry will kiss me. I wonder if it's possible for Lesley and me to be kissed on the very same night. That way we won't have to worry about who was first.

I don't care what Mom says, I'm not going into that bomb shelter without Lesley. We've been friends our entire lives and I refuse to let her die because her family can't afford to build a bomb shelter.

Pine Ridge Herald
May 29, 1962
Top Ten Students From
St. Mary Junior High Named

The Sisters of Providence have named the top ten students from the eighth-grade graduating class. They are listed in order of ranking: Jillian Lawton, Lesley Adamski, Jerry Englehardt, Marilyn Andrews, Bonnie Gamache, Bernard Simmons, Yvette Dwight, David Thoma, Steve Bounds and Diane Kerry. Each student received a twenty-five dollar scholarship toward tuition at either Holy Name Academy or Marquette High School.

July 10, 1962

220 Railroad Avenue
Pine Ridge, Washington

Dear Judge and Mrs. Lawton,

Thank you so much for inviting me to the Seattle World's Fair with you and Jillian. I had a wonderful time, even if we didn't get to see Elvis. I especially loved taking the elevator to the top of the Space Needle and riding on the monorail. I'm sorry I can't go to Hawaii with Jillian, but my mom and dad need me at home. It was very nice of you to include me. Perhaps someday I'll see the islands.

Thank you again.

Sincerely,

Lesley Adamski

August 8, 1962

Dear Jillian,

Summer is so boring without you. I wish I could be with you in Hawaii, but I need the baby-sitting money for my school uniform. Did you hear that Marilyn Monroe died? Mom didn't like her because she was too sexy.

Susan and I went to the movies last Saturday and saw John Wayne in *The Man Who Shot Liberty Valance.* It was good, but I would've had more fun with you than my little sister. Dad said spending 25¢ to see a movie is a waste. I didn't tell him popcorn went up to 10¢ a bag.

Call me over at Mrs. Johnson's house the minute you get home. I have a lot to tell you.

Your Best Friend Forever,
Lesley

❖

September 4th

English Class

Lesley,

Here we are, the first day of HIGH SCHOOL. Don't you just want to die with happiness? I was disappointed we aren't in the same homeroom, though. Someone must have told

Sister Anna Marie that you and I are best friends. They want to keep us apart, but nothing ever will. At least, we've got English and Algebra together.

Can you meet me after school? We need to practice the watusi. I can do the bossa nova but this new dance is more complicated. Thank you for saying I can twist better than Chubby Checker. Now all we need is for a couple of boys to invite us to a dance so we can show everyone how good we are.

I heard Sister Bernice grades easy in English.

Jillian

October 22nd

Algebra Class

Jillian,

Do you think we're going to war? This is so scary. Even my dad was talking about it. I can't concentrate on Algebra, can you? Mom went to Mass this morning to pray for peace. Cuba wouldn't really bomb us, would they?

Lesley

Algebra Class

Lesley,
I don't know if there will be a war or not, but if there is you can come in the bomb shelter with me. I've already told my parents that I refuse to go inside without you. Do you want to sleep over tonight? We can camp out in the shelter. In case something does happen, we'll be safe.
Jillian

P.S. If the politicians listened to the music of Joan Baez and the New Christy Minstrels, I bet this wouldn't be happening.

Holy Name Academy
230 First Street
Pine Ridge, Washington 98005

November 1, 1962

Dear Judge and Mrs. Lawton,
Thank you for your generous financial contribution to Holy Name Academy. It is because of benefactors such as yourselves that the Sisters of Providence are able to offer high-quality education to the young Catholic women of Pine Ridge.
You can trust that the matter of the scholarships for Lesley and Susan Adamski will be handled in the most discreet manner possible.

Neither the girls nor their parents need ever know that you have paid their tuition in advance. I have discussed the matter with Mother Superior; she felt it would be best if the girls were awarded scholarships and nothing more was said. I'm confident, however, that if Lesley and Susan Adamski were aware of your generosity, they would express their gratitude personally.

Again, your generous check is appreciated.

In Christ's Service

Sister Martin de Porres

Lesley's Diary

December 4, 1962

Scott kissed Jillian and she said it was the most romantic, wonderful event of her entire life. She asked Scott McDougal to the Sadie Hawkins dance and I asked Roy Kloster. Jillian's dad picked us all up in his new Cadillac. It was my first official date and Roy brought me a corsage. My mother pinned it on my dress — and then embarrassed me by saying in front of Roy how pretty I was.

Jillian and I spent all afternoon with our hair in pink rollers, the hard plastic ones. Her mother said we used enough hair spray for our hairdos to survive hurricane force winds.

I was barely home from the dance when

Jillian phoned to tell me that Scott kissed her. She described everything he did, and it sounded better than anything we've read in *Modern Screen Magazine* or *Movie Life.* I don't think I'll ever be kissed. I'm planning on joining the Peace Corps and dedicating my life to helping children in Africa.

I wanted Roy to kiss me, but all he did was hold my hand. He barely spoke to me all evening. I didn't talk much either. I knew Roy from Junior High and when I called to ask him to the dance, he sounded like he wanted to go. Mikey has a paper route now and he delivers to Roy's house on Maple Street. He thinks Roy wants me to be his girlfriend.

Mom said Roy is shy, but I am, too. If we're both afraid to talk, we could be seventeen before either one of us gets up the courage to do more than gawk at the other. I want romance and music, the same way Jillian had with Scott. Maybe someday I'll meet a boy who won't be afraid to kiss me . . . and I won't be afraid to let him. Until then I'm keeping the idea of joining the Peace Corps in the back of my mind.

Even if Roy didn't kiss me, I had a wonderful time at the dance. I'm going to sleep now and dream about being kissed. Susan's still awake and she keeps pestering me. She thinks I should kiss Dr. Kildare. If I can't get Roy Kloster interested in me, there isn't much chance a famous television star like Richard Chamberlain would want to kiss me. Besides, I like Ben Casey better.

1963

Lesley's Diary

January 1, 1963

Mom and Dad had another one of their fights. They woke all us kids in the middle of the night, ranting and raving at each other. Lily and Bruce came racing into Susan's and my bedroom and climbed into bed with us. I don't know what the fight was about this time. Probably money. Or Dad's drinking. I wish he didn't drink so much, but he says a beer or two never hurt anybody. Only it does. It hurts Mom when Dad gets so mean. It frightens Lily and Bruce. They're too young to understand what's happening or why Dad gets the way he does. All he cares about is his beer, his Legionnaire friends and watching *The Beverly Hillbillies*.

Christmas was awful. Dad got laid off at the mill before Thanksgiving, and we couldn't afford gifts. Mom wrapped up empty boxes with handwritten promises. She promised me a new pair of shoes and a Beatles album after Dad goes back to work.

She promised Susan a perm and Mikey a used bike for his paper route. Joe got a picture of a fire truck and Lily a doll that cries Mama when she's turned upside down. Bruce didn't understand why he couldn't have his big red wagon now. I don't know what we would have done for Christmas dinner if Catholic Charities hadn't dropped off the food basket. I'd hate it if anyone at school found out how poor we really are. I'd die before I'd tell Jillian about my pretend gift. Her parents had 22 gifts under the tree for her. I can't imagine what it must be like to have that many presents.

They're so nice, her mom and dad. They always give me something for Christmas — I got this new diary with my name on it, just like last year, and a beautiful blue sweater. I know envy is a sin and Jillian's my best friend but I wish I had parents like hers.

I'm sure the nightmare Lily had was caused by Mom and Dad's argument. She slept with me the rest of the night and woke up sobbing and wouldn't tell me what was wrong. Then she clung to me and made me promise I'd never grow up and move away. She wouldn't stop pestering me until I told her I'd live at home forever, but I crossed my ankles when I said it. I want to leave. I can't wait to get away from my father. Jillian and I talk about college. Her parents want her to attend Barnard College in New York. Everything's already been settled for her. She has a big trust fund to pay for college. I pretend there's a chance I'll be able to go. But Mom and Dad could never afford to send me. Jillian doesn't realize how lucky she is.

Even if we were rich, I don't think Dad would let me go to college. He told me he didn't plan on wasting money to educate girls, seeing that we wouldn't be the ones supporting a family. I wanted to stand up to him and tell him that plenty of girls go to university these days, but I knew it wouldn't do any good to argue. He'd only get mad at what he calls my "smart mouth" and belittle me. I think it's because he didn't graduate from high school and is afraid I'll be smarter than he is.

Mom said if I continued to get good grades there's a possibility I might get a scholarship. She said that if I did, she'd do whatever was necessary to find a way for me to attend college, even if that meant taking a second job. I know how much she hates working at the school cafeteria, but Mom said she'd be willing to work there and scrub floors, too, if it meant I could go to college. I wanted to cry I was so happy. Mom was serious, too. I could see it in her eyes. Then she held me against her, tight as could be, and said where there's a will there's a way. A hundred gifts under the Christmas tree couldn't have made me happier than I was at that moment.

February 20, 1963

Dear Ann Landers,
I've tried to write this letter a dozen times. Please help me. My husband's involved with another woman. I pretend I don't know about her but I do and it's eating me up inside. We have six children. Don't tell me to leave him, because I can't. I feel trapped and miserable, and stupid.
Dorothy A. from the Seattle area

March 7th

English Class

Les,
Wanna spend the night on Friday?
Jillian

P.S. Why do elephants have trunks? Because they don't have glove compartments.

English Class

Jillian,

I'll have to clear it with my mom first, but I think so. Let's stay up all night and talk, okay? Do you have any new records? Did you notice the new boy at First Friday Mass? He's cute!

Lesley

P.S. Why do elephants climb trees? To hide.

❖

Jillian's Diary

March 10, 1963

Lesley and I had the best time ever! Mom and Dad were involved in some social function at the Country Club all weekend, so we had the house to ourselves. On Friday we stayed up all night and read *Profiles in Courage* by John F. Kennedy. We did it for extra credit in Sister Sebastian's English class, but it was the best book I ever read on purpose about history. First Lesley would read a chapter aloud and then I'd read the next one. We didn't mean to finish the entire book, but we couldn't stop reading. Lesley said I look a little bit like Jackie Kennedy. Jackie's much prettier than I am and so graceful and elegant.

The only reason Lesley said that is because Jackie and I both have dark hair. It would be like me saying Lesley looks like Marilyn Monroe did (before she died!) because she's blond.

Anyway, after we read, we listened to the radio. My favorite singer is still Roy Orbison and Lesley likes Peter, Paul and Mary. We talked for a long time afterward. Mostly it was about boys and school. I'd rather go to a co-ed high school, but an all-girl is okay, too. I bet we'd meet more guys, though, if we went to a regular school.

I wonder what it would be like to fall in love and marry. Lesley insists that she doesn't want to get married until she's out of college, but I do. I want a romance just like John and Jackie Kennedy's. I don't know anyone I'd want to marry yet. Not even Scott. I asked Mom how she knew Dad was the right man for her and she got a goofy look on her face and said she just knew. That didn't tell me anything. It was the same way last year when my periods started. Mom hardly explained anything. She seemed embarrassed about it, mumbled a few words and then handed me two safety pins and a pad. If it hadn't been for Lesley starting first, I wouldn't have known what to do. In biology class, Sister Mary Clare said that our periods tie in with having babies but I'm still not sure how. It's like a deep, dark mystery no one wants to talk about. Lesley tried to check out a book at the library that explained everything but the librarian said she had to be eighteen to take it out of the building. When we went back to read it together, the book was missing. Lesley thinks the librarian saw us coming and hid it.

Oh, I almost forgot! My birthday gift finally arrived. I have my own television now. I don't know anyone else in school who has her own TV. Dad had it built right into the wall. Lesley's going to spend the night next month so we can watch the Oscars. I really hope Sidney Poitier wins Best Actor for *Lilies of the Field*. Lesley and I liked that movie better than any of the other movies we saw this year. Everyone talked about how wicked *Tom Jones* was, but I just thought it was silly. Lesley and I both learned something valuable from that movie. Neither of us can tell a lie and not feel guilty about it. We told our parents we were going to some other show and instead we went to *Tom Jones* and we both regretted lying. It was hard because Dad picked us up afterward and I wanted to blurt out the truth the moment I saw him. I didn't, but he knew something was bothering me. Dad didn't pressure me into telling him and I'm glad he didn't. I wouldn't want to see the disappointment on his face when he learned I'd deceived him.

This summer, instead of going to Hawaii, Dad said we might go to Disneyland. I said that would be fine as long as Lesley gets to come. Last year in Hawaii, Mom insisted Kathy Galloway tag along so I'd have company. Mom's friends with Mrs. Galloway and she thought I'd enjoy having someone close to my own age. I would've liked company, but it didn't work out. Kathy's three years older and wasn't interested in hanging around the hotel swimming pool with me. She was after *men.* Mom figured that out soon enough when she found her in the cocktail lounge flirting with a businessman. I bet Mom won't invite Kathy again for anything, which is all right by me.

❖

Holy Name Academy				
Freshman Report Card				
Lesley Adamski				
Subject	**1st Quarter**	**2nd Quarter**	**3rd Quarter**	**4th Quarter**
Religion	A+	A	A	A
French	A	A	A	A
Biology	A	A+	A	A
English	A+	A+	A+	A+
Algebra	A-	A	A	A
Comments: Leslie is a good student and works hard. It is recommended that she be placed in the advanced class, geared toward those considering a college education.				

Bell's Book Store
455 Main Street
Pine Ridge, Washington 98005

July 29, 1963

Dear Mrs. Lawton,

The Feminine Mystique is in. At your request, I have set aside a copy for you. We look forward to seeing you soon.

Ethel Cowin, Manager

Lesley's Diary

August 29, 1963

The most incredible thing happened yesterday. Hundreds of thousands of people gathered around the Washington Monument in our country's capital in a Civil Rights demonstration. It was on television and on the radio. Mom and I talked about what it meant to be a Negro in America. Several colored families live on the other side of the railroad tracks. Dad works with colored men at the mill. He calls them names Mom won't let me repeat. Mom said they're like everyone else. They bleed and sweat and breathe the same as us, despite what Dad says. I can hardly believe that the South treats people so differently just because their skin is a different color, and I told Mom that. I read that Negroes have a hard time finding a job or getting an education. That isn't fair. Mom was born and raised in Mississippi, and she said the Civil War was about more than slavery. She explained some of the South's history since the War Between the States (that's what she calls it), and she helped me understand how much courage it took for this rally in Washington to happen. Then she recited a quote from an English writer named Samuel Johnson. I'm writing it down because I don't ever want to forget it. COURAGE IS THE GREATEST OF ALL VIRTUES, BECAUSE IF YOU HAVEN'T COURAGE, YOU MAY NOT HAVE AN OPPORTUNITY TO USE ANY OF THE OTHERS. I don't think I've ever realized how smart my mother is about life. (And I didn't know who Samuel Johnson was until she talked about him.)

There's going to be a colored man speaking at the Pine Ridge Emmanuel Church on September 6th and I told Mom I'd like to hear what he has to say. She didn't think that was a good idea because it wouldn't be right for a Catholic girl to be seen inside a Protestant Church. Although

Mom said I couldn't go, I had the feeling she'd like to attend the meeting herself. If I had my driver's license and a car, I'd do it. Jillian's taking Driver's Education this summer. She thinks her parents might buy her a car. As it is now, her mother drives her to school every morning and her father picks her up every afternoon.

I hate being fourteen. I want to be sixteen and to be able to drive and hear the people I want to hear and meet the people I want to meet.

Jillian's Diary

November 22, 1963

President Kennedy was killed today. Lesley and I were in Religion Class when the news came over the loudspeaker that the President had been shot. Sister Dorothy immediately had us get down on our knees and pray. No one knew then how serious it was.

It wasn't long before we were released from school. Lesley and I went right over to church and it was already full of people pleading with God to save our President. By the time I got home, I learned he was dead. I can't stop crying. Even my dad had tears in his eyes.

Poor Jackie. She's the one I'm crying for. I can't bear this. It's so terrible. Everyone is watching television. Everyone is weeping. I can't sleep. I can't eat. I can't believe President Kennedy is dead.

Farewell from John Kennedy
by Lesley Adamski

Sorry I had to leave right away.
I look down and smile at you each day.
Little Patrick says to say "Hi"
And so, my darlings, please don't cry.

Caroline, I'd like to say,
How proud Daddy was of you that day,
When you stood like a lady
and watched me go by,
And doing like Mommy, you tried not to cry.
John John, now you're the big man.
Take care of Mommy the best that you can.
You were just like a soldier, that salute was so brave.
Thank you for the flag you put on my grave.

And Jackie, I had no time for goodbyes,
I'm sure you could read the "Farewell" in my eyes.
Watch over our children, and love them for me
I'll treasure your love through eternity.

Please carry on as you did before,
Until we all meet on heaven's bright shore.
Remember I love you, remember I care.
I'll always be with you though you don't
see me there.

(This is in Memory of the late
John Fitzgerald Kennedy,
whom I loved more than words can say.
I pray that I will meet him in heaven
one day.)

1965

Holy Name Academy

January 20, 1965
Demerit Slip
Student: Jillian Lawton
Offense: Rolling up the uniform skirt above the knee.

Holy Name Academy
230 First Street
Pine Ridge, Washington 98005

January 20, 1965

Dear Judge and Mrs. Lawton,

Enclosed is the demerit slip for Jillian, which I have had no choice but to issue. She has had repeated warnings about the length of her uniform skirt. Several of the Junior girls have defied the rules and each will be obliged to remain after school the first Friday of February to polish the gymnasium floor.

I appreciate your cooperation in this unfortunate situation.

Sincerely,
Sister Agnes, Principal

Jillian's Diary

January 23, 1965

This whole detention thing is juvenile, and all because I rolled my skirt up. First, I detest wearing a uniform. I told Mom how much I hated it but she didn't care. She says that a lot. "I don't care" and "We aren't going to talk about it." Sometimes I swear she treats me like I'm ten years old. The other day I wanted to stand on my chair at the fancy new dining-room table and scream to get her attention. How else can I get her to recognize that I'm sixteen years old?

The state of Washington trusts me enough to give me a license to drive a motorized vehicle. Dad even bought me a car to go back and forth to school. It seems that if the government thinks I'm mature enough to drive, I should be smart enough to figure out what to wear to school. Apparently they think that if I had a choice, I'd wear something obnoxious like jeans and a sweatshirt. The truth is, my choices have been completely taken away from me, since I'm forced into a ridiculous school uniform. My closet is full of dresses I never get a chance to wear. I have this fear that I'll be wearing a blue skirt and red blazer my entire life!

I love my parents, especially my dad. Both

Mom and Dad are swell, but at times they can be completely irrational. They're no better than my teachers when it comes to this uniform thing. Girls attending school in Communist Russia wear uniforms. (I don't know that for a fact because no one really knows what's happening in Russia except spies.) We talk about the Berlin Wall and the struggle for freedom, but we're not all that different right here in Pine Ridge.

When I insisted that wearing uniforms was a form of Communism because it enforced sameness and obliterated personal identity, Dad said he wasn't going to argue with me. I told him he was a coward but in a joking way, since everyone knows my dad is probably one of the truest, kindest, fairest men in the entire courthouse. I could see that he was amused and I know why. By proving my point with such a smart argument, I'm showing my parents that I'd be a good attorney. Actually I like to argue. I enjoy flustering people and proving my point. It gives me a sense of satisfaction.

I flustered the kid at the gas station the other day, but I didn't mean to. He was young, probably about thirteen. He wanted to wash my windshield, but couldn't reach the middle of the glass so I got out of my car and did it for him. Then his big brother showed up and finished the job for us both. I don't think any boy has ever affected me like this. His name was embroidered on his coveralls. **Nick.** He's the sexiest guy I've ever seen. One look told me he was a break-all-the-rules kind of guy. My heart was going crazy. I wasn't about to let him know the effect he had on me, so I casually stepped aside and let him take over.

When he was finished, I paid him the $3.09 to fill up my tank. As soon as I pulled away, I looked in my rearview mirror and found Nick watching me. Then he grinned – and I nearly steered off the road. I felt that smile go right through me, the same way I do when the cat lies across my chest and purrs. I think I might be buying gas at the Texaco station a lot more often. Not soon, though. My driving privileges have been suspended for two weeks because of that demerit slip. I'm furious about it, but no amount of arguing would change my mother's mind. As far as I'm concerned, Mom is the unreasonable one in our family.

P.S. I found out that Nick goes to Pine Ridge High and he's a Junior (same as me).

Lesley's Diary

February 5, 1965

Jillian had a detention because of her skirt length and had to stay after school to polish the gym floor this afternoon, so I walked home alone. Buck Knowles saw me and stopped to offer me a ride. Buck is twenty-one and works at the mill with Dad. Because I kinda know him, I thought it would be okay to accept. He didn't remember that I was Mike's daughter and then tried to pretend that he did. He said he's noticed me before, looking all "virginal" (his word) in my Academy uniform. It sounded like he's been interested in me for a long time. I've noticed him, too.

Last week Mom sent me down to the mill to collect Dad's paycheck and I saw Buck. He looked at me and I looked at him. I had my school uniform on then, too. The way he stared made me feel older than sixteen. Mom didn't see him drop me off at the house today and I didn't mention that Buck had given me a ride. After I closed the car door, he leaned over and rolled down the side window and said he'd see me around. I know I'll be looking for him.

❖

March 4th

Religion Class

Jillian,

Guess what? Buck Knowles came home from work with my dad last night and had dinner with the family. He's the guy I was telling you about who gave me a ride home last month. I haven't seen him since and I was beginning to wonder if I ever would. Neither Buck nor my dad get along with the foreman and they spent the entire night complaining about him.

The best part is that Buck said he's coming to pick me up after school, so I won't need you to give me a ride home. I'll call you as soon as I can. Buck is so-o-o-o handsome.

Lesley

P.S. I signed up for Driver's Ed, but I sure won't be driving any fancy cars!

Murphy's Texaco
Charge Slip
April 3, 1965

Quantity	10 gal
Per Gallon	.309
Total	$3.09
Attendant:	Nick Murphy
Signed:	*Jillian Lawton*

April 12, 1965

Dear Buck,

Dad said he'd make sure you got my note. I'm sorry to hear about the foreman's accident. I hope he's on the mend soon and won't miss much work. I know how hard it is on our family when Dad's off for a long period of time. Dad said that both of you would be working a lot of overtime in the next couple of weeks, so I'll understand if I don't hear from you for a while.

I did enjoy seeing your apartment and watching television with you. The news about Vietnam doesn't sound good, does it? Your place is small and a little messy, but that's okay. Arranging the empty beer cans like a pyramid against the wall is a clever idea. You're right, I haven't had much experience with kissing but I did like it. Well, most of it.

Lesley

Murphy's Texaco
Charge Slip
May 7, 1965

Quantity	9.5 gal
Per Gallon	.309
Total	$2.94
Attendant:	Nick Murphy
Signed:	*Jillian Lawton*

Dance Card for
Jillian Lawton
Junior/Senior Prom
"Moulin Rouge"
May 15, 1965

1. Scott McDougal
2. Scott McDougal
3. Scott McDougal
4. Marvin Watterman
5. Scott McDougal
6. Scott McDougal
7. Scott McDougal
8. Scott McDougal
9. Buck Knowles
10. Scott McDougal

June 4th

Latin Class

Dearest Lesley,

Can you believe this is our last day of school? As of this afternoon we're officially Seniors. We should celebrate. Mom and Dad want me to go to Hawaii with them again, which means no real job for me. I hate Hawaii. I don't understand why we can't go to San Francisco instead. I'd love it there, I know I would. Did you hear that *My Fair Lady* with Audrey Hepburn is starting next Wednesday? Do you want to go or do you have a date with Buck? You're still seeing a lot of him, aren't you? Meet me after school and we'll celebrate being Seniors.

Jillian

French Class

Jillian,

Sorry, I can't go out with you after school this afternoon. I got a call from the library — I have an interview for a summer job. I'd just about given up hope of getting hired. Say a prayer that I get the job. This is important. Besides, the library pays more than baby-sitting. I'll call you the minute I know. Buck said he'd take me to the drive-in tonight. Are you and Scott doing anything special?

Lesley

<table>
<tr>
<td>
August 10, 1965

Dear Lesley,
Here I am in Hawaii again. (Sigh.) I wish you were here. I can't tell you how bored I am with nothing to do but read and laze around the beach every day. I miss you and Scott so much. I'm counting the days until I return. I hope your summer is more exciting than mine. See you soon.
Love,
Jillian
</td>
<td>
U.S.
Postage
3¢

Miss Lesley Adamski,
220 Railroad Ave.,
Pine Ridge, Washington
98005
</td>
</tr>
</table>

August 25, 1965

Dear Jillian,

I was so glad to hear from you. Is the water in Hawaii truly that blue? I'm sorry you're bored, especially when there's so much happening elsewhere. Did you hear about all the rioting in California? The television news has been full of it every night. Last night they reported that there were 20,000 National Guard troops in Watts. So far, 34 people have died, and after five days of rioting it's still going on. I didn't think anything this terrible would ever happen in our country. Mom said it all has to do with civil rights and moral wrongs. I won't tell you what my dad and Buck said, but I think you can guess.

Every day before I start work at the library, I've been checking into different kinds of scholarships. You wouldn't believe how many are available. Mom's been encouraging me to apply at the University of Washington. I know your parents are set on you going to Barnard College, but that's in New York and Jillian, I just can't afford it. At the same time, I can't imagine attending college without you.

The Soroptomists offer a thousand-dollar scholarship. A thousand dollars would pay all my expenses for the first year at the state university. I've been thinking about it and

I'd like to get into the nursing program. My mom thinks nursing would be a good choice for me. My dad doesn't know anything about this yet. Mom said she'd deal with him when the time came. I'm so excited to think about where we'll be a year from now. But we have to finish high school first and I'm going to need top grades if I plan on getting any scholarships.

I'm putting every cent I earn into a savings account, but I did buy myself a pair of bellbottom trousers. Buck said I have a cute behind, and he'd like me to wear miniskirts. Can you imagine what Sister Agnes would say if she saw me in one of those??!

I miss you so much. At least ten times a day I think of something I want to tell you. Five weeks has never seemed so long. I know you're sick and tired of Hawaii and that you're missing Scott, but do try and have a good time. Call me the minute you're back. Until then, I remain . . .

Your Friend Forever,

Lesley

August 27, 1965 Dear Scott, Just a postcard to let you know how much I miss you. Before you ask, I'm wearing your class ring so every guy will know I'm your girl. Tell everyone hello for me. See you soon. Love, Jillian	U.S. Postage 3¢ Scott McDougal, 4520 Country Club Lane, Pine Ridge, Washington 98005

Lesley's Diary

October 13, 1965

Buck phoned twice, but I had Susan tell him I wasn't home. I don't want to talk to him, not after what happened last week. When he picked me up for our date he'd been drinking, but I thought everything would be all right. It wasn't, and Friday was the worst night of my life.

He said it was my fault, and that I can't lead a man on and then turn him off. He was so rough and angry and it hurt so badly.

Jillian and I used to discuss what it would be like the first time and this wasn't anything beautiful or tender. Buck hurt me.

I know I should go to confession, but I don't want to talk about this. Father Morris wouldn't understand. He's a man and he'd say I was as much to blame as Buck. It wasn't my fault! I didn't do anything to lead Buck into thinking that was what I wanted. We started kissing and when I saw he was getting really worked up I tried to stop, but that only made Buck want me more. Next thing I knew, his hands were on my breasts and then he pinned me down on his davenport and he'd shoved my panties down.

When Dad came home from work tonight, he wanted to know why I wasn't talking to Buck. I told him we'd had a fight, which we did, and Dad got mad at me. My own father sided with Buck! I've decided to have nothing to do with Buck ever again. I don't think I can forgive my father for thinking I was the one in the wrong. He doesn't even know what happened. No one does. I can't talk to Mom about this, or Susan. My sister has barely been kissed. As much as I'd like to tell Jillian, I can't. I can't even tell my best friend! My dress is ruined and even if it wasn't, I'd never want to wear it again. I feel ugly and dirty and so ashamed.

October 14th

Latin Class

Lesley,

Are you all right? You've been so quiet lately and that isn't like you. Is your dad out of work again? I bought an album yesterday by a new group called The Rolling Stones. My dad listened to "Satisfaction" and ordered me to destroy the record because he considers the lyrics indecent. I think they're swell.

Have you seen the show *Get Smart*? I laughed all the way through it. It's so much better than *My Mother the Car*.

Jillian

Lesley's Diary

October 26, 1965

Buck phoned and this time I was unlucky enough to answer. He begged me to see him. I said no, but he turned up at the house anyway and insisted on taking me to the Dairy Queen for a Dilly bar. I didn't want to go, but my dad asked me if I considered myself too good for a man who worked at the mill. I told him not seeing Buck didn't have anything to do with his job.

Buck and I sat and talked at the Dairy

Queen and he apologized over and over. He promised me nothing like that will happen again. He seemed so sincere. Tears came to his eyes and I wanted to believe him. Then, when we got in his car, we started kissing. Before I realized what he was planning to do, he had his hand up my dress. I could see he was getting excited and I immediately put an end to our necking. Buck got mad and what he said made me feel kind of guilty. He kept saying how crazy he is about me and how much he needs me. We ended up doing it again. I could've stopped him, but I didn't. At least it didn't hurt this time. When we finished I started crying. Buck didn't understand why. I'm not sure I do, either, but I couldn't make myself stop. I told him it would be better if we didn't see each other again and he said it's because I think I'm too good for him, just the way Dad claimed. He dropped me off at the house and then took off with his tires squealing.

Murphy's Texaco
Charge Slip
November 20, 1965

Quantity	9 gal
Per Gallon	.309
Total	$2.78
Attendant:	Nick Murphy
Signed:	*Jillian Lawton*

Jillian's Diary

December 14, 1965

I stopped at the Texaco station with a fruitcake for Mr. Murphy. He seemed surprised that a customer would remember him at Christmas and gave me an entire set of matching juice glasses. Jimmy knew I'd been collecting them whenever I filled up my tank and must have told his father. I was disappointed Nick wasn't there.

Last week I saw him riding his motorcycle in front of Holy Name Academy and wondered if he was looking for me. I hope he was. My heart beat so fast when I saw him. He pumps my gas almost every time I come to the station now. Sometimes we talk, but he's usually too busy to say more than hello.

Lesley warned me that I'm flirting with danger. She says Nick is dangerous. I see it in his eyes and the way he looks at me, as though I'm the only girl he's ever wanted. Whenever he focuses on me, I can actually feel it. The air between us gets hot and heavy like it does before a big storm. This shivery feeling goes all through me and doesn't stop for a long time afterward.

I'd be a fool to break it off with Scott. I don't know what I'm going to do. I don't want to hurt Scott's feelings, but I'm drawn to Nick the way a moth is to a flame. Scott has been a good boyfriend and I'm the envy of every girl at school. I know if I broke up with him, he wouldn't have any trouble getting a new girlfriend. That makes me wonder if I should stop seeing him.

Nick has never asked me out, never called me at home. For the longest time I didn't even think he remembered my name. The most he's done is fill up my car with gas and flirt a little. I can't hurt Scott over that. Not when he's been so sweet and considerate.

Speaking of breaking up, I wish Lesley would dump Buck Knowles. He treats her terribly. At first it was exciting that Buck wanted to date Lesley. He recently turned twenty-two and no one else in class is dating anyone that much older. The fact that he's so attracted to her tells us all that we're no longer girls; we're women now. But I don't care how much older and more sophisticated Buck is. He doesn't treat Lesley the same way he did when they first started seeing each other.

I don't know what's wrong with her lately, but she hasn't been herself. She tells me she's going to break up with Buck and then she never does. When I ask her about it, she always has some excuse for why she can't. It's like she's caught in a trap and doesn't know how to break free.

The whole world seems to be in turmoil. The war in Vietnam is heating up and there was a huge protest rally in Oakland. When I asked my dad about it, he said it was vital that we wipe out Communism. He thinks it's a good idea for the United States to be involved in the war. My father is the smartest man I know. If he believes in this war, then I'll do whatever I can to support it.

I finally figured out what I'm getting Mom for Christmas — a book. I know that sounds boring, but she enjoys reading and *The Shoes of the Fisherman* by Morris West is one I know she'd enjoy. Dad subtly dropped that hint, and I was grateful.

Les and I should be able to spend time together over Christmas break, and maybe then she can tell me what's wrong, because something definitely is. I've been her best friend since first grade. I know her as well as she does herself. Whatever it is has to do with Buck, I'm convinced of that.

1966

January 3rd

Latin Class

Dear Jillian,

You want to know what my New Year's resolution is? First and foremost it's getting that scholarship from the Soroptimists. I want to be a nurse. Secondly, I'm going to break up with Buck. I mean it this time. Meet me after class.

Lesley

Latin Class

Les,

Where have I heard that before? I've got a dentist appointment after Latin. Call me tonight, okay?

Jillian

Jillian's Diary

January 3, 1966

Today was the first day back at school following Christmas break, and it was hectic. Lesley and I had lunch together and we passed notes in Latin class. Sister Angelica is half-blind and hasn't got a clue what's going on behind her back. I'm so happy Lesley is breaking up with Buck. This time she sounds serious about it. I hope so.

She told me her resolution for this year, but I didn't tell her mine. I haven't told anyone. I can't. *I want Nick Murphy to kiss me.* He's so cute and he's got that dangerous kind of sexiness. He even looks like trouble in his black leather jacket, riding his motorcycle. He makes me go all shaky every time I'm near him.

I know Mom and Dad would never let me date him. In their view, anyone who drives a motorcycle is part of a biker gang. I think Nick might've gotten into some sort of trouble with the law, too. Dad mentioned that he didn't think I should gas up at the Texaco station anymore. I asked him why and he said those Murphys were hotheads. I didn't dare show too much curiosity about that, but I'm paying cash for my gasoline these days instead of using credit.

One kiss is all I want and then I'll be satisfied. Then I can go on with my life and he can continue with his. My curiosity will be satisfied and Scott need never know.

❖

January 20, 1966

Dear Lesley,

You won't answer my phone calls so I'm forced to write you a note and bribe your little sister into giving it to you. The least you can do is talk to me! How are we going to solve our problems if you refuse to have anything to do with me? I know you're upset about what's happened the last few times we went out. But you've got to understand, baby, that kind of frustration can lead to serious physical problems.

Can't you tell I'm crazy about you? You're the smartest girl I ever met and you go to that fancy Catholic girls' school. I felt like the luckiest man alive when you said you'd date a high-school dropout like me. I can't let you go. You're the most important thing in my life.

Are you going to the school dance Friday night after the basketball game? Your brother said he could find a way to sneak me into the gym. I'll look for you there. Whatever's wrong, I'll make it right. You have my word on that.

Buck

January 21, 1966

I am so stupid. I can't believe what a disaster tonight was. I swore to myself that if Buck showed up at the school dance, I wouldn't talk to him. Sure enough, he was there. He's everywhere lately. Last Sunday he sat in the pew behind me during Mass. He must be leaving work early because he's parked outside the Academy most afternoons, waiting for me. Thank goodness Jillian's been driving me home. Apparently he had words with my dad about the job, because he hasn't been coming over to the house much. That helps. It's been three weeks and I've managed to avoid him thus far. Still, he won't leave me alone. No one knows how awful it is to keep looking over my shoulder, worrying and wondering if he's following me.

Then he came to the school dance and it seemed everyone there was watching us. Jillian was with Scott or she would've helped me. I didn't want to create a scene and I was afraid Buck was going to pick a fight with Roy Kloster, so I agreed to dance with him. It was awful, a slow dance by *The Mamas and The Papas.* Buck held me close, closer than I wanted, and he kept whispering in my ear how crazy he is about me and how he can't sleep nights because he needs me so much.

I was proud of myself because I told him I don't think we're good for each other. It's true. All we do is argue. We don't view life the same way. When he drinks it's like seeing my dad. I told Buck that, and he got mad. He said I was playing hard to get and there were plenty of other girls interested in him. That's when I said those other girls were welcome to him and walked off the dance floor.

Buck left the dance in a huff, but waited for me outside the gym. When I didn't come out soon enough to suit him, he found Mikey and sent him inside to get me. Buck threatened to yell until I agreed to come out and talk to him. I should never have done it, especially alone, but I couldn't find Jillian and I didn't want to involve Mikey or Susan in this. I could tell Buck had fortified his courage with beer. I realize now it would've been better to return immediately to the dance. Instead I tried to reason with him, but Buck was angry just like Dad gets angry and in no mood to listen. He wanted what he's always wanted from me. Before I could stop him, Buck shoved me against the side of the school and kissed me. I tried to break free, but he tore open the front of my blouse and started mauling my breasts. I don't know what would've happened if Father

Morris hadn't happened upon us. He told me to straighten my clothes and get back to the dance.

I don't know what he said to Buck afterward. I don't want to know. Father Morris. Ye gads, how am I going to look him in the face again? When I got home from the dance, I wanted to talk to Mom, but she'd had another fight with Dad and was trying to hide that she'd been crying. I sat with her while she talked about *Star Trek*, this new television series she likes. Mom has troubles enough of her own without listening to mine, so I didn't tell her anything.

My life is awful. All I want to do is graduate and get away from home.

❖

February 5, 1966

Jillian,
Be my Valentine. Meet me behind the snack booth after the hootenanny.

Nick Murphy

February 6th

Latin Class

Jillian,

You're not going to do it, are you? What will Scott say?

And Jillian — these verbs are impossible! I might as well give up and just accept that I'm going to get a C.

Lesley

Les,

Scott's visiting the University of Oregon this weekend. He'll never know. I haven't decided if I'll go or not.

And Lesley – I'll help you with the verbs. We're going to be co-valedictorians, remember?

Jillian

You've got that look in your eyes. You're going to meet him, I can see it. Just promise me one thing. BE CAREFUL and for heaven's sake, don't let your parents find out about this!

Lesley

No one else knows. I promise I'll give you a full report afterward.

Jillian

Jillian's Diary

February 11, 1966

Nick Murphy has never lacked nerve – that's for certain. My dad would have a conniption if he found out I was planning to meet Nick. My stomach was in knots the entire hootenanny even though we sang all my favorite songs: "*Kum-ba-yah*," "*Where Have All the Flowers Gone*" and "*If I Had a Hammer*."

Everyone was there . . . except Nick. I kept looking around for him and after a while I realized he'd stood me up. I'd agonized for days about whether I should meet him or not, and then Nick Murphy didn't even have the common decency to show up.

After the hootenanny Cindy wanted me to drag the boulevard with her, but I made up some excuse and headed toward the parking lot, half expecting and desperately wanting to find Nick waiting for me. He wasn't there, either. I'd been torn about meeting him behind Scott's back, but Nick made the decision easy.

I was furious when I left the football field. Then I thought I might've gotten the day wrong or the time or something. Mostly I was disappointed and angry. How dare he! Just to be on the safe side, though, I decided to double back.

Sure enough, there he was, leaning against the snack booth, confident as anything. He had his motorcycle and looked so cool in his leather jacket. He smiled that sexy smile of his when I pulled into the parking lot. It was almost as if he knew I'd come back looking for him.

One thing I can't tolerate is arrogance, and Nick's got so much it's practically coming out his ears. I almost drove away right then and there, but thank goodness I didn't. Before I could tell him how mad I was, he reached for my hand, kissed it and asked if I'd be his Valentine. I must've looked terribly silly — I know I was confused. Somehow I managed to stutter that I wasn't sure yet. He laughed. I should've told him Scott's already given me a box of chocolates, but just then my steady was the last person on my mind.

We sat in the bleachers and Nick said he'd ended up having to close the station and that was why he'd been late. He said he was glad I'd come back. Then he talked about his family. He mentioned his dad some, but mostly he talked about his mother who died of cancer when he was ten and Jimmy was five. I wasn't sure what I expected when he asked to meet me, but I didn't think all we'd do was talk. That was exactly what we did. It was as though we'd been waiting all these months and we both had all this information stored up inside us that we had to get out first.

Later he gave me a ride around the field on the back of his motorcycle and I slid my arms around his waist and held on. I loved the feel of the wind in my hair and the smell of his leather jacket. Afterward, I was so hoping he'd kiss me, but he didn't. He wanted to. I could tell by the way he kept looking at my lips. When we left, he followed me most of the way home to make sure I got there safely, which made me feel really good. Cherished. He didn't ask to see me again, and that disappointed me.

Now that I'm home and in my room, I can't sleep. This excited, happy feeling is keeping me awake. I knew I had to write it all down. I want to remember every last detail. I told Lesley I'd report back everything that happened, but I don't know if I will. This is the first time I've kept anything from her. I know something's happening in her life that she hasn't told me about, and I understand that now. I like Nick so much I can hardly think of anything without him popping into my mind. My New Year's resolution hasn't been fulfilled yet, but I'm positive it's going to happen. The only thing that remains a mystery is when Nick will kiss me. It's no longer an if – he wants to kiss me as much as I want him to. I just hope it's soon.

March 10th

Latin Class

Verb conjugations are so boring. Isn't it great that the Beatles are coming to Seattle? I'd love to go to the movies with you on Saturday, but I can't. My mom needs me to help around the house with spring-cleaning. What's *Charade* about, anyway? I think Cary Grant is so handsome! If Sister Angelica finds this note, we're both going to end up with a detention.

Love,
Lesley

❖

March 15, 1966

Dear Lesley,

I've missed you! School was a real drag while you were out. There's no one to pass notes to when you're not here — no one I like, anyway! I've been worried about you. Is everything all right? We hardly talk anymore. I know you're upset about seeing Buck with that other girl, but isn't that what you wanted? Sister Angelica said you look pale and you do. You've lost weight, too. (Lucky you!) I'll see you at lunch.

Jillian

March 17th

Buck, we need to talk. Please phone me right away.
Lesley

❖

Soroptimists International of Pine Ridge
200 Sixth Avenue
Pine Ridge, Washington 98005

March 20, 1966

Miss Lesley Adamski
220 Railroad Avenue
Pine Ridge, Washington 98005

Dear Miss Adamski,

It is a great pleasure to inform you that we have selected you as this year's recipient of our $1,000 college scholarship. The committee was impressed with your essay about your desire to further your education. It's bright, responsible young women like you who are the hope and future of our country.

Congratulations!
Sincerely,
Sarah Janus,
President

March 23, 1966

I met Nick again and, of all places, in the town cemetery. He showed me where his mother's buried and we left flowers there. We walked through the cemetery, holding hands, and talked for a long time afterward. He told me his dad fought in World War II and has a medal for distinguished service. My dad was in the war, too, but he never talks about it.

This is the third time Nick and I have met on the sly like this. I love it when he takes me out on his Harley because I can put my arms around his waist and press my cheek against his back. Nick admitted that riding his motorbike gives him a surge of power and freedom and he says it's a real high.

What's strange is that so far, all we've done is hold hands. Every time we're together I'm convinced he's going to kiss me and it hasn't happened. Not from lack of wanting on my part. Sometimes I wonder why he keeps asking me to meet him. The last person I expected to be the perfect gentleman is Nick Murphy! Tonight, I finally got the courage to ask him if he ever intended to kiss me. He didn't answer right away. In fact, it took him so long I thought he might not have heard me. Then he said he wanted to kiss me more than anything, but he refused to do it while I'm wearing Scott's class ring.

I wish now that I hadn't asked. Not because I dread breaking if off with Scott. It's always been understood that we'd eventually go our separate ways. He'll be attending the University of Oregon in Eugene and I'll be either at Barnard or the University of Washington. I dread returning Scott's ring because I know what will happen between Nick and me once I do.

The electricity between us is so strong I swear it sometimes crackles. Up until now, we've both pretended it isn't there, but it is. Some nights I lie awake and try to imagine what it would be like to have Nick Murphy make love to me. Then I feel guilty for thinking such impure thoughts and immediately say the rosary.

Before we parted, I told Nick we probably shouldn't meet again. I hoped he'd argue and tell me how badly he wanted to be with me. Instead he agreed – but we *will* continue seeing each other and meeting whenever we can. He knows it and so do I. I can't stay away from him any more than he can stay away from me. As different as we are, we both recognize that we were meant to be together.

I've dated Scott forever, but I've never felt like this about him. Every moment I'm with Nick I feel this intensity, this wonder. It's strange that we could be so different and yet so alike.

March 24, 1966

Dearest Lesley,

Surprise! Remember when you were a little girl and I used to tuck notes inside your lunch box? I bet you'd forgotten. Lesley, I found the letter from the Soroptimists in your room and no, I wasn't sneaking through your chest of drawers! I read it and almost burst with pride. Why didn't you tell me? I'm so excited, it was all I could do to keep from shouting.

Oh Lesley, if only you knew how thrilled I am that you have a chance to attend nursing school. I always wanted to, but as you know your father and I got married instead.

Were you afraid to tell us about the scholarship? Or did you want to surprise us later? We both know how your father feels about you girls getting a college education, but he can't argue with a scholarship, can he?

You've been so quiet lately, not like yourself at all. If you were afraid to mention the scholarship, I want to assure you how delighted I am. Don't worry about Dad, I'll make sure he doesn't stand in your way.

I'm so pleased for you, sweetheart, and so very proud.

Love,
Mom

March 31st

Latin Class

Lesley,

What's wrong? I haven't been your best friend all these years without knowing when something's bothering you. Tell me. Did your dad lose his job again? Meet me after drill team practice.

Jillian

Lesley's Diary

April 1, 1966

I don't know what I'm going to do. I couldn't put off telling Buck any longer. I'm pregnant. I thought he'd be angry and yell at me, but instead he seemed almost glad. No one knows, not even Jillian. I can't talk about it to anyone. The minute I start thinking about what this means for my future, I start to cry. That's all I seem to do lately.

As soon as the words were out, Buck held me and kissed me and told me how happy he was to have me back. He doesn't care if the only reason I'm his is because of the baby. Now he wants us to get married. I don't know if that's the best answer for either of us. He wanted to elope, drive to Idaho right away, but I refused to do that. It seems like an easy out, but if we marry now I won't be able to graduate. If I can't have college, then at least I can get my high school diploma.

Buck has been really good about everything. He's been over to the house almost every night since I told him. He and my dad seem to be getting along better now, and Mom's already treating him like another son. I'm beginning to think he's right and we should get married. Tonight he told me he's got the whole thing worked out. He talked to an Army recruiter this afternoon and decided enlisting would be the best solution for us. That way, all the medical expenses for the baby will be covered. I don't want Buck to enlist. There's so much talk about what's happening in Vietnam, although Buck said the recruiter told him he could get an assignment in Germany — but only if he enlists within the next month. With the way things are developing in Vietnam, Buck thinks he should take the Germany assignment while he can. I agreed, but I feel guilty about him maybe risking his life for the baby and me.

Buck and I do it all the time now; there doesn't seem to be any reason not to — that's what Buck says. I don't mind so much, I guess, but I find it hard to go to church or explain why I can't take communion.

Jillian's Diary

April 12, 1966

Something's up with Lesley. Weeks after breaking up with Buck, all of a sudden she's seeing him again. For a while, she was almost her old self — and then, without warning, he's back. I've tried to talk to her, but she insists everything's all right and that I'm imagining things. Maybe so. Whatever's bugging her she's keeping to herself. I've never seen her so secretive. *The Sound of Music* is coming to town, and we've both been waiting to see it for weeks. Now she has some hokey excuse about why she can't go. I'm worried about her and I wish she'd talk to me.

Things aren't right with Scott, either. Someone must have told him about Nick and me, because he's been acting possessive and unreasonable lately. It all started when I told him I didn't want to go to the Junior/Senior prom. He seems to think it's a foregone conclusion that I'll be his date. I probably should attend the dance with him, but I don't think I can pretend to be his girl when my heart belongs to Nick.

Everything is so much worse since Scott's been nominated for Prom King. I'm pleased for him, I really am. He deserves it and is a wonderful athlete, but now there's all this pressure on me because I'm supposed to be his girlfriend. Scott can't believe I'm turning down the opportunity to be Prom Queen.

I haven't heard from Nick, either. It seems he took my suggestion that we not meet again seriously. I got tired of waiting for him to contact me and went to his dad's gas station. As luck would have it, Nick was working the pumps. Other than asking if I wanted him to fill up my tank, he didn't say one word.

Everyone's treating me like I have the plague. First Lesley, then Scott. Even Nick's mad at me. And I don't know what I've done!

April 20, 1966

Dear Jillian,

I was your first fool and I sincerely doubt I'll be your last. If you want to break up right before prom and graduation, then that's just fine. There are plenty of other girls interested in going to the biggest dance of the year with me.

Since you weren't inclined to explain this sudden change of heart, all I can say is goodbye. Thanks for the prompt return of my class ring.

Scott

May 1, 1966

My dearest Lesley,

It seems odd to be writing my own daughter a letter, but I know if I try to talk to you I'll never get through this without crying. To say that your news was a surprise would be an understatement. How I wish you'd come to me months ago so we could've talked things out and decided what to do before dragging Buck and your father into it.

If you'd prepared me, I might've been able to break the news to your father more carefully. If you remember anything from tonight, please don't let it be the terrible names he called you. He didn't mean them. Not a one. He was upset and angry . . . you know how he gets after a few beers.

What I'm about to tell you now may come as a shock. Years ago your father and I found ourselves in exactly the same predicament. Yes, Lesley, I was pregnant with you when your dad and I married. You were born six months after the wedding. (One day, you would've checked the dates and figured it out on your own.) My father said those same hateful things to me. He threw me out of the house and said I was never to come back. I didn't speak to either of my parents again until after you were born.

I didn't want to get married — like you, I had my own dreams — but at the time it seemed best for all concerned. So often in the years since, I've wondered what my life would've been like had I taken a different path. I've worked hard to be a good wife and mother to you kids, but every now and then I look back on the girl I once was and remember the precious dreams I held so dear. I married so young, barely sixteen, and it seemed those dreams went up in smoke the minute your father slipped the wedding band on my finger. Little did I realize then that along with everything else you inherited from me — your blue eyes and blond hair — you'd be stuck with repeating my mistakes, too.

Look at my life, Lesley. Is this what you want for your future? Six kids and a husband who has a hard time holding down a job? A husband who has a harder time refusing a bottle. I look at Buck and I see your father all over again. It seems so clear to me now. You're smart, just like I was back in high school. Don't you know how proud I felt when you were invited to join the National Honor Society? Don't throw away your dreams the same way I did!

Lesley, despite what your father insists, the thought of you marrying Buck leaves me shaking with fear. Look at me, sweetheart, because I'm terribly afraid that your future is my past. I'm pleading with you not to make the same mistakes I did. Think hard and long before you decide to marry Buck. I'll deal with your father and do whatever I can to help you.

Love,

Mom

May 1st

Nick,
Meet me behind the snack booth on prom night.
Jillian

Lesley's Diary

May 5, 1966

I felt my baby move for the first time and it surprised me so much that I stopped ironing and pressed my hand to my stomach. In the last few weeks, I thought that light fluttering might have been the baby, but there was no mistaking it this time.

I don't know what I'm going to do. Mom wrote me a letter and said she was afraid I was making the same mistakes she did and urged me not to marry Buck. I wish I was stronger. Not physically but emotionally. Everyone's pressuring me. Dad and Buck are adamant that marriage is the right thing. More and more, Buck acts like we're already married. Just when I thought I could go away and have the baby in a home, I learned that Buck had enlisted in the Army — without any of the guarantees that will keep him out of Vietnam. He did it for the baby and me. He loves me, I know he does. I'm so afraid he's going to end up fighting in that horrible war and all on my account.

So many people are against the war. There's talk of a huge rally at the Washington Monument protesting our involvement. Now that Buck's enlisted, I can't turn my back on him. Even if I found the strength to go away to one of those homes, I'd never have the courage to give up my baby for adoption. But I can't raise a child all by myself. Even though Mom would help me, there's only so much she can do. I already know my dad's thoughts on the subject. I feel like there's no solution to this. Whatever I decide will bitterly disappoint one of my parents.

I finally told Jillian about the baby and she burst into tears. I wept, too, although I've long recovered from the shock. She's sworn to secrecy. She knows if anyone at school ever found out, I wouldn't be allowed to graduate. Like everyone else, Jillian wants to know what I plan to do, as though I had a limitless number of options. Dear God in heaven, how I wish I did! She broke up with Scott and although she didn't say why, I knew it was over Nick Murphy. He's all she thinks about.

Lately I've been listening to the radio, just lying on my bed and staring up at the ceiling. The Beatles have a song, "Eleanor

Rigby." I'm beginning to feel like the girl in that song. Susan comes in and talks to me and we cry together. If this was happening to her, she wouldn't listen to either Buck or Dad. She's always been stronger than me. I told her that, and she stunned me by crying. She said she'd drop out of school and get a job and support me and the baby if I asked her to. I couldn't, but I love her all the more for offering. The other kids don't know yet, although I'm sure Mike suspects. We don't talk about it. We can't.

I saw Mom talking to Father Morris on Friday. I think she was talking about Buck and me. If we do marry, I want it to be in the Church. If I have anything to be grateful for, it's that my parents didn't kick me out of the house the way Mom's parents did to her.

Jillian's Diary

May 15, 1966

Prom Night

This had to be one of the most incredibly romantic nights of my life. Nick was waiting for me when I arrived at the football field and he was dressed in a suit, complete with tie and shiny new shoes. I was in my prom dress.

I lied to Mom and Dad about meeting Scott at

the prom. They seemed a little suspicious that Scott wasn't picking me up, but I explained that he couldn't because he's one of the King nominees. I hated lying, but they'd flip if they found out I was meeting Nick Murphy at the football stadium instead.

Nick set up his transistor radio and held out his arms to me and we danced beneath the stars. Just the two of us. He held me so close I could feel his heart beating. Even when a fast song came on, we danced slow, right through the commercials and everything. Neither one of us spoke for a long time.

After a while, he asked me what excuse I'd given Scott for not attending the prom. That was when I confessed I'd returned Scott's class ring. I've never seen anyone's eyes light up the way Nick's did once I told him. It didn't take him long to kiss me after that. Scott's kissed me plenty of times. I've been kissed by other boys, too, but this is the first kiss I've felt from the top of my head to the tips of my toes. I think Nick was just as surprised. We both trembled afterward, and he didn't kiss me again until it was time to leave. All the while we were together, I kept thinking how silly it is that we're meeting on the sly like this, but I didn't say anything for fear of breaking the mood. I like Nick so much, but I'm worried about how my parents would react if they knew I was dating him, especially my dad. He's got the wrong impression of Nick. I don't know how to convince Dad what a wonderful man Nick Murphy is. I don't dare say a word, but I hate deceiving my parents like this. It's even worse to feel that I need to.

❖

The Class of
Nineteen Hundred and Sixty-six
Holy Name Academy
Announces its
Commencement Exercises
Saturday evening, May twenty-eighth
At seven o'clock
Pine Ridge Community Center
Pine Ridge, Washington

❖

June 1, 1966

Dear Jillian,

You know I can't stand it when we argue. You're my best friend and we mean too much to each other to let anything or anyone come between us. That said, I want you to know I do believe you. If you say you saw Buck with some other girl on graduation night, then I know you did. But couldn't it have been someone who *looks* like Buck?

I asked him about it and he claims you couldn't have seen him. He swears he wasn't with any other girl. He implied that you're jealous and trying to make trouble for him. I know it isn't true, but I also know you don't think I should marry him. All I can say is that it must've been someone who looked a lot like him. Please, let's put this incident behind us. You're my best friend and I love you.

Lesley

P.S. I thought your Valedictory speech was wonderful. You did a much better job of it than I would have. I know it was our dream to be co-valedictorians, but that wasn't meant to be.

Mr. and Mrs. Michael Adamski
request the pleasure of your company
at the marriage of their daughter
Lesley Louise Adamski
to
David James Knowles
Saturday, June 11, 1966
at two o'clock in the afternoon
St. Catherine's Catholic Church
404 Mitchell Avenue
Pine Ridge, Washington
Reception immediately following the ceremony

MR. AND MRS. BUCK KNOWLES

July 2, 1966

Dear Mom and Dad,
I'm busy writing thank-you notes for the wedding gifts and I realized I hadn't sent one

to you. Buck and I owe you both so much and are extremely grateful for everything you've done. The pot and pan set is wonderful, and far and above what Buck and I expected, especially after you paid for the wedding.

We're very grateful for the used crib, too. Buck is going to refinish it once he's back from basic training. I love you both so much.

Buck, Lesley & ?

Jillian's Diary

August 3, 1966

I don't think I've ever been more disappointed in my mom and dad. I finally convinced Nick that my parents prize honesty above all else and that we should simply tell them we're going steady. He came to the house just the way I asked and Dad answered the door and almost didn't let him in because of his police record. (He was once charged with assault. It happened during a fight three years ago, and he was actually defending another boy. He got a suspended sentence.)

I stood with Nick and we held hands, but I could see that Nick was close to losing his cool. Mom wouldn't even look at him. And Dad treated him like a criminal for having the audacity to ask his little girl out on a date. What neither of my parents seems to understand is that I'm not a child. I'm eighteen years old and perfectly capable of making my own decisions, and I reminded my father of this before he had time to tell me otherwise. Dad insisted that it didn't matter what age I am. As long as I live under his roof, I have to do what he says and he doesn't want me dating Nick Murphy. Then Nick and Dad started shouting at each other and Nick stormed out. I haven't spoken to Mom or Dad since, but they can't stop me from seeing Nick and they know it.

They think that just because I'm leaving for college in a few weeks, what Nick and I feel for each other will end. I haven't told Nick yet, but I've decided I'm going to marry him. I knew it the first time he kissed me. No, even before that, when he *wouldn't* kiss me because I was wearing Scott's ring. He's everything I want in a husband. Three girls in our graduating class are already married. Lesley, Judy and Pam. Soon it will be Nick and me, and then we'll see what Dad has to say.

NAME: DAVID MICHAEL KNOWLES
BORN: SEPTEMBER 29, 1966
WEIGHT: 6 LBS, 7 OUNCES
LENGTH: 20 INCHES
PARENTS: BUCK AND LESLEY KNOWLES

JILLIAN LAWTON
BARNARD COLLEGE
PLIMPTON HALL
NEW YORK, NY 10025

October 10, 1966

Dearest Lesley,

I can't believe it, you're a mother! I opened the birth announcement and nearly screamed with excitement. I loved the picture, but really, Les, little David's going to be mortified when he's older and sees this photo of him only a few hours old with a blue ribbon in his hair. The poor thing. You didn't say a word about labor. Was it horrible?

I hate school. Well, not exactly hate it, but I miss everyone so much. Mostly Nick and you, of course. I'm living in a big dorm and sharing a room with Janice Stewart, a girl from Florida. She seems nice, but she isn't you. We talk some but we don't seem to have a lot in common. She doesn't have a boyfriend back home and doesn't understand what it is to miss someone the way I miss Nick.

Speaking of Nick, he can't afford phone calls and he doesn't want me "wasting" all my allowance on phoning him, so we write nearly every day. Don't be shocked if I tell you how much I love him. Please don't be like everyone else. Just be happy for me the way I am for you and Buck.

You asked about my classes, and thus far everything's going all right, I guess. The classes, especially history, are wonderful, with lots of discussion. If it wasn't for those I think I'd go nuts. Dad suggested I fulfill all the course requirements in my first year and I followed his advice, but I did sign up for one psychology class, which I'm really enjoying. New York isn't so bad, either, not the way I thought it would be. Last weekend, Janice and I went into Manhattan and took the ferry over to Ellis Island and climbed the Statue of Liberty.

Gotta scoot, but I promise I'll write again soon. I hope David likes the baby blanket. It's handmade (although not by me!).

Love,
Jillian

DEPARTMENT OF THE ARMY
Detachment C, 500th Personnel Services Battalion
Unit 20121
APO AE 09107

ORDERS 65-10 22 December 1966

KNOWLES, DAVID JAMES, 522-02-3776, SFC 587TH SIG CO 9WFTXAAO APO AE 09131

You will proceed on permanent change of station as shown. Information concerning port call will be provided separately.

You are hereby ordered to report for active duty in Vietnam.

Reporting Date: 26 December 1966

1967

JILLIAN LAWTON
BARNARD COLLEGE
PLIMPTON HALL
NEW YORK, NY 10025

January 16, 1967

Dear Nick,

I know we only said goodbye a few days ago, and already I find myself missing you so much I don't know how I can possibly go back to school. I can't bear to be this far away from you! The Christmas holidays were wonderful because of all the time we were able to spend together, despite my parents. You'd think that by now they'd realize you and I are serious.

I've always thought of my father as a man of wisdom, but these last three weeks have opened my eyes. Okay, he's right, you do have a record, but that happened years ago when you were fourteen. Everyone makes mistakes and your record's been clean ever since. I hate to say this, but my father is a fool.

I don't want you to feel bad about the argument between me and Dad. It's been building for a long time. I tried to talk to Mom and she listened, but I know she immediately told my father everything I said. I can't trust her. The only people I can talk to anymore are you and Lesley. How different all our lives are from just a year ago! Last year at this time the most pressing problem was what theme to choose for the Junior/Senior Prom.

Lesley looked good, don't you think? I didn't mind that Buck wasn't there when we went to visit. Little Davey is a beautiful baby. Holding him made me long for a baby of my own. I'd need to think about who his daddy would be. Any volunteers?

Again, I want you to know that I truly love the medal of the Virgin Mary you gave me. I'll treasure it forever. It's especially dear to me because it once belonged to your mother. Every time I miss you, I reach for it and hold it tight and am instantly reassured of your love. It's on a long chain and falls close to my heart. That's where you are, even though we can't be together.

You don't need to say the words, Nick. I already know how you feel about me because that's the way I feel about you. I love you, Nick, heart and soul. I don't care what my parents say. I don't care what anyone says. I'm crazy in love with you.

I want you to seriously consider what I mentioned on New Year's Eve. I know Pine Ridge is your home and where your dad's gas station is, but at least consider moving to New York. Just think of all the money we'd save on phone calls and stamps!! I can't imagine what life will be like without you for the next three and a half years. I'm not sure I can continue with school if it means we can't be together.

Promise me you'll think about it, okay? And write me soon. I live for your letters.

Hugs and kisses,

Jillian

❖

January 27, 1967

My dearest Jillian,

Me move to New York? I thought you were joking when you suggested it earlier, but I can see now that you were serious. Sweetheart, I can't. Not because it isn't tempting — I'm here to tell you everything about you tempts me and has since the first moment I saw you. More than anything, I want to be close to you, but Dad needs my help at the gas station. Jimmy's getting to be a handful, too. He's fourteen and the kid needs his big brother around to keep an eye on him. Besides, my dad's working out a deal with one of his buddies who teaches at Bailey's Trade School to get me my mechanic's certification. I'll be taking some night classes. Seeing that I've been tinkering with cars since I was twelve, it seems a waste of time for me to go to some school when I already know practically everything there is to know about engines.

But there's more to my decision than sticking around Pine Ridge to help Jimmy and to work with my dad. Me going to New York wouldn't be right for us.

We both know what would happen if I found a way for us to be together. First thing, your grades would fall. You're smart, really smart. Sometimes I have to pinch myself to believe that the valedictorian of Holy Name Academy is dating a hellion like me. The temptation would be too much for us, and that wouldn't be good for a couple of Catholic kids who have enough trouble keeping their hands off each other. Feeling the way I do about you, I should be canonized! You don't make it any easier, either. If you think your parents disapprove of me now, you can bet your bottom dollar they'd really hate me if your grades dropped and you turned up pregnant. The last thing I want to do is alienate them completely.

Talking about your parents, I'm going to say something I should've said when you were home. Don't concern yourself with this business between your old man and me. I don't mean to be a chump, Jillian, but he is your father. Looking at it from his perspective, you have to admit he's got a point. I have a juvenile police record. Your father wants what's best for you. It's my job to prove to him that what's best for you is *me*. In other words this is between your dad and me. Not between your dad, you and me. Understand?

In time, I'm going to prove to your parents that I'm worthy of their beautiful daughter. My dad drilled into me a long time ago that anything of lasting value is worth waiting for. You, Jillian, are worth waiting ten lifetimes for.

Another thing, and I know you don't want to talk about this, but we can't ignore it any longer. I registered for the draft last year and who knows what's going to happen with that. My dad's worried about it and he's got enough on his plate without me leaving because I want to be with my girl.

I love you heart and soul, too. I love you enough to do what's right for us, even when it isn't easy.

Study hard. You're going to be a terrific lawyer one day.

All my love,
Nick

P.S. God bless the families of Virgil Grissom, Edward White and Roger Chaffee. What a horrible way to die. When I go, I pray it isn't in a fire.

❖

February 4, 1967

Dear Buck,

I haven't heard from you since Christmas

and I hope everything's all right. Almost every night the television is filled with stories about what's going on in Vietnam. Two of the boys in Susan's class have already decided to enlist as soon as they graduate.

Little David is getting big and sassy, just like his daddy. He'll be five months old soon and already has a tooth coming in. I'm sending along a few more pictures so you can see for yourself how much he's changing. He's a good baby.

I know you don't approve of my part-time job at the library, but the extra money is a blessing. You don't need to worry about strangers watching David, either. Mom baby-sits for me. I've been putting the money I earn aside so I can join you in Hawaii the way you mentioned in your last letter. Don't be angry about me having a job. I like getting out of the house and you know how much I enjoy reading.

Dad wanted you to know there'll be a job for you at the mill once you're out of the Army. He'll make sure of that. You can be on the same crew as before.

Write me soon, okay?

Your wife,

Lesley

JILLIAN LAWTON
BARNARD COLLEGE
PLIMPTON HALL
NEW YORK, NY 10025

March 9, 1966

Dear Lesley,

It was great to hear from you. I loved the photograph of Davey with his one tooth. And I loved the picture of you holding him on your lap. You look radiant, like a classic madonna with child. I'm so glad everything's working out for you, and I'm glad Buck's okay.

The news is full of Vietnam. I'm worried about what's happening with our country. I don't understand why we're even there. My parents support the war. They say it's important to wipe out Communism before it overtakes the world. I don't know what I believe. I don't want Communism to spread, either, but I'm not sure it's worth this horrible war.

I've been so homesick all week and your letter went a long way toward cheering me up. I've been in the doldrums ever since Christmas vacation and the disagreement between Nick and my parents. Nick told me to stay out of it but it's hard not to defend him. Speaking of Nick, did I mention he's in trade school? Plus, he works long hours at his dad's service station. Because he's so busy, he can only write three times a week. I miss him so much. It kills me the way Mom and Dad act toward him.

When I asked to come home for spring break, they said no, that I'd be home soon enough. Can you believe it? They seem to think that if they keep Nick and me apart I'll forget about him. Since I can't fly home, I've decided to attend a protest rally and peace march in the city. Janice, my roommate, asked me to go with her. We're making a banner that says MAKE LOVE, NOT WAR. Pete Seeger's going to be there and Martin Luther King, Jr. and Benjamin Spock, the famous pediatrician. The crowd should be huge. Everyone's already talking about it and the rally isn't even happening until next month. I can't go home, so why shouldn't I attend a peace march?

Did I tell you in my last letter how Mom and Dad tried to fix me up with a friend of theirs? He's over thirty! He phoned and invited me to dinner. Montgomery Gordon — even his name is boring. I don't need to meet him to know he's a stuffed shirt. I'm not actually sure why he's in town. He told me but I've forgotten. I guess that tells you what I thought of him. Needless to say, I declined the invitation.

On another subject, I think it's great that you're working at the library part-time. Remember how we used to stay up all night to read books out loud to each other? I miss those times.

I'm lonely and miserable and I hate everything about New York. I never wanted to attend

Barnard College. It was Dad's idea. I'm nineteen and legally an adult, but my parents continue to control my life. Why can't they accept that I'm my own person?

It isn't only being stuck here during spring break, it's Nick, too. I want to be with him, but the minute I mention his name my parents get all uptight. Dad constantly reminds me that Nick has a police record. Then I remind him that everyone deserves a second chance.

You'd think that after spending nineteen years raising me, they'd have some faith in my judgement. Oh well, crying on your shoulder doesn't change anything, but it does help. You were always the one friend I could talk to, no matter what.

I'm so happy you're finally going to see Hawaii. I know you and Buck will love it. You both need a little R and R. I knew you'd get to the islands sooner or later! Waikiki can be wildly romantic. How I envy you spending a whole week with the one you love.

Although it seems like forever, I'll be home in June. We'll spend lots of time together then, I promise.

Love,
Jillian

A Message from Southeast Asia

March 28, 1967

Dear Lesley,

Baby, I'm crazy to see you again. Everything's been arranged. When you arrive in Hawaii, take the shuttle bus from the airport to the hotel. I'll land the next morning, but the way things happen around here, it wouldn't surprise me if I didn't make it to the hotel until late afternoon. Be waiting for me! I've got six months of loving to make up for, so if you're thinking about wasting time sunbathing on the beaches, you can forget that.

Give Davey a hug and kiss from his old man.

Love,

Buck

Lesley's Diary

April 10, 1967

I can't believe I'm really here in Hawaii! It's just like Jillian described it, with the tall palm trees, pearly sand and lush orchids. I can hear the sounds of the ocean from my room, which has a balcony that faces — well, sort of faces — the beach. Normally we'd be staying in a military hotel, but with so many servicemen coming to the islands from Vietnam, Buck was booked into a civilian hotel. This is going to work out just great.

My plane landed at four and I took the shuttle, just the way Buck said in his letter. Unfortunately he didn't tell me what to do about dinner. The room service menu is much too expensive. It'll be a cold day in hell before I pay $1.00 for a cup of coffee! Mom and Dad repeatedly warned me against going out at night by myself, so I don't feel comfortable leaving the hotel. I stayed in my room and went without dinner.

I miss Davey so much. This is the first time we've been separated for more than a few hours. I feel like I left part of myself in Pine Ridge. I want to call home and tell everyone I'm here, but Buck told me not to use the phone. He said it costs an arm and a leg to make long-distance calls from a hotel room.

I stood out on the balcony in the dark and sang torch songs at the top of my lungs. No one could hear me, not with the surf pounding against the sand below. I'm so anxious to see Buck again. It's been nearly eight months since we were together. He doesn't write often, but I understand how difficult it must be when he's so far from home and everything.

I'm hungry, but sleepy too. Since I skipped dinner, I'll have a little extra money to buy

Mom something special for watching Davey. She's a wonderful grandma. I'll write more later.

❖

Barbara Lawton
2330 Country Club Lane
Pine Ridge, Washington 98005

April 11, 1967

Dear Jillian,

It was good to talk to you this afternoon, and I'm sorry the conversation took such an unpleasant turn. I don't know what it is with you and your father lately. You two clash at every opportunity, but I suspect it's because you're so much alike. You might resemble me in looks, Jillian, but I fear you were cursed with your father's stubbornness. Sometimes I swear I don't know what I'm going to do with the two of you.

I know how unhappy you are and that you want to transfer to the University of Washington next autumn, but your father is adamant you continue your studies at Barnard. Although you didn't actually say it, I'm wondering how much this desire to change schools has to do with that boyfriend of yours. You know how Dad and I feel about Nick Murphy. Jillian, the boy has no future. His father is a grease monkey and from all appearances, that's Nick's future, too.

There's nothing wrong with a man who works with his hands. It's just that your father and I want better for you. You may be right when you say we're snobs, although we don't mean to be. You're our only child. Try to understand. Be patient with us and make an effort to see the situation from our point of view. Your aunt Jillian, God rest her soul, set aside these funds for your education. Both your father and I feel the best place for you is Barnard College. We can't allow you to do something now that you're sure to regret later, and all because you miss your boyfriend.

If you and Nick truly love each other as you claim, then he'll wait for you. These years will fly by so quickly you'll barely notice. It might not seem like it now, but you have your whole lives ahead of you. What are a few years?

You talked a great deal about being an adult and you say you're capable of making your own decisions. Your father and I are giving you the opportunity to live up to that. Be adult about this, accept the wisdom of what we're saying and stay at Barnard College.

Love,
Mom

April 15, 1967

Dear Mom,

Isn't Hawaii beautiful? I thought you'd enjoy this postcard of the beach. Buck didn't arrive until late the afternoon of the 11th. I stayed in my room until I got so hungry I couldn't wait to eat, then I went down to the beach. I met a really wonderful Navy Officer who sat with me. His name is Cole Greenberg. We talked about books and music and life. He hates the war too. Cole knows a lot about the history of Vietnam and Southeast Asia. We talked for a long time and he said he'd like to report the news on television one day. He wanted to buy my breakfast but I told him he shouldn't because I'm married. He said Buck is a lucky man. I have lots to tell you. Give Davey a big kiss for me.

Love, Lesley

U.S.
Postage
3¢

Mrs. Dorothy Adamski,
326 Front St.,
Pine Ridge, WA
98005

JILLIAN LAWTON
BARNARD COLLEGE
PLIMPTON HALL
NEW YORK, NY 10025

April 20,1967

Dear Mom and Dad,

Sometimes I wonder if I could truly be your daughter. For the first time in my life, I'm ashamed of you both. After our "discussion" last Christmas, Nick said this matter was between you and him. He asked me to stay out of it. I've tried to do that, but you make it impossible. How dare you judge Nick because he's a mechanic! The term is mechanic, Mom, not grease monkey. And he has a name, a very nice name, I might add. Nick Murphy. You'd better get used to hearing it because I fully intend to marry him with or without your approval.

You say I should start acting like an adult and accept your decision. You've given me no alternative. How convenient. The trust fund is in my name but you control it. Either I attend the school of your choice or else. Well, thanks for nothing!

Jillian

A Message from Southeast Asia

May 15, 1967

Dear Lesley,

Listen, baby, I got some unpleasant news. There are all kind of weird diseases a guy is susceptible to here in the tropics, and it looks like I might have gotten a dose of something bad. Now don't get upset, but there's a chance I might have given you this disease so I need you to go to the doctor and tell him what I wrote. He'll know what to do. It's nothing to worry about, baby. All you'll need is a few shots of penicillin.

I'm sorry if I was too demanding of you physically, but you have to understand it's been a long time since I was with my wife and, baby, I missed you. Seeing all that tourist stuff didn't interest me, anyway. I don't know what's the big deal with the Pearl Harbor Memorial. I see enough of war now without being reminded of it. There was no reason to get your nose out of joint over it. Besides, I said you could keep that job at the library as long as you're a decent mother to my kid.

Write me soon.

Buck

June 17, 1967

Dear Jillian,

I need a shoulder to cry on. If I had the money I'd phone, but our budget just doesn't allow for long-distance calls. There's a reason you haven't heard from me. Oh, Jillian, I'm pregnant again.

I couldn't see any reason to go on the pill with Buck in Vietnam. Besides, it's a problem with the way the Church feels about birth control, and I was hoping to avoid facing the issue. Then I met Buck in Hawaii. I know my postcard made it sound like I had the time of my life, but I didn't.

The first day was wonderful. Buck was delayed and I got tired of sitting in the hotel room by myself and wandered out to the beach. I met a Naval Officer there, someone who likes books and music. We sat and talked for the longest time. Later I wondered what would've happened if I'd met Cole before I met Buck. He'd read the same books as me. Michener's *Hawaii* and Leon Uris's *Exodus*, and he carefully follows world news, just like I do. We got into a big debate about what's happening in the Middle East, and that was just before the Six-Day War in Israel. He knew about the Palestine Liberation Organization, which I'd never heard of until then. Meeting him made me realize how much I've missed by marrying Buck.

Oh, Jillian, I'm afraid I've made a terrible mistake.

What I'm about to write next you have to promise never to tell anyone. Time slipped away from me while I was talking to Cole and I hurried back to the hotel to see if Buck had arrived. When I passed through the lobby I caught sight of him in the cocktail lounge. He was necking with a woman in the far corner. He didn't see me and I pretended not to see him.

I know I should've confronted him about that woman right then and there, but I didn't. I knew that if I asked about her, we'd spend the entire seven days arguing. I couldn't bear it. Instead I'm pregnant again.

To make things worse, he wrote me the next month and said I should see a doctor because of some tropical disease he picked up. The doctor didn't answer my questions directly, but I think it might have been V.D.

Oh, Jillian, I'm so humiliated and upset and worried. I can't stand it anymore. I know you'll be home from school soon. I've never needed to talk to you so much. Please call me as soon as you're in town.

Lesley

July 1, 1967

Dear Lesley,

So you're knocked up again. Hey, that's great! Davey could use a little brother or sister. Don't you worry. Take care of yourself, you hear?

I love you.

Buck

P.S. I don't think it's a good idea for you to continue working at the library in your condition.

July 3, 1967

My darling Nick,

It doesn't look like I'm going to be able to get out of this 4th of July outing with my parents. We'll make our own fireworks later. Meet me at midnight at the snack booth behind the football field.

Jillian

Jillian's Diary

July 5, 1967

Mom and Dad and I are barely on speaking terms. They caught me sneaking into the house at three a.m. after meeting Nick. From the way they acted, you'd think they found us in bed naked! Dad lectured me for an entire thirty minutes and when he finished, Mom started in. Finally I couldn't take it anymore and exploded. I'm almost twenty years old!!!

Dad threatened to throw me out of the house. My own father! Mom was sobbing and I was too angry to be careful of what I said and I told them what I really thought. They are such snobs.

I wish I could talk to Lesley, but she's got enough troubles of her own. She's as miserable with this second pregnancy as she was with the first, perhaps more so. It isn't just the pregnancy, either. This marriage is all wrong. I knew it the day I saw Buck with Tessa McKnight, but Lesley didn't want to hear the truth. Not when she was six months pregnant with Buck's baby and the wedding invitations were in the mail. I can't say I blame her. What a mess and now, God forbid, she's pregnant again.

I wish I knew how to help her, but I can't even find solutions to my own problems. Nick wants to talk to my parents again, face to face, and have this out, once and for all. I don't see how it'll do any good, but he thinks it might help. I don't know anymore. I just don't know.

One thing I'm going to do is take a stand. I refuse to return to Barnard College this September. If Mom and Dad won't let me attend the University of Washington, then I'm dropping out of school. I never knew my parents could be so unreasonable. I refuse to be that far away from Nick any longer. We've spent almost the entire year separated from each other and we're more in love than ever. That's got to prove something. What I feel for him isn't just an infatuation. I love him heart and soul. Sometimes it frightens me how deeply I feel. He's my everything.

❖

July 15

Nick,

I'm leaving a note on your windshield to let you know Dad took the phone out of my room so I won't be able to call you without them listening in on our conversation. Not to worry, I think I've found the solution to our problems.

Let's get married.

Do you realize nearly one third of my high-school class is either married or engaged only 14 months after graduation? It'll work. We'll make it work. I'll phone you as soon as I'm home from Republican headquarters. Dad volunteered me to fold brochures with Montgomery Gordon. I hope you're insanely jealous.

Lots of love,
Jillian

July 15, 1967

Jillian,

It isn't every day a man gets a marriage proposal taped to his windshield. Sweetheart, be serious. I've got two months of mechanic's school left. I need that stupid certification if I'm going to get a decent job. I want to marry you but I'm not prepared to propose until I can support you and buy a decent engagement ring. I want to buy you a diamond big enough to impress your daddy's friends. Besides, you need to finish school first.

I know you don't want to wait that long to get married; I don't either, but we have to. When we march down that church aisle, it'll be with your parents' blessing. That's a must for you and for me. All I need is time to prove myself. Let's both be patient, all right? I know it's hard, but it's necessary.

So your phone's gone. You're the only girl I ever knew who had a phone in her bedroom, anyway, so it's no big deal. We can still talk. Meet me at the dance in the park on Friday night — and be sure to wear some flowers in your hair.

Nick

September 15, 1967

Jillian left for college this morning. I didn't get a chance to ask her why she decided to return to New York, especially when she was so adamant about transferring to the University of Washington. But I have my suspicions. I think Nick felt that her going back was the best thing. I think they must've made some sort of pact. Jillian desperately wanted them to run away and get married, but Nick refused. He wants to marry her, but he won't officially propose until he's gained her parents' blessing. I admire him for that. Still, I know Jillian convinced him to make love to her. I never thought I'd be a mother before my best friend lost her virginity. Jillian didn't tell me much, but she said it was as beautiful as she always dreamed. I try not to think about my first time with Buck because all I can remember is the pain and the humiliation.

Davey and I rode to the airport with Jillian and her mother. The air was thick with hostility between the two of them. I wanted to tell Mrs. Lawton that Nick is a wonderful man if only she'd give him a chance to prove it to her and Judge Lawton.

Mrs. Lawton plied me with questions on the drive home. She's worried about Jillian seeing so much of Nick, but I didn't tell her anything. Nick and Jillian are deeply in love and it hurts me to see Jillian this unhappy. I think her parents are all wrong about Nick. He won my respect this summer just because of the way he treats Jillian. I never thought of Judge Lawton as unreasonable but he certainly is as far as Nick is concerned.

These last three months have flown by much too fast. I didn't get to spend nearly enough time with Jillian. It was a long, hot summer of urban anger and violence all across the country. It seems like the whole world is angry. I'm angry over giving in to Buck and quitting my job at the library. He insisted because of the baby and all the problems I'm having with this pregnancy, and I finally agreed. Jillian's angry about the way her parents treat Nick. Judge and Mrs. Lawton are angry with Jillian because she's in love with Nick.

I've been feeling sick and I worry that all those shots the doctor had to give me might have hurt the baby. Twice now I've had spotting episodes, which frightened me. The last time I was in to see the doctor, the blood tests said I was anemic. This pregnancy feels different, but I'm in and out of the doctor's so fast I hardly have a chance to ask him anything. I wonder if the baby knows how much I don't want to be pregnant.

God forgive me, some nights I lie awake and think about Cole Greenberg and dream about that morning on the beach in Hawaii. I wonder if he remembers me. Those few hours with him were like an oasis in some vast desert. It's a memory that's sustained me these last months.

Now Jillian's gone back to school again. Buck will be home from Vietnam soon, but he doesn't have any idea where he'll be stationed. I don't want to think about that, or this baby or anything else. I just want to close my eyes and remember sitting on the beach talking about books with a Naval Officer who made me smile and encouraged me to express my opinions. Who made me wish my life was different . . .

❖

October 1, 1967

Dear Susan,

Well, little sister, you're off to start your life in the Navy. It seems like only last week that we shared a bedroom. Now I'm a mother and you're going away to serve Uncle Sam. You'll be a wonderful corpsman. I'm proud of you, Susan, and happy you have this opportunity. I know you're going to prove yourself and get picked for nursing school. Write when you can.

Love,
Lesley

October 16, 1967

Dear Jillian,

It's official now. I got my mechanic's certification in the mail and graduated at the top of my class. Dad still wants me to work weekends for him, but the guy from the Chevy dealership offered me a job starting at $5.00 an hour. With that kind of money I'll be able to buy a special Christmas gift for my girl.

Life feels damn good just now. I wish like crazy you were here to share it with me. Was I really the one who convinced you to return to Barnard College? I should have my head examined. Christmas can't come soon enough to suit me.

Remember how much I love you.

Nick

Approval Not Required.

SELECTIVE SERVICE SYSTEM

ORDER TO REPORT FOR INDUCTION

The President of the United States,

(Local Board Stamp)

To Mr. Nicholas Murphy
247 Virginia Court
Pine Ridge, Washington
98005

....
(Date of mailing)

SELECTIVE SERVICE NO.

GREETING:

You are hereby ordered for induction into the Armed Forces of the United States, and to report

at...
(Place of reporting)

on.................................at.................................
(Date) (Hour)

for forwarding to an Armed Forces Induction Station.

....
(Member, Executive Secretary, or clerk of Local Board)

Birth Announcement

I'm so excited

I just had a Mom and Dad

Name: Lindy Marie Knowles

Born: December 15, 1967

Weight: 4 lbs., 3 oz.

Length: 17 inches

Parents: Buck and Lesley Knowles

1968

Lesley's Diary

January 15, 1968

My Lindy, born five weeks premature, is officially one month old today. I go to the hospital every morning to spend time with her, touch her, reassure her of my love. The poor thing is so tiny and she's got all these tubes coming in and out of her. I've learned that those last few weeks of pregnancy make all the difference.

Everyone is amazed that Lindy's managed to hold on this long, but not me. This child has grit. I feel it in her, this determination, this overpowering will to beat the odds. Buck says I should be more realistic and accept the fact that we're probably going to lose her. I refuse to think that way. If he spent more time with her, he'd know how badly our daughter wants to live, how fiercely she's battling for life each and every day.

I go to Mass every morning to ask God to be merciful to my little girl. I love her so much I can barely bring myself to think about the possibility that she might die. Dad said it'd be for the best. I couldn't believe my own father would say such a thing! More and more I find myself unable to cope with my father and avoid him as much as I can. It's because of Dad that Susan joined the Navy. His unwillingness to educate his daughters is barbaric. Dad continues to insist that if anyone gets a higher education in this family, it'll be Mike or Joe or maybe Bruce. But not Susan, Lily or me. I had my chance and often wonder what would've happened had I been able to accept that scholarship from the Soroptimists.

With Dad forcefully reminding her that college was out of the question, Susan became more determined than ever to make something of her life. When she talked with the Navy recruiter, she saw a way to forge a future for herself. She joined the Navy because she wanted out from under our father's thumb. She couldn't tolerate his views toward women any longer. The military is the only means she has of getting an education and becoming a nurse. It frightens me that she might end up in Vietnam, but I refuse to think about that. She's doing what Mom and I can only dream about now.

The Army gave Buck compassionate leave after Lindy was born, but he doesn't like spending time at the hospital. Sometimes Mom or a friend will drive me there and back. Or else Buck drops me off and then comes back later to pick me up. He doesn't like to be without a car. I'm so grateful Mom's been able to watch Davey for me.

It looks like Buck's going to be stationed in California for the rest of his stint in the Army. I've already decided to stay here in Washington in order to be close to my family. Buck would rather I joined him, but he understands. He's been really good with Davey. These last few weeks are the first time he's had a chance to know his son. For all his faults, Buck can be sweet when he wants to. Davey idolizes his father.

❖

January 21, 1968

Dear Jillian,

I know you were upset with me because I refused to move to Canada after my draft notice arrived. I prefer to believe you weren't serious. Remember how I told you everything would work out? Well, now it's happening just the way I said it would. I have terrific news.

First, you'll notice that the return address on this envelope is different. I'm at Fort Rucker now and I was pegged for the infantry in AIT — Advanced Individual Training. Yesterday I learned I'd been selected for training to be a helicopter pilot.

You said when you gave me back my mother's medal that it would protect me. I think you must be right. It's certainly bringing me luck. Still, I can't wait for the day I can put it back around your neck where it belongs.

Anyway, here's the best part about me being a pilot. As soon as I'm finished with this training, I'll become a warrant officer. Soon they'll be saluting me. Before long I'll be piloting a Huey and, sweetheart, it's a beaut. I was sure the Army would want me as a mechanic, since I'm already qualified in that area, but not so. Just think. Me, a pilot! This is great news, isn't it? I couldn't be more excited.

Basic training was hell, but your letters got me through it. The BS in the Army is neck-deep, and that isn't going to change any time soon. But damn it all, I can put up with just about anything if they're gonna make me a pilot.

I start training right away. I called my dad and he's so damn proud it's a wonder the buttons didn't bust right off his shirt. I talked to Jimmy, too, and told him that if he didn't shape up in school I was personally going to rip him a new set of lips. That kid's a handful.

Be pleased for me, Jillian, and don't worry. Nothing's going to happen to me. A year from now, I'll be finished with my tour of duty in Vietnam and we can talk about setting a date for the wedding. Your father might have trouble accepting a mechanic as a son-in-law, but my guess is he'll find a pilot far more palatable.

Remember how much I love you.
Nick

❖

February 19, 1968

Dear Jillian,

Oh, Jillian, you'll never guess what! I won $350 at St. Catherine's Friday night bingo. Mom talked me into going with her and had Mike and Joe watch Davey. The hospital said I can bring Lindy home next week and bingo was a time for us to celebrate. I was just thrilled. We could use that money for a hundred different things, but I didn't dare tell Buck about it. Guess what I did? You won't believe it. I bought myself a car. I've needed one so badly these last few months and Buck took ours to California. I've had to rely on Mom and anyone who was willing to drive me to Madegan Hospital in order to be with Lindy.

I know what you're thinking, that for $350 I wasn't able to get much of a car, but I got an excellent buy. It's a brownish 1957 Chevy with a stick shift. I took it over to Nick's father and had him check it out. He said it was in decent shape. All it needed was new brakes and a couple of other things to make it run really well. I'm so grateful for his help.

You know, my mother's something of a surprise to me. While I was growing up, I didn't understand or appreciate her the way I do now. It angered me that she let Dad drink so much. I hate to say it, but I blamed Mom for Dad's drinking — for putting up with it and not forcing him to stop. I saw her as weak. I view things differently now. Mom isn't weak at all, but strong, so much stronger than I gave her credit for. She's the one who held the family together. When she needed Dad to do something, it got done. I'd never have had the wedding I did without my mother. She stood up to Dad. She told him she wasn't going to let him treat me the way her father had treated her. She's got a part-time job now, too, and she keeps that money for herself.

I know you're worried about Nick going to Vietnam, and I don't blame you, especially since the situation seems to be heating up. I heard on the news last week that we might have as many as 500,000 troops there by the end of this year. What's happening in our world? Remember how the riots in Watts shocked us in 1965? Then Detroit and Newark followed. Students are demonstrating against the war, too.

Even though this Vietnam mess is scary, Nick will be all right, I'm sure of it. Buck returned safe and sound and he'll be discharged before long. Those twelve months he was in Vietnam went by fast. Nick's year will, too.

I was excited about the bingo win and wanted to let you know.

Loads of love,

Lesley

JILLIAN LAWTON
BARNARD COLLEGE
PLIMPTON HALL
NEW YORK, NY 10025

April 7, 1968

Dear Mom and Dad,

I've made a decision about this summer. I won't be coming home the way I'd originally planned. After last summer, I suspect you're both relieved. While I might be too young to vote in this year's election, I can still volunteer to work for the candidate of my choice. I know this will come as a surprise, but I'll be working to get Robert Kennedy elected as president of the United States.

Yes, Dad, I'm fully aware that Robert Kennedy is a Democrat. I'm also aware that our family has voted Republican since time began. But I refuse to blindly step into line and vote a certain way simply because that's the way you and Mom vote.

I realized I was a Democrat three days ago, when Martin Luther King, Jr. was assassinated. What is wrong with our country that people are killed in the streets because of what they believe? For the last couple of years, I haven't said anything because I wanted to maintain our fragile peace. Unlike you, I've kept my opinions to myself. Martin Luther King, Jr. is dead. 125 cities across the country are in flames. Federal troops and the National Guard are patrolling our streets. As I thought about it, I realized that at some point this summer you'd volunteer my services to the Nixon campaign. In good conscience, I can no longer support your political choices and I can no longer remain silent. Yes, Daddy, I'm staging my own personal demonstration for truth.

Although you haven't asked, I want you to know that Nick has completed his pilot training at Ft. Rucker and is shipping out to Vietnam within the month. My heart goes with him. I urged him to move to Canada, but he refused. He insisted that since he enjoyed the benefits of this country's freedom, he felt obliged to fight when called upon. If anything happens to him, I'll never be able to forgive the establishment.

I don't expect either of you to agree with my politics, but I'm hoping you'll respect my right to make my own decisions.

Your daughter,

Jillian

May 8, 1968

Dear Buck,

Everything's set for the kids and me to join you in California. I would've preferred to remain in Washington State, but you're right: a wife's place is with her husband. Davey, Lindy and I are taking the train down and will arrive on the afternoon of the 21st.

Mom, Mike and Joe are driving down in my car for a short vacation without Dad. They're following the van that's hauling our furniture. I'm anxious to see you, too. I'm so glad you were able to get base housing for us.

Lindy weighs almost ten pounds now and is growing every day. She might have been born five weeks premature, but she's made up for it ever since. In the early days, shortly after she was born when we didn't know if she'd live or die, I pleaded with God to let her live, and He answered my prayers. On her last visit, Dr. Owen said Lindy shouldn't suffer any permanent damage from being a preemie.

One reason I mentioned Lindy is because of an issue you and I haven't discussed before, and that's birth control. We've had two children in two years. I might want another baby later, but I don't right now. I'm sure you agree. Davey and Lindy demand all my attention. At the same time, I don't want to go against the teachings of the Church. God answered my prayers with regard to Lindy, and it seems selfish of me to disregard the Church's teaching in the area of birth control now. What I'm asking, Buck, is that we practice the rhythm method. It means that during certain times of the month, we have to abstain from intercourse. I know you, Buck, and you won't want to wait, but for the sanity of your wife you must. Please think about this, all right? I'm bringing it up now because, as best as I can figure, my fertile time begins the day we arrive. So don't get any ideas about me falling into bed with you that night. We aren't doing it until I can be sure I won't get pregnant again.

I look forward to seeing you, and the kids are anxious to be with their daddy.

Love,

Lesley

❖

Outside Khe Sanh in South Vietnam

June 15, 1968

Dearest Jillian,

I got your letter written June 5th just this morning. It's hard to believe that Robert Kennedy is dead. Assassinated like his brother. I didn't see any of the news about the train crossing the country with his body or how people came to stand and watch it pass. Unfortunately, we don't get much news here of what's happening back home. In some ways that's a good thing, but in others it isn't.

I can't blame you for wanting to stay in New York this summer, but, sweetheart, perhaps it would be best if you went home for a while. You've had a shock. The entire country has. Go home, make peace with your parents. They love you, just as I do.

You asked how I am, and I can honestly say that I'm doing all right today. Yesterday was a different story. We got orders to fly into this valley where 50 VC were reported on the ridgeline outside our position. It was raining like nothing I've ever seen but I managed to get the chopper in. The soldiers I was flying were able to jump free. That was when I spotted the VC hiding in the bushes. Before I knew it, all hell had broken loose.

I don't know who said 50 VC, but I'd say the count was off by a hundred or more. By that time, other choppers were coming in and there was shooting from all directions. I got the hell out of there, but it wasn't pretty.

Our crew chief was shot up and I managed to get him out before we were completely surrounded. He says if it wasn't for me he'd have died. When they carried him to the hospital, he grabbed my hand because he was hurting so bad.

His leg had been shot to hell and his blood was mixing with the rain. I told him he had a million-dollar wound. He had his teeth clenched against the pain, but he smiled at that. If you have a million-dollar wound, you get sent back state-side so if you're going to get hit, you want one that'll send you home.

Yesterday is over, and today is better. I'm fine, don't worry about me. I probably shouldn't have told you about the battle. I'm gaining more experience all the time and becoming a better pilot. I like flying. I get a thrill out of it, a rush of excitement whenever I lift that Huey off the ground. What really excites me is that once this insane war is over, I can continue being a pilot.

I'd like to pursue a career in aviation once I'm a civilian again. A married civilian. Each day I find reasons to regret not running away and marrying you last summer when you proposed. I can hardly wait to tell our children that their mother was the one who first popped the question.

I've made some friends here. We watch each other's back, so you don't need to worry. Enclosed is a photo of me — I'm the tall, handsome one and the ugly guy standing next to me is Brad Lincoln from Atlanta, Georgia. He's another helicopter pilot. The two of us have been talking about starting up a business together. Brad's a good friend and like I said, we look out for each other. It helps knowing he's there for me.

Don't forget how much I love you.

Nick

JILLIAN LAWTON
BARNARD COLLEGE
PLIMPTON HALL
NEW YORK, NY 10025

August 1, 1968

Dearest Nick,

Tell me about your bad days. I want to know everything.

I had a rotten day today. I wasn't sure coming back to Pine Ridge was the right thing to do, but I felt so lost after what happened to Robert Kennedy. Being around my friends sounded like a wonderful idea; now I'm not so sure.

Lesley is in California and my other friends are all married or engaged. I saw Cindy briefly, but we didn't have anything to talk about. Most days I wander down to the gas station and visit with your dad and Jimmy.

Missing Lesley is bad enough, but then my dad tried to arrange a date with that friend of his again. I was rude to them both. It angered me so much that my father would do such a thing when he knows how I feel about you.

That's not the worst of it. Mom suggested I shop for new clothes for school and it sounded like fun. I decided to drive into Seattle, to the Jay Jacobs store, which has always been a favorite of mine. At the Seattle Center I ran into a group of war protesters. I know it was foolish of me, but I couldn't allow them to say the things they were saying. They called our troops "baby killers" and I couldn't let that go and got into a shouting match with them. They have it all wrong, but before I could explain myself, one of the demonstrators threw a tomato at me. Oh, Nick, it was just awful.

I'm fine. All the tomato did was stain my dress. But it showed me how heated people's feelings are about this war. I tried so hard to get them to understand how important it is for everyone at home to support our troops. The war is wrong, but our men are only doing what our government has ordered. It was stupid to try to reason with a crowd – I had a lot of insults thrown at me, as well as the tomato. As you might guess, my father was terribly upset by the entire incident. Now he doesn't want me driving into Seattle unless Mom accompanies me.

I probably shouldn't have told you this. Don't be like Dad and get upset, okay?

I love you so much, and am counting the days until you're home. If you don't marry me the instant you step off that plane, I'll never forgive you.

Remember how much I love you.

Jillian

August 3, 1968

I'm so furious with Buck I can hardly think straight. The minute he got his paycheck he disappeared with his drinking buddies and didn't return until the wee hours of the morning. He crawled into bed, smelling of beer, and immediately wanted to make love. I told him we couldn't because it was my fertile time of the month. He knows I don't want another baby so soon after Lindy. He kept insisting we do it, and wouldn't take no for an answer. He tried sweet-talking me into it, but I repeatedly said no. Eventually he got mad and said he might as well find himself a real woman. That was when I suggested he search in the cocktail lounge in Waikiki.

He didn't understand I was telling him I'd seen him necking with that woman in Hawaii. Instead, he insisted he didn't want any woman but his wife. Like a fool, I agreed to let him make love to me as long as he withdrew before he ejaculated and he promised he would, but then he didn't. If I turn up pregnant again, I don't know what I'll do. With the future as uncertain as it is, with assassinations, race riots and the war in Vietnam, I don't want to bring any more children into the world.

In the morning, his head hurting from a hangover, Buck told me over and over how sorry he was and promised it wouldn't happen again. As far as I'm concerned, there won't be an opportunity for another "accident."

❖

Outside Khe Sanh in South Vietnam

August 19, 1968

Dearest Jillian,

Your letters were waiting for me when I got back to base. Right away I read each one twice. Jillian, I agree with your father — stay away from those protesters. You put yourself in a dangerous situation and for no reason. You aren't going to convince them to change their minds, so play it safe. I need to know you're safe, sweetheart! So promise me you won't do anything that foolish again. I appreciate that you want to support us, though. I agree with you — this war is wrong. We shouldn't even be here. If the demonstrators manage to bring us home, then more power to them.

I can't tell you how much getting mail means to me, especially after a day like today. I won't describe what happened. Not all of it, anyway, but I watched a brave man die this afternoon. A good man and, honey, it really shook me up. It shook us all up. It could've been any one of us. I've seen death before, but I haven't felt it the way I did this afternoon. It was like a giant hand reached out and grabbed Bob, completely at random. Why Bob and not me? None of it makes any sense.

Then later, after we got back, one of my buddies read a letter from his girl. I knew something was wrong when he threw it down and walked outside. His fiancée broke off the engagement and he was crying. Not so anyone could see, but when I found him he had tears running down his face. It wiped him out emotionally. This war is hell enough without hearing shit like that.

No one slept much last night. I kept thinking about you and me and how much I love you. I know I shouldn't think this way, but I was glad it wasn't me that got killed. I love you too damn much to leave you. Right now, I want to hold you so much my arms ache. I'm sorry Bob is dead, sorry Larry's girl dumped him. I want to get out of this hellhole. When I close my eyes all I see is war. All I hear is the rapid fire of guns and the cries of men like me just hoping to get out of here alive. All I dream about is getting home to you.

Remember how much I love you.

Nick

Jillian's Diary

September 14, 1968

I'm so glad to be back at school. Dad and I can barely look at each other. It's impossible to carry on a civil conversation with him. At one time I idolized my father, but I don't anymore. Nick keeps telling me that I'm going to make a great attorney. I refuse to even consider a career in law. If being an attorney means I'll start thinking and acting like my father, then I don't want any part of it. Mom, who attempts to play the role of peacemaker, says it's because Dad and I are so much alike.

I sincerely hope she's wrong. My father actually told me to my face that he didn't raise his daughter to be a Democrat. He spits out the word as if it's going to dirty his mouth.

Politics is only one of the things we fight about. He knows I love Nick and that we're planning to get married once he's home from Vietnam. But my father still refuses to accept him and insists on introducing me to other men. Men he considers more "suitable" than Nick. Rich boys who'd race to Canada at the hint of a draft notice.

He doesn't like my music. He thinks *The Doors* and *Jefferson Airplane* are tools of the devil. My wardrobe upsets him, too. What's so revolutionary about bellbottoms and sandals? Anyway, I don't care what he thinks. I'm just grateful to be out from under his domination.

Nick thought coming home for the summer would be good for me, but he was wrong. I doubt I'll return for Christmas, feeling the way I do about my father.

This wasn't a good summer for Lesley, either. Selfishly Buck insisted on uprooting her and the kids and making them move to California to be with him. That meant we hardly had a minute together at all. Lesley's life is so different from mine. I was afraid that after her marriage we'd drift apart, but she's still the only person in the world who truly understands my feelings. She's the only one who accepts my love for Nick.

In her last letter, Lesley said she's scared she might be pregnant again. I hope not, for her sake. Buck's the kind of man who likes his women barefoot and pregnant. With two babies already, the last thing she needs is a third child. I don't know why she refuses to take the pill. The Catholic Church's stand on that issue is right out of the Dark Ages.

I've got to stop watching the television news about Vietnam. Last night there was all this talk about the aftermath of the Tet Offensive and how the death toll keeps rising. My dreams were filled with war and worries about Nick. I woke up in a cold sweat with my heart pounding so hard I could barely catch my breath. It took a long time before I was able to calm down and remember it was just a dream and that Nick's perfectly fine. If anything happened to him my heart would know it, I'm sure of that.

❖

Outside Khe Sanh in South Vietnam

September 15, 1968

Dear Jimmy,

I promised I'd write as often as I could, but it's been a while. I've discovered that jotting down a few lines to send home helps ease the tension. We all look for ways to keep our minds off the war. That's one reason getting mail from home means so much. I carry the letters from you, Dad and Jillian with me. I've read them all so many times they're falling apart. The ones from Jillian I've committed to memory. Her letters, and yours and Dad's, too, are the only way I have of staying sane here. I haven't been as faithful as I wanted to be in writing you, but I know you understand.

By the way, I got word of your recent "troubles." What the hell are you doing hanging around with Dirk Andrews? You didn't learn your lesson about him the last time? We both know Dirk's bad news. He's already been arrested twice. I didn't realize you had a hankering for jail food. Thank God Dad was able to get you out of this scrape, but don't count on being that fortunate again. Before you decide to step out of the house or do *anything,* stop and consider the consequences of your actions. Dad only said one thing to me before I left for Nam. "Be a man." Then he hugged me and asked me to come home. I'm asking you to be a man now, Jimmy, and ditch Dirk before you end up doing jail time for being stupid.

I don't mean to come down too hard on you. You're my kid brother and I've always looked out for you. It's harder now with me being so far from home, so I'm relying on you to keep your own nose clean. In other words, stay away from Dirk, and stay out of trouble. I've got to end this if it's going to make today's mail.

I don't say this often, Jimmy, but I love you.

Your brother,

Nick

October 1, 1968

Dear Susan,

It was so good to hear from you. I knew you'd like the Navy, and if everything goes according to plan, you'll soon be in nursing school. I envy you the opportunity.

Buck, the kids and I are doing great. We're anxious to move back to Washington. Dad said there's a job waiting for Buck at the lumber mill once he's discharged, but you know Dad, he's always full of talk. However,

Buck worked at the mill before he enlisted, so we're hoping he can get back on.

Lindy is growing by leaps and bounds. Davey, too. I don't know how Mom did it with six of us constantly underfoot. Mom wrote and said Mike has a job at the Albertson's store this summer and Joe's hoping they'll hire him next year when he's old enough to work. He took over Mike's paper route and has his own money for school clothes. That helps Mom. Bruce and Lily spend most of their time at Lion's Park swimming, just the way we did when we were their age.

Your sister,
Lesley

❖

JILLIAN LAWTON
BARNARD COLLEGE
PLIMPTON HALL
NEW YORK, NY 10025

October 6, 1968

Dear Mr. Murphy,

I hope you don't mind that I'm writing you, but I haven't received a letter from Nick in almost a week. Have you heard from him? It isn't like him not to write. Ever since he was stationed in Vietnam, he's made a point of writing me at least every other day, just so I won't worry.

At first I thought there might be some confusion with the mail because I recently returned to school, but my mother assures me nothing's been delivered to the house, either.

I'll await your reply.

Sincerely,

Jillian Lawton

From the Department of Defense

Addressed to: Mr. Patrick Murphy
It is with deep regret that we
inform you of the death of your son
Nicholas Patrick Murphy
September 16, 1968
in Vietnam

JILLIAN LAWTON
BARNARD COLLEGE
PLIMPTON HALL
NEW YORK, NY 10025

October 8, 1968

Dear Nick,

I screamed when I heard you'd been killed. Screamed and screamed and screamed. My heart has yet to stop screaming. I don't sleep. I don't eat. This can't be happening, this can't be real. Tell me it isn't real! It's like my chest has been caught in a vise that grows tighter and tighter. Sometimes it even hurts to breathe.

My mother was the one to tell me. Your dad phoned her and explained that two soldiers had arrived at the gas station to deliver the news. He was too broken up to tell me himself, so he phoned my mother.

I knew something was wrong when she called, because she was crying and trying to hide it. Only I thought it had to do with my dad. I never dreamed she was calling to say you'd been taken away from me. Never dreamed that a phone call from home, from my own mother, would change my life forever.

Following your funeral, Mom wanted me to stay home for the remainder of the semester and return to school after the Christmas holidays, but I'll go crazy sitting around the house for the next three months. Dad seemed relieved when I told him I'd decided to go back. He said he thought that was probably for the best. I can't talk to my father at all. But don't worry, we didn't fight. I haven't got the strength for it.

I'm writing this on the plane, flying back to the East Coast the day after your funeral. It all seemed so unreal until yesterday morning, when I sat in church between your father and Jimmy. Your father looked old and frail. It was the first time I'd ever seen him in a suit. He tried to be brave for me and Jimmy. You would've been proud of your brother. I don't think your father would have made it through the funeral if not for him. It wasn't until we reached the cemetery that Jimmy started to cry.

Your family loved you, Nicholas Patrick Murphy. I loved you, too. Oh Nick, tell me what I'm supposed to do without you. Tell me.

Please, please tell me.

Jillian

❖

October 9, 1968

Dearest, dearest Jillian,

Oh, how I wish I could be with you. I'm so sorry I couldn't make it to Nick's funeral. Even now I find it hard to accept that he's really gone. You see, I came to love him myself when I saw how much he loved you.

I remember when you told me you'd met Nick behind the snack booth on Valentine's Day, back when we were still in high school, and how you spent prom night with him instead of going to the dance. I knew when you broke up with Scott that Nick wasn't just a fling. It hurts so terribly, doesn't it? The only thing I can compare it to would be losing David, Lindy or Buck.

Jillian, how can I help you? What can I do to ease this pain? We've been best friends our entire lives and have seen each other through everything. You were the first person I turned to when I discovered I was pregnant with David (just as I did last month, when I thought I was pregnant again — which, thank God, I'm not). You were maid-of-honor at my wedding. You've been with me through good times and bad, but how can I possibly see you through something like this? How can I help you?

Your tears are my tears. Your pain is mine. Our friendship is stronger even than the bonds I share with my own sisters. Let me help you. Just tell me how.

With all my heart,

Lesley

JILLIAN LAWTON
BARNARD COLLEGE
PLIMPTON HALL
NEW YORK, NY 10025

December 1, 1968

Dearest Lesley,

Thank you for your letters. I don't know how I could have survived these last months without them. I received a letter from Nick's friend Brad Lincoln this week. He'd wanted to write sooner, but was badly injured and dictated the letter to a hospital volunteer. It took me a long time to find the courage to read it.

Deep down I knew what Brad wanted to tell me, and I was right. Nick died a hero. The news didn't comfort me. Knowing that Nick died saving someone else angered me so much I went on a rampage through my dorm room. It's hard to believe I'd do such a thing, isn't it? The anger pounded inside me until I had to do *something*. I know it sounds crazy, but I tore the sheets off the beds and sent every book in the room crashing against the wall. Then I collapsed and wept until my throat was raw. Later Janice came in and knelt on the floor, held me and cried with me. Afterward I showed her Brad's letter.

The last thing I wanted to read was how Nick saved his friend's life. If Brad is waiting for me to absolve him from his guilt, then he has a very long wait.

You asked what you can do to help me. I don't know, Les, I just don't know. I've never experienced this kind of pain before. I feel like I'm walking in a fog. People talk to me and I don't hear. I read, but I don't understand the words. I look, but I don't see. Everyone tells me time is the great healer, as though everything will be all right again in six months. Nothing in my life will be the same without Nick. Nothing ever again, and I know it.

This has been a year of death. First Martin Luther King, Jr., then Bobby Kennedy and now Nick. And all the other soldiers in Vietnam . . . Oh, Lesley, so much death! I'm not sure I want to live anymore. You're the only person I can tell how I really feel. I think about dying and wish I could end everything just so this pain would stop.

I continue to write Nick letters – please don't tell me I shouldn't. Sometimes it's the only thing that gets me through the night. I wrote him every day for months, and now it seems only natural at the end of each day to share my thoughts with him. Sometimes I can almost make myself believe he isn't really dead and that he'll be coming home soon.

I don't sleep well. When I do manage to drift off, I wake with a start and then I remember that Nick is dead. And my heart wants to stop beating. A dark, heavy sadness settles over me, a sadness too great to carry on my own.

Yes, I'll be home for Christmas and I'm so grateful you will be, too. It'll be good to hold Davey and Lindy. My prayer is that they won't have to grow up and worry about fighting wars.

I love you.

Jillian

❖

December 4, 1968

Dear Jillian,

Hi. Thanks for your letter. Dad's not doing well since Nick died. My mother died and now Nick's gone, too. I'm all right, I guess, but,

Jillian, I need you to be strong because I don't think I can hold Dad together much longer. He doesn't sleep very much and I can't remember the last time he sat down for dinner. He barely knows I'm around and yesterday he called me Nick and then realized what he'd done and began to cry. Customers are starting to complain, too. Will you be home soon for Christmas? Can you come by the station and visit once you arrive? Can you do that? Please?

Jimmy Murphy

1970

Invitation to a Retirement Party

For: Judge Leonard Lawton
At: Pine Ridge Country Club
140 Country Club Lane
Pine Ridge, WA
When: Sunday, January 4, 1970
Time: 2–4 p.m.
To celebrate 25 years of service
No gifts please

January 12, 1970

Dear Jillian,

By the time you get this, you'll be in the midst of your other life — classes and essays and (I hope) parties.

Having you home over the Christmas holidays was wonderful. It felt more like Christmas this year, didn't it? The mood was certainly lighter than last year, when the holidays came so soon after Nick was killed.

Davey and Lindy already miss you. Lindy moped around the trailer all morning, wondering when her Aunt Jilly was going to visit again. It'll be summer before you're back, won't it? It seems much too long to wait for another chat fest. I marvel at how wonderful you are with the children — and oh, how they took to you!

You look good, Jillian, more like yourself than you have in a long while. I know how difficult the last fifteen months have been without Nick and have kept you constantly in my prayers. I couldn't find the words to say it when you were here, possibly because talking about him always makes me cry. What I wanted most to tell you is how very proud I am of you. Proud that you loved Nick despite your parents' attitude. Proud of the way you stood up to them and believed in him and in your love.

I'm sure Nick would be pleased that you've kept in touch with his dad and Jimmy. You've made a point of being there for the two of them and being part of their lives. They've needed you just like you've needed them. Nick's death hit his dad and Jimmy hard. I don't think Mr. Murphy will ever get over this. I know you won't, and helping one another is the only way to see all of you through this.

I don't know what would've become of Jimmy without you. My brother Joe is in the same class with him and told me Jimmy's almost been expelled several times. I do hope he holds on long enough to graduate this June. Speaking of graduation, I can hardly believe that in a few months you'll be a college graduate! I understand why you decided to change your major from law to education, but try as I might, I can't picture you as a teacher. I know your father's disappointed and I trust my honesty won't offend you, Jillian, but are you sure you didn't change majors just to get back at him for his attitude toward Nick?

We've been friends far too long for me not to express my opinion. Now, I'll give you the opportunity to do the same. There's something I should've mentioned when you were here and didn't. Surprise, surprise, I'm going to be a mother again this August. This baby wasn't planned, but for that matter, neither were Davey and Lindy. We've been careful, but apparently not careful enough. I've tried to be faithful to the Church's teachings on birth control, but the thought of three children in four years is enough to make me consider changing religions! Naturally Buck's delighted with the news. The health insurance at the mill is pretty lousy, so it looks like we'll need to pay a large portion of the expenses for this pregnancy ourselves. The doctor's fee alone is $300. That's highway robbery. Oh well, I'm not going to worry about it.

Write me soon.

Love,

Lesley

JILLIAN LAWTON
BARNARD COLLEGE
PLIMPTON HALL
NEW YORK, NY 10025

January 12, 1970

Dearest Nick,

It's been a couple of weeks since I last wrote, and that's the longest period I've gone without writing you since your death. A shrink would suggest my not writing was a sign I'm getting over you – as if that were possible. All it really means is that I've been especially busy over the Christmas holidays. I saw your dad and Jimmy several times while I was at home. They both did a good job of pretending. I did, too, for their sake. I'm worried about your father, Nick. He's so thin, and Jimmy says all he does these days is work. It's as if he's convinced himself that if he spends eighteen hours a day at the station he'll forget that his wife and oldest son are dead. I don't fault him. I've never had better grades, and I study and work hard for all the same reasons as your father. I'm desperately searching for a way to forget how empty my life seems without you.

Jimmy's adjusted the best, I think. Your brother's over six feet tall now, and when I first saw him, I did a double-take. He looks so much like you. I had a rough couple of minutes, but managed a fast recovery.

On Christmas Eve, the three of us assembled at your gravesite. We formed a circle and held on to one another. New Year's Day, I found your father sitting on a bench near your mother's grave. I gave him his privacy and sought my own.

I knew the holidays would be difficult, but I'm happy to report that I didn't get into a single argument with my dad about politics or the war or anything else. I feel sorry for my mom. She's always trying to bring the two of us together and is miserable when her efforts fail. Loving us both makes this tension between Dad and me extrahard on her.

I played the role of the good daughter and went to Dad's retirement party. I smiled when it was required of me and socialized to the best of my ability. Dad's friend Montgomery Gordon attended the function, too, and I passed the time chatting with him. He's as stuffy and full of himself as my father is.

Lesley wants me to come back to Pine Ridge this summer, but I can't. I don't belong there any more. Besides all the tension between Dad and me, Pine Ridge holds too many memories. Anyway, I'll be busy applying for teaching positions around the country. As of right now, I don't have a clue where I'll end up.

Oh, Nick, you'd be amazed at Lesley's babies. Davey is three and Lindy two and they're both so precious. I fell in love with them all over again this Christmas. We would've had beautiful children, you and I. My heart aches for the babies we never had.

I saw a few friends from high school while I was home, mostly to satisfy my parents who are subtly pressuring me to date again. I don't know why I should. I don't plan to marry. No one knows that except you and Lesley. It would sound rash and melodramatic to anyone else. How could I possibly love anyone but you? I can't. No one could ever take your place.

Remember how much I love you.

Jillian

We are pleased to announce that
Retired Judge Leonard Lawton
Has rejoined the Shields & Ellis Law Firm

Leonard Lawton is available
For mediation and arbitration,
consultation and legal representation
in business, real estate and civil matters

JILLIAN LAWTON
BARNARD COLLEGE
PLIMPTON HALL
NEW YORK, NY 10025

February 1, 1970

Dear Monty,

Forgive me, but I can't make myself address

you as Montgomery. I received the letter telling me you're going to be in New York next week. Thank you for the invitation to dinner, but unfortunately I've already made other plans for the evening.

I understand congratulations are in order. My mother told me you'd recently been made a full partner in Lawton, Shields and Ellis. My father's mentioned your name often and with great fondness. I'm sure the law firm will benefit from your expertise.

Once again, I'm sorry I'll miss seeing you next week. I hope you enjoy your stay on the East Coast.

Sincerely,
Jillian Lawton

❖

JILLIAN LAWTON
BARNARD COLLEGE
PLIMPTON HALL
NEW YORK, NY 10025

February 1, 1970

Dear Mom and Dad,

I insist you stop. I know you asked Montgomery Gordon to invite me out for dinner while he's in New York. He couldn't have been any more obvious. I'm not over Nick and I will never be over Nick. Please don't make this more difficult than it already is. I'm not interested in seeing your friend (especially since he's nearly fifteen years older than me!)

Because he is your friend, I refused him politely, but I would appreciate it if you'd see that this sort of thing doesn't happen again.

Jillian

❖

Pine Ridge Mills
Pine Ridge, Washington
Reduction in Force Notice
Effective March 1, 1970
Attn: Buck Knowles

❖

PINE RIDGE
COMMUNITY BULLETIN BOARD
Day Care Available
All hours
Contact Lesley Knowles
555-6766

April 22, 1970

Dear Lesley and Buck,

I suppose by now you've heard from Mom and

Dad that I'm married. I've known Bill Lamar for three years. We both joined the Navy at the same time. This isn't a sudden decision and we're both very happy.

Mom wrote that Buck got laid off at the mill. I'm sorry, Les, but it's not really surprising, seeing how Dad's job has been on and off for as long as I can remember. I realize another pregnancy now is going to cause you financial hardship. Apparently that's a prerequisite for babies! We haven't told Mom and Dad yet, but I'm pregnant too, almost four months, the same as you.

Bill isn't Catholic and we didn't get married in the church. Dad had one of his temper tantrums when we told him we were married by a Justice of the Peace. He said he didn't scrimp and sacrifice all those years to send us girls to Holy Name Academy only to have us marry outside the faith. That's a real laugh! If it wasn't for the tuition scholarships, neither one of us would've been able to attend parochial schools. And we both know it was because of Mom that you and I were able to accept those scholarships. She took in ironing and later worked in the school cafeteria to pay for our uniforms and whatever else we needed. As for Dad defending the faith — what a joke. I doubt either of us can remember the last time he darkened a church door.

But I didn't write to complain about Dad. I wanted you to know about the baby and to tell you that Bill and I are hoping to visit Pine Ridge sometime this summer.

I miss Joe, Lily and Bruce, and I worry about them at home with Dad. At least Mike got out of the house as soon as he graduated — like you and me. I never hear from him. Do you? The last thing I heard, he left town with a couple of friends and was headed for California. I can't believe Joe's a senior this year. What are his plans, do you know? Lily writes me every once in a while and tells me about school. She's as smart as you were. I miss you all so much.

Write me soon.

Susan, Bill and ?

JILLIAN LAWTON
BARNARD COLLEGE
PLIMPTON HALL
NEW YORK, NY 10025

May 4, 1970

Dear Dad,

I just finished watching the evening news. The anger inside me refuses to be silenced. Four students were killed at Kent State today and nine others wounded. Shot by the National Guard. Are you proud, Daddy? Does the sight of those protesters being gunned down satisfy your sense of justice? How dare the youth of America voice their dismay over the escalation of the war in Vietnam. Is that what you think? I can almost hear you say those students got what they deserved.

From the first, you've made your hawkish views on Vietnam very clear. You and your cronies are convinced of the importance of wiping out Communism, but so far all you've done is wipe out the youth of America. How many mothers weeping over the caskets of their sons will it take to prove the craziness of this war to you and your friends?

I was in grade school when you so eloquently explained to me the importance of the law and how it was based on our Constitution. I was probably the only third-grader in the entire state who could recite the entire Bill of Rights from memory. Apparently the rights you were so proud of no longer apply in our country. Apparently freedom of speech is so dangerous to our society it must be silenced by gun-toting soldiers firing blindly into a crowd of college students. Free speech is so dangerous it must be stamped out.

You once disdainfully told me you didn't raise me to be the wife of a mechanic. That mechanic died in a fiery crash on foreign soil because our country asked it of him. Nick didn't hide from what he considered his duty. He went willingly and fought with pride. Tell me, Dad, where are the sons of your friends? You don't need to answer that because I already know. Harvard. How many of your pompous friends are willing to lay the lives of their children on the line in an effort to wipe out the spread of Communism? Not a one.

As long as Nick was on the battlefield, I supported our troops, and although I disagreed with our presence in Vietnam, I supported that war. I won't any more. Not after today. The demonstrators are right: It's time we got out of Vietnam and Cambodia. I only regret that our withdrawal didn't happen sooner, so I could have married the "grease monkey" you scorned.

Jillian

Mrs. Leonard Lawton
2330 Country Club Lane
Pine Ridge, Washington 98005

May 11, 1970

Dear Jillian,

Your letter deeply upset both your father and me. Neither one of us condones what happened at Kent State. You so distressed your father that he locked himself in his study.

He didn't want me to say anything, but his health hasn't been good, which is what led to his early retirement. I cannot express how much this unpleasantness between the two of you grieves me. You seem intent on blaming your dad for

Nick's death, as if he were personally responsible for this terrible war. I doubt that you realize how unfair you've been.

Another point. Montgomery Gordon has been like a son to us in recent years. He contacted you last February before his trip east as a courtesy and certainly not because of any prompting on either your father's part or mine. Although I was infuriated by your accusation months ago, I bit my tongue. I can no longer remain silent. You told us earlier that you have no interest in dating Montgomery and that, as always, is your choice. But don't blame him or us for transgressions we haven't committed.

You implied that your father and I are a bitter disappointment to you. I wish you'd look at the situation from our point of view. Remember you are our only child. We invested all the love we had in you, nurtured you, supported and educated you — and all we've received back for years now has been your contempt.

I find it painful to speak of such matters. All I ask is that you not write such cruel, hateful things to your father again. His heart can't take much more of your venom.

Mom

May Protest Rally
Against the War in Vietnam
Sunday, May 17, 1970
12–3:00 p.m.
Student Union Building

May 15, 1970

Jillian,

If you want to see an end to the war, join me in making our voices heard. The killing must stop at home and in Vietnam. If you believe this, as I do, join the march on Sunday. You must be willing to risk the chance of arrest.

Following the incident at Kent State, we are placing our lives on the line in support of our belief.

Too many have already died. Don't let the Kent State student deaths be in vain. Join me in taking a stand against the establishment.

Thom Eliason
ASB President

ARREST/BOOKING INFORMATION
DEFENDANT: *Jillian Lynn Lawton* DOB: *01/15/48*
AKA(S):
CHARGE(S): 1: *unlawful assembly* COURT: BAIL: *$500*
2:
3:
DATE & TIME OF ARREST: *17 May 1970*
NEXT COURT DATE IF BAIL: *10 June 1970*
ARREST LOCATION: *Student Union Building, NYU Campus*
ARRESTING AGENCY:__________________
ARRESTING OFFICER: *Sgt. Bodine* BADGE #*3967*
OUT OF COUNTY/STATE HOLDS (If NOT primary charge):
VEHICLE IMPOUNDED? Y N
IF YES, WHERE LOCATED:__________________

(continued from previous page)

BAC READING(S): 1: ________ 2: (If Needed): _____
I CERTIFY THAT THE DEFENDANT HAS REFUSED TREATMENT BY MEDICAL PERSONNEL. (If applicable).
TIME ARRIVED: ______________________________
ARRESTING/TRANSPORTING
OFFICER SIGNATURE ____________________

May 23, 1970

Dearest Jillian,

Arrested — you! I could hardly believe my eyes when I read your letter. What a ghastly experience that must have been. Of course I won't say anything to your parents, or anyone else.

Something good has come out of it, though. I applaud your decision to apply to law school. I imagine your parents were elated with the news. That has been their dream for you from the beginning. You would've made a good teacher, but you'll be a brilliant attorney.

Thank goodness you're familiar with the law, otherwise who knows how long you and the other students would've been detained.

Both Dad and Buck are back working at the mill. I'm grateful. It's hard enough to get anything done around the trailer with four kids constantly underfoot. My own, plus the two daycare children I've been looking after.

With Buck home, it's impossible to accomplish anything. Although, to be fair, he wasn't actually around all that much. He was off doing his "guy things," as he calls them.

I recently met a few of Buck's friends and made sure he understood that he's not to bring any of them to our home again. He plays poker a couple of nights a week with his buddies, but I don't mind. I get out myself, thanks to Lily who loves to watch the kids. Mom and I are taking decoupage classes and I've made several things for the living room. It's an inexpensive way to decorate. I knit a baby blanket for Susan, too. I have several left from Davey and Lindy and don't need any new ones myself.

This pregnancy is less troublesome than the first two. I'm much bigger this time. I asked the doctor about twins and he measured my tummy, did a few calculations and said there's a real possibility this could be a multiple birth. I was joking when I suggested it! There's no way to tell until July, when I'm seven months along and it's safe for me to have an x-ray. Until that point, I refuse to worry about it. Naturally Buck is ecstatic, as if twins would prove his virility. Men! Sometimes I think their brains are located below their belts.

I want to get this in the mailbox before the postman arrives, so I'll end for now. Thanks for your letter. I'm proud of you, Jillian! You stood up for what you believe in — enough to risk arrest.

If I wasn't so busy taking care of my family and doing daycare on the side, I'd march in a protest rally myself. This war has robbed our country of so much already. I'm grateful Mike didn't have to go to Vietnam, but then I think of all the young men who have, including Buck and Nick. It isn't right that we're fighting someone else's war.

I've got to scoot; Lindy's up from her nap and needs lots of attention.

Lesley

❖

The Class of
Nineteen Hundred and Seventy
Barnard College
announces its
Commencement Exercises
Sunday afternoon at three p.m.
June seventh
Nineteen Hundred and Seventy
At Altshul Court, facing Barnard Hall
By invitation only

June 25, 1970

Dear Jillian,

Dad's been after me to write you a thank-you note for the high school graduation present. I should've done it a long time ago, but I've been real busy. It was groovy of you to send me the money, as well as Nick's certificate from helicopter school. You're right. I do want it. I got the unspoken message, too. Nick achieved something after graduation and so can I.

You'll be glad to know I've got a real job with potential. (I'm defining a real job as one that isn't at my own dad's service station.) Care to guess what I'm doing? I'm building houses. I'm good with my hands and always did enjoy seeing stuff come together.

It's funny how it happened. I was pumping gas for a guy who turned out to be a building contractor and he started asking me questions and said he had his eye out for someone he could train to be a carpenter. He said he was looking for someone with a strong work ethic and a willingness to learn. I told him I'd be interested and he told me to come down to the job site the next day and fill out an application.

I was there bright and early, before any of the other workers arrived. Sure enough, Brian shows up. He said he liked my enthusiasm and gave me a job on the spot. Here's the best part. Brian is a union contractor, which means I'm making union wages. He personally took me down to the union hall and signed me up. There's a fee but he paid that, too, only it's a loan that'll be deducted from my wages.

You'll never guess who I saw talking to Brian a few days ago. Your dad! Apparently they're friends. I think your dad might've put in a good word for me because I saw Brian nod and look in my direction. Your father's all right. I know he and Nick didn't see eye to eye, but then us Murphy boys sometimes rub people the wrong way. I bet that if Nick was alive, he and your dad would be okay with each other.

Sorry it's taken me so long to send you this thank-you. Dad's doing better, I think. He still goes out to the cemetery a lot, but he's eating more. Be sure and stop by the house the next time you're in town.

See ya,
Jim Murphy

P.S. Since I'm a high school graduate and a union carpenter, I decided it was time to be Jim instead of Jimmy.

❖

Pine Ridge Library Request Form

Name: Lesley Knowles
Books Requested:

1. *Everything You Wanted to Know About Sex But*

Were Afraid To Ask by Dr. David Reuben
2. *Bury My Heart at Wounded Knee* by Dee Brown

❖

JILLIAN LAWTON
BARNARD COLLEGE
PLIMPTON HALL
NEW YORK, NY 10025

July 12, 1970

Dear Lesley,

It was great to chat with you this afternoon. We don't talk nearly often enough. Now that I have a summer job that pays real money, I can afford to call you once in a while. Actually, I didn't think I was going to enjoy working in a law library, but I do. My first apartment is so dinky I barely have room to turn around, but that's New York.

Okay, what's up? I haven't been your best friend all these years without knowing when you're upset about something. You might be able to hide it from everyone else, but not me. I know you far too well. It was in your voice when we spoke this afternoon. I could always detect when there's a problem, so 'fess up.

Are you worried about the baby/babies? Buck's job? The kids? I've spilled my guts to you often enough that you shouldn't have any

trouble unburdening yourself to me.
I'll look for a letter soon.
Love,
Jillian

P.S. I guess it's time I changed my stationery, isn't it? I'm no longer a student at Barnard College and I'm no longer living in residence. Watch out, Harvard! Here I come.

❖

July 24, 1970

Dear Jillian,
You do know me, don't you? Sometimes I forget how well. When you phoned Sunday afternoon I'd just finished dealing with an unexpected visitor. He'd come to the door and knocked and seemed surprised when I answered. I was holding Lindy in my arms and had Davey clinging to my side. He took one look at my belly and didn't seem to know what to say. Then he asked if this was where Buck Knowles lived and I told him it was. He asked to talk to Buck, but Buck was out fishing with his buddies. The man introduced himself as Sam Gavin and said he'd come to deliver a message to Buck. I told him I'd make sure Buck received it. That was when Sam said I should tell my husband to stay away from his wife. If he caught

Buck anywhere near her again, he'd rearrange his face.

Jillian, I was stunned speechless. Buck is seeing another woman? Naturally I'd find this out when I'm big and pregnant and feeling incredibly ugly. I felt as if the floor had opened up.

Now you can understand why I didn't sound like my normal self. Buck didn't get home until late. He'd caught his limit of fish but none of his buddies had even a nibble, so he gave them his catch. (Sometimes I wish he wasn't so generous.) When I told him Sam Gavin stopped by, Buck didn't give any indication that he knew who the man was. When I relayed Sam's message — word for word — Buck looked dumbfounded. He told me that he had no idea what the hell Sam was talking about.

I know what you're going to ask me. It's a question I've asked myself a hundred times. Was Buck telling the truth? I don't know. I just don't know. He vows he isn't seeing anyone else. With two kids, another on the way and no means of supporting myself, I can't afford not to believe him.

Since that night he's been wonderful with the kids. He picked up some spare wood at the mill and built Davey a clubhouse. It's really cute and Davey is thrilled. He hammers the nails for hours and is so proud of himself. For the last week Buck's been home every night and even helped with the dinner dishes once. Lindy is a real daddy's girl and he can charm her out of a temper tantrum without trying. All I can say is, if he was actually seeing this woman, he isn't any longer. Don't tell me I'm turning my head and blindly looking the other way. I'm not. Buck is my husband and the father of my children and I believe him. I have to.

On a brighter note, I was finally able to have the x-ray and all the doctor saw was one big baby. I'm sure it must be a boy, although I think Buck would almost prefer another girl.

Don't work too hard this summer and promise me you'll stay in touch. I'll be sure and let you know when the baby's born.

Love,
Lesley

BIRTH ANNOUNCEMENT
It's a bouncing baby boy
Douglas Steven Knowles
Born on
August 1, 1970
8 lbs, 14 oz.
21" long
The happy parents are:
Buck and Lesley Knowles

Lawton, Shields, Ellis & Gordon
600 Main Street
Suite 302
Pine Ridge, Washington 98005

September 1, 1970

Dear Jillian,

I'm writing you at the risk of offending both your parents. As you may or may not know, your father has experienced a number of health problems in recent years. This past month he's undergone several medical tests. As a result of the doctor's findings, it's been decided that your father needs heart bypass surgery. Your mother wanted you to know, but your father insisted you not be told.

Since I'm a close family friend, I've taken it upon myself to inform you of this. Apparently your father's condition makes it necessary for the surgery to be scheduled almost immediately. He goes into Seattle General Hospital on the afternoon of Tuesday, September 8th, with surgery scheduled first thing the following morning. At this time, Seattle General is the only hospital in the Puget Sound area that performs these surgeries.

Your mother would never go against your father's wishes. I, on the other hand, feel you have a right to know.

I realize you and your father have had your differences over the last few years, but I didn't think you'd allow a disagreement to stand between you at this crucial time in your father's life.

Forgive me if I've spoken out of turn.

Sincerely,

Montgomery Gordon

Classified ad in
Pine Ridge Newspaper

Hunting Rifle, barely used
$150 or best offer
Contact John Smithson
777-7078

Posted at Laundromat

Sewing machine —
$75.00

Rainier Bank

Savings Passport

Lesley Knowles

1/1/70—	$10.00	
2/1/70—	$10.00—	$20.00
3/5/70—	$5.00—	$25.00
Interest	*.15—*	*$25.15*
4/15/70—	$3.00—	$28.15
6/1/70—	$20.00—	$48.15
Interest	*.36—*	*$48.51*
7/30/70—	$5.00—	$53.51
9/1/70—	$40.00—	$93.51
Interest	*.70—*	*$94.21*
10/22/70—	$10.00—	$104.21
11/1/70—	$5.00—	$109.21
12/26/70—	$25.00—	$134.21
Interest	*1.01—*	*$135.22*

❖

Rainier Bank Withdrawal Slip
$130.00
Signed: Buck Knowles

Rainier Bank
1321 Main Street
Pine Ridge, Washington 98005

Dear Mrs. Knowles,

Thank you for your letter, concerning the recent withdrawal from your savings account. According to our records, the $130.00 in question was withdrawn at the request of Buck Knowles. As you have a joint checking account with your husband that is linked to your savings account, he is granted automatic access to your account.

I apologize if this misunderstanding has caused you any inconvenience.

Sincerely,
Peter Johnson
Customer Service Manager

1973

Jillian's Diary

January 1, 1973

Dearest Nick,

I woke up early this afternoon after a late New Year's Eve party at a friend's house. As I lay in bed, my thoughts were on the new year, but my heart drifted back to you. I guess I've been feeling guilty because of Thom and me. I've been seeing quite a bit of Thom Eliason. We met a few years ago at a protest rally and we're both attending Harvard Law School. You and Lesley always said I'd make a great attorney and I'm beginning to realize how right you were.

I love the law and am working hard to grasp its principles. I long to make the laws of our land more equitable for women. It'll happen in time. The changes of the last few years would shock you, but I don't think you'd be upset, the way some men are. (It won't surprise you to learn that my father is one of them!) Honest to God, I don't know what men are so afraid of.

I don't want to get sidetracked on the issue of

women's rights. My feeling is that the Equal Rights Amendment will eventually pass. Too many women have put their hearts behind this constitutional amendment for it to fail now. As you can see, I've become more politically minded than ever. Law school has had that effect on me.

About Thom. I figured I should tell you I've been sleeping with him. It's nothing like what we shared. It happened the first time after a few joints, when my inhibitions were lowered. It's continued because . . . well, because it feels good to have someone hold me. Thom seems to understand that this is a physical thing and my emotions aren't involved. We don't talk about it.

Marriage isn't a subject I even consider, although according to Lesley, who keeps track of this sort of thing, nearly ninety percent of the girls in our high school class are now married. Lesley's worried that unless I find a husband soon, I'll end up an old maid. As a mother of three, she has difficulty accepting the fact that I have no interest in marriage or a family. Good grief, I'm only twenty-five! I've repeatedly told her I never intend to marry, but (like my parents) she doesn't believe me. It isn't an issue with us, but I do find her attitude amusing.

I have big expectations for this new year. I only wish you were here to share them with me. I think of you, and talk to you so often in my head that sometimes I can almost believe you're still alive. Sometimes I indulge in the luxury of pretending that you came home to me and that we're married and we've had a baby or two. I think about you and Brad Lincoln starting up your own business, the way you so often mentioned. But sooner or later, reality hits. You never came home and the happy life we planned is nothing more than the lingering memories of a dream that died with you.

Please don't mind about Thom and me. You're the only man I've ever truly loved. The only man I ever will. I'm not the girl I was back when you knew me. I'm a woman now, and I'd like to believe you'd approve of the changes.

Remember how much I love you.

Jillian

❖

February 14, 1973

Dearest Jillian,

Happy Valentine's Day! I hope you like the big red heart Davey made you. He's so proud of it. His was the best-looking one in his entire first-grade class. (But then, you could say I'm prejudiced.) Lindy made you a valentine, too. She's thrilled that she can print her own name now. I haven't the heart to tell her that Ydnil isn't quite right. (Her kindergarten teacher told me not to worry — left-handed children often do this.) It's amazing to think that my children are attending the same parochial school you and I did. St. Catherine's is letting me work part-time in the cafeteria to help pay for Davey and Lindy's tuition. The timing is perfect for me. It's during Dougie's naptime and Mom puts him down at her house and he barely knows I'm gone.

Buck is back at work now and I'm relieved. Not knowing where the money's going to come from for the next trailer payment was such a worry. The food stamps helped with the groceries, but accepting charity, even from the government, mortifies me. I could barely show my face in the Albertson's Store. It bothered me to the point that Buck volunteered to do the shopping. Okay, he didn't exactly volunteer, it was a trade-off. Buck invited his cousin Moose Garrison from Montana to live with us until he found a job. This guy eats like a moose, too, and it didn't take much to envision him chomping his way through my weekly grocery allotment.

You'll love this. At dinner the first night Moose showed up, Lindy sat down at the table, looked him square in the eye and said, "My mom says you're gonna eat us out of house and home." I could have died!

Moose ended up staying two weeks and expected me to wait on him hand and foot. I put up with him, but in exchange Buck started doing the grocery shopping. He didn't like it, but I told him the job was his until he returned to work. Three weeks later, the mill called. I've never seen Buck this eager to get back on the job.

Did you see the television news the other night about the released American POWs landing at Clark Air Force Base in the Philippines? I sat there and wept for joy. Thank God this horrible war is almost over. It's hard to believe anyone could survive such a horrendous ordeal as a prison camp. These men say a great deal about the strength of the human spirit, don't they?

Jillian, something you said when we talked at Christmas has stayed on my mind. You told me you'd stopped attending Mass because of the Catholic Church's stand on birth control and other issues regarding women. I've thought a lot about our discussion and I don't agree, especially with what you said about birth control. Do you sincerely believe the Church would attempt to subjugate women by burdening them with more children than they can handle? As you know, Buck and I have struggled with this very issue. We've practiced the rhythm method all these years — with limited success.

Right before Dougie was born, Dr. Boone suggested I have a tubal ligation. I refused. As a practicing Catholic I just couldn't. I'm as careful as I can be, but I feel God knows how many children Buck and I should have. It's more than the Church's stand; it's a matter of faith, too.

Your not attending Mass wouldn't bother me as much if you'd decided to join another church, but you haven't. (Sister Martin de Porres would swallow her tongue if she heard me suggest anyone step inside a Protestant church!) From the way you were talking, it's almost as if you believe God is against women. I refuse to even consider such a thing. I need God in my life and I need my faith. I couldn't manage to survive a single day without getting down on my knees and saying the rosary. All I'm asking is that you not be too quick to abandon your faith.

I know you think I'm hopelessly naïve and perhaps I am, but I *choose* to believe. The alternative would destroy the very foundation of my life.

Keep in touch. You have no idea how much I enjoy your letters.

Lots of love,
Lesley and all

JILLIAN LAWTON
330 FAIRCHILD AVE.
APARTMENT 3B
BOSTON, MASS. 02138

February 17, 1973

Dear Thom,

I don't know where to start other than to say how sorry I am. The engagement ring you bought me for Valentine's Day was lovely. But I don't think I've ever been more surprised.

Actually, it came as a complete shock, since we'd never discussed marriage. I suppose I should've realized that all the talk about our moving in together was your way of leading up to the marriage proposal. Thank you for your patience and for giving me time to think this over.

Please don't be angry with me, but I'm simply not interested in marriage. I don't want to marry anyone. I've got another year and a half of school before I take the bar exam. (We both do!) Also, I don't know if I mentioned that my father's health hasn't been good, which is the reason I've made frequent trips to the west coast. Once I do pass the bar, I'm contemplating a move back to Washington State, to work at my father's firm.

I'm not the right wife for you. I've enjoyed your friendship, especially in the last six months, but I can't accept your proposal.

Please try to understand.
Jillian

February 24, 1973

Dear Jillian,

Your letter told me how difficult you found my marriage proposal. The fact that you chose to write me instead of talking this out, face to face, tells me you're upset. I don't want you to be. I certainly didn't intend (or expect) my proposal to send you fleeing in the opposite direction!

What did you think, Jillian? Are you afraid my ego's too fragile to handle rejection? I'd hoped that you, of all people, would know me better. But don't worry, I'm cool with this. If you just want to live together for a while, that suits me fine. Call me and we can talk.

Thom

Mrs. Leonard Lawton
2330 Country Club Lane
Pine Ridge, Washington 98005

March 1, 1973

Dear Mr. Brad Lincoln,

Your letter addressed to Jillian arrived at the family home this past week. Please forgive me for reading something that wasn't addressed to me. You see, I recognized your name. Jillian told me about you shortly after Nick died.

She's had a very hard time dealing with the loss of her high-school sweetheart and is only now starting to adjust and date again. I was afraid your letter would distress her. As her mother, I was trying to prevent that. I hope you'll forgive me for intruding in this manner.

After careful consideration, I have decided against forwarding your letter to my daughter. I'm afraid that your contacting Jillian now would do her more harm than good. I understand your guilt over Nick's death, but I don't believe Jillian is the one who can absolve it. For whatever reason, God chose to let you live. Who is either one of us to question His will? Who are we to know His reasons?

Nick's death nearly destroyed our daughter. It's taken her five years to deal with her loss. Currently she's dating another law student, and her father and I are encouraged by the relationship.

As her mother, I beg you to leave her alone. Please don't attempt to contact her again. I will pray for you, and I hope this mental anguish will abate in time.

Try to understand why I'm doing this.

Thank you.

Sincerely,

Mrs. Leonard Lawton

❖

March 4, 1973

Dear Jillian,

So we're back to letter-writing. I'm disappointed, but if this is the way you want it, then this is the way it'll be.

I thought you loved me, but I'm not sure anymore. Perhaps you care for me, but not in the same way as you loved the boy from your hometown who died in Vietnam. You didn't think I knew about him, did you? I never mentioned it, but you talk to him in your sleep. It took me a while to put two and two together. I loved you enough to hope that eventually you'd be willing to let go of the past and live in the here and now. Apparently I've been wasting my time.

I'm sorry, Jillian, for believing you'd want to marry me. Obviously I was wrong. Perhaps some day you'll have a clearer picture of what you really want in life.

I agree. It would be best for all concerned if we no longer saw each other.

Thom

❖

March 10, 1973

Dear Buck,

Seeing that you won't phone me and have dropped out of the bowling league, you give me no choice but to write you a letter. The last time you stopped off at the house, I told you I was late. You acted like it didn't worry you and said that you were crazy about me. I was stupid enough to believe you. I'm still late and the virus I picked up appears to be the nine-month variety. I'm pregnant, Buck, going on two months, and I want to know what you intend to do about it.

Moose finally broke down and told me you're married. That's just hunky-dory! You might've mentioned it. Later I learned I'm not the only woman you've fooled around with behind your wife's back. Denise Gavin told me all about your fling with her, only she was married herself. Well, I'm not married and I didn't know you were. If I'd known, you can bet we'd never have ended up in bed together, but it doesn't matter now. Right? You got what you wanted, and then some. Congratulate yourself because you fooled me into believing you actually cared.

I went to a clinic and found out an abortion

will cost $150. Either I receive the full amount by next Monday or I'm going directly to your wife. I wonder if she realizes her husband sleeps around? First Denise and now me, and God knows how many others. Maybe it's time someone told your wife exactly what kind of man you are.

Terri

❖

April 11, 1973

Lesley,

Let's make one thing clear right now. There's no way in hell I'm moving out of this trailer. It was thanks to my sweat and blood that we made each and every one of those payments. If you're so keen on filing for divorce, go ahead, but I'm keeping what's mine, including the trailer. You can have the kids and what you need for them, but everything else is my property. Blame me if you want for what happened with Terri, but a man needs a real woman in his bed, not one who's constantly worried about getting pregnant.

If you insist on leaving, I say fine. Just go.

Like you said, there's no reason for us to talk again. That's fine by me, too. Have your attorney contact me. One question — how are you going to afford an attorney? I can tell you right now, I'm not paying for it.

Buck

April 14, 1973

Dearest Jillian,

The siege at Wounded Knee is finally over, and the news is filled with talk of the break-in at Watergate and President Nixon's involvement. I wish I could tell you that my own life has settled down, but it's gone from bad to worse. For once, the house is quiet. The kids are all sleeping and the television is off. I'm not writing this from home, though. The kids and I are doubled up with my brother, Mike, who recently moved back from California. He's letting us stay with him until things get straightened out between Buck and me. There are five of us in a one-bedroom apartment, so you can imagine what it's been like for the last few days.

This letter is to tell you what's been happening and also to apologize. I've owed you an apology for nearly eight years. Do you remember the summer after graduation when you saw Buck with Tessa McKnight shortly before he and I were married? Buck convinced me it must've been someone who looked like him. Then, three years ago, a man came to my door and left a message saying that Buck had better stay away from his wife. I remember how shocked he looked when he saw me. He didn't have any idea that Buck was married.

Neither did Terri Noble. I received a letter from her last week, telling me Buck got her pregnant. He claimed because he was Catholic he was against abortion and wouldn't pay for one. The church takes a similar view of infidelity, but apparently that didn't bother him.

When Buck came home from the mill, I showed him the letter. He blew up and asked how I could possibly believe this woman. A stranger I didn't even know. He was hurt and offended that I'd take her word over his. Frankly, it never occurred to me not to believe her. I asked Buck to move out and he refused.

I'm filing for divorce as soon as I can afford an attorney. I have to, Jillian, in order to maintain my sanity. I wanted this marriage to work, but not at the price of my dignity.

The peace this evening feels like the lull before the storm. I can't continue to burden my brother with my problems. Mike barely makes enough to support himself, let alone three children and me. Mom wants to help, but my dad's forbidden her to speak to me. All he's done, from the moment I told him I'm divorcing Buck, is quote chapter and verse about how it's a woman's duty to stand by her man, regardless of his faults.

At this point, the future looks like a constant battle but I don't care. All I know is that I can't stay in this marriage. I'm sorry for not believing you all those years ago. I would've saved myself a lot of grief if I had. Please don't send mail to the trailer. I sincerely doubt he'd give me any letters from you, especially since he knows how much I treasure them.

Love,

Lesley

❖

May 1, 1973

Dear Lesley,

I'm sorry to hear about you and Buck. I wish we lived closer so I could really help you. It makes me mad that Dad won't let you live at the house, but it upsets me even more that he won't allow Mom to see you and the kids. That's downright cruel.

I remember how he was when Bill and I came to visit shortly after we got married. Dad refused to meet my husband. He refused to have anything to do with Bill or me. His excuse was that Bill and I were married outside the Church. The real reason was because I got out from under his unreasonable, fickle thumb. He always disapproved of me joining the Navy. He did everything he could to stop me from leaving home. He didn't get the opportunity to choose my husband for me, the way he did you. Dad didn't give you any choice but to marry Buck. I know what happened, Les. I figured it out. Buck raped you, didn't he? Then you ended up pregnant with Davey and you were trapped. Well, I saw what happened to you and got out before Dad could mess up my life, too.

You didn't ask for help, but you're my sister and I can't bear the thought of you and the children hurting or hungry. Bill and I talked it over and we're enclosing a check for $100. It isn't much, but it'll help a little.

I'm so proud of Mike for stepping in and helping you. He said Joe and Bruce and Lily are giving you whatever spare cash they can. We're behind you 100%. Don't worry, Les. Everything's going to work out. Buck doesn't deserve you. He never did.

Love,
Bill, Susan and Aaron

❖

JILLIAN LAWTON
330 FAIRCHILD AVE.
APARTMENT 3B
BOSTON, MASS. 02138

May 2, 1973

Dearest Lesley,

Your letter was waiting for me when I returned from a week in Nantucket. Oh, Les, I am so sorry. I never tried to hide my feelings about

Buck. I didn't want you to marry him. I didn't feel he was anywhere near good enough for you. It's true; my reasons weren't entirely self-less – I wanted you to attend the University of Washington, or any college for that matter. I wanted us to be together the way we'd been since we were kids.

You're a wonderful mother, Lesley. I've often admired that about you. Your children are as dear to me as if they were my own, especially Lindy, who holds my heart in the palm of her hand.

I know how difficult all of this has been. I'm impressed by your courage, especially in light of all the opposition you've faced. I also know this decision wasn't made without a great deal of thought. But, Lesley, Buck is no kind of husband.

Now, here's what I want you to do, and please, for once, don't argue with me. This isn't charity. I talked to my mom this afternoon and she's going to give you a job. Her house-keeper has retired and she needs a replace-ment. She wants to hire you, and before you say no, it was her idea, not mine. The money probably won't completely support you and the kids, but that's what child support pay-ments are all about.

I have an attorney for you. Montgomery Gordon is the best attorney in town and quite possibly the state. He's one of my dad's part-ners and a bit of a stuffed shirt, but he's good.

Mom mentioned your case to him and he's offered to represent you without charge. Personally, I can hardly wait for him to get his claws into Buck.

I'll be in touch. Don't worry, Lesley, everything's going to work out.

Love,

Jillian

❖

June 1, 1973

Dear Mr. Gordon,

Thank you so much for your efforts on my behalf. I know you felt bad that you weren't able to remove Buck from the trailer, but you did accomplish what you set out to do. The children and I now have a place to live without needing to rely on my brother.

You asked me to think about having the judge issue a restraining order against Buck. I've given this serious thought, but I don't believe it's necessary. Even though Buck sometimes blows up like that, his temper tantrums generally end quickly. He was upset because the judge ordered him to pay the rent on the apartment for me and the kids.

Having to pay the rent and the amount of child support the judge ordered until the divorce is final was a shock to him. Apparently he assumed he wouldn't be asked to accept financial responsibility because I was the one who filed for divorce. With the rent covered, plus Buck's payments and what I'm making as a housekeeper for Judge and Mrs. Lawton, I'll be able to support my children. Unfortunately it was necessary to withdraw them from the Catholic school, but that couldn't be helped. They'll start public school in September.

Again, my appreciation.

Sincerely,

Lesley Knowles

Dorothy Adamski

July 2, 1973

My dearest Lesley,

I can't tell you how much I've missed you and the children. Your father has been extremely unreasonable about this. When he learned I'd been over to see you and the kids, he got into such a state, he nearly had a heart attack. He's absolutely forbidden me to contact you again. This situation with the long gas lines isn't helping his temper any. He waited two hours to fill up yesterday and came home in a horrible mood. As far as I'm concerned, OPEC is a four-letter word!

Does Jillian know about Mr. Murphy's gas station closing down? It's the saddest thing to see a man's lifework disappear because of foreign greed.

I'm miserable without you and dreadfully miss seeing my grandbabies. Lily has agreed to deliver this note to you, plus the ten dollars. I wish it was more, but that's all I was able to get this week without your father suspecting.

Buck was here for dinner yesterday. I could hardly look at him, and I was disgusted that your father would have anything to do with the man. Buck and your dad sat around all afternoon watching baseball and drinking beer. Buck complained the entire time about that highfalutin attorney you've got working for you. It was all I could do not to stand up and cheer. He's let himself go, I noticed. His shirt needed washing and he hadn't shaved in a couple of days. Your father assured Buck you'd come to your senses soon.

Don't give in, Lesley. Your father would probably put his fist through the wall if he knew I'd said that. You have more courage than I ever did. I'm proud of you.

I love you, sweetheart. Stay strong.

Love,

Mom

July 5, 1973

Dear Daddy,

I miss you. I saw fireworks at the park.

Love,

Davey

❖

July 10, 1973

Dear Lesley,

Okay, baby, you win. I miss you and the kids too damn much to pretend I don't. I wake up in the morning and there's no reason to crawl out of bed. For years this trailer didn't seem to have an inch of extra space. Now it feels big enough to drown in.

I'm sorry about Terri, sorrier than you'll ever know. I'm not going to offer any excuses — it happened and I was the one at fault. I regretted it all along. I never meant to hurt you or the kids, and I can see that I have.

Can we talk? Please? I miss my family. Nothing is right without you. The kids miss me, too. I want to see them. Let me visit, okay? How about if I come this weekend? I'll take Davey fishing. You know how he's always wanted to go with me. Later I'll take Lindy and Dougie for ice cream so they won't feel left out. Afterward, you and I can talk. Say I can come, Lesley. Don't keep me away from my children.

I don't deserve you, but I'm begging you, baby. Talk to me, that's all I'm asking. Give me a chance to make it up to you and the kids.

Buck

❖

JILLIAN LAWTON
330 FAIRCHILD AVE.
APARTMENT 3B
BOSTON, MASS. 02138

August 4, 1973

Dear Montgomery,

Just a note to thank you for all the work you've put into helping my friend in the matter of her divorce. In her last letter to me, Lesley mentioned that she and Buck were talking about reconciling. I'd hate to see that happen, but I can't make the decision for her.

I appreciate the updates on my father's health. He does seem more chipper these days and I'm sure that's because you've taken over a number of his professional responsibilities. But it won't be forever; if everything goes according to schedule, I'll be joining the firm about this time next year.

My parents consider you a valued friend and I want you to know that I do, too.

Sincerely,
Jillian

September 12, 1973

Dear Jillian,

I'm enclosing a picture of me and the kids. I'm the one with the big hair. I love this new style! All I have to do in the morning is wash it and let it dry. Of course, my head looks like a dandelion gone to seed, but that's beside the point.

The kids look happy, don't they? Davey has missed his father something fierce — his daddy and his clubhouse. Davey was barely three when the two of them built that rickety old shack, but it remains my son's retreat from the world. Without his clubhouse, he's been a lost soul.

Lindy has taken to sucking her thumb again. I'm sure the divorce proceedings were responsible for that. And predictably Dougie started wetting the bed. Children need their father.

I'm telling you all this for a reason. I imagine you know what it is. Buck and I are getting back together. I didn't make this decision lightly, any more than I made the decision to leave.

You and I both know Buck has his faults, but every one of us does. I have his word that he'll never cheat on me again. He begged me to give him one last chance to prove himself. He begged me not to break up our family.

For weeks I've been torn, not knowing what to do. My children cry at night after Buck comes to visit, because they miss him so much. They all want to move back home.

I used to think I was smart, but solving algebra equations is a whole lot easier than making decisions that affect the lives of my children. Maybe I'm weak. I don't know anymore. I wouldn't take him back if I didn't firmly believe he's learned his lesson. I've made it clear that if he has another affair, it's over — right then and there.

Thank you for your support and love during this time. You're the best friend I've ever had, Jillian. I don't know what I would've done without you.

Your mom is interviewing other women for the housekeeper position. There's a reason I'm not going to continue with the job. Oh, Jillian, I did something terribly stupid. You don't need to be upset with me, because I'm upset enough with myself.

Earlier in the month, Buck stopped by the apartment one night. The kids were all asleep and he said he wanted to talk. We did talk, but then he spent the night and, well . . . you guessed it. I'm pregnant. I haven't told Buck yet, but I already know he'll be absolutely delighted.

We're both going to give this reconciliation everything we have. I wouldn't do this if I had a single doubt of his love for the children and me. We're both going to try harder to make our marriage work.

I'm grateful to Montgomery Gordon. He was wonderful through all of this. I know he's disappointed but he'd never openly admit it. He doted on the kids and they took a shine to him, too. You said he's a stuffed shirt and I agree he is a bit stiff before you get to know him, but he's a very nice man.

Thank you for being the best friend I've ever had.

Love,
Lesley

1974

Jillian's Diary

January 1, 1974

Dear Nick,

Here it is, the start of yet another year. I always believed that once I was practicing law, I'd join my father's firm. Instead I moved back to New York and I'm volunteering with the National Organization for Women. Dad encouraged me to go ahead and do that, knowing how strongly I feel about women's rights.

Surprisingly, I get along better with my parents these days, especially my father. I'm not sure who changed and would prefer to think we both have. He remains a staunch Republican despite the Watergate mess, although his defense of Nixon isn't as loud or as adamant since Agnew resigned and the Watergate hearings have started. Montgomery Gordon works closely with Dad, and part of me feared a power struggle would develop between us if I returned to Pine Ridge. I still view him as stodgy, but I've revised my opinion of him. He represented Lesley last year when it looked like she was going to divorce Buck and she couldn't say enough good things about him.

My decision to remain on the East Coast also has to do with the fact that I no longer think of Pine Ridge as home. I associate the town with you and that glorious summer we shared before I left for college. The summer before you went to Vietnam. We were young, innocent and so much in love. That time, that innocence, is gone forever now.

I enjoy visiting Pine Ridge and cherish my friends, especially Lesley, but I don't fit comfortably into that small town anymore. Besides, I love living in New York.

Oh Nick, you wouldn't believe the gas lines! People are waiting two hours and longer for gasoline. The newspaper had a picture recently of people parking their cars outside the service station the night before it opened, hoping to get in early before the pumps ran dry. There's even talk of rationing. Supposedly it all has to do with OPEC, but almost everyone believes it has more to do with greedy oil companies than with any foreign government.

I haven't seen Thom since we graduated from law school. He phones every once in a while, we chat for a few minutes and then I hang up feeling guilty and frustrated. I treated him badly. I know I hurt him. He still holds out hope that one day I'll change my mind about the two of us, but I won't.

I've been seeing Curtis Chandler, another attorney. I'm not sleeping with him, although I know he'd enjoy a sexual relationship. I'd enjoy it, too, but I learned a valuable lesson with Thom. Contrary to what I'd assumed, there's more to sex than the physical aspect. I only wanted to involve my body and not my heart; while I succeeded, it left me feeling empty. Thom held me, but it wasn't enough. In the end, all I did was hurt someone I considered a friend. The truth is, I'm not as sophisticated as I once believed. I know lots of women who've had multiple sexual partners. We are, after all, part of the "free love" generation. However, I've decided I can live without sex. I'll never recapture what you and I once had. Frankly, what's the point? Sex complicates everything.

Another truth I've recently owned up to: I don't have many friends. Plenty of acquaintances, but few real friends. Lesley is my closest and dearest friend and probably always will be. Our lives have taken diverging paths, but we understand, accept and love each other like sisters.

The only real disagreement we've had since I left for college has to do with the Catholic Church. I no longer consider myself a Catholic. In fact, I don't really consider myself anything. For lack of a better word, I suppose I could say I'm a Christian, but one who carries a deep-seated anger at God for taking you. My attitude toward religion, God and anything spiritual is bitter. I'd feel like a hypocrite attending Mass. Lesley thinks I'll find peace in church, but I don't want peace, I want you.

Lesley and I've talked about my attitude several times. Her situation is vastly different from my own. She finds solace in attending Mass and it's important to her, but not me. Besides, she has three children, with a fourth on the way. Yes, a fourth – she insists on using the rhythm method, although I think (despite the Church) she's convinced Buck to get a vasectomy after this latest surprise.

I went to see your father and Jimmy over the holidays. Your dad's old service station is a plant store now. I went there and talked to the woman who bought the building and she has plants hanging in every conceivable location. She teaches macrame classes on the side. I know that your father finds it difficult to go past the old station. He's driving a milk truck now, but he didn't talk about his job much. On New Year's Day we went out to the cemetery together. That's become tradition for us. You'll be pleased to know that Jimmy's working steadily and seems happy. He's serious about a girl from his high school class.

I love you, Nick, so much. I refuse to forget you. The war is over now, the POWs have been released, and our troops are home. Saigon has fallen.

Regardless of the general sense of relief – a relief I share – I feel cheated and so very alone. Because you didn't come back to me . . .

Remember how much I love you.

Jillian

February 28, 1974

Dear Jillian,

I'm being lazy this afternoon and just woke up from a nap. Earlier Dougie and I baked chocolate chip cookies and ate our lunch underneath the kitchen table. (That's where his fort was and we were on the lookout for an Indian attack!) Then we snuggled together in my bed, with the blankets pulled over us (hiding from marauding Apaches). It's astonishing what a mother will do to convince her child it's naptime.

This pregnancy has been more difficult than all the others combined. I'm tired most of the time and listless. My ankles are swollen and the doctor has taken me completely off salt, which I love. There are only five weeks before my due date and we haven't registered with the hospital yet. It might have something to do with the fact that we haven't paid off the bill for when I had Dougie.

I have wonderful news. Buck attended his first Alcoholics Anonymous meeting last month and now has thirty days' sobriety. He talks to his sponsor every day, reads from what he calls the Big Book (not the Bible, in case you're wondering) and faithfully attends his meetings. His efforts have convinced me I made the right decision in sticking with him. He's serious about doing whatever he can to save the marriage and keep our family intact. The kids rush to him every night when he gets home and he's been wonderful with them. Lindy adores her daddy.

Judging by the information he brought home from his meetings, I realize my father is an alcoholic, too. Buck's been encouraging me to attend Al-Anon meetings, for family members of alcoholics, and I will as soon as the baby's born. As it is now, taking care of the house and the kids is all I can manage.

Just my luck that of all the men in this world, I had to choose one who has the same problem as my father. I'm positive the reason Dad liked Buck so much is because he saw a drinking buddy in his future son-in-law. Buck never told me what prompted him to seek help, but I thank God he did. I wish my dad would join him, but he refuses to believe he has a problem with alcohol.

I see changes in Buck each and every day. He's a better father and husband since our reconciliation. Here's another first. Buck attended Mass with the children and me last Sunday morning. He was surprised to learn that I actually take part. Remember how I used to pick at a guitar in music class when we were teenagers? Well, I've managed to learn a few chords, and I play and sing at the 9 a.m. Folk Mass. After church, Buck told me how proud he was of me, but I'm the one who's proud of him. It meant the world to me that he came to Mass with us.

I was going to save this as a surprise, but I can't wait. If the baby's a girl, I'm naming her after you. Jill Marie. (Buck insists we can't name a child one thing and call him or her another, so Jill it is!)

I saw your parents at Mass last Sunday, and your mom told me how busy you are. She looked good as always, elegant in her hat and white gloves. Your dad looked wonderful, too. He surprised me. He squatted down so he was eye-level with the kids in order to talk to them. He's going to make a wonderful grandfather once you decide to marry and have your own children.

I know you find a lot of satisfaction in your work, but don't get so involved that you forget about everything else. Take time for yourself, too.

Write when you can.

Love,

Lesley and all

Pine Ridge Herald

March 12, 1974
OBITUARY COLUMN

Patrick Francis Murphy, 56, owner of Murphy's Texaco Full Service Station, died on Monday, March 11 1974 of a heart attack. His son, James Murphy of Pine Ridge, and one brother, Matthew, in Dallas, Texas, survive him. Mr. Murphy is preceded in death by his wife, Eileen, who died of cancer in 1964 and his son, Nicholas Murphy, who was killed in Vietnam in September of 1968. Patrick Murphy was an active member of St. Catherine's Catholic Church and the Veterans of Foreign Wars. Burial Mass is scheduled for Thursday at noon.

❖

BIRTH ANNOUNCEMENT
CHRISTOPHER JAMES KNOWLES
BORN MAY 8, 1974
9 LBS, 3 OZ.
21"
HAPPY PARENTS:
LESLEY AND BUCK KNOWLES
BROTHER TO
DAVID, LINDY AND DOUG

June 12, 1974

Happy 8th anniversary to my beautiful, wonderful and forgiving wife. I'm sorry I forgot, but I have a lot on my mind lately. Don't be mad, all right?

Buck

❖

June 13th

Buck,

The carnations are lovely, but it's too little too late. The least you could've done was let me know you didn't plan on coming home after work. I'm glad you're attending your meetings, but you should've told me. I went to a lot of trouble to make our anniversary dinner special and then sat up for hours waiting for you. I had a horrible night.

Lesley

❖

Sweetheart,

How many times do I have to tell you I'm sorry? Next time you plan on cooking a fancy dinner, you might let *me* know. Okay, you've made your point. I've never seen you this angry over something so petty. Let me make it up to you, okay? I'll do anything. Tell Lindy I appreciate her making my lunches for me, but I'd rather you did it. Yesterday she packed me two licorice sticks, a plum and a carrot. I work too hard to survive on that. Come on, baby, be reasonable.

Buck

Lesley's Diary

June 26, 1974

It's been ages since I wrote. My last entry was early in 1973 and here it is halfway through 1974. Four children are demanding, and I have so little time to myself these days. (They're occupied for the moment watching *Little House on the Prairie.* I'm grateful we could finally afford to have the television repaired.)

I guess I feel the need to write because of my disastrous anniversary. Buck claims he forgot all about it, but I'm never completely sure if he's telling the truth. It's difficult to admit that even to myself. With all the lies he's told me over the years, I'd be a fool to believe his lame excuses the way I did when we were first married. Time has taught me to question everything he says.

When Jillian and I were teenagers, we sometimes stayed up all night reading books aloud to each another. In the wee hours of the morning, when we were so tired it was hard to keep our eyes open, we'd talk about what our lives would be like ten or twenty years into the future. The scenes we created in our minds have nothing in common with what has come to be. We both saw ourselves married with children, as well as maintaining our own careers. I was a nurse with two perfect children and a husband who adored me.

Jillian is the attorney she used to say she'd be. She learned a lot when she volunteered at NOW and has taken her experience to a NY law firm that's prestigious enough to do her father proud. She's a polished professional, shining like a gemstone, a brilliant attorney — sharp, quick, relentless. She's told me about a few of her cases and I almost feel sorry for the defendants. On rare occasions as a teenager, I saw that ruthless, angry side of Jillian. These days, that part of her is all the world sees. But beneath her hard-edged determination, she remains the friend I remember from my childhood. My best friend in the whole world.

Losing Nick changed her. It's almost as if she's shut herself off from love. Yet when she's with the children and me, the old Jillian quickly resurfaces and she's once again the girl she used to be. How I wish she'd marry and have children of her own. In my heart I know that's what Nick would want for her, too. I've tried to talk to her about it, but she closes up so tight there's no reaching her.

My own dreams of attending college vanished when I learned I was pregnant with Davey. I love my children and I wouldn't change anything. My life with Buck is the hand fate dealt me and I'm determined to make the best of it. That, however, doesn't make me blind to my husband's faults. He can be wonderful one day, and the next he'll treat me with thoughtless cruelty. Our anniversary is a prime example of that. Although Buck claims he's attending AA meetings most evenings, I'm pretty sure he's elsewhere, at least some of the time. But I refuse to be the kind of wife who follows her husband around, trying to catch him in a lie. And yet I won't bury my head in the sand again, either. Finding the balance isn't easy.

I suspect one of the reasons I'm writing all this down has to do with something I saw on television. Or rather, someone. The other night, Buck was gone as usual and I was hurrying to get dinner on the table when a news bulletin flashed across the screen. It had to do with Patty Hearst and the Symbionese Liberation Army. I nearly dropped the pan of tuna casserole. Not at the newsflash about Patty Hearst, but at the man reporting it.

Cole Greenberg. He was the Naval officer I met on the beach in Hawaii back in 1967. I've never forgotten him, and although it's probably wrong of me, I've always regretted not giving him my address. In all likelihood, he won't even remember me. Three hours out of a lifetime was all we shared. When Cole's face came on the screen, I could hardly stop myself from telling the children that I knew him and he was my friend. I didn't, of course, and it's not really true — but it could have been. And I wish it was. . . .

I wonder if he's married and if he's happy. For my own peace of mind, I pray he is. I remember I marveled at how smart he was and how much we had in common. He was so easy to talk to, and he said the same thing about me. He was at the top of his class, the one everyone called a "brain." He told me he'd never dated much and I could see he was telling the truth. He said that one day he wanted to report the news on television and now it's happening. I was so excited to see him, so pleased that the things he'd talked about have come to pass.

The only real boyfriend I ever had was Buck and I married him. I so want Cole Greenberg to be happy and married and successful, which he appears to be. I feel a bit silly writing this but the last two nights I've dreamed of Cole. The dreams have been wonderful. We're on the beach again, talking about the war in Vietnam and the books we've read. It's as though I was single and the two of us were falling in love.

This must stop. It has to; I can't allow myself to indulge in this kind of escape. It's too dangerous to my mental health and to my marriage. My reality is that I'm married to Buck, and we have four beautiful children.

❖

August 10, 1974

Dear Jillian,

This letter is long overdue, but I want you to know how much I appreciated you flying home for my dad's funeral. It would've been a lot rougher on me if you hadn't been there. Thank you for helping me with everything, like choosing the coffin and arranging the wake.

I didn't expect Dad to die this young, but he was never the same after we learned about Nick. None of us were. Losing the service station was another blow. He hated his job driving a milk truck. He said it paid the bills, but it was as though there wasn't any joy left in him anymore.

The doctors said his heart attack was brought on by years of cigarette smoking and I'm sure that had something to do with it. But you and I both know the real cause. Vietnam. It killed my father the same way it took my brother.

Nick's been dead nearly six years now and I still miss him. Sometimes I think about telling him something, and it hits me that I can't, my brother is dead. And then I feel a shock and this sadness that sucker punches me. I can tell it's going to be like that with my dad, too. I'm really gonna miss him.

I gotta tell you, it's a weird feeling being an orphan. First my mom, but I barely remember her, then Nick, and now Dad. If it hadn't been for you and Angie, I would've stood alone in the family pew at the funeral Mass. You're like a sister to me, Jillian, and I want you to know how grateful I am for everything you've done for me over the years. Both you and your parents have been like family to me. I think your father's done a lot of things in the last six years to help my dad and me. He's never admitted anything, but I'm sure of it, and I believe it's his way of letting us know that if he had to do it over again, he wouldn't have been so critical of Nick. Deep down, I've always had that feeling. We ran into each other recently and he made a point of saying hello. I appreciated that. I appreciate you, too.

There's something else you should know. I was going through a bunch of Dad's business papers and came across two loans he'd taken out when the energy crunch first hit. Your father co-signed on those loans. It looks like Dad paid off all his financial obligations when he sold the service station to the plant lady. If he didn't, I'll make sure everything is square with the bank and your dad.

I know you've had your differences with your father, but Judge Lawton is a good guy. It was because of him that I got my first job with D & D Construction. I asked Judge Lawton about it once, but he denied he had anything to do with me being hired. I know better, though.

I'm glad you were finally able to meet Angie. She felt bad about being away over the holidays, because I talk about you so much. She sure is pretty, isn't she? We started dating last summer and I'm pretty sure we're going to get married. What do you think? You liked her, didn't you?

She graduated from college this summer and wants to be a teacher. Angie and I've been talking about a lot of things. She's encouraging me to give community college a try. Since Mr. D made me a foreman, I've discovered how much I enjoy working with blueprints. Someday I might think about all of that. Kind of an exciting idea, isn't it?

Thanks again, Jillian, for everything.

Your "adopted" brother,

Jim Murphy

P. S. Isn't it something about Nixon resigning as President? When they got rid of Agnew, Dad told me Nixon was next and he was right. Who will it be now? The Pope?

JILLIAN LAWTON

September 18, 1974

Dear Mom and Dad,

Thank you for the radar range, which I'm using and enjoying. I don't know how I lived this long without one. If only I could find a way to make popcorn in it, I'd really be in heaven.

But the gift isn't the only reason I'm writing to thank you. I recently realized how much I have to be grateful for. Loving parents, good friends, an exciting new job and much, much more.

Dad, I want to thank you for your patience with me, especially in the late sixties. It's taken me four years, but I want to apologize for the letter I wrote you after the shootings at Kent State. You received the brunt of my pain and anger, and I thank you for loving me through those turbulent years. Mom always claimed you and I have the same personality and that's the reason we sometimes clash. It's taken me this long to recognize how right she is. Where those words once made me cringe, now they make me so very proud. It's an honor to have my name mentioned in connection with you. I want to be a good attorney, the same way you were. You've been a wonderful role model for me, and I'm proud to be your daughter.

Much love,
Jillian

P.S. By the way, I'd love it if you and Mom could fly east next month. There's a revival of Gypsy starring Angela Lansbury on Broadway. Let me know as soon as you can and I'll order tickets.

❖

JILLIAN LAWTON

October 20, 1974

Dearest Lesley,

It's a lovely Sunday afternoon and I'm indulging myself by being completely and utterly lazy. Mom and Dad were in New York last week, and it was great to see them. I spent as much time with them as my schedule would allow. My law firm is one of the largest in the city and the long hours are unbelievable. But that's how it goes, and I have to pull my share. I'm making incredible money; now all I need is time to spend it!

Everything went exceptionally well with my parents until Mom mentioned Nick. She thinks I've buried myself in work because I'm still dealing with my grief. This was her subtle way of letting me know she'd like me to get married, I guess. Frankly, I don't have time for a man in my life, which I suppose is Mom's point.

Nevertheless, I've given our conversation some thought. The problem is, I haven't met a man who makes me feel the way Nick did. I don't know if it's even possible to find that level of love and communication with anyone else. I'm over the tears, and the grief is no longer so brutal. Sometimes I'll remember something Nick said or did and I catch myself smiling.

I told my mother I haven't ruled out marriage, which I know pleased her. I'm not sure, though. The thing is, I just can't imagine loving anyone with the same intensity I loved Nick – and still do.

Thanks for the pictures of the children. Christopher's so cute I just might forgive him for not being a girl. I did a double-take when I saw the one of Lindy. Lesley, she looks so much like you! It's hard to believe she's almost seven. Davey's quite the little gentleman, isn't he? He looks so grown-up in his suit and tie. Little Doug stole my heart, holding on to his blankie with one hand and sucking his thumb with the other. I suppose it's only natural that he wanted his blankie back after Christopher was born.

Buck never followed through with that vasectomy, did he? I applaud your decision to handle the matter of birth control yourself.

No, I'm not attending Mass. I haven't in years and you know that. I realize you feel I should make peace with the Church. The problem is, I don't think I can. I no longer think of myself as Catholic. For a while, I was bitter because of Nick, but I'm not any more. After working with NOW, my views of male-dominated religion have simply made it impossible for me to join any church, Catholic or otherwise. We've had this discussion before and I think it'd be best if we avoided the subject. I know you're committed to the Church and I respect that. Unfortunately, it just isn't the same for me.

I might be able to fly home for Christmas. No promises, but I'm working on it. New York is an incredible city, especially in December, so if my schedule won't permit me to travel, you don't need to worry about me being here alone. I won't have a problem spending the holidays by myself. The fact is, I've come to quite enjoy my own company. My parents seem to have a hard time believing it, but for the most part I'm actually happy. For six years I'd lost that joy but slowly, surely, it's returning. Life does go on, although it can take a long while to realize it.

Enough about me. I noticed that you didn't mention one word about Buck. What's going on? You should know by now that there isn't anything you can't tell me.

Write soon. I love getting your letters and hearing about the children. And NO, you can't tell me not to spoil them at Christmas. I have way too much fun shopping for them.

I think I'll see a movie tonight, even if I have to go by myself. I can't remember the last one I saw and I've been hearing good things about *Alice Doesn't Live Here Anymore*. I'll let you know what I think.

Kiss the kids for me.
Love,
Jillian

MONTGOMERY GORDON, ESQUIRE
248 Phillips Avenue
Pine Ridge, Washington 98005

November 12, 1974

Dear Jillian,

It only took ten years to convince you to have dinner with me. I want you to know I consider our night on the town worth every minute of that wait.

To say I was surprised when you agreed to dine with me on my recent trip east would be an understatement. I can't tell you how much I enjoyed your company.

Sincerely,
Montgomery

DWI FOR BUCK KNOWLES

THE UNDERSIGNED CERTIFIES AND SAYS THAT IN THE STATE OF WASHINGTON

Drivers License No. KNOWLES*DA461TB **State** WA
Expires 5/75 ID #533-24-6009
Name (last) KNOWLES **First** DAVID **Initial** J.
Address KNOTTY PINES TRAILER COURT
City Pine Ridge **State** WA **Zip Code** 98005
Employer PINE RIDGE LUMBER MiLL
Race W **Sex** M **Date of Birth** 02/28/43
Height 6.1 **Weight** 200 **Eyes** BLU **Hair** BRO
Residential Phone 206-458-0522
Violation Date: Month 12 **Day** 24 **Year** 74 **Time** 10:30 PM
At Location STATE ST **City/County of** Pine Ridge

DID OPERATE THE FOLLOWING VEHICLE/ MOTOR VEHICLE ON A PUBLIC HIGH WAY AND

Vehicle License # 478GZR **State** WA **Expires** 06/75 **Veh.Yr.** 1960
Make CHEVY **Model** IMPALA **Style** 2 DOOR **Color** BLU

DID THEN AND THERE COMMIT THE FOLLOWING OFFENSES

OPERATE A MOTOR VEHICLE WHILE INTOXICATED
Appearance Date: Mo 01 **Dy** 07 **Yr** 75 **Time** 9:30 AM
Date Issued 12/24/74

WITHOUT ADMITTING HAVING COMMITTED EACH OF THE ABOVE OFFENSE(S) I PROMISE TO RESPOND AS DIRECTED ON THIS NOTICE X__________________
Defendant

I CERTIFY UNDER PENALTY OF PERJURY UNDER THE LAWS OF THE STATE OF WASHINGTON THAT I HAVE ISSUED THIS ON THE DATE AND AT THE LOCATION ABOVE, THAT I HAVE PROBABLE CAUSE TO BELIEVE THE ABOVE NAMED PERSON COMMITTED THE ABOVE OFFENSE(S) AND MY REPORT WRITTEN ON THE BACK OF THIS DOCUMENT IS TRUE AND CORRECT. X__________
Officer

1976

Jillian's Diary

January 1, 1976

Dear Nick,

Can you believe it's been nearly ten years since we graduated from high school? Lesley is already dutifully at work, rounding up everyone for an August reunion. She's always so organized. Where she finds the time and energy to be a wife, a mother and to do everything else she does is beyond me. I might be a corporate attorney, but she's turned into an earth mother who runs circles around me. Ever since the energy crunch back in 1974 she refuses to be at the mercy of anyone for her family's basic needs. She has a garden that's the envy of anyone who sees it. She raises a few chickens and sells the eggs she doesn't use. Most recently, she started baking her own bread and is active in a huge co-op. Reading *Diary for a Small Planet* by Frances Moore Lappé had a powerful influence on her. In addition, she sews many of the kids' clothes, knits and crochets, and puts up preserves. Like I said earlier,

I'm exhausted just listing all the things she does.

Buck's a complete waste of time, but you and I knew that years ago. In my opinion, she should have divorced him when she had the chance. He works four or five months in a row and then is either laid off or comes down with a mysterious ailment that forces him to take several weeks off. His affliction coincidentally appears around the same time as hunting season, and he goes off with his worthless friends and stumbles around in the bush. He's back on the booze, too, with intermittent periods of sobriety.

Why Lesley puts up with him, I'll never know. I don't agree with her choice, but my admiration for her grows whenever we're together. She's coping with a difficult situation and doing a wonderful job raising those kids. I keep pictures of David, Lindy, Doug and Christopher on my desk at work and I love them as if they were my own. What beautiful, sweet children they are.

While I was home over the holidays, I went to see Jimmy, oops, Jim. Oh, Nick, you'd be so proud of him. He's married and attending night classes in business management. I spent a day with him and Angie and was impressed with what a nice couple they make. It's become tradition for the two of us to visit the cemetery. We placed flowers on your dad's gravesite. The marble grave-marker, with both your parents' names engraved on it, is in place now. Jim insisted he pay for that himself although I was more than willing to help with the expense. He left me to spend some time alone with you, knowing I'd want a few moments before he joined me.

You don't need to worry about your little brother, Nick. He's responsible and wise beyond his years.

I suspect you're wondering why I'm chatting on endlessly about Lesley and Jim instead of telling you about myself the way I normally do the first of every year.

Nick, something's happened to me that I thought would never happen again. I've fallen in love. So deeply in love it shocks me. I didn't think it was possible after losing you. You'll probably get a good laugh when I tell you who it is. Montgomery Gordon. (I'm the only person in the world who calls him Monty.)

You can't tell me anything I haven't already told myself. I'm fully aware that he's too old for me. I'm still in my twenties and he's forty-four. Not only that, we live on opposite sides of the country. Now here's the part you'll find really amusing. He's a Republican and as chauvinistic as my own father – well, almost. He's learning.

It all started in the autumn of '74 when he flew to New York for a business meeting and we had dinner together. As you know, Monty's been a good friend of my parents' over the years. You'll remember how Mom and Dad attempted to pair us off soon after you died and even before. I resented their interference and refused to date him. In fact, I was downright rude to him.

Then back in '74, in a moment of weakness, I agreed to meet him for dinner while he was in town. It was a surprise to discover I actually enjoyed his company. When he returned to Pine Ridge he wrote me the sweetest letter. I wrote him back and, well . . . that was the beginning.

Last year on Valentine's he came out here expressly to spend the day with me. We talked until the wee hours. That night, after walking through the snow in Central Park, he kissed me. I didn't feel completely shaken the way I did the first time you and I kissed, but it was a nice kiss.

After Valentine's Day, Monty and I spent a fortune talking on the phone. (I wish to hell someone would take on the telephone company's monopoly. Long-distance rates are ridiculous, even after business hours.) Now it's become habit to check in with each other at the end of the day. Our conversations sometimes last two and three hours. It's crazy, I know.

With our hectic schedules, it's impossible for us to get together very often. We're both involved in cases that demand time and dedication. The earliest I can take a few days off to actually see him is June.

I never expected to fall in love again, Nick. But I've discovered something — I don't love you any less. Perhaps more, because it's given me a glimpse of the adult relationship you and I might have shared. It's as if loving you has enabled me to open my heart to Monty.

Just last week when I was home for Christmas, Monty mentioned marriage for the first time. I've thought about marriage, too; it seems a natural progression for this relationship. And yet I froze up the moment he uttered the word.

Marriage frightens me. I love you, Nick. My love didn't die when your casket was lowered into the ground. It's been eight years now and you're as much a part of me as you ever were. But I love Monty, too. It's taken me all these years to reach this point – this ability to love another man. I'm not sure I'm ready for marriage and all the changes it would bring to my life. I said I need time to think about all this, but I could see Monty was a little impatient. I'm afraid I'm going to lose him. Oh, Nick, what should I do?

I love living on the East Coast and I don't want to abandon my career. I've worked too hard and too long to walk away from it. Monty prefers life on the West Coast. I don't know what to do. Then I look at the pictures of Lesley's babies, and I feel this deep hunger. I yearn for children of my own. I don't want to be alone any more.

This doesn't mean I'll stop loving you. But Nick, if it's at all possible, find a way to let me know you approve of Monty. I need that.

Remember how much I love you.

Jillian

February 4, 1976

Dear Susan,

I've just got Christopher down for his nap, so I'm taking a few minutes to write and tell you how pleased I am about your pregnancy. I'll bet Aaron and Jessica are excited about being a big brother and big sister.

I certainly understand how you feel about three children being your limit. Mom and Dad don't know, but I had a tubal ligation when Christopher was born. Father Morris would strongly disapprove if he learned what I'd done, but Father Morris and the Catholic Church aren't raising these children. Buck and I are the ones responsible for the size of our family. (You can see that my views have changed somewhat!) I figure God gave us a brain and a budget, and we have to work with both.

There's a reason I mentioned God. Recently a woman in the trailer park invited me to a Bible study in her home. The only reason I attended was so I could make friends with the other mothers. The socializing is good for me, but I soon discovered how much I enjoy reading the Bible.

When Father Morris found out I was meeting with Protestants, he paid me a visit, his first in several years, and assured me the Church would teach me everything I needed to know about God. He said it's better to have a priest explain the Scriptures to laymen. He went on to say I was treading dangerous waters by attending a Bible study, especially one conducted by someone other than a Catholic priest.

His attitude rankled. It seemed as if he was saying I wasn't intelligent enough to make these decisions on my own — or to understand what's written in the Bible. After his visit, I realized how much I've accepted in my life simply because a man insisted that was the way things should be. Then I got angry. Angry with Father Morris, angry with Buck and with Dad and almost every man who's ever been in my life.

Jillian's worked hard to enlighten me on the issue of women's rights and for the first time it started to sink in. I stood up to Father Morris and informed him that I had no intention of leaving the Bible study. Wouldn't you know it, he went straight to Mom and Dad, as if I were a disobedient child.

The very next day, our own mother phoned and cautioned me against this group. I couldn't believe my ears. I'm enjoying these sessions, and the other women are becoming my friends. I certainly don't need Father Morris telling me who can be my friend! I do a slow burn every time I think about what he said and did. Now I'm going to say something else that will shock you.

I've stopped going to Mass. There's a small nondenominational church down the road that I've been going to for the last couple of weeks. Buck doesn't care one way or the other. I haven't told Mom or Dad yet. I'm sure you'll hear about it but I figure I'm twenty-seven years old and this is my business.

Speaking of Mom and Dad, they're well. Dad's eager to attend the Legionnaires' convention this summer, which will take place in Philadelphia in July. My ten-year class reunion happens the first week in August. Oh, Susan, tell me, where did all those years go? It seems only a short while ago that we were fighting over whose turn it was to use the bathroom mirror. Remember those huge spongy pink rollers we faithfully wore to bed?

I'm glad we keep in touch. I hardly ever hear from Mike since he moved to Nevada. The last time he wrote, he was dealing blackjack in Vegas. Mom hasn't heard from him at all, and I don't think she will as long as Dad is alive. Dad's never forgiven Mike for helping me when I left Buck. Ever since then, the two of them can't be in the same room without yelling and arguing.

You asked about Joe and he's fine. I like his new girlfriend. I hope Karen encourages him to get a job other than the one he has at the mill. That's a dead end, and he's too smart to waste his life there the way Dad and Buck have. Lily's great. It's hard to believe our baby sister will be twenty-one this year, isn't it? She's still working as a beautician, which is a real bonus to me. According to Mom, Bruce has turned into a real heartthrob. He worked for a contractor this summer and earned enough money to buy his own car. Can you imagine either of us driving our own car at sixteen?

Buck is drinking again and is fool enough to think I don't know. We don't have much of a marriage, although we both do a good job of pretending otherwise. I suppose he's the reason I need that Bible study as badly as I do. I want so much to be a good wife and mother.

The kids are awake, so I'll have to end this for now. You're my sister and I love you. If you need anything for the new baby, be sure and let me know.

Love,

Lesley and all

MONTGOMERY GORDON, ESQUIRE
248 Phillips Avenue
Pine Ridge, Washington 98005

March 19, 1976

My dearest Jillian,

I know you're away for the weekend. Not talking to you doesn't seem right, especially on a Friday evening when we've so often chatted. But perhaps it's for the best. I'll write everything down so you can read this over carefully and think about what I have to say.

All those years ago when we first met, I knew I was going to love you. I realize it makes you uncomfortable when I tell you this, but I can't deny what I know to be true. After all this time, it seems like a miracle that you feel the same way about me.

If you remember last Christmas, I mentioned marriage in hopes of gauging your reception to the idea. You immediately tensed up, as though you were afraid I'd press the subject. Your reaction told me everything I feared. You listed all the reasons talk of marriage was premature. You live on the East Coast, while I live on the West. Your job, my job. Your friends, my friends. Within five minutes, you had me believing a marriage between us would be impractical and improbable. It made me see what a persuasive attorney you are.

In the months since, I've had time to think about your objections. True enough, there are several considerations that require discussion. But nothing so major it can't be resolved. It occurred to me recently that we can find a solution to any one of these issues. The real reason is Nick Murphy, isn't it? I know you loved him, Jillian, and that you love him still.

I can't compete with a dead man. I won't try. But I can assure you that I don't intend to replace Nick. He's part of you. His love for you and yours for him shaped you into the woman you are. The woman I love. I don't love you the same way as Nick did. What you had with him is unique. But I can and will love you as me. And the love we share, while completely separate, will be unique in its own way.

If you do agree to marry me, I want you to know I don't expect you to stop loving Nick.

That said, I also want you to know I put out a few feelers on the East Coast to see what kind of response I'd get on the job market. To my delight, I've been offered an excellent position with the Justice Department.

If I could be certain you'd accept my proposal, I'd leap at the offer. I love you, Jillian, and want nothing more than to be married to you. But I can't, I won't, uproot my entire life unless you're sure this is what you want, too. Think about it. Consider it seriously. The problem is, I need an answer soon. Will you marry me, Jillian? Tell me. Yes? No?

Love,
Montgomery

JILLIAN LAWTON

March 21, 1976

My dearest Monty,

Forgive me for being such a coward and writing instead of telling you personally or over the phone. Your letter arrived this afternoon. I knew it was coming and had guessed at its contents. Nevertheless I was stunned. You want an answer right away. I understand, and you deserve one, but I can't make a decision like this under pressure.

Before I write any more, it's important that you know how deeply I've come to love you. I love you so much . . . and yet, I'm afraid. I have never completely understood what frightens me about marrying you, but the fear is there. I suspect you know what's coming.

I'm grateful you had the courage to bring up Nick. Few people do. Your tenderness toward my feelings for him touched my heart, and has helped me sort through my feelings about you and me. In my own defense, I never expected to fall in love again. I certainly didn't anticipate this. Perhaps such thinking was shortsighted. If I were to see a counselor, I'm sure he or she would advise me to let go of the past and get on with my life. Unfortunately I seem incapable of that, especially if it means letting go of Nick. I'm so grateful you understand and accept my love for him.

Heaven knows my parents will make a fuss, but what I'd like to suggest is this. Accept the job with the Justice Department and move in with me. Let's give this marriage idea a trial run first.

I'm sorry, but that's the best I can do for now.

Love,

Jillian

❖

WU **Telegram**
Western Union

TO: JILLIAN LAWTON

FROM: MONTGOMERY GORDON

I'M TOO OLD TO PLAY HOUSE. THE QUESTION REMAINS THE SAME: YES OR NO?

MONTGOMERY

Pine Ridge Herald
May 29, 1976
Neighbors Section

Jillian Lawton Marries Prominent Local Attorney

Judge and Mrs. Leonard Lawton are pleased to announce the marriage of their daughter, Jillian Lynn Lawton, to Montgomery Gordon.

The bride is a 1966 Graduate of Holy Name Academy in Pine Ridge, a 1970 graduate of Barnard College, and has a Harvard Law degree. She is currently residing in New York City. She is an associate at Kline and Shoemaker, Attorneys at Law.

The groom has recently accepted a position with the United States Justice Department. The couple will make their home in New York City.

Lesley Knowles, a lifelong friend of the bride, served as matron-of-honor and Charles Johnson, the groom's cousin, served as best man. The bride's gown featured French lace and beaded pearls over satin.

A reception was held immediately following the ceremony at Pine Ridge Country Club.

June 19, 1976

Dearest Lesley,

I'm taking a moment to jot you a long-overdue note. Monty and I are settling into married life. I love my husband, but even now I'm not sure I did the right thing.

I agreed to go through with the wedding because I didn't want to lose him. I've never had anyone love me like this. Not even Nick. Monty is completely and totally dedicated to me. I'm telling you all this as a preface to describing our first fight. I had my hair cut and it never occurred to me that I should mention my plans to Monty. It's trimmed like Dorothy Hamill's and I love its short, easy-to-care-for style. Monty was so upset he barely said a word to me all night. I'm not accustomed to having a man tell me how to wear my hair. I let that be known in terms he was sure to understand. He got huffy and I got huffy right back. I learned one thing. I hate the silent treatment. We patched it up fast enough and I lured him to bed to prove all was forgiven. We so seldom bicker and this has taught us both some valuable lessons.

Speaking of "bed," we're hoping I'll get pregnant soon. With Monty turning 45 this year, we don't want to wait much longer. You, my dear and fertile friend, never seemed to have a problem with that. Any hints you care to pass on? I'll let you know at reunion time how successful we are.

Monty and I will be staying in the city for the bicentennial celebration. Already there's talk about security around the United Nations building against possible terrorist attack. We don't have any definite plans for the rest of the summer, other than going to Pine Ridge in early August.

So Buck bought himself a CB radio. Yes, I can picture it! What's his "handle"? I'll bet Davey and Dougie love riding around in his pickup chatting with the big truckers on the Interstate. You haven't said much about Buck lately, which leads me to think he's up to something unpleasant.

My mom and dad are enjoying their retirement to the fullest. Monty and I are picking them up at the airport tomorrow. They've spent the last two weeks in Italy. Speaking of traveling, your father will love Philadelphia. It's a fabulous city. I'm sorry your mother won't be attending the Legionnaires' convention with him, but from what I understand men rarely bring their wives to these things.

I can hardly wait for our class reunion, but I'm far more interested in spending time with you.

Promise me you'll write soon.

Love,

Jillian

HOLY NAME ACADEMY AND
MARQUETTE HIGH SCHOOL
ANNOUNCE
THE TEN-YEAR REUNION OF THE
CLASS OF 1966
AUGUST 6–8, 1976
PINE RIDGE, WASHINGTON

FRIDAY NIGHT GET-TOGETHER
SATURDAY DINNER AND DANCE
SUNDAY PICNIC
RSVP Lesley (Adamski) Knowles

IN MEMORY OF
MICHAEL JOHN ADAMSKI

March 10, 1925–July 6, 1976

SERVICES
Emerson Mortuary

ORGANIST
Sally Johnson

CASKETBEARERS

Michael Adamski, Jr.	Clarence Behrens
Joseph Adamski	David "Buck" Knowles
Bruce Adamski	Roy Bensen

INTERMENT
Pine Ridge Cemetery
Pine Ridge, Washington

August 9, 1976

We are all reeling from the sudden and unexpected death of my father. Off he went with his beer-drinking buddies to Philadelphia for the American Legion convention. Mom drove him to the airport and kissed him goodbye, never dreaming that the next time she saw him would be in a casket. Dad was one of the first to come down with the mysterious ailment and one of the first to die. He was gone even before Mom could make arrangements to fly east. The shock of it rippled through our community. Bud Jones, Dad's roommate at the convention, got sick too, but he survived. No one's sure what happened to cause this — it's still being investigated. All I know is that my father is dead, and my mother is grieving.

I have a lot of mixed feelings about my father. Sometimes I thought I hated him. He was never the kind of father I needed, and we disagreed on many things, but I did love him. Not until he died did I realize how much. He may not have been the greatest dad, but he *was* my dad. I'm grateful I had the reunion work to keep me busy. As long as I was involved with those arrangements, I didn't need to deal with my feelings about him.

Now that the ten-year high school reunion has come and gone, I can say that all the committee's hard work paid off. It was wonderful to see everyone again. The girls looked basically the same; it was the boys who were different. Most had filled out and looked more mature, more muscular.

After literally weeks of work, I came down with a terrible case of nerves. Not everyone knew I was pregnant when we graduated, and now Buck and I have four children. Not surprisingly, I received the award for the one with the most kids.

Although it was less than three weeks since we buried my dad, Mom insisted I have a new dress. All at once I felt like prom night all over again. I modeled the dress for Buck and he growled and chased me around the house. The kids loved it and laughed with delight as they watched their father sweep me off my feet.

The night of the dinner and dance it was an entirely different story. Buck knew I was supposed to be at the hall early to help set up, but he was late and then had to shower. All in all, we arrived thirty minutes late and the entire evening started on a negative note.

Then Buck disappeared and was gone for more than an hour. When he returned he had liquor on his breath and no one needed to tell me he'd been in the parking lot with a bottle, joking with his loser buddies. I tried not to let it bother me. This was *my* class reunion and if he wanted to spend it in the parking lot making crude jokes with his friends, that was his choice. I guess some of what I'm learning at Al-Anon is finally sinking in!

The highlight of the evening was dancing with Roy Kloster. Dr. Roy Kloster these days. I've known Roy nearly all my life. We met in first grade and went through the first eight years of school together. Then he went to Marquette and I moved on to Holy Name Academy. I asked him to the Sadie Hawkins dance when we were freshmen and desperately wanted him to kiss me. He didn't. After that, we saw each other at sporting events and such, but neither of us ever had much to say.

Now, ten years following graduation, Roy confessed he'd had a major crush on me all through high school. On me! He was the Valedictorian of his class and I was the Salutatorian for mine. Jillian and I had always planned to be co-Valedictorians, but with the pregnancy and all, I let my last quarter's grades slide. Roy isn't married, and he came to the reunion alone. He teased me about getting the award for the ten-year graduate with the most kids.

Afterward I sat and chatted with Jillian and Cindy and Judy and some of the other girls. At one point, I found a quiet corner to sit and watch my friends, people I knew as a child. The oddest sensation came over me. I suddenly realized I was close to tears and I wasn't sure why. I've been overly emotional lately, which is understandable, seeing that I recently lost my father, but this sadness was part of something else. I guess I'd have to call it regret. Regret about bad decisions and lost dreams.

From the age of six, I thought Roy was wonderful. He doesn't remember this, but he defended me against Todd Kramer in the third grade and got a black eye for his efforts. In eighth grade, he secretly put a valentine and a small box of chocolates on my desk during recess, but I always knew he was the one. What I didn't know about Roy was that he wanted to be a doctor. He never knew I dreamed of becoming a nurse.

I know this is wrong, and may God forgive me, but when I first heard the news about my dad I wished it had been Buck who'd died. I've felt guilty about that ever since. Buck is my husband and the father of my children. I married him, not Roy Kloster and not Cole Greenberg. I've got to accept reality and quit playing these ridiculous games in my mind. If I hadn't married Buck, there'd be no Davey, Lindy, Doug or Christopher. My children are my everything.

It's nearly two in the morning and I'm exhausted. Buck still isn't home, but I refuse to guess where he might be or with whom. It's best not to scratch too deeply below the surface because I know I won't like what I find. I'm trying hard to hold on to the happy memories from the reunion and not to think about anything else. I'm not going to hear from Roy again, and that's for the best.

❖

Bumper sticker on Jillian's car:

NIXON'S FORD — A LEMON

Bumper sticker on Buck's pickup:

BOZO FOR PRESIDENT

1978

Jillian's Journal

January 1, 1978

Dearest Nick,

I'm still not pregnant. Monty and I are so discouraged. We've been married almost two years now. We don't know what's wrong. Both of us have been tested, a humiliating experience which we endured because we desperately want a child. I couldn't bear it if Monty and I can't have children. As you can see, I'm very distressed about this. However, my parents waited years for me and I eventually came along. I take hope from that.

Married life is surprisingly good. Monty wants me to cut back on my work hours. He believes it's the stress of my job that's keeping me from getting pregnant. I suspect he's right, and as of the first of the year (today!) I'll be in the office only three days a week. We moved into a wonderful new apartment and absolutely love it.

I feel this urgency to hurry up and have children. Monty's age is a factor and my parents' ages, too. Both my mother and father are anxious for grandchildren. Dad's turning seventy this year, and he'd like the opportunity to watch them grow up.

Monty and I spent four days in Pine Ridge over the Christmas holidays. Last year Mom and Dad flew to New York, but Dad hates to fly. He does it for Mom and me. He has this theory about all those germs floating around and infecting everyone unlucky enough to share the flight. His theories are often amusing. I sit and listen, nod at the appropriate times and pretend to agree. I wonder if I'll be anything like him at that age. In many ways I hope I am.

Unfortunately, because of our abbreviated visit, I only had a few hours with Lesley. Buck was off work because of a bad back but was feeling well enough to leave his sickbed to go bowling with his buddies. (Need I say more?) I can't tell you the number of times I've had to bite my tongue when it comes to the subject of Buck Knowles. Lesley is more religious than ever, which I can understand. If I was married to Buck, I'd find God, too.

She's clever at crafts and sews these cute little Tooth Fairy pouches from leftover material. She sells them at Christmas bazaars and other craft shows. Apparently she's doing quite well with that. I wish we'd had more time, but Christopher had an ear infection and she had to take him to the doctor on the 26th, when we'd originally planned to get together. Luckily Pine Ridge now has a free health clinic.

Buck hasn't worked enough hours for the mill to cover his health insurance so Lesley had to wait her turn, which took hours. She was there nearly all of one day before the doctor could see Christopher and write a prescription. I did visit the next day. David, Lindy and Doug were so enthusiastic about the gifts I brought, so pathetically grateful, it nearly broke my heart. You'll note Davey now prefers to be called David. He's a lovely child, although that isn't generally the way I'd describe an eleven-year-old boy. He's sensitive and caring, gentle-spirited and protective of his younger brothers and sister. I can already see that Lindy's going to be a handful. I don't envy Lesley, especially when her daughter hits the teenage years. Dougie is in first grade and a real charmer. Because his ear hurt, three-year-old Christopher clung to Lesley and refused to have anything to do with me.

I was sorry not to have time to visit Mrs. Adamski. Although she didn't say much, Lesley alluded to the fact that her mother's life is vastly different now that Mr. Adamski is gone. Apparently she's dating and has a regular beau. Good for her!

Jim and I met Christmas Eve Day at the cemetery and placed flowers on your parents' graves and on yours, too. We were only together an hour, but as far as I could tell, he's happy. I'm delighted that he married Angie, and you would be, too. She's been good for him. It wouldn't surprise me if they made you an uncle soon.

I thought that after this year, I wouldn't write you any more letters. I'm married now and somehow it didn't seem right that I should continue this. I loved you so completely, Nick, but you left me. It's been almost ten years since you were killed. As much as I thought everything would stay frozen in that time and space, it hasn't. I've aged ten years, and the world is changing so fast I sometimes feel I can't keep up. Most importantly, I have a husband now, whom I truly love. Still, I couldn't bear the thought of letting you go completely. At one time you were my whole world, and I was yours.

I decided this morning, as I reached for my new journal, that one day a year, just one, I would invite you back into my life. Once a year, on January first, I will sit down and talk to you, just as if you were here with me.

You see, Nick, I've discovered that life does stagger forward and there's a certain beauty in that. Because in a way, I experience the past and the present at once. When I write you, I force myself to look back through time at the girl I was. I'm a woman now, and I'd like to think I'm wiser and a bit more pragmatic. Still, part of me continues to hold on to you. For now that's the right thing to do, but at some point in the future, I might choose to release you. Just remember that won't mean I've forgotten you or stopped loving you.

I know this sounds a little crazy, but I swear there are moments when I feel you're with me. Not in a physical sense, but a spiritual one. It's the sort of thing Lesley probably believes. She's so into the Bible and her new church. Her life is chaotic, mostly due to Buck, but she remains outwardly calm and serene. I wish I could be more like that. Perhaps one day I'll find that serenity myself. Perhaps next year when I write you, I'll be pregnant. That's my prayer.

Until then . . .

Jillian

P.S. You'll note that this is a "journal" and not just a diary — or so the clerk at the stationery store informed me. Does that mean my thoughts and observations are supposed to become more impressive?

❖

January 15, 1978

Dearest Jillian,

Happy birthday! Just a short note inside this card to wish you a happy 30th. We're all doing fine. Buck still isn't working. I've learned fifty different ways to cook beans. Thank God for food banks.

Write soon.

Lesley

SURPRISE!
Happy 2nd Anniversary
(a little early!)
Love,
Monty

Caribbean Cruise Specialists

Itinerary for passengers:
Jillian Gordan and Montgomery Gordon

Your Ship: the Grand Prince Rupert

Thank you for booking our
premier 10-day package.

Welcome aboard!

Lesley's Journal

March 26, 1978

This hasn't been a good day. I woke up early and sat with my coffee and my Bible in order to clear my head. It was necessary, otherwise the anger would've consumed me. Buck crawled into bed at two in the morning, reeking of cheap cologne and stale beer. He's doing everything I swore I wouldn't put up with. Not only is he doing it, he's flaunting it, as if he wants me to challenge him. Instead I gather my children around me and pretend I don't notice. I'm sick of my life, sick of swallowing my pride and struggling to hold up my head in public. God knows I've done everything I can to save this marriage.

Buck is a practicing alcoholic. These days when he's drinking, he becomes irrational and angry. He's rarely home and when he is, he's verbally abusive to the children and to me. It's almost as if he's asking me to kick him out.

I never dreamed it would take such courage. My greatest fear about staying with Buck is that the children will grow up believing this is the way a man treats his wife and family. I can't allow his ugliness to taint my children the way my father's alcoholism tainted my brothers, sisters and me.

I've got to get out of this marriage! I made a mistake five years ago by taking him back, but I'm stronger this time. Buck has broken every promise he's ever made to me. I deserve better. I've learned my lesson. If this is what marriage is like, then I'll never again risk such unhappiness.

Leaving Buck means putting Christopher in day care and taking a job outside the home, but I'll do it. I'd do a whole lot more than that to protect my children.

WANT ADS

Cashier — 7 to 11 p.m. swing shift. Minimum wage to start. Ask for Jan. 784-2387

East Park Dry Cleaners seeks part-time employee. Can become full-time for right worker. $2.65 784-2665

Oaks Convalescent Center — Housekeeper needed. Flexible hours for mother with school age children. $2.75 per hour. Apply at Personnel Office. 784-7549

New York Cornell Medical Center
505 East 70th Street
New York, NY 10021

April 27, 1978

Dear Mr. and Mrs. Montgomery Gordon,

Congratulations! It is with extreme pleasure that we confirm your pregnancy. Your expected delivery date is November 15th.

Sincerely,

Dr. Oliver Keast

❖

May 1, 1978

Dear Lesley,

Okay, you've made your point. You can call off your rabid dog of an attorney. I'll agree to the terms of the divorce, but in return I want you to do something for me.

Wait.

I know you're set on this divorce. I don't like it, but you have cause. All I ask, and I'm begging you, baby, is that you give me time to pull my life together. Give me one last chance to prove to you that I'm sincere. I need you and my family.

Don't take my children away from me. You might not think it's true, but I love you. I've always loved you and you can't doubt the way I feel about our children. All of you are my life.

I wish to hell I knew why I do the things I do. I don't blame you for kicking me out. I suppose that's what I get for cheating on you. But you're the only good thing I've ever had in my life. Without you and the kids I might as well give up.

Think about it. Please? What will six months matter, anyway? That's all the time I'm asking. Six lousy months. I'm going to prove to you that I can stay sober and faithful. I don't deserve another chance, but I'm begging you to give me one.

In case you're interested, I'm living in Tom Cullen's basement. You might remember Tom. He and I went hunting together last fall. He's only charging me $50.00 a month, which is all I can afford with what the state's taking out of my check for child support. I hate the thought of you working at that convalescent home, Lesley. Our children need their mother. But if this is what you want, then go ahead.

Please don't do anything rash. Give me six months. Is that so much to ask after nearly twelve years of marriage? Please, baby.

Buck

❖

May 14, 1978

HAPPY MOTHER'S DAY.
WE LOVE YOU.

David, Lindy, Dougie and Christopher

CARD ON BOUQUET OF RED ROSES
Happy 12th Anniversary!
I love you.
Buck

HAPPY FATHER'S DAY
David, Doug and Christopher

I love you, Daddy
Lindy

JILLIAN LAWTON GORDON
331 WEST END AVENUE
APARTMENT 1020
NEW YORK, NY 10023

June 15, 1978

Dearest Lesley,

I'm four wonderful months pregnant as of today! You can't begin to imagine how excited Monty and I feel. My parents are thrilled, and Monty's mother, who's never been quite sure about me, is leaping up and down for joy. I have a few of the negative symptoms but I can't remember a time my appetite's been healthier. Manhattan offers the most incredible assortment of ethnic food and currently I'm into anything Italian. Last week we ordered out from Balducci's three times.

You should see Monty. He's so protective of me it's not even funny! I guess that means dancing at Studio 54 is out until after the baby's born. As if I could ever have convinced Monty to bump and grind with what he calls "the libertine elite." (Have you heard of Studio 54? It's a trendy disco with strobe lights and computer-programmed synthesizers and a drum machine. Think Donna Summers, Andy Warhol and John Travolta all in the same place at once!)

I have your last letter here in front of me. You're right, I am disappointed that you've decided to delay the divorce. Do you seriously believe Buck is going to change in six months? He's already had twelve years! But this is your life, so I won't say any more.

Still, I want you to know I'm proud of you, Lesley. The decision to separate from Buck couldn't have been easy. I don't mean to suggest otherwise. I know it's hard on the children but as you explained, they rarely saw Buck anyway and when they did, he was usually in a foul mood.

Mom mentioned bumping into you at Oaks Convalescent Center. She was at the Center as part of her work with Catholic Charities (but you probably know that). Her ladies' group from the church took on the project several years ago. She said you looked wonderful and that the staff and patients already love you. When she asked her friend who works in personnel about you, Mrs. Wagner said you're terrific with the patients. Cheerful, sympathetic and compassionate. Apparently all the retired men are in love with you.

And speaking of love . . . Remember what Roy Kloster told you at our class reunion? He's not married. Write him, why don't you? This isn't an idle suggestion. I've been thinking about it for quite a while. I've resisted the urge to contact him myself on your behalf — don't worry, I won't. This is something you've got to do on your own. My guess is he'd be thrilled to hear from you.

How are the kids? I'm glad your mother agreed to watch Christopher while you work. It helps that the three oldest can drop by her house on their way home from school, too. What would we do without our mothers?

It must be a hoot to see your mother date. I can't imagine mine going out with any man other than my dad. Still, it's a good thing your mom isn't sitting at home pining after your father. What's this about her dating a former priest???

I'll be able to write more often now that I've stopped working. I do intend to go back to the firm after the baby's born. Just part-time at first.

Keep me informed. You're going to be fine,

Lesley. Write or call me anytime. What are friends for?

Love,

Jillian, Monty and Jr.

Pine Ridge Herald

July 16, 1978

Judge Leonard Lawton
Succumbs to Sudden
Heart Attack

Former Superior Court Judge Leonard Lawton, 70, succumbed to an apparent heart attack at his home on July 15. Judge Lawton is a native of Pine Ridge and served on the bench for twenty-five years before retiring in 1970.

As a Lieutenant during the Second World War, he was stationed in the South Pacific and was decorated for bravery. He is survived by his wife, Barbara Lawton, and one daughter, Jillian, (Mrs. Montgomery Gordon). Mrs. Gordon currently resides in New York City.

Judge Lawton was a member of

the Bar, St. Catherine's Catholic Church, The Veterans of Foreign Wars and the Moose Lodge.

The family asks that in lieu of flowers a donation be made to the American Heart Association.

Funeral services will be held at St. Catherine's Catholic Church on July 19, 1978.

Jillian's Journal

August 1, 1978

Dearest Dad,

I'm still having trouble believing you're gone. This was all such a terrible shock to Mom and me. When the phone call came, Monty went pale and then he could barely tell me the news. None of this seems real, or right. I know how much you looked forward to holding your first grandchild, and now you'll never have that opportunity. How unfair, how wrong. If ever a grandfather deserved to know his grandchild, it was you. You would have made such a wonderful grandpa. I know this because you were a wonderful father.

We had our differences. I think back to those turbulent years during Vietnam and my radical political views while I was in college. So much of the pain and anger I felt at losing Nick was directed at you. You were the "establishment" that had ripped away the person I loved. Blinded by my loss, I lashed out at you and everything you stood for.

It wasn't until years later that I told you how sorry I was. I cringe now when I remember the awful things I said and wrote to you. What I didn't say, I shouted with my attitude. You didn't deserve it.

Daddy, I'm so sorry for hurting you and blaming you for what happened to Nick. I wanted to talk to you about him, but every time I tried, I couldn't get the words out. They sat like an anchor on my chest and refused to budge. Now I'd give anything to have settled that pain between us, once and for all.

There must have been things you wanted to say to me, too. You never spoke about it but I know you regretted your attitude toward Nick. You wanted to ask my forgiveness for that. I know because of the way you've helped Jim and Nick's father. If there'd been time, you would've asked me to take care of Mom. I will. You can count on Monty and me to see to her needs.

I suspect you would've wanted me to know how much you loved me. The words aren't necessary. You said it in a thousand ways. I knew, Dad. I always felt your love.

I'm in Pine Ridge now, settling your affairs. I'll be with Mom for the next couple of months. I've started going through your papers, and it doesn't surprise me that everything is in immaculate order.

Life won't be easy for Mom without you. She relied on you for everything. Monty and I understand that and will look after her with the same dedication you did.

Daddy, I'm sorry we can't move back to Pine Ridge. I know you would've preferred that, but with Monty's job and mine in New York, that just isn't possible. Lesley has promised to check in with Mom every week and report back to me. If there's the slightest hint of a problem, I'll take care of it right away.

I love you, Dad. Rest in glory.

Jillian

Dorothy Adamski

September 14, 1978

My Dearest Lesley, Susan, Mike, Joe, Lily and Bruce — My Children,

I hope you can forgive me for writing instead of calling each of you personally. For reasons you will understand in a moment, I thought this was the best approach.

Lesley, you've probably already guessed what I'm about to tell you. Susan, you too. I've talked to you both so often in the last few weeks because I couldn't hold such happiness inside me.

Mikey, I'm delighted that you've moved back to Pine Ridge. I never did understand what was so attractive about life in Las Vegas. It's a desert there, in more ways than the obvious. As your mother, I welcome you with open arms, even if it took your father's death to bring you home to Washington.

Mikey, we've had many a discussion since your return and not all of them have been pleasant, especially over the issue of my seeing Eric. Son, I know you don't think I should be dating a younger man. I agree it might seem a bit silly, but if it doesn't bother Eric and me, then it shouldn't bother anyone else. Ten years may seem like a lot, but when I'm with Eric I feel young again. I'm happy with him. I realize it troubles you even more that Eric was once a priest. Of all my children, you're the last person I expected to be judgmental about something like this. Try to keep an open mind.

Joe, although you haven't said anything negative about Eric, I've felt your disapproval — and yours too, Bruce. You boys haven't been as vocal about your feelings as Mikey, but you've made it plain you think I'm an old fool. You could be right, but if that's the case, I'm a happy old fool. In fact, I'm absolutely giddy with joy.

Of all my children, it's been my three daughters who have encouraged me to live my life as I see fit. Lesley, Susan and Lily. God love you for your support and encouragement. I'm forever grateful to each one of you for your understanding.

As you know, life with your father wasn't easy, but he's gone now and I don't intend to live the rest of my days grieving for a man who mentally and emotionally abused me. I've still got a lot of life left in me and I intend to make the most of it.

The reason for this letter is to tell you that Eric has asked me to be his wife. Yes, children, we want to marry. But there's something else you need to know. Eric isn't a former priest. He *is* a priest. This is a shock, I'm sure. Eric never misled me, so please don't accuse him of lying. I was the one who told you he was a former priest. I stretched the truth a bit. He's no longer connected with a parish and has been living on his own for the last eighteen months. He's waiting for dispensation from Rome.

Father Morris knows Eric and isn't in favor of our relationship. If you decide to talk to someone objective about the situation, I wouldn't recommend him.

My children, all I'm asking for is your support and your prayers as God guides Eric and me in the direction He wants us to go.

Whatever happens, I pray that all six of you will stand behind my decision.

I love you all.

Mom

Birth Announcement
Montgomery and Jillian Gordon
Joyfully announce the birth
of
Leni Jo Gordon
Born
November 20, 1978
7 pounds, 15 oz.
19" long

❖

Lesley Knowles

December 5, 1978

Dearest Jillian,

Congratulations to you and Monty! Leni Jo is a beautiful baby girl. Those pictures taken at the hospital are normally so dreadful, but I can already see she's going to be a beautiful, intelligent woman. How proud you must be.

I'm glad you received the baby blanket I knitted for Leni Jo. Every stitch was made with my love for you and your daughter. Don't you dare be afraid to use it! You're right, it's an heirloom piece — and her baptism will be the perfect occasion. (Yes, I know you gave up attending church services years ago, but there's no better time to return to God, my friend.)

You asked about your mother and my last visit with her. I wish I could tell you she's doing better than she is, but she still seems lost and confused without your father. She does try, however, and is making progress. I've gone out with her several times and showed her how to pump her own gas. Writing checks completely frazzles her, but she's becoming more accustomed to it. I've written up a list of phone numbers and set it in a handy place in case she needs someone or something when I'm not available.

Now on to my news. Yes, it's true, my mother is dating a priest and it looks as though they'll marry. Eric, however, has to get some sort of dispensation from Rome and that could take a few months. They're very much in love and despite the local gossip and the disapproval from my brothers, they intend to spend the rest of their lives together. More power to them both is what I say.

Buck was over to visit the children the other night. He stops by two and three times a week, but I've resisted giving him dinner. It would be far too easy to let him slip into the habit of eating here and eventually working his way back into the family without anything ever changing.

The good news is that report cards are out and David got straight As. We celebrated with Spanish rice (his favorite) and homemade tortillas. Then Buck arrived and claimed he'd had nothing but a bowl of cornflakes for dinner. It put a damper on the entire evening. After he left, Lindy had me feeling so guilty that I made him a plate of leftovers and drove over to Tom's place. That was a mistake. He lured me into his room and it took all my strength to refuse him sex. It would've been so easy to fall into bed with him, Jillian, so easy. When I'm not at work, I have no adult companionship and I'm dying of loneliness. Some nights I just crave the feel of his arms around me. We had problems in our marriage, but for the most part the sex was good.

Halfway home, I weakened. I sat and thought about it for several minutes, then decided to go back. I intended to invite him to the house for the night. I didn't want this to become a regular thing, but I was lonely and my resolve was fragile. Oh, Jillian, what a good lesson that was! When I got to Tom's, there was another car in the driveway. I parked and peeked in the basement window and sure enough, there was a woman with Buck. In the space of thirty minutes he had another woman in his bed!

This was exactly the prompting I needed to proceed with the divorce. This marriage is over. I'm calling Janis Bright today and filing the last of the paperwork.

I should feel a sense of relief, I suppose, but I don't. Instead, all I feel is sad. So terribly, terribly sad.

Keep in touch, and don't worry about your mother. She's going to be fine, and so will I.

Love,

Lesley

1980

Jillian's Journal

January 1, 1980

Dear Nick and Dad,

The thought of you two together never fails to bring a smile to my face. It's been a comfort to me in the last eighteen months to imagine Nick waiting to greet you when you passed into the afterlife. I picture Nick standing there, dressed as I remember him best — in his black leather jacket, looking like Joe Cool. Then you arrive and Nick sees you and extends his hand, offering his friendship as he so often tried before. Then I envision you looking at Nick's outstretched hand, and instead of exchanging handshakes, you hug. What a creative imagination I have! Still, it gives me a sense of peace to think of the two of you, looking down on me, knowing how much I love you both.

Another decade starts today. I can only speculate on what the 1980s hold for us. Leni Jo is the joy of our lives. She's a cheerful, happy child and very bright. Oh, Daddy, how I wish you'd had the chance to see her and hold her. Every day she does something that reminds me of you — the little frown when she's puzzled, the grave expression on her face as she's concentrating on one of her picture books, the delighted laughter when something amuses her. Mom's the perfect grandmother. She'd love to spend more time with Leni Jo, but that's difficult, so she spoils her. Mom's biggest competition in the "who can spoil Leni Jo the most" contest is my husband.

Speaking of Monty, I'm worried about him. He's working far too many hours. Especially since the American embassy hostages were taken in Iran — this is so outrageous! It infuriates me that something like this could happen. To make things even worse, the Iran situation appears to be having a ripple effect throughout the federal government, and as a result Monty is working a great deal of overtime. Some nights he isn't home until long after Leni Jo's asleep and I'm in bed. He has most of his meals out. When he is home, he's wiped out, emotionally and physically. I've insisted he go in for a physical right after the first of the year.

I'm back to working three days a week. We have a wonderful nanny for Leni Jo. I love my job, but I'm constantly wondering if I'm doing the right thing in leaving my daughter's care to someone who's essentially a stranger. I never expected to feel this emotional tug whenever I walk out the door. Perhaps this guilt is the result of having been raised Catholic, but I tend to think every mother experiences these ambivalent feelings, torn between being a good mother and a good employee. I suppose that eventually it will be easier, particularly once Leni Jo's at school. I know Monty would prefer that I gave up practicing law for a few years, but I'm afraid I'd go stir-crazy at home. I need the intellectual stimulation, the interaction with other adults. My co-workers assure me it's better for Leni Jo, too. But these women are mothers themselves and they've had to justify leaving their own children.

I don't know how Lesley does it. Monty and I have one baby, and Leni Jo ran us ragged for the first six months. Neither of us got a full night's sleep. We were forever checking to make sure she was still asleep (and still breathing. As new parents, we experienced every fear out there!). It took us all those sleepless months to figure out we were the ones waking her up.

Lesley did everything practically by herself — Buck was no help — with four children. Four. I am in awe of my best friend. I don't know how she managed — correction, manages!

Now that she's divorced, Lesley is making a new life for herself. She's attending Puget Sound Community College every morning and working toward a nursing degree. The convalescent center gave her a glowing recommendation and she has a part-time job with a physician in the afternoons. I'd hoped that once she was free of her useless ex-husband she'd start dating again. To my disappointment, she hasn't. I was afraid Buck might still be in the picture but she assures me he isn't.

I think Lesley's frightened of dating again. I wish she'd meet someone who deserves her. She never did write Roy Kloster, even after I encouraged her. My friend should follow her own mother's example. I don't mean to imply that she should date or marry an ex-priest, but I do wish she'd put her marriage behind her and search for some real happiness.

From what I understand, Buck is still around. He sees the kids when it's convenient for him, and that isn't often. Long before Buck and Lesley were divorced, she came up with ways of paying the bills without relying on him. She baked and sold her own bread, became a remarkable seamstress and offered day care. She's still got those extra sources of income – except for looking after kids – and it's a good thing, too, because God knows she's not getting much support from Buck. He was never inclined to work if he could avoid it.

I hear he's got a different woman every week, but still comes to Lesley when he's down and out. She listens, pats his hand and tells him everything's going to work out, then sends him on his way.

Thankfully, David is far more like Lesley than his father. He's studious and serious and quiet. Lindy is just the opposite. At twelve she's already a flirt and announced over Christmas that she intends to marry Greg Brady from *The Brady Bunch* or the Fonz from *Happy Days.* Doug is all boy and involved in soccer and softball, and sweet, sweet Christopher is in first grade. He lost his front tooth and lisps when he speaks. (He kept pronouncing Santa as "Thanta" — it was the cutest thing.)

Dad, you'll be pleased to know Mom's making new friends. She's terribly lonely, but she's met other widows and has joined that social circle. The ladies travel together; they've been on several brief trips to places like the Napa Valley and Victoria, British Columbia. Every Wednesday afternoon, they play canasta. One day last fall, Mom looked at your old painting easel and decided to try her hand at it. Dad, you'd be amazed at how talented she is. I remember you enjoyed your art, especially your oil landscapes, but I never dreamed Mom had an artist's soul, too.

Nick, you're an uncle. Jim and Angie had a baby boy in October. They named him Ryan Patrick. He's a chubby one, with a birth weight of over ten pounds. Jim was so pleased and proud he phoned me from the hospital just minutes after Angie delivered. We stay in touch and speak often. I love Jim like a brother.

This is the report of my life for another year.

Remember how much I love you both,

Jillian

Park West Medical
284 Central Park West,
Suite 1A
New York City, NY 10024

February 11, 1980

Dear Mr. Gordon,

The results of the blood work from your physical examination have been received from our laboratory and everything looks to be in order. Dr. Lyman has granted you a clean bill of health for the upcoming year.

Sincerely,
Joan McMahon, R.N.

❖

LESLEY KNOWLES

March 10, 1980

Mr. Cole Greenberg
ABC News Network
7 West 66th St.
New York, NY 10023

Dear Cole,

I don't know if you'll receive this letter, but after watching the news today, I felt compelled to write. We met in 1967 on a beautiful Hawaiian beach. You were a Navy officer and I was a young wife who'd flown to the island to meet my husband. That was fourteen years ago, and I've never forgotten those few hours we shared, talking and laughing. In all the years before or since, I've never bonded with anyone quite the way I did with you that magical morning.

A few years back, by chance, I happened to catch you on national television reporting the news. It thrilled me to see how well you've done. Just this evening, I saw you again, reporting on the hostages in Iran. Each time I see you on the news, I feel a renewed sense of pleasure and pride.

I realize it's presumptuous of me to contact you, and I hope you'll forgive me for intruding on your life after all these years. I wanted to let you know how happy I am about your success. You told me back in Hawaii that becoming a television news reporter was your goal, and you've managed to achieve that on a national level. Congratulations!

Like all Americans, I'm praying for the hostages in Iran. I pray for your safety, too. I've never forgotten you.

Sincerely,

Lesley Knowles

From: COLE GREENBERG
ABC TELEVISION NEWS CORRESPONDENT

Date: April 17, 1980

Dear Lesley,

Of course I remember you. How could I forget the most stimulating conversation during my entire tour of Vietnam? I would've answered you immediately but the mail here in Tehran is understandably unpredictable. I, too, have thought of you often over the years.

You didn't tell me anything about yourself, but I assume, since you wrote, that you're single. I am, as well. Constant traveling isn't conducive toward developing long-term relationships.

I know this sounds a little crazy, but there were times I faced a camera wondering if you'd see me and what you'd think. I can't tell you how pleased I am that you've contacted me.

So you're living in Washington State. I understand Mt. St. Helens is making rumbling noises. As a senior reporter, I'm given a choice of assignments. If at all possible, I'll see what I can do to steer a path to your mountain.

Nothing seems to be happening with the hostages. There's been speculation about a a rescue attempt, but if it hasn't happened by now, it probably won't.

Write again, and I'll be in touch as soon as I'm stateside.

Sincerely,

Cole Greenberg

JILLIAN LAWTON GORDON
331 WEST END AVENUE
APARTMENT 1020
NEW YORK, NY 10023

April 25, 1980

Dearest Lesley,

You heard back from Cole Greenberg? I'm so excited I can hardly stand it. I'm trying to remember every word you read me over the phone. I knew it had to be something big for you to call, but this is bigger than big. I'm sorry I couldn't talk longer.

What are you going to do now? Answer him, right? You have to! Oh, Lesley, this reminds me of when we were in high school. I got such a giddy, happy feeling just listening to the excitement in your voice. It seems like a very long time since I heard you this enthusiastic about anything.

Isn't it dreadful what happened yesterday?

The failed rescue attempt in Iran was humiliating. Eight brave, good men died a horrible fiery death in that helicopter. It brought back memories of when I lost Nick. I couldn't even watch the news. I held Leni Jo close to my heart, wanting to protect her from all the horrors in this world. I can't, I know that.

With this latest crisis, it appears Cole might be stuck in Iran for a while. Let me know as soon as you hear from him again. Oh, how I pray the hostages will be released soon.

Are you following the campaign news? Believe it or not, I like what I'm hearing from Ronald Reagan. I can only imagine how happy my father would be if he even suspected I was thinking of voting Republican.

Call me the minute you hear from Cole Greenberg. Promise!

Jillian

❖

May 12, 1980

Dear Daddy,

Mommy's got a boyfriend. He calls her on the phone and he writes her long letters. I thought you should know.

Love,

Lindy

Barbara Lawton
2330 Country Club Lane
Pine Ridge, Washington 98005

May 20, 1980

My dearest Jillian, Monty and Leni Jo,

I'm fine, children. I don't want you to worry. Mt. St. Helens' eruption was terrifying, although we should have seen it coming. The mountain has been dormant since 1857, and despite recent activity, no one expected anything of this magnitude. Certainly not our governor! Dixie Lee Ray recently opened up an area of the mountain that had been closed off because of the rumbling and earthquakes. That was a mistake that cost people's lives.

I don't mind telling you all of this has shaken me badly. Ash fell heavily across the eastern half of the state. The newscast showed incredible scenes of raging rivers and devastating mudslides. The city of Yakima was as dark as night with ash raining down like something from a Biblical plague. I read in the paper this morning that the National Guard is going to help the families shovel off their rooftops. You wouldn't believe what a mess all that ash has created. I'm so grateful the western half of the state was spared. All we had here in Pine Ridge was a light dusting.

Never having lived through a volcanic eruption, I wasn't sure what to expect. I thought we'd see lava flows the way you do on the Big Island of Hawaii. This horrid ash took everyone by surprise. Did you hear that at last count there were sixty deaths attributed to the eruption? How terribly unfortunate and how tragic, since some of them, at least, could have been prevented.

Thank you for your phone calls, but as I said, there's no need to concern yourselves. It looks as though the worst of it has passed.

In the enclosed Baggie is a sample of ash. An enterprising young man in the neighborhood brought some back with him. He and his wife drove to the Yakima and Ellensburg area to collect ash to use for figurines. They're new to the neighborhood. Both Skip and his wife are artists, and I wish them well in this venture. Who knows what will come of it?

Love,
Mom

❖

LESLEY KNOWLES

June 5, 1980

Dear Cole,

Thank you for your call. It didn't matter that it came in the middle of the night. I was awake, anyway, trying to figure out who shot J.R. It's wonderful to hear your voice any time. As I explained, we're none the worse for wear following the eruption. The children are upset because we got so little of the ash. Dougie would have considered it a real windfall (so to speak). Heaven only knows what he would've done with it, but knowing my son, he would have thought of something.

My David, the most enterprising of the four, raises guinea pigs. He's got quite a thriving business, selling them to pet stores. The guinea pigs do all the work and he collects the money. Hmm, that's an interesting concept. He's the animal lover in the family. I've been forced to limit him to one dog and one cat and, of course, the two guinea pigs.

I'm sure you've heard of President Carter's decision to boycott the Moscow Olympics. The Soviets are learning more than one hard lesson in Afghanistan without us snubbing them like this. They should've learned from our mistakes in Vietnam. I've never been a political person, but I think this is wrong. The Olympics shouldn't be about politics.

Anything new with the hostages? The days must seem endless to them. They continue to be in my prayers. You, too.

Yours,
Lesley

DWI FOR BUCK KNOWLES

THE UNDERSIGNED CERTIFIES AND SAYS THAT IN THE STATE OF WASHINGTON

Drivers License No. KNOWLES*DA461TB **State** WA

Expires 5/75 ID #533-24-6009

Name (last) KNOWLES **First** DAVID **Initial** J.

Address KNOTTY PINES TRAILER COURT

City Pine Ridge **State** WA **Zip Code** 98005

Employer PINE RIDGE LUMBER MiLL

Race W **Sex** M **Date of Birth** 02/28/43

Height 6.1 **Weight** 200 **Eyes** BLU **Hair** BRO

Residential Phone 206-458-0522

Violation Date: Month 06 **Day** 10 **Year** 80 **Time** 1:05 AM

At Location COLUMBIA ST **City/County of** KING

DID OPERATE THE FOLLOWING VEHICLE/ MOTOR VEHICLE ON A PUBLIC HIGH WAY AND

Vehicle License # 259TIM **State** WA **Expires** 06/82 **Veh.Yr.** 1974

Make FORD **Model PINTO** **Style** 2 DOOR **Color** BRN

DID THEN AND THERE COMMIT THE FOLLOWING OFFENSES

OPERATE A MOTOR VEHICLE WHILE INTOXICATED

Appearance Date: Mo 06 **Dy** 18 **Yr** 80 **Time** 9:30 AM

Date Issued 06/10/80

WITHOUT ADMITTING HAVING COMMITTED EACH OF THE ABOVE OFFENSE(S) I PROMISE TO RESPOND AS DIRECTED ON THIS NOTICE X____________________

Defendant

I CERTIFY UNDER PENALTY OF PERJURY UNDER THE LAWS OF THE STATE OF WASHINGTON THAT I HAVE ISSUED THIS ON THE DATE AND AT THE LOCATION ABOVE, THAT I HAVE PROBABLE CAUSE TO BELIEVE THE ABOVE NAMED PERSON COMMITTED THE ABOVE OFFENSE(S) AND MY REPORT WRITTEN ON THE BACK OF THIS DOCUMENT IS TRUE AND CORRECT. X______________________

Officer

July 6, 1980

Dear Lesley,

I imagine it's a surprise getting a letter from your ex-husband. I'm in a rehab center. The courts sent me here after my second drunk-driving charge. I'm not proud of that, but then there's a great deal in this life I regret.

I'm working with a counselor and have been dry for two weeks. My head is starting to clear and I realize what a mess I've made of my life. The counselor tells me that unless I'm willing to be honest with myself, there's no hope of ever kicking the booze. I didn't know honesty was this damned hard.

I've been doing a lot of talking and soul-searching. You and the kids are the best thing that ever happened to me. I know I've told you that before. It was true then and it's even truer now.

There are things I never told you about my childhood. I'm not offering any of this as an excuse, but I feel you have a right to know. Working with the staff here I've been able to face my past and most of it is ugly.

My dad didn't die when I was young. He deserted my mother and us three kids. Another thing I lied about was how my mother worked to make ends meet. She hooked on the side to put food on the table for my two older sisters and me. By the time Anne and Lois were in their teens, Mom had grown hard and mean, and she set them up with johns. She kicked me out when she found me stealing money from her purse to buy beer. She slapped me around some and then threw me into the street and said that was where I belonged. She was probably right. Soon afterward, I drifted into Pine Ridge and got a job at the mill.

I heard from Lois a few years after Mom died. Anne came down with a liver ailment at 30 and never recovered. No one knows what caused it, but the doctors told my sister it had something to do with her immune system.

When I met you and your family, I couldn't get over how you all looked after one another. No one looked after me. Your father was one of the best drinking buddies I ever had. When you agreed to date me that first time, I nearly burst with pride. You've always been a classy girl and you being interested in a lowlife like me gave me hope that I might turn into something good.

I never wanted you to know about my past. I never wanted anyone to know.

It's funny how life catches up with you, isn't it? It sure as hell caught up with me. I lost you and the kids, and painful as this is to admit, I realize I'm to blame for everything.

I pulled a lot of stunts while we were married. Emptying out your savings account to buy that hunting rifle is only the tip of the iceberg. There were other women, Lesley. More than I care to remember, but not a one of them meant anything to me. I know that doesn't excuse cheating on you, but even when I was with someone else, it was always you I loved.

When you left me the first time, I went into a panic. I couldn't believe you'd actually follow through with it and I thanked God a thousand times over when you agreed to take me back. I tried, baby, I really did. For you and the kids I managed to stay sober for a year, maybe more. I don't remember exactly how long it was, but longer than any period before or since.

This last time, I knew you meant to go ahead with the divorce. You had a look in your eye that told me nothing was going to change your mind. I didn't fight you as hard because I knew I deserved to have you walk out on me. My life's been on a downward spiral since that day.

No one's ever loved me like you did. No one ever cared what happened to me. Not my bastard of a father and not my bitch of a mother. Only you, and I killed that love because of the way I treated you.

I understand you have a new man in your life. I only hope he treats you better than I did. I hope he appreciates you.

Thank you for reading this, Lesley. I'm going to make a determined effort to be a better father to my children. They've got the best damn mother in the world and it's time I showed them I'm capable of being a good father. I might have failed you as a husband, but I'm not going to fail my children.

Buck

July 10, 1980

Dear Dad,

Mom said you were in the hospital. I hope you get well soon. I have a paper route now, but I only have to deliver two days a week. It's mostly advertisements and some local news. Mrs. Dalton gave me a $1.00 tip when I went to collect. I'm saving my money to help Mom.

I hope you're better soon.

David Knowles

❖

544 Klondike Avenue #304
Fairbanks, Alaska 99701

August 1, 1980

Dear David, Lindy, Doug and Christopher,

Thank you for your cards and letters while I was in the hospital. They meant a lot to me. I'm feeling great now. Thank your mother for me, too.

I'm going to be much better now. I heard about a job in Alaska and that's where I'm living. The money is good and if I get on this crew, I'll be able to send a check to your mother on a regular basis.

I love you. Be good for your mom.

Love,

Dad

JILLIAN LAWTON GORDON
331 WEST END AVENUE
APARTMENT 1020
NEW YORK, NY 10023

October 3, 1980

Dearest Lesley and Kids,

It was so good to hear from you. It's been far too long. We can't let this much time go by without at least a quick phone call.

Life just doesn't seem to slow down for me. I know it's the same for you. You're a marvel; you always have been. I didn't fully appreciate everything you accomplish until Monty and I had Leni Jo.

By the way, I've learned something about Monty that completely took me by surprise. He wasn't free to tell me until a few days ago, but he's been deeply involved in the ABSCAM investigation. That's the reason he was working so much overtime during the past few months. His office cooperated with the FBI to catch legislators taking bribes from rich Arabs. Just this afternoon Representative Myers was expelled from Congress, the first member since 1861.

Now that the worst of it is over, he's taking a vacation at my insistence. We both desperately need one. Leni Jo barely knows her father.

This is incredible news about Buck. He's actually paying you child support? I don't know how he managed to get that job in Alaska, but I'm grateful he's taking some responsibility for supporting his children. Just beware, Lesley – we both know him, and a leopard doesn't change his spots. His intentions might be good now, but don't forget how unreliable he's always been.

You haven't mentioned our friendly international newscaster lately. What do you hear from Cole? I realize he's probably traveling back and forth between New York and Tehran, but surely he's been able to squeeze in a trip to the West Coast? Tell me everything!

Thanks for checking up on my mother. The Mt. St. Helen's eruption is the first time she's had to deal with anything major since we lost my dad, and she appears to be handling things quite well. I don't know what I'd do if I had to rely on strangers for information about her. I know you aren't afraid of telling me the truth about her condition.

I only wish I could get back to Pine Ridge more often. We'll be there for Christmas, and you and I can talk then. I do worry about her.

I'm sorry this is so short. Keep in touch.

Monty and I send our love, Leni Jo, too.

Jillian

October 21, 1980

The kids got another letter from Buck. They love hearing from their father and get so excited when the mail brings them even the briefest of communications. Dougie and Christopher immediately sat down and wrote him back. I found David reading his father's letter again after dinner, and Lindy was in a bad mood all evening. Unfortunately that's all too common these days. When I tried to find out what was troubling her, she screamed at me that the divorce was all my fault. I was the one who wanted it. I was the one who'd ruined our family.

Her accusations shocked me. I didn't defend myself, and I didn't enlighten her, either. For reasons I've never understood, she's always been close to Buck. Of all my children, she's the one who found our divorce the most difficult to accept. I left her sobbing pitifully in her room and then later went back to try to reason with her. That was a mistake. She threw Cole in my face, telling me how wrong it is for me to have another man in my life. She as good as threatened me. My daughter, blood of my blood, heart of my heart, said that if I married Cole she'd make sure our lives were a living hell. I have no intention of marrying Cole, but her words shook me.

I refuse to allow a child — a girl who hasn't even turned thirteen — to dictate how I live my life. Despite that, I've been giving my relationship with Cole a lot of thought. We've written and he's called several times, although the conversations have always been short, but we haven't had a chance to meet. We both know that given the opportunity, we could so easily let ourselves fall in love. It's premature to even think about this, but I know I'd be tempted if he asked me to marry him. However, that's not likely to happen. Cole's already married — to his career. Not only that, I'm coming into this relationship with four needy children. David's already a teenager, and Lindy might as well be. This daughter of mine is full of attitude, all of it bad. God help me. Dougie and Christopher aren't far behind.

I no longer know what's right. I shouldn't be making decisions for Cole. But I don't want this to go any further. The minute we see each other again, I'll convince myself we could make it work, and we can't. I know that already even if Cole doesn't.

In any event, my one experience of marriage has left me doubting myself — and doubting my ability to make the right choice.

Buck seems so genuine these days, but

then he always does when he's afraid he's going to lose me for good. I'll never forgive him if he builds up the children's hopes and then doesn't follow through on his promises. I've seen him do that countless times. If I could protect the children, I would, but he's their father and they love him and need him.

One way and another, the subject of marriage is definitely on my mind. A wedding announcement arrived in the mail, along with Buck's letter to the kids. Roy Kloster. He's married now, to another doctor. I'm pleased for him and equally pleased that he considers me enough of a friend to send an announcement.

I'm grateful to be in school. I love every minute of it. I gave up my dream of being a nurse fourteen years ago and I'm not going to let anything destroy it a second time. Dr. Milton and his staff have been wonderfully supportive. Dr. Milton's promised me a full-time position with his office once I graduate. His wife's been working with him for years and wants to quit. They're counting on me to step into that vacancy.

I may never find love or romance again, but I'll have a fulfilling career. I've got my friends, my family and — finally — a healthy measure of self-respect.

Cole Greenberg
ABC News Network
7 West 66th St.
New York, NY 10023

November 5, 1980

Dear Lesley,

I haven't heard from you in a couple of weeks and wasn't sure if the mail had been delayed or if there was some other reason. That's why I phoned. When we spoke, I heard the hesitation in your voice. You don't need to explain or apologize.

Getting your letters and talking to you, however briefly, while I was in Tehran has lifted my spirits immensely. It's made these long months reporting on the hostage situation more bearable.

You didn't say why you don't think it's a good idea to continue this relationship, but I suspect I know. You're looking for someone who can be a father to your children and a husband to you. I don't blame you for that.

I have to be up-front with you, Lesley. I doubt that I'm husband or father material. My schedule takes me all over the world. I need the freedom to leave at a moment's notice. I'm away so much of the time that relationships just don't seem to work, no matter how hard I try.

I realize all this talk of the future is premature, as you said yourself, but you were wise to bring it up. I value your honesty and your willingness to confront this now, before we invest our emotions in a relationship that's headed down a dead-end road.

Perhaps the best way to close this letter is to let you know I've enjoyed your friendship these last few months.

God bless you, Lesley. I think we could have recaptured what we found in each other that day in Hawaii. The question is, would it have been the best thing for either one of us? You believe it wouldn't, and I suppose you're right. I have my work, and you have your children and the promise of a career.

When we first met in 1967, I found you smart and sweet and oh, so genuine. I was impressed by your honesty and your wisdom. That hasn't changed.

Fondly,

C. Greenberg

❖

December 11, 1980

Dear Daddy,

Someone shot John Lennon. I love his music. I'm really bummed and so are all my friends.

School is all right, I guess. David is the brain in the family.

Mom doesn't have a boyfriend anymore.

Lindy

1982

Jillian's Journal

January 1, 1982

Dearest Nick and Daddy,

Happy New Year. Leni Jo is three, and Monty and I would very much like to have a second child, but it just doesn't seem to be happening. The medical advancements in infertility are incredible, but they're expensive, time-consuming and they have a negative effect on my emotions.

Monty claims he's content with one child if I am. The problem is, I was raised an only child and although I appreciate the advantages, I'm also well aware of the disadvantages. I'd so hoped for more children. I envy Lesley her siblings. Even now, as adults, they remain close, although Lesley and Mike are the only two who still live in Pine Ridge.

At this point, Monty and I have decided to leave the matter of more children in God's hands, and I'm comfortable with that. I couldn't have imagined myself making a statement like this even a year ago. It's the kind of thing Lesley has often said and I've usually ignored. In fact, as I ease into my thirties, I'm more and more comfortable with the subject of God. The anger I felt toward Him (Her?) isn't as strong as it was during my college years. Lesley's never questioned her belief in a Supreme Being who guides our lives. She's so confident, so secure in her faith. I wish I could be more like her in that regard, but I'm not.

As Leni Jo grows up, I find myself thinking more seriously about attending Mass again. Perhaps I will. That would make you happy, wouldn't it, Daddy?

Lesley continues to thrive. Her ex is still in Alaska, although the pipeline work is complete. Buck seems to have a job of sorts, but he isn't making the big money he was a couple of years ago. I don't know exactly what he's doing and I don't care. Unfortunately, the family's financial welfare still depends on Buck, although that's less and less the case since Lesley will be working full-time by summer. I'm so proud of the way she's managed to keep up with school, her job and the children's needs. She'll graduate in June and I'm hoping to surprise her and show up for the ceremony.

It's hard to believe David's in high school. What's not hard to believe is the fact that he's getting top grades. He reminds me so much of Lesley at this age.

Lindy is just the opposite. I worry about her. Lesley told me at Christmas that her fourteen-year-old daughter has driven her to her knees in prayer. The two of them are constantly at odds. She's the most like Buck in attitude, and the kid knows exactly what buttons to push to upset Lesley. The "guilt" one appears to be her favorite, and she uses it frequently.

Dougie is now called Doug or Douglas, and he's in junior high. Christopher is nearly eight and crazy about sports. He's the team's top soccer player and shows real promise as an athlete. No matter how tight her school and work schedule is, Lesley makes an effort to attend his games. Dr. Milton's been very good about allowing her the flexibility to do this. I think Lesley's found herself a wonderful boss. Mom tells me he's a respected OB/GYN and is well liked by the hospital staff.

I was disappointed when Lesley broke off the relationship with Cole Greenberg. Apparently it was a mutual decision, but Lesley hasn't really said much about it. I suspect she's in love with Cole, but couldn't see involving him in her life with four children and their constant demands.

I wish I knew what she was thinking. I'd write Cole myself if I could be assured Lesley would speak to me again. She'd consider that a betrayal and I would never do anything to threaten our friendship.

The best news has to do with Monty. He's leaving the Justice Department and interviewing with several firms. It'll be nice to have a husband again! I swear he's nearly worked himself to death.

I still hate leaving Leni Jo every day, but I enjoy my job, too. Law is exciting work. It seems that I read about a landmark case at least once a week. I'd love to have been in court when Lee Marvin was sued for "palimony." Actress Carol Burnett's libel suit against the *National Enquirer* was in the headlines for months. This year it's going to be the deregulation of AT&T. President Carter opened the door when he deregulated the airlines. While I enjoy the challenge of being an attorney, I love being a wife and mother, too. It's finding the balance between my job and my role as Monty's wife and Leni Jo's mother that has proven to be the most difficult.

Dad, you'll be reassured to learn that Mom is doing very well. She's grown accustomed to living alone and seems emotionally stronger with every year. I'm proud of her and I know you would be too. She's handling her own financial affairs now. I check the numbers every three or four months, and so far everything looks great. She's willing to travel alone, too. You can thank Leni Jo for that. These days Mom hops on a flight to New York with barely a pause. I can remember when she wouldn't dream of calling a cab on her own, let alone navigating her way around an airport.

Jim and Angie had a second child last year, Nick. A little girl this time, and you'll be as excited as I was to learn that they named her Nickie Lynn after you and me. I wept when they told me. We're part of this child, Nick, in her name and in the family stories she'll grow up hearing. I look forward to being her "aunt."

Jim and I stay in touch, mostly by phone. (As Jim is quick to tell me, he isn't much of a letter-writer.) It's always good to hear his voice. He sees me as a big sister and I consider it an honor that he would.

This is going to be a good year, I can feel it already.

Remember how much I love you both.

Jillian

❖

We are pleased to announce that
Montgomery Gordon,
has joined the Beckham Law Firm.
Montgomery Gordon is available
for mediation and arbitration,
consultation and legal representation
in business, real estate and civil matters.
Beckham, DiGiovanni, Zimmermann,
Johnson & Blayne
652 Park Avenue
New York, NY 10021

Park West Medical
284 Central Park West,
Suite 1A
New York City, NY 10024

February 19, 1982

Dear Mr. Gordon,

The blood test results are back from your annual physical with Dr. Lyman. Your cholesterol count is 342. Dr. Lyman requests a follow-up appointment. Please contact our office between the hours of 9 a.m. and 4 p.m. to schedule your visit.

We look forward to seeing you again soon.

Sincerely,

Joan McMahon, R.N.

❖

LESLEY KNOWLES

March 7, 1982

Dear Buck,

I'm writing because I'm at my wits' end with Lindy. I simply can't control her. Last Friday night, I happened to check on her and discovered she wasn't in bed. She'd crawled out her bedroom window and didn't return until four the next morning. She was pretty surprised to find me sitting in her room when she climbed back in. I have no idea who she was with or where she went. She refuses to answer both questions. Our daughter is only fourteen years old.

I've restricted her comings and goings and taken away phone privileges, but all that's done is create more friction between us. I don't know how to reach her. Perhaps you can succeed where I've failed.

I'd appreciate your trying.

Thank you.

Lesley

❖

March 9, 1982

Dear Daddy,

Mom is being totally unreasonable and mean. She wouldn't let me phone you and she's forcing me to stay in my room. This is child abuse. I can't take it anymore. You've got to do something. I can't live with her.

David is so perfect. He's gag-me perfect. I don't get along with Mom, and I never have. Let me come live with you, all right? I won't be any trouble, I promise. You've got to help me, Dad. You've just got to.

Love,

Lindy

Your only daughter

April 6, 1982

My dearest Monty,

If you're wondering why your wife is sending you flowers, think back two weeks to our weekend trip to Boston. Can you guess? If you need a further hint . . . I suggest you schedule time away from the office eight and a half months from now.

There should be maternity leave for fathers! If you don't know a good lawyer who can argue the case, I just might.

Hurry home! We have some celebrating to do.

Your loving, pregnant wife

Lesley's Journal

May 6, 1982

I saw Cole on the evening news tonight. He's in Port Stanley on the Falkland Islands, waiting for the approaching British fleet. When I saw him, I felt as if someone had punched me hard. Everything around me started to fade. Thankfully Christopher was there and brought me a glass of water.

My head can't deal with the romantic fantasy I've built in my heart. I'm raising four children on my own, and I'm in love with a man I only saw once for a few hours when I was still a teenager. It doesn't make sense to feel this way about him. No man could possibly live up to the cherished memories I have of Cole. I think I've needed that fantasy version more than reality. After being married to Buck all those years, I pictured Cole as the ideal husband and father: loving, patient, dedicated to his children. And employed!

I regret my lack of faith in us both. I spelled out my fears, anticipated all the problems and made a decision based on my limited experience with men. He accepted that decision, and now it's too late. It wouldn't be right to pop back into his life.

It's more than seeing Cole and reliving the grief I brought upon myself that's getting me down. I thought this last year of school would be easier than the previous four and a half. I assumed it'd be a downhill slide from this point. I was wrong. The hours are long, the professors demanding and I'm so far in debt it'll take me fifteen years to pay off the student loans.

Lindy's rebellious attitude toward me doesn't help. I don't know what happened between her and Buck. I suspect she asked to move in with him, but he didn't write back, which was an answer in itself. I've never worried that Buck will send for any of the children or want custody. He couldn't be bothered with them while we were married;

he certainly isn't going to let one of his children disrupt his lifestyle now. Lindy hasn't mentioned his name in weeks and snarls whenever the boys talk about their dad. But then, her reaction to me is much the same.

Jillian invited Lindy and me to New York this summer as a graduation gift. She's planning to pay for our tickets, and I just might take her up on this more-than-generous offer. Mom and Eric have agreed to watch the boys for me. I haven't said anything to Lindy yet for fear of disappointing her if it doesn't work out. First I've got to get through school. Then and only then will I feel like celebrating. One thing's for sure: I don't want my daughter hanging around the house with nothing to do all summer. That's a guarantee of trouble.

David is taking Driver's Education and is eager to get his license in September. I can't wait! Once he's driving, I won't have to spend as much time taking the two younger boys to one sporting event or another. Two years ago, Buck promised to buy Davey a car. For David's sake and mine, I hope he follows through, but I have serious doubts. Of course, David knows better than to count on anything Buck tells him. Still, hope springs eternal.

May 20, 1982

Dear Lesley,

Bill and I talked it over and wanted to know if you'd agree to send Lindy to us for the summer. With me working full-time at the hospital and Bill putting in long hours at the office, we're concerned about day care during the last part of June through August. We'd pay for her airplane ticket and give her $5.00 a day.

Get back to me ASAP so we can make other arrangements if we need to.

Love,
Susan

❖

June 6, 1982

City of Sitka Jail
304 Lake Street
Sitka, Alaska 99835

Dear Lesley,

I hate to ask this, but I need a loan. As you can see, I'm in a bit of a jam here. I swear to you, Les, I'll pay you back. On my sister's grave, I'll find a way to get the money to you as soon as possible.

This isn't an easy letter to write, but I'm not afraid to admit I need help. If I don't get out of here by Tuesday, I won't be able to fish. If I don't fish, I can't pay child support. Getting me the money will help you and the kids. You know I wouldn't ask if there was any other alternative.

Buck

P.S. Wire the money directly to the jail, all right? And listen, I know I'm a few months behind on child support, but I'll make that up as soon as I'm back fishing.

THE PRESIDENT, FACULTY AND THE GRADUATING CLASS
OF SEATTLE UNIVERSITY, PINE RIDGE EXTENSION, ANNOUNCE THAT
LESLEY L. KNOWLES
IS A CANDIDATE FOR
REGISTERED NURSING DEGREE
AT THE FIFTY-FIRST COMMENCEMENT EXERCISES
SUNDAY AFTERNOON, JUNE SIXTH
NINETEEN HUNDRED AND EIGHTY-TWO
AT THREE O'CLOCK

A RECEPTION WILL FOLLOW
THE COMMENCEMENT EXERCISES

LESLEY KNOWLES

June 11, 1982

Dearest Jillian,

I can hardly express my delight about seeing you at my graduation. I know I embarrassed myself by bursting into tears right in the middle of "Pomp and Circumstance," but I didn't have a clue you were doing this. To think David knew all along! You really know how to surprise a girl, don't you?

If all goes according to plan, Lindy and I will fly out the third week of August. She'll be back from California then, with her baby-sitting money burning a hole in her pocket. I've always wanted to see New York, and before you suggest it, NO, I refuse to contact Cole.

I'm so excited about this trip! But are you sure you're going to want company so close to when the baby's due? Let me know if you have any concerns. If you prefer, we could postpone our visit.

Thank you for the wonderful, wonderful surprise. You were right when you said, back in 1966, that I was college material. It only took me fourteen years to prove it!

I start working full-time with Dr. Milton immediately. Mrs. Milton is more than ready to have me take her place.

Love,
Lesley and all

JILLIAN LAWTON GORDON
331 WEST END AVENUE
APARTMENT 1020
NEW YORK, NY 10023

July 7, 1982

Dear Mom,

Please come. I haven't been able to stop crying since the miscarriage. Monty doesn't know what to say to me anymore. It was a little boy, did I tell you that? It seemed like a miracle that I was pregnant again, and we were so happy. Monty and I were so thrilled. How cruel of God to do this to us. How heartless and mean to build up our hopes and then bring us such pain. I didn't expect this, didn't even consider that I'd lose my baby.

You never told me you miscarried. Three times before I was born? Oh Mom, how did you bear such grief? I feel empty inside. My arms ache to hold this child I'll never know. I feel lost and afraid of the future. The doctors told me it was normal to grieve, but I can't seem to let go of my son.

I want my mother.

Jillian

Card on floral arrangement sent to
Jillian Gordon
Mt. Sinai Hospital

Jillian, Montgomery and Leni Jo:
I'm so very, very sorry.
I love you. Call if you need anything
Lesley

❖

July 14, 1982

Dear Mom and Everyone,

Hi. I thought I'd write and let you know that everything's all right here in Sacramento. Aunt Susan and Uncle Bill asked me to tell everyone hi from them. I thought Sacramento was on the ocean and that I'd meet some guys with surfboards. It's not! Did you know that when you sent me here?

I'm really sorry to hear about Aunt Jillian and her baby. I guess you're right and this probably isn't the best time to visit, especially with her mother there for the summer. We will visit another time, won't we? Actually I don't mind so much because — this will probably surprise everyone — I've missed being home. I've saved almost all my money for school clothes.

When I get back I want to take everyone to dinner. A real sit-down restaurant, too, like Denny's. I bought a *Culture Club* cassette last week, but that's been my only extravagance. I think Boy George is radical. If you want, Doug, I can dress you like a girl, too. Just kidding!

Has anyone heard from Dad? I wrote him from here and the letter was returned. What's up with him?

I get home on Friday, August 20th. Who's going to come to the airport to pick me up? Will everyone? I miss you all. I didn't think I would, but I do.

Love,
Lindy

P.S. Christopher, would you like to see the movie *ET*? I'll treat if you buy the popcorn.

WASHINGTON DRIVER'S LICENSE

STATE OF WASHINGTON
Department of
LICENSING

NUMBER	ISSUE DATE	EXPIRES
KNOWLES*DJ459TK	092782	09287

CDK END RES

SEX	HEIGHT	WEIGHT	EYES	BIRTH DATE
M	6-01	192	BRO	092966

KNOWLES, DAVID MICHAEL
KNOTTY PINES TRAILER COURT, #14
PINE RIDGE, WA 98005

X *David Michael Knowles*

Barbara Lawton
2330 Country Club Lane
Pine Ridge, Washington 98005

October 7, 1982

My dearest Jillian, Montgomery and Leni Jo,
I'm home and settling back into my normal routine. In spite of the circumstances that brought me to New York, I had an enjoyable visit. I miss you all dreadfully. The house feels empty without the sound of Leni Jo's laughter.

Jillian, this has been a hard summer for you with the loss of your pregnancy. Time is the great healer; it might be a cliché but it's true. I'm glad you're wise enough to recognize this. Taking a three-month sabbatical was exactly the right thing to do at this juncture. Learning to take care of your emotional needs is as important as anything physical. I learned that lesson after your father died.

Grief, my children, is part of the healing process. When Leonard died, I didn't think I could possibly recover. We'd been married forty-five years and he was as much a part of me as my own hands and feet. I felt lost without him, abandoned and confused. Those first two years of widowhood were a challenge I don't care to repeat. I managed nicely once I found my balance, but it took quite a while. That sense of balance will come back to you, too. Be patient with yourself, deal with one day at a time and be grateful for the beautiful daughter you already have.

Montgomery, if you don't mind my saying so, you're working too hard. Jillian's been telling me this for years and I agree with her. Don't make the same mistake Leonard did. Take care of yourself, will you?

Leni Jo, you're the most brilliant, beautiful grandchild in the universe. I don't know a single three-year-old nearly as wonderful as you. I want to remind you how much your Grandma Lawton loves you. I miss reading to you at bedtime and cuddling with you during our afternoon naps, but I won't stay away long, I promise.

Cheers will be on soon, and you know how much I enjoy that show. Mark my word. Ted Danson is going to be a big star. His co-star, Shelly — oh dear, I can't recall her surname at the moment, but she's quite good too.

I'm looking forward to seeing you all at Christmas.

Love,
Mom

P.S. I liked Anne Tyler's *Dinner at the Homesick Restaurant*, which I read on the plane home. I'll give it to you at Christmastime.

P.P.S. My land, what is this world coming to that people are tainting headache pills with cyanide?

Whoever's doing this is a very sick person and should be prosecuted to the full extent of the law. I only hope that Johnson & Johnson survives this mess. God help us all.

❖

LESLEY KNOWLES

November 1, 1982

Dear Buck,

I don't make a habit of opening your letters to the children. You were probably counting on that. This latest letter, however, came with a Sitka County Jail stamp on the envelope. I hoped to spare them the knowledge that their father is currently incarcerated.

How dare you blame me for your situation! I didn't do anything to cause you to be arrested or jailed. It wasn't me behind the wheel of that car. You were the one who got into an accident. You were the one with the high blood alcohol count. You landed behind bars without any help from me. It's time you accepted responsibility for your own actions.

I've been angry with you before, and always with good reason, but you've sunk lower than I dreamed possible. I refused to send you money, and now you're asking your teenage children. It's bad enough that you blame me for your jail sentence, but asking David to send you cigarette money is unconscionable.

From this point forward, I will be censoring all your mail to the children. You won't get a dime from me and you won't get a penny from your son. As far as I'm concerned, jail is exactly where you belong.

Lesley

Jillian's Journal

November 13, 1982

My dearest Nick,

I watched the dedication ceremony for the Vietnam War Memorial on the news this evening. It's stunning in its simplicity. The black granite wall has your name engraved on it, along with those of the 52,000 other young men and women killed or missing in the Vietnam War. Each life lost is marked there. Each one will be remembered and honored. I'm so grateful, Nick. I don't want anyone to forget you or what you did. I hate it when I'm in Pine Ridge and someone mentions your name and then casually comments that you never returned from Vietnam. They don't know that you died a hero and that because of you, other men lived.

When I watched the news, Leni Jo was down for the night, thank goodness, and Monty wasn't home. The tears and the grief came so fast and furious that for a few moments I was overwhelmed. I turned off the television and sat for a while, immersed in the memories.

Oh, Nick, I loved you so much. I remember how I felt when my mother phoned to tell me your helicopter had been shot down and you'd been killed. At that point in my life, I'd never known such grief. It seems all too familiar now that my father's gone, too, and I've miscarried my son. But you, Nick, oh dear God, how I've missed you through the years.

My mother wrote last month soon after she returned home and said that time heals broken hearts. She's right — it blunts the pain and allows you to go on, to create a life. But it hasn't healed mine, Nick. It hasn't stopped me from loving you. It hasn't made me forget. I love my husband, but there have been nights, both before and after I married him, when I'd wake up, often in tears, because I'd been dreaming of you.

I've never told anyone this, not even Lesley.

There's irony in all this. The newsman who gave the report was in Vietnam himself. His name is Cole Greenberg and he's the man Lesley met in Hawaii. He's very good at his job, but I could see he was deeply moved by the ceremony. His facial expression revealed little, but his words came from the heart. He knows.

He's been there. He saw it with his own eyes. He lived the nightmare, too.

I can't visit the Vietnam War Memorial now. I might never be able to stand in front of that wall without breaking down. It was hard enough saying goodbye to you the first time. Remember how much I love you.

Jillian

❖

LESLEY KNOWLES

November 20, 1982

Dearest Jillian,

I've been meaning to write all week, but this is the first free moment I've had. I can't tell you how eager I am for your visit next month. Save as much time as you can for me, will you? I need one of our good, old-fashioned gabfests.

This has been a quite a year, hasn't it? A mixture of the good, the bad and everything else. You've been in my thoughts almost every day since June, when you lost the baby. Then I read about the dedication of the Vietnam War Memorial and realized how hard that must have hit you.

I've put in a request with Dr. Milton for time off the week between Christmas and New Year's. Following graduation, he gave me a substantial raise, which the children and I are putting to good use. I sold the trailer and paid off part of my school loans, as you know. After that, we moved into this rental home and now we have an opportunity to purchase it. I'm thrilled! The owner has made the terms very advantageous, asking for a relatively small down payment. The place is in good shape, has a yard and a convenient location. I'm so happy we can actually do this. All the kids are equally excited and they're pulling together to make it happen.

David is working thirty hours a week at the Albertson's Store and still manages to get top grades. I don't know what I'd do without him. Lindy's a social butterfly, but she's adding her baby-sitting money to the pot. Doug has David's old paper route and Christopher is walking dogs. Together we'll have enough for the down payment and the closing costs.

Lindy's attitude is a little better since she went away for the summer. She has a boyfriend, but at least he's in school and as far as I can tell, drug-free. For her fifteenth birthday, she wants to pierce her ears. I never thought I'd agree to that but I have. You've got to choose your battles and this one's not important enough to risk our fragile truce. Can you imagine what the nuns would think if we'd pierced our ears?

How times have changed! In our day, we were considered hussies if we rolled our socks down to show our ankles. We'd get kicked out of class for chewing gum, while now . . . Well, never mind.

I try to spend extra time with Lindy, but that doesn't help. She'd rather listen to her music than talk to me. It seems she's never going to forgive me for divorcing her father. Perhaps some day she'll understand the reasons I left Buck. I want so much for her, and I'm so afraid she'll make the same mistakes I did.

On to more positive news. Doug made the varsity basketball team and we had a party to celebrate. He isn't as athletic as Christopher, but he shot hoops every night after practice. I'm really proud of him.

I realize I'm talking about myself when it's really you I'm anxious to hear about. I know this has been a hard six months for you and Monty.

Write soon — and take care of yourself. You're the only best friend I have.

Love,
Lesley and the kids

P.S. I saw a bumper sticker the other day that made me smile. It said: GOD BLESS AMERICA — AND PLEASE HURRY!!!

HOSPITAL EMERGENCY ROOM CHART SHOWING MONTGOMERY GORDON HEART ATTACK

<table>
<tr><td colspan="2">New York Hospital ER
100 Madison Street
New York, NY 10029
212-555-5555</td></tr>
<tr><td>Date: 12/08/82

Time seen: 2100 hrs.

PMD: R.Lammers,MD

Chief Complaint: Chest pain, cold sweat, nausea

BP: 220/125 T: 147
P:140 R: 12
Pulse OX: 92%</td><td>Name: Gordon, Montgomery

DOB: 9/22/30 Age: 52

MRW: 123456789
Sex: Male

WEIGHT: 210 lbs</td></tr>
<tr><td>History of Present Illness:

Onset/Timing: 2 hrs PTA

Location: heart muscle, left arm

Quality: “squeezing”

Severity: Severe

Duration: 2 hrs.

Context: Reading at home

Modifying Factors:</td><td>Allergies:

Current Medications:

Ibuprofin, antacids</td></tr>
</table>

1986

Jillian's Journal

January 1, 1986

Dear Nick and Daddy,

I'll just bet you're cheering up a storm in heaven, aren't you, Daddy? There's a Republican in the White House, inflation is down and there's talk of eliminating the national debt by 1991! For the second time in my voting history, I chose to cast my ballot for the former Hollywood actor. So go ahead and gloat!

This is going to be an exciting year. Lesley and I are attending our twenty-year class reunion in July, and Lindy will be graduating from high school. Since I'm her official godmother, I plan to be at the graduation exercise and I'll sit proudly beside Lesley. The dates are already written in my schedule, which I'm finding more and more crowded since I was elected to the bench last year.

Nick, I'm sure Dad is being a real bore about that. You'll need to forgive him for being embarrassingly smug about his daughter, the judge. Dad knew, I swear he did, from the time I was three years old, that I'd follow in his footsteps.

Leni Jo is the smartest seven-year-old in her second-grade class. She's already reading at fifth-grade level. Monty and I have resisted placing her in an advanced schooling program because we prefer that she socialize with children her own age. We take pains to make sure she's intellectually stimulated both inside and outside the classroom. I'm still struggling with the conflict between the obligations of motherhood and career. I haven't found any easy solutions — only compromises.

Monty's law career is still going well. Last November he was approached about becoming a full partner. The heart attack in December of 1982 frightened us both. I have no desire to be a widow, and Monty doesn't intend to make me one anytime soon. I'm grateful to report that as of last February, he is physically fit with a normal cholesterol count. Whether or not he accepts a partnership with the Beckham firm is completely up to him. I'll support his decision either way. If he says yes, then I'll cheer him on just as enthusiastically as he encouraged me when I entered the race for Superior Court Judge.

I'm more in love with my husband every year. Monty and I have a good life. This isn't the passionate love I shared with you, Nick, but a mature love, one that developed slowly and steadily.

Now that Leni Jo is a bit older, we feel more comfortable leaving her with Mother and when our schedules allow, Monty and I enjoy traveling. Mom is in her glory when she can spend "quality time" with Leni Jo — that's a catch phrase of the 80s!

I've come to believe that our daughter has given Mom's life new purpose. She's incredible, Dad. When we were in Pine Ridge last summer, she decided it was time Leni Jo learned how to swim — and decided to teach her at the Country Club pool. Before she knew it, Mom had a whole class of six- and seven-year-olds. I think it's wonderful. Leni Jo talks to her on the phone every weekend and misses her terribly. I'm so grateful they had three weeks together this summer.

I was only able to see Lesley once this year, but we're as close as we ever were. She hasn't heard a word from Buck in almost four years. No real loss there. The last time he wrote, he was still in Alaska — in jail for reckless driving, reckless endangerment and driving while under the influence. I understand there are also a whole slew of property damage claims against him. As far as I'm concerned, she's better off not hearing from him, and so are the children.

David is attending classes at Pine Ridge Community College and working part-time for a computer store. He loves his job and apparently the owner relies on him quite a bit. He told me recently that he'd like to design software. I'm not entirely sure what that means, but then I barely even know how to operate a computer. They certainly seem to be taking over the world, though. Monty swears by his and claims it won't be long before every home has one. That'll be the day! I remember when everyone told us we'd have settlements on the moon by the year 2000. It isn't going to happen. Space travel isn't for me, and neither are computers.

Some time this month the *Challenger* is lifting off with the first private citizen aboard. A schoolteacher was chosen. Needless to say, I didn't apply, but what an experience. Christa McAuliffe will have a lot to share with her students when she returns.

Now that interest rates have fallen, Jim and Angie bought a house. (I don't think we can totally attribute lower interest rates to a Republican White House, Dad!) Lesley and the kids have been in their house for almost four years. It took her so long to buy a home of her own (other than the trailer) that she takes care of it as though it were one of her children. The yard is immaculate and the inside is decorated in a charming country style that is so Lesley.

Yes, life is good and I'm happy. Every year seems better than the one before. Monty and I have given up hoping for another child, (I'll be thirty-eight in a few days and Monty is fifty-six,) but that makes us all the more grateful for Leni Jo.

Remember how much I love you both,

Jillian

Barbara Lawton
2330 Country Club Lane
Pine Ridge, Washington 98005

January 5, 1986

My dearest children,

Jillian, I'm considering a major decision and I want to discuss it with you before I proceed further. I'd like to list the house with a real estate broker.

When the John L. Scott representative came today for what he called a "walk-through" he told me the house was worth over $200,000. Can you imagine? He suggested I list it at a slightly higher price to leave room for negotiations. My goodness, I nearly wet my drawers when he said what we could get for it. I didn't dare tell him that your father and I paid only $15,000 for it back in 1947.

I suspect you're asking yourself why I'd want to sell the house now. First and foremost, it seems ridiculous to heat 3,000 square feet for just one person. The place is just too big for me. My friends told me not to make any major decisions the year following your father's death. I doubt that I could have, but it's been almost eight years and I'm finally ready.

Jillian, I can hear you asking me where I intend to move. This might come as a surprise, but I'm seriously thinking about New York City. Manhattan in particular. To be a bit more specific — an apartment within walking distance of you.

Having Leni Jo with me for three weeks this summer is what prompted this. She's the joy of my life. The house seemed so dull and empty without her. The sound of her laughter faded from these rooms far too quickly.

Now, I don't want you to worry that I'll intrude on you and Montgomery. I intend to maintain my privacy and will respect yours. I trust you know me well enough to realize that.

I hope to hear back from you soon so I can make my plans. If you have any objections, I do hope you'll be honest enough to tell me now.

I love you all.

Mom

Park West Medical
284 Central Park West, Suite 1A
New York, NY 10024

February 10, 1986

Dear Mr. Montgomery Gordon,

The results of your blood work are back, following your annual examination with Dr. Lyman. Your cholesterol count is 190. We look

forward to seeing you again next year.
Sincerely,
Joan McMahon, R.N.

❖

March 3, 1986

Grandma Lawton,
I'm glad your house sold and you're moving to New York. There's an apartment for sale in our building. It's on the fifth floor. We live on the tenth floor. I could take the elevator down to your apartment and you could take it up to see me.
Love,
Leni Jo Gordon

❖

LESLEY KNOWLES

April 1, 1986

Dearest Jillian,
There's a reason I chose to write on April Fool's Day, and that's because I feel like a fool. While sorting through the laundry this afternoon, I found a package of birth control pills in Lindy's sweater pocket. She apparently got them at the Planned Parenthood Clinic behind my back.

Well, I suppose I don't feel so much a fool as a coward. I should have confronted her immediately, but I didn't. Instead I poured myself a glass of iced tea, sat down and cried. My daughter has lost her innocence — and it isn't just her virginity I'm referring to. She's sexually involved with a young man I barely know and she's unwilling to discuss her situation with me. She's dating Carl Kennedy and as far as I can discern he's a decent enough young man. But the thought of them having sex just freezes my blood.

Buck and I were sexually active my senior year, but the memories are not happy ones. As a result I ended up pregnant with David. I love each of my children — but not one of the four was planned. Buck wouldn't allow me to take the pill and at the time I was struggling to be a good wife and a good Catholic. I sometimes think I failed on both counts.

I wish Lindy had waited for the right man and the right time. I long to tell my daughter these things but I won't. I can't find the words. The pill might prevent a pregnancy, but sex won't give her the love she craves, or whatever else she's seeking. It will only complicate her life and possibly her future. Carl isn't any more ready for a committed relationship than Buck was at his age. Or me for that matter.

The first few years Buck and I were married, and for a long time afterward, I lived in denial. I became accustomed to ignoring ugly or difficult situations — like this one with Lindy. I was afraid to confront him the same way I'm afraid to confront my daughter. Because once the reality is acknowledged, you have to do something about it. I can remember nights when Buck would come home reeking of another woman's cologne. Although he disgusted me, I'd pretend not to notice. I got so good at that. So good at turning a blind eye to the truth, because the truth was just too damn painful. Now I'm doing it again, only this time my eyes are wide open and it isn't Buck I'm dealing with but our daughter.

As you know, Lindy has always been a difficult child. She was a problem even before she became a teenager. Even though there's been a slight improvement in her attitude in the last couple of years, she seems to think she can do whatever she wants. But she's still a child, still living in my home. Living under my rules and under my protection. And Jillian, I do long to protect her. Which means I'd have to insist she own up to what she's doing — but I'm afraid of the consequences of a confrontation. Just like I was with Buck . . .

What should I do? Confront her, no matter how hard that is, or ignore what I found? Risk having her walk out or put up with behavior I find appalling?

What do you say, oh wise and trusted friend? How should I handle this one?

On a totally separate subject, I talked to your mother this week and learned she put down earnest money on an apartment five floors below yours. My fear is that once she moves to New York, you won't be as inclined to visit Pine Ridge. Jillian, if only you knew how much your visits mean to me! I don't know what I'd do if I didn't have that time to look forward to.

I have some good news. Mom and Eric bought a Winnebago. They invited the boys to join them for a short trip this summer during the week of our class reunion. They'll drive down to Susan and Bill's place in Sacramento and stay there for a few days. You can't imagine how excited Doug and Christopher are. Doug will be 16 in August and he thinks Eric might let him do some of the driving. Fat chance! Christopher thinks he might be able to persuade them to head from Sacramento to Disneyland. More power to him if he succeeds.

I'm sorry I got so long-winded, but this thing with Lindy really upsets me. She's too young to be having sex. I don't want her to repeat my mistakes and my mother's, as well. I don't just mean the teenage pregnancy — thank God for the pill. But the tendency to get trapped in a marriage or a relationship that will stifle her at best, destroy her at worst. I want so much more for her!

Write me soon.

Lesley

❖

20 YEAR REUNION
FOR
HOLY NAME ACADEMY AND
MARQUETTE HIGH SCHOOL
JULY 18–20
HOLIDAY INN,
PINE RIDGE, WASHINGTON

FRIDAY NIGHT SOCIAL
At
TINK'S SPORTS BAR
2210 Pine Ridge Way
369-7895

SATURDAY DINNER AND DANCE
At
PINE RIDGE COUNTRY CLUB
Featuring
Dion's 60s Revue Band

SUNDAY AFTERNOON PICNIC
At
LIONS FIELD
231 8th Avenue

R.S.V.P. Diane Andrews Coleman
Lesley Adamski Knowles

March 1, 1986

Mom,

You're being completely unreasonable. You leave me no choice but to move out of the house. I'm staying with Shannon and her parents until Carl and I can find a place of our own.

I am not a child and I refuse to let you treat me like one.

Lindy

May 2, 1986

English Assignment
Christopher Knowles, Grade 7

WHY MY MOM IS THE BEST MOM IN THE WORLD

My mom is super cool. She does fun things. In the summer, in the middle of the night, she wakes us all up and takes us outside to lay in the grass and look at the stars. She calls these Surprise Pajama Parties because we never know when the night sky will be clear enough. Then she gives us ice cream cones.

One time when I was little and my brothers and sister were in school and there was only Mom and me, we had Backwards Day. We had a hamburger for breakfast and cereal at dinnertime and dressed funny all day. Everyone wished they could be home with us instead of going to school.

When my dad left, my mom volunteered to be the assistant coach on my soccer team. She didn't know the rules, but she learned them because she wanted to be part of my team. Twice a week, when she wasn't going to classes, she left work early so she could get to the soccer field in time for practice.

Everyone loves their mom because they are their mom. I love my mom because she's fun, too. She's cool.

❖

LESLEY KNOWLES

May 7, 1986

Dear Lindy,

The choice to leave home was yours. I told you this when you left and I'll say it again: you're welcome back at any time as long as you're willing to abide by my rules. Despite what you think, I'm sorry Carl broke up with you. Sweetheart, trust me, I know how much it hurts to have the person you love dump you for someone else.

I really miss you, and the boys miss their sister. Come home and we'll talk again without the anger and the threats. I think we've both learned a valuable lesson.

I love you.

Mom

❖

The Class of

Nineteen Hundred and Eighty-six

Pine Ridge High School

Announces its

Commencement Exercises

Sunday afternoon, June eighth

At three o'clock

Invited guests only

BANK OF AMERICA

Jillian Gordon **16062**

Montgomery Gordon

331 West End Ave.

Apartment 1020

New York, NY 10023 Date 6/5/86

Pay to the order of Lindy Knowles $100.00

One Hundred and 0/00

Jillian Gordon

June 10, 1986

Dear Mom,

I'm writing because I want to thank you for everything. I hated it when I was away from home. I thought you were being unreasonable and stupid to demand that I break up with Carl. But I was the stupid one. You never even asked for an apology for all the ugly things I said.

I do want to apologize, though. I'm sorry, Mom. You were right about Carl. I would never have been able to graduate if it wasn't for everything you did to help me catch up with my schoolwork. I feel so much better now that I'm home.

I waited until after graduation to apologize because I didn't want us to get all emotional. I know forcing me to make a decision was hard for you. You might not think I mean this, but I'm glad you stuck to your guns. You're right, I was hoping Carl would marry me. I thought we'd run away to Reno or someplace like that but he wasn't interested, and after a few days I knew neither one of us was ready. I'd prefer to marry David Cassidy, anyway. PSYCH!

I was pretty upset when I left, but I appreciate that you gave me the freedom to make my own choices, right or wrong. I learned a lot about myself while I was with Shannon and her family. I always thought it was great that her parents let her do anything she wanted, but when I was living with her I realized that what seems good from the outside often isn't good at all.

I had a great party after the graduation ceremony. Thanks, Mom. I wish Dad could've been here, but I learned a long time ago that I can't depend on my father. Still, if I could change anything about graduation, it would be having Dad there. Do you think he got the invitation? Probably not, seeing that the last address we had for him was the jail.

Love,
Lindy

JILLIAN LAWTON GORDON
331 WEST END AVENUE
APARTMENT 1020
NEW YORK, NY 10023

July 8, 1986

Dearest Lesley,

I know this is short notice but I'm not going to make it to the reunion. Monty hasn't been feeling well. He insisted I buy the airline tickets, but I told him I wasn't going anywhere until he saw Dr. Lyman. He went in last week and the test results are back.

Monty has cancer. Even as I write the word my hand is shaking. I've never been more terrified. My husband has cancer. Oh, Lesley, I don't think I can bear this. Monty is confident that everything will be fine. I'm not.

I remember the first week I didn't get a letter from Nick when he was in Vietnam. A terrified sensation came over me at the absence of his letter – a premonition, I later realized. I have that same feeling now. Dear God, I hope I'm wrong. I don't know what I'd do without Monty. Haven't I lost enough already?

Please pray for us, Lesley. You're so much closer to God than I am. He'll heed your prayers far more than He will mine.

Mom has been wonderful through all of this. She immediately took charge, sat me down and made us both a cup of tea. Then she chatted on about medical advances these days and how I'm probably panicking for no reason. By the time she left, she had me believing that Monty's surgery will be no more serious than having a mole removed. It'll be followed by a series of chemotherapy treatments.

The surgery's scheduled for the Wednesday before the reunion. I won't leave him. I know you understand, but oh, Lesley, I will so miss seeing you.

Please, please keep us in your prayers. I don't want to lose my husband.

Jillian

Dear Daddy,

Get well soon. I drew the picture of the flowers for you.

I love you.

Leni Jo

Lesley's Journal

July 21, 1986

The reunion was wonderful, although it seemed odd being there without a husband or a date. I was a little intimidated at first, but as soon as I arrived, I started talking to my classmates and before long I forgot I was alone. It really didn't make any difference.

As luck would have it, one of the first people I bumped into was Dr. Roy Kloster. His wife, the other Dr. Kloster, is pregnant with their third child and they looked blissfully happy. Roy introduced me as his high-school heartthrob.

Bob Daniels asked me where Buck is. I told him his guess was as good as mine. I didn't pursue the matter because I had the sinking feeling that Buck owes him money. Bob tried to flirt with me, but I've never liked him and quickly made an excuse to talk to someone else.

A lot of people wondered about Jillian. She was missed. Unfortunately, the news about

Monty isn't good. The surgery was a success, but his colon was full of cancer and it's spread to several of his organs. The surgeon removed what he could and as soon as Monty's recovered his strength, he'll undergo both chemotherapy and radiation treatments. Naturally Jillian is worried. She said she knew this was going to be bad and she was right. How I wish I could be with her.

Despite my constant worry about them, I managed to have a good time. Several people asked me who I'm dating or if I'm available. I wasn't sure how to answer. This whole dating scene unnerves me. There's only been one man in my life. After Buck, I was terrified of getting involved again. I've definitely been scarred by my marriage. Anyway, taking care of my children is what's most important right now. I am certainly capable of living my life without a man. I've proved that from the beginning. I could never rely on Buck.

When my former classmates pressed me about the dating issue, I told them I preferred the quiet life. Quiet? Not likely! I have four children at home, three of them teenagers. People who believe my life is serene would probably fall for any outlandish sales pitch!

If I were to get married again, I'd want a man like Jillian's Monty. Or Jillian's dad. Or

Dr. Milton, who's sane, sensible and happily married. Or Susan's husband, Bob. (See? They do exist!)

I refuse to think about Cole Greenberg. I built a fantasy around him and I have absolutely no idea what the real man is like.

All in all, the reunion was wonderful, but I missed Jillian.

JILLIAN LAWTON GORDON
331 WEST END AVENUE
APARTMENT 1020
NEW YORK, NY 10023

August 15, 1986

Dear God,

Let's make a deal. Save my husband and I'll start attending Mass again. I'll sing in the choir. Become a lay minister, feed the hungry, do anything else You ask of me.

Please Lord, let Monty's body respond positively to all these horrible treatments. Don't let him be this sick when there's no hope.

Cure him, Lord. I believe in miracles. Perform one now.

Sincerely,
Jillian Gordon

September 16, 1986

Dear Daddy,

Mommy said I can't go to the hospital to visit you. I think the rules are wrong. I want to see you. I hope you're feeling lots better. Grandma took me to the Park and we saw a dog. Can I have a dog soon? I want to name him Blackie.

Love,
Leni Jo

❖

Dr. Steven Milton
Doctors' Clinic
100 Spruce Avenue
Pine Ridge, WA 98005

October 12, 1986

Dear Lesley,

To celebrate your eight years of dedicated service, I'm giving you one week's extra vacation. Gloria and I know that your friend in New York is going through a very rough period just now. As a thank-you for all you've done for my office, Gloria and I would also like to give you this airline ticket to New York.

Sincerely,
Dr. Steven Milton, OB-GYN
And Gloria Milton

Park West Medical
284 Central Park West, Suite 1A
New York, NY 10024

November 7, 1986

Dear Judge Jillian Gordon,

I'm sorry I haven't been in the office to personally return your phone call. Perhaps that worked out for the best because it's given me time to think over your difficult question.

Although I was Montgomery's primary physician before the cancer surgery, I am only one member of the medical team that is currently treating him. I understand the cancer hasn't responded as we'd hoped to the chemotherapy and radiation. I'm very sorry to hear that. I was able to check with my colleagues and learned that Montgomery has refused any further treatments. I concur with his decision.

Now to your question. No, I can't persuade him to continue. Nor do I recommend any type of experimental treatment available in other countries. I can understand how painful this is for you. Unfortunately it is too late. Your husband wants to die with dignity. My suggestion is that you call a Hospice team and take him home.

With deepest regrets,

Dr. Larry Lyman, MD

In Loving Memory
Of
Montgomery Charles Gordon
September 22, 1930–December 23, 1986

1989

Jillian's Journal

January 1, 1989

Mom and Leni Jo are spending the day together, and this gives me a few moments to myself. Since Monty's death, the holidays have been especially difficult. Being alone has been a painful adjustment. I never thought I'd be a widow at thirty-eight, but then I didn't expect Nick to die at age twenty, either. Life is full of unpleasant and unwelcome surprises.

Even now, a little over two years after Monty died, I struggle with bitterness and self-pity. My emotions are like an undertow, and the current is deadly and silent. Just keeping my head above water is a struggle. The only one who knows how hard these last years have been is Lesley. I dare not let on to Mom or Leni Jo how I feel. For them I put on a smile and pretend.

I've discovered something noteworthy about pretending. It's a highly underrated skill. I've gotten quite good at it. Good enough to almost fool myself into believing I've adjusted to widowhood. There are days I pretend I'm happy to such a successful degree, I actually feel that way. Some days it completely slips my mind that Monty won't be walking in the door just in time for dinner. It's late evening before I remember that my husband and I won't be snuggling in front of the fireplace or reading briefs together. For Leni Jo and my mom, I can pretend, but at night, when I'm alone in our bed, the reality chokes me.

I don't believe I've slept an entire night since Monty was diagnosed with cancer. Certainly not since his death. Some nights I wake and just stare at the wall. Every man I have ever loved has died. Nick, my father, my unborn son, and now my husband. But I can't allow the losses in my life to diminish the good things. It's times like this — when the weight of my grief nearly overwhelms me — that I pause and remember everything I do have. My daughter is my very heart, and my mother is healthy and whole. I have a satisfying career that keeps me focused and challenged. Lesley has been my best friend my entire life, and without her I don't know what I would've done.

Monty left me well enough off that I need never worry about money. I can work or not, whatever I desire. Yes, there's been great pain in my life, but on the other hand I have much to be grateful for.

Okay, onward and forward. This is the dawn of yet another year. Leni Jo turned eleven in November and astonishes me with her wonderful, wry sense of humor. Not surprisingly, my daughter and my mother are the very best of friends. They spend at least part of every day with each other. Often when I get home, the two of them already have dinner started. Mom is currently teaching Leni Jo to embroider tea towels and pillowcases. Their relationship is strong, bonded by love and laughter. In ways I can't, Mom has helped Leni Jo deal with the loss of her father.

My antidote to grief has been painting. Daddy took up oil painting after he retired, and later Mom dabbled in it for a while. When Mom moved east, she sold quite a few of Daddy's things, rather than transport them across the country. But she couldn't bring herself to get rid of the oils and brushes. Not knowing what to do with them, she gave the whole kit and caboodle to me. I put the equipment in a closet and completely forgot about it until just recently.

To my surprise, I've discovered I enjoy painting. I don't think I'm particularly gifted, but it calms my spirit. So far, I haven't shown anyone my paintings (other than Leni Jo and Mom). I've done several small canvases now and am taking classes on Saturday afternoons. It's my one indulgence.

I wonder what 1989 will hold. More work, of course! I'm grateful to have a demanding career, otherwise I might have allowed the tide of loss to sweep me beneath the surface. My friends are few in number, mostly peers and attorneys. My life is so hectic I can't take the time to develop deep relationships. Lesley is and always will be my best friend.

Soon all her children will be raised and out of the house. David's in the Army. He enlisted last year when the military offered him a way to receive advanced computer skills. He jumped at the opportunity, certain that computers are the wave of the future. Lesley wasn't happy, since he didn't discuss the decision with her or anyone else. He's stationed in California and although he misses his family, he loves the work.

As for computers, I swear they're taking over the world. Monty claimed that by the end of the century there'd be one in every home and I'm beginning to believe he is (was) right.

Lindy's a sophomore, attending Pine Ridge Community College. Her note at Christmas mentioned that she's considering medicine, but she enjoys her drama classes, too, and joined a community theater group. It wouldn't surprise me if she went into nursing, like her mother and her aunt Susan; perhaps she'll even become a doctor. I'm sure Lindy could accomplish anything she set her mind to. For years Lesley said that her daughter was the one most like Buck and in some ways she's right. But Lindy has a lot of her mother in her, too, and no one should discount her ambition and drive.

Doug graduates from high school this year

and is already talking about joining the military like his older brother. He sounds pretty determined. I doubt Lesley will be able to dissuade him.

Christopher is in his last year of junior high and making quite a name for himself as a cross-country runner. He's good enough to run varsity for the high school, although technically he's still in junior high. Last spring he was eligible to compete in the state tournament. Lesley derives a lot of pleasure from attending his meets. Dr. Milton has always been very flexible and accommodating, so there's no problem about leaving the office early to watch Christopher run.

It won't be long now before all the kids are gone and Lesley will be alone. I wonder if she'll think about dating then. I hope she does – but if not, I'll understand. I've been a widow for just over two years, and the thought of another relationship has no appeal. I can't imagine that it ever will.

Brad Lincoln
30 Market Street
St. Simons Island, GA 31522

February 8, 1989

Dear James Murphy,

This address came from an old telephone book, so I don't know if you'll ever actually see my letter. I'm looking for the brother of Nicholas Patrick Murphy. The Nick I knew died in Vietnam in 1968. He often talked about his little brother, and I'm hoping you're him.

Let me start by introducing myself. My name is Brad Lincoln. I don't know if you remember Nick mentioning me, but I suspect he wrote home about me the same way I did him. After all these years you've probably forgotten my name. I'm hoping your memory will kick in, though. Your brother was the best friend I ever had. He saved my life and died doing it. I took his death hard. The only thing that kept me sane for the next few years was the knowledge that I would've done the same for him had the situation been reversed.

In the twenty-one years since Nam, I've married, had a couple of kids and made a decent life for myself. For the most part, I buried the experiences of war as deep inside me as I could. In other words, I did my damnedest to forget. But I want you to know I never forgot Nick. Not one day in all those years.

Last summer I visited the Vietnam War Memorial with my wife and kids, and made a point of looking up Nick's name while I was there. I have to tell you I got pretty broken up when I saw it. You don't need me to tell you that your brother was a good man. An honorable man. Plenty of guys cheated on their wives and girlfriends while they were in Nam, but not Nick. He loved his Jillian heart and soul. That's what he always used to say — heart and soul — and it was true.

This brings me to the reason for my letter. I think Nick must've had an intuition about what was going to happen because he gave me something that belonged to Jillian and asked me to return it to her. He wrote a letter to go along with it. I've never opened the envelope.

When I got out of the hospital and home from the war, I tried to contact her, but her mother wrote and asked that I leave her alone. It'd only been a couple of years and Jillian was just beginning to get on with her life. Her mother didn't want me disrupting whatever peace she'd found. I understood. I always intended to deliver this to her, but set it aside and waited for the right time.

She's had more than twenty years to heal and so have I. At the Wall in Washington, D.C., Nick reminded me that I still hadn't done the one thing he asked of me.

I wrote Jillian at the address I had for her, but the letter was returned. Apparently she doesn't have any family left in Pine Ridge. Do you know where she is and how I might reach her?

Your help would be greatly appreciated.

Sincerely,

Brad Lincoln

❖

LESLEY KNOWLES

March 5, 1989

Dear David,

It was great to hear your voice yesterday. You sounded so excited — although I have to tell you I don't have a clue what you were talking about. I'm sorry, but the announcement of a million-transistor microchip doesn't mean much to me. Thank you for explaining that a million transistors can fit on a surface half the size of a postage stamp, but I don't see how that's going to affect my life. Still, if you're excited about this, it must mean good news for all of us.

I know it's more than the news from Intel that prompted your phone call. You might not think I picked up on the fact that you mentioned your girlfriend. Meagan, you said her name was? It sounds as if this is more than a casual relationship. I'd love to meet her. You like this girl, don't you? I've waited a long time for you to mention someone special. We're very much alike, David. You're careful and deliberate in your choices, which is the same way I approach relationships. Life has taught me that. And yet . . . there are chances worth taking. I don't have a great deal of experience with falling in love, but I know you didn't come to me for advice. You'll have to trust your own emotions. Protect yourself — but not too much.

If Meagan's the one to bring that smile to your voice, then I love her already. I want for you what every mother wants for her son — your happiness.

We're all doing fine. There's no need to rehash the news, but I will tell you that Lindy applied for the summer session at the University of Washington in the pre-med program.

Doug talked to a Navy recruiter yesterday. He'd enlist right now if it didn't require my signature. I hope to God we don't go to war any time soon with two of my sons in the military.

Christopher sends his love and says he wishes you were home again. So do I.

Some sad news. Dr. Milton's wife was recently diagnosed with a brain tumor. Please pray for her. Both Dr. Milton and Gloria have been very good to all of us. I'm not sure what's going to happen, since Dr. Milton isn't one to bring his personal problems to the office, but her condition is obviously serious.

Take care of yourself and write when you can.

Love,

Mom

❖

Leni Jo Gordon

April 3, 1989

Dear Exxon Company,

The pictures on television showed what happened when your tanker spilled 11 million gallons of oil in Prince William Sound in Alaska. You should be ashamed of yourself. My mother is a judge. You're lucky you won't appear in her court because she's as angry with you as I am.

Sincerely,

Leni Jo Gordon

Age 11

LESLEY KNOWLES

May 14, 1989

Dearest Jillian,

Help, I'm in a panic! I just got word that the Army is transferring David to Panama.

My son's going to be down there with those rebels! From what the evening news said, we already have ten thousand troops in place. This is sounding scary.

David's work so far has been with computers, but now he's in the field and not behind some desk. You can understand why I'm freaking out. The kids think I worry too much. How can I not?

I'm still a little shell-shocked over David's transfer, but your news was just as unsettling. So Brad Lincoln contacted you after all these years. Incredible! You're going to meet him, aren't you? Promise me you won't let whatever he says upset you. It goes without saying that if you need to talk you can phone me any time, day or night.

I have an idea. Last year we both turned 40 — without any fanfare. It occurred to me that it's been ages since the two of us had any serious time together. I'm thinking white sandy beaches, pina coladas and lots of sunshine. I generally take my vacation in October, but I'm game to go whenever you can fit me into your busy schedule.

Dr. Milton has been preoccupied with his wife's condition and I don't think he'll care when I take my vacation. However, I do feel it's important for me to be here during the next few months. Unfortunately things aren't going well with Mrs. Milton. The tumor is inoperable and growing. I don't need to tell you how devastating this is to their family. No one's saying very much here at the office.

Get back to me about a "We're 40 Getaway" vacation as soon as possible. Let's kick up our heels and enjoy life while we can. The one truth I've learned is that life is both precious and fragile and needs to be grasped with all the passion we have inside us.

What's that old saying? Life Begins at 40? Are you ready? Because I am!

Love,

Lesley

Outside Khe Sanh in South Vietnam

September 15, 1968

My dearest Jillian,

Word came just after dark that we'll be lifting off at first light. The fighting lately has been fierce. I've seen good men die. The fact is, Jillian, I might not come home. Holding you, loving you and marrying you is all I care about. But the way things look here, I don't know if that will be possible.

If you read this, the worst has happened. I know Brad will find a way to get this letter and my mother's medallion back to you. There's one thing I want you to know, and I hope you find peace with it. I'm not afraid of death. Not when it's been an unwelcome passenger on damn near every mission I've flown. I don't want to die, but I've come to believe in God and accept His will in my life, however long or short that is. Personally, I'd choose to end my days in some rocking chair with you at my side and a grandchild on my knee.

Your love for me is everything I'll ever need. You believed in me and showed me I could be and do anything I want. If I die, Jillian, I want you to know that I will love you through eternity.

Remember how much I love you.

Nick

❖

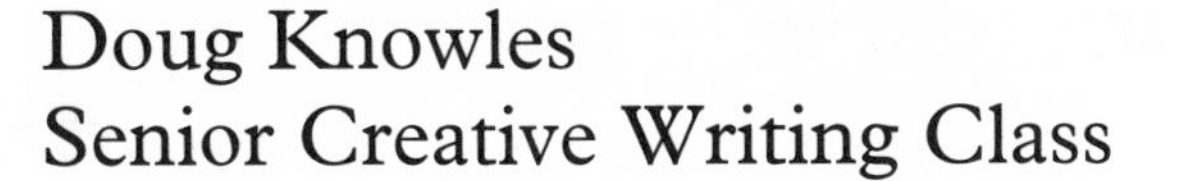

Doug Knowles
Senior Creative Writing Class

DYING TO BE FREE

It happened 200 years ago,
And it's happening today.
In Boston it was a Tea Party
And freedom fighters of yesterday.
Now students stand in Tiananmen Square,
And their hearts are filled with dreams.
They have hopes for Democracy
And all that it brings.
The fire in their hearts
Is reflected in their eyes.
The rage of the army
Is heard in battle cries.

Their Goddess of Democracy
Lies crushed in the square.
She symbolized their purpose;
Now she warns each to prepare.
The cry for freedom is louder
Than any bell can toll.
The government can murder people
But never destroy their goal.
What began as a demonstration
Has begot civil war.
Deng hoped that by killing,
Things would return to ways before.
But people are no longer happy
With what used to be.
They are ready for a change.
They are dying to be free.

❖

The Class of
Nineteen Hundred and Eighty-Nine
Pine Ridge High School
Announces its
Commencement Exercises
Sunday afternoon, June fourth
At three o'clock
By Invitation only

June 5, 1989

Dear Doug,

Congratulations! You did your mother and your family proud this afternoon.

It looks like I'm not going to be able to change your mind about joining the Navy. All right, Doug, go ahead with my blessing. You're a strong, capable young man, and you have a lot to offer.

Love,

Mom

Six-Year Obligation Program

Name (Last-First-Middle-Jr-Sr, etc.) SSN
KNOWLES, DOUGLAS STEVEN 528-94-7995

I. I am enlisting in the U.S. Navy for four (4) years and at the same time signing an agreement to extend my enlistment for twenty-four (24) months to guarantee assignment in the ADVANCED ELECTRONIC FIELD program.

Nuclear Field (AF)
Advanced Electronics Field (AEF)
Advanced Technical Field (ATF)

II I understand that my selected program includes the following ratings:
N/A Nuclear Field. Electrician's Mate (EM), Electronics Technician (ET) and Machinists Mate (MM).

XX Advanced Electronics Field. Avionics(AC, AT, AM), Data Systems Technician (DS), Electronics Technician (ET), Crypotologic Technician Maintenance (CTM), Electronics Warfare Technician, Fire Control Technician, Sonar Technician (STS), and Strategic Weapon System Electronics

N/A Advanced Technical Field. Interior Communication Electronics, Hull Maintenance Technician, Hospital Corpsman, Radiology, Gas Turbine Systems Technician and Boiler Technician

III. Training Guarantees

XX 1.Assignment to Class A School for a rating within my program will be made after my classification interview at recruit training and will be based on my test scores, personal desires, and the needs of the Navy.
OR
2. I have been guaranteed assignment to STS Class "A" School

IV. I understand that my eligibility for my guaranteed program will be rechecked during recruit training and subsequent schooling. I must, at all times, remain eligible for the required security clearance and physical qualifications of my guaranteed program. If it is determined that I am ineligible to continue in this program, any one of the following courses of action will be taken:

1. If I become ineligible for my guaranteed program because of personal facts(s) of which I knew and did not include in my application for enlistment, I may be assigned to an alternate Navy program for which there is a vacancy and which I am qualified

2. If I become ineligible for my guaranteed program because of a personal fact(s) of which I did not know or which I knew and included in my application for enlistment, I will have the following options:

a. Reassignment to a Navy Program in which a vacancy exists and for which I am qualified and desire,

OR

b. Honorable discharge from the Navy.

3. If my guaranteed program training is stopped because of disciplinary reasons or failure to meet the Navy's academic or professional standards during any phase of my training, I will be assigned as the needs of the Navy required.

Douglas Steven Knowles
Signature of Enlisting Officer/Date

____

Signature of Enlistee/Date

____

July 14, 1989

Dear Mom and Christopher,

Davey was right, Basic Training is hard. It's probably the hardest thing I've ever done, but I'm going to see it through.

I have some news. We were tested last week and remember how I always got top grades in French with hardly any studying? Well, it seems I have a flair for languages. That's what the tests say. I talked with the Staff Sergeant, and he says I'll probably be sent to Linguistic School. I asked him what languages I might be learning. I don't hold out much hope that I'll be taking French again, but who knows. It seems there's an emphasis on the Middle Eastern languages, especially Arabic.

I got a letter from David and he's hoping to get out of Panama soon. He complained about the heat and the bugs, but I think he's missing Meagan more than anything.

Hey, Christopher, have you moved into my bedroom yet? You'd better not, 'cause I'll come back and kick your butt if you do. I've learned a hundred different ways to maim and kill and I have no qualms about using any of them on you. PSYCH! It wouldn't hurt to write your big brother once in a while, you know.

Take care,

Doug

LESLEY KNOWLES

August 4, 1989

Dearest Jillian,

I just got back from the travel agent's and I've booked everything on my end. I'm so excited I feel like a kid again. The last real vacation I had was when I was thirteen and our family went camping.

I fly into Miami on October 17th with a plane change in Atlanta. My flight lands just fifteen minutes after yours. I'll meet you at the gate and we can go collect our luggage together. We pick up the rental car at the airport. I don't mind driving as long as you navigate.

I've never heard of the resort, but then how would I? Marathon Key. Any reason it's named that? Not that it matters. I'd go just about anywhere as long as we could be together for nine glorious days. I've already got a few books I'm saving to read. One I'm bringing is *The Joy Luck Club* by Amy Tan. It really looks interesting.

Taking this time off isn't going to be a problem at the office. Dr. Milton has booked a two-week cruise for him and his wife, also in October. She appears to be responding to the treatments. Dr. Milton is devoted to her. I've always respected him, but seeing how much he loves his wife gives me faith that there might be a good man in my future.

Christopher thinks it's ridiculous that he has to go stay with Mom and Eric while I'm away. But I don't feel right about leaving a fifteen-year-old boy on his own. I'm determined not to give in, even though he has a way of talking me around. I remember how Mom spoiled Bruce, and now I catch myself doing the same thing with my youngest.

I'm so anxious to see you, I can hardly stand it. Just two more months!

Love,

Lesley

1991

Jillian's Journal

January 1, 1991

At the start of a new year I'm usually filled with enthusiasm and energy. This year is different. What I feel now is dread and worry. Not since Vietnam have I been this afraid. It's almost certain that we're going to war against Iraq. The coalition has been building up its forces for months, and the deadline for Iraq to withdraw its troops from Kuwait is looming closer, although there's been no movement at all. Apparently James Baker, the Secretary of State, is meeting with the Iraqi Foreign Minister early in the month, but no one's holding out much hope of a peaceful resolution.

I can feel tension everywhere on the streets of New York, where security has never been higher. There's fear of terrorist activity all across America, but a lot of people believe that if and when it happens, it'll be here in New York. An uneasy feeling comes over me every morning when Leni Jo leaves for school. I couldn't bear it if anything happened to my daughter.

Speaking of children, I'm sick with fear for Lesley. Both David and Doug are in the Persian Gulf. David is with the ground forces and Doug's aboard one of the aircraft carriers. Lesley is frantic. She's dedicated her entire life to her children. The thought of either boy being killed is enough to start her weeping uncontrollably. This brings back all the angst I endured when Nick left for Vietnam. I remember how high his morale was when he flew to Southeast Asia. He was confident that he'd put in his time and get the hell out of there and return home safe and whole. I see that same enthusiasm in the faces of our young men and it terrifies me. These boys have no idea what they're headed for, no idea at all. Dear God, this is insanity!

Mom and Leni Jo are walking down to St. Patrick's every afternoon to pray for peace. Leni Jo tells me the church is bright with all the votive candles people have lit. My daughter astonishes me with her understanding of this situation. Her teacher has gotten the entire class involved in a letter-writing campaign to our troops. Thank heaven she has Mom to talk to about this war, because I can't seem to manage more than a few coherent words at a time. This is all too familiar, and all too real. In my heart I know that Saddam Hussein intends to play this out to the bitter end, whatever that might be. Everyone's biggest fear is that he'll use biological warfare, which he's done in the past against Iran.

I don't know what the future holds for our country, my family or for me. When life was riding along fairly smoothly I didn't give peace much thought. Now worries consume me and the unknown future is a frightening prospect.

❖

Pine Ridge Herald

January 7, 1991
Obituary

Services are being held for Gloria Milton, 50, who died at her home Sunday January 6th. Mrs. Milton succumbed after a long illness. The service will be held Wednesday, the 9th, at 1 p.m. at Our Lady of the Woods Mortuary. Burial will be in Pine Ridge Cemetery.

Mrs. Milton was born August 10, 1942 in Portland, Oregon. She attended the University of Oregon where she met Dr. Steven Milton, OB-GYN. They were married in 1964.

Survivors include her husband and two daughters, Maryanne Steadman and Sandy Princeton; two grandchildren, Bryce and Jay Ann; one sister, Joan, and one brother, Ken, in addition to several nieces and nephews.

Mrs. Milton was an active volunteer in the community. She was a member of the Regular Baptist Church, and sang with the choir. She taught first-grade Sunday School for twelve years.

In lieu of flowers the family requests donations to the American Cancer Society.

unteer in the community. She was a member of the Regular Baptist Church, and sang with the choir. She taught first-grade Sunday School for twelve years.

In lieu of flowers the family requests donations to the American Cancer Society.

❖

SOMEWHERE IN SAUDI ARABIA

January 14, 1991

Dear Mom and Christopher,

Thanks for all the mail. I can't tell you how great it is to hear from you. They're keeping us busy here, so we barely have a moment to ourselves. It's hot and miserable, but the desert has its own beauty, too. (Or so they say. I haven't discovered it yet, but give me time.) We're all working together toward a common purpose and because of that, everyone's pretty much able to look past any discomfort.

I know you don't want to hear this, but it looks like we're going into battle soon. The brass haven't discussed their battle plans with me, but war seems inevitable. I don't want to die. If it happens, though, I want to be prepared for it. That's one of the reasons for this letter. Mom, you've been the greatest. I couldn't have asked for a better mother in the whole world and I'm not just saying that. I mean it with all my heart. I know that life with Dad was never easy for you, but you did everything you could to hold the family together. Lindy might not believe that, but Doug, Christopher and I do.

I haven't heard from Dad in years. None of us have, but I feel like I should make my peace with him. I talked to a lady who works with the Red Cross and she said she could help me locate him. I've written him a letter and given her all the information I had. The last thing I remember, he was in Sitka, Alaska. That's right, isn't it? She said she'd do everything she could to find him and give him my letter.

Thanks, Mom, for phoning Meagan. She said it meant a lot to her. If I come out of this alive, I'm going to ask her to marry me. Do you have any feelings about that? I'd like to make you a grandmother within the next few years.

Don't worry about me, Mom. I mean that. We

each have a job to do on this earth and it could be that mine has been accomplished. You raised me as a Christian so I know where I'm headed if this is the end.

I'll write more as soon as I can, but I wanted to tell you that I've sought out Dad. I don't expect a reply, but there were things I needed to settle between him and me, just in case . . . I know you'll understand.

Love,
David

Lesley's Journal

February 4, 1991

I'm addicted to the television, watching news of the war. Desert Storm is a good name for it. It feels as though my entire life has been caught up in a sandstorm, a whirlwind of chaos and uncertainty. First David and Doug being shipped to the Middle East to fight for a country I'd never heard of until last year. Then Mrs. Milton died, and although it was expected, her death hit me hard. She was such a gracious, kind and generous woman. Poor Dr. Milton seems lost without her. He's only been back to work these last two weeks and just isn't himself. This is such a difficult time for him.

Cole Greenberg is one of CNN's correspondents from inside Baghdad. Whenever his face flashes on the screen, I feel breathless. I'm instantly flooded with all these emotions I'd prefer not to confront. He was sincere with me, and I was young, foolish and afraid. My divorce from Buck left the children so needy, shaken to their core, and I had to be there for them 100%. I still believe it was best to cut things off when I did, even though I have my regrets.

Everyone expects the ground war to start soon. So far, it appears we have reason to be optimistic. Hussein is doing everything he can to draw us into battle on the ground, which includes turning Kuwait into an environmental disaster area. I realize that as soon as the war starts, David will be in the thick of it. All I can do is pray and trust in God. Living hand to mouth the way we did when Buck was part of the family, I thought I knew what faith was about. But leaving the lives of two of my children in God's hands — that's *real* faith.

Jillian and I talk nearly every day now. She tries to hide how concerned she is about the war and David and Doug. She's afraid my sons won't be coming home. She's terrified of history repeating itself. I remind her that this isn't Vietnam, but I don't think she hears me.

She's coming for a visit in August. We have a condo booked in Mexico for a week.

No kids, no worries, just sunshine and laughter while we create more happy memories. My prayer is that by then, this terrible war will be behind us.

❖

P. O. Box 984
Lubbock, Texas 79460
February 11, 1991

Dear Lesley,

Surprise! I bet I was the last person you expected to hear from. It's been a while, hasn't it?

Listen, I owe you a shitload of child support, but the last few years haven't been easy. I had enough trouble supporting myself, let alone four kids. It looks like you did all right without me, though. I probably won't ever find the money to pay you what I owe. I wish things were different but they're not, and you might as well accept that. Knowing you, I suspect you already have. You were never one to hold a grudge.

After my stint in Alaska I headed for Texas, which was a mistake. I won't go into my troubles here, but there were reasons other than the child support issue why you didn't hear from me. I've been sober for six months and think I've finally got my problems with booze licked. I've got a job and a decent place to live. I was married a second time but that was another mistake I made in the last thirteen years.

Enough about me. I had the surprise of my life when I heard from David. His letter arrived last week and I have to tell you it shook me up pretty bad. I had no idea he was over in the Middle East. Doug, too, he said.

I'm concerned about David. What he said in his letter led me to believe he doesn't expect to come home. I've probably told you this before, but I've done a lot of things I regret. I'm not ashamed to admit it. Hell, everyone makes mistakes. But marrying you and fathering four children are the things of which I'm proudest. You did one hell of a good job raising 'em, and you did it with damn little help from me.

Getting David's letter made me realize everything I walked away from when you asked for that divorce. I talked with my AA sponsor, and one of the twelve steps to recovery has to do with making retribution wherever possible. If it takes me the next fifty years, I swear I'm going to make up to you for all the grief I caused you and the kids.

I guess what I'm saying is I want to be part of the family again. David said you'd never remarried. I'm glad, Lesley, because that means I have a chance. Tell me I do. It would mean the world to me.

I handed in my notice at work this morning. It won't take much to pack up everything I have. I'll probably have to nurse my truck along the way, but it should get as far as Washington. If all goes well, I'll be back in Pine Ridge before March 1st.

For the first time in a lot of years, I have hope. I gotta tell you, it feels damn good.

See ya soon.

Buck

❖

February 15, 1991

Dearest Dad,

I don't know if this will reach you before you leave Texas, but I had to try. Mom has let it be known that you aren't welcome to live with her and Christopher, but you can stay with me if you want. I have a cat and it's just a small studio apartment, but we can manage, don't you think? It will be good to see you again.

Your daughter,

Lindy

❖

From the Department of Defense

Addressed to: Mrs. Lesley Knowles

February 16, 1991

It is with deep regret that we inform you that your son David Michael Knowles

Is Missing in Action

In

Iraq

JILLIAN LAWTON GORDON
331 WEST END AVENUE
APARTMENT 1020
NEW YORK, NY 10023

February 20, 1991

Dearest, dearest Lesley,

I can't sleep. I know we talked for an hour already, but I'm still in shock. I can't accept this is happening. The ground war has yet to start. How can David be missing? You explained everything to me, but I'm having a hard time taking it in.

At least there's hope. We know that when the helicopter went down, there were men seen on the ground who survived the crash. I have to believe David was one of those men, otherwise I think I'll go crazy. I can't allow myself to remember what happened to Nick. But as you've reminded me so often in the last few months, this isn't Vietnam and David isn't Nick.

I haven't stepped inside a church since Monty's funeral. I felt that God turned His back on me and to be honest, I haven't missed Him. You've always maintained your faith, and while I considered all that Bible talk fine for you, I wasn't interested. Religion is not the answer for me. But Lesley, I don't mind telling you how afraid I am, for David and for you. This situation is forcing me to relive the biggest nightmare of my life.

You say the word and I'm on the next flight out of here. If there's anything and I mean ANYTHING I can do, let me know. You're as close as any sister I could have had.

Love,

Jillian and Leni Jo

❖

LESLEY KNOWLES

February 25, 1991

Dear Cole,

In 1980 I decided it would be best if I didn't contact you again. The decision was difficult, and I made it at a particularly rocky time in my life. Now I find that I'm changing my mind.

Two of my sons are part of Desert Storm. David is with the 101st Airborne Division and Doug is aboard the aircraft carrier *Independence.* Last week, two men came to the house bearing news that David is Missing in Action. There is strong evidence that he was taken as a prisoner of war. At this point, Iraq is refusing to release any information pertaining to him or his welfare, if he is indeed a captive. You can imagine what not knowing is doing to me.

Cole, is there any possibility that you can discover anything about his whereabouts and condition? I've faithfully followed your reports from Baghdad and am praying that you might know someone, someplace, who can give you information regarding my son.

I've thought of you often through the years and wondered how life is treating you. I'm well, but I don't know how much longer I can hold on to my sanity if I can't find out what's happening to my son. I would be deeply grateful for anything you're able to learn.

I ask your forgiveness in advance if I'm imposing on our friendship. I don't know where else to turn or who else I might ask.

I can't thank you enough,

Lesley Knowles

❖

JILLIAN LAWTON GORDON
331 WEST END AVENUE
APARTMENT 1020
NEW YORK, NY 10023

February 20, 1991

Dear God,

I've come to You before. When I didn't get a letter from Nick, I prayed. When my husband was gravely ill, I pleaded for a miracle. The deepest prayers of my heart have gone unanswered. Now the oldest son of my dearest friend is missing, half a world away. I feel lost, helpless and empty. This is the same feeling I had all those years ago with Nick, and it's tearing me apart.

I have been so angry with You. You're supposed to be a God of love. Well, thanks very much, but I haven't felt Your love in a very long time.

In the past, I've tried to bargain with You. If You do this for me, then I'll do that. My "Let's Make A Deal" attempts have failed, haven't they? You don't want or need anything I can give You. I realize that now. Lesley says that all You've ever wanted was for me to surrender myself to You. Well, I'm desperate enough to give it a try.

So here I am, God, willing to do as You ask, willing to place David's fate in Your hands. It isn't easy, but I'm ready to let go and to let You take over now.

Judge Jillian Gordon

❖

COLE GREENBERG
CNN CORRESPONDENT

March 1, 1991

Dear Lesley,

Thankfully, we were able to connect by phone, so most of what I found out you already know. I can appreciate your relief after learning that

David is alive and reasonably well. Given the rate at which the ground war is proceeding, it shouldn't be much longer before he's released with the other captives.

As I explained earlier, I wasn't able to speak with him directly, as David is being held in a restricted area. But through my contacts I did get a message to him and I got one in return.

It's selfish of me to be grateful for this opportunity to speak to you again. Has it really been eleven years? It seems just a short time ago that you and I were corresponding, doesn't it? You didn't ask and I didn't volunteer this, but I want you to know I've never been married. It appears you haven't married again. For my part, I've been too involved in my career, traveling constantly, landing in one trouble spot after another. I assume you've remained single because of your children. You made it clear even back then that your family was your priority. I understood that because I felt the same way about my career.

As I said earlier, this war is just about over. It'll be a pleasure to leave Baghdad and return to New York. I've got plenty of vacation time accrued and I'd like to see you, Lesley. You asked a favor of me and now I'm asking one of you. Have dinner with me? As soon as I hear from you, I'll make my flight arrangements.

Until then,
Cole Greenberg

March 5, 1991

Dear David,

Your mother said she talked to you this morning after the Iraqis released you. It's good to learn you got through all that and you're okay.

I never had a chance to answer your letter, which found me in Lubbock, Texas. I've been living there for the last five years.

Like you wrote, our relationship hasn't always been the best. I accept responsibility for that. I was the one who let you kids and your mother down. I've had a problem with the bottle that dates back to before you were born. You were kind enough not to list all my faults and I thank you for that. Everything you said was right on.

Your letter arrived when I was at a low point, crawling out of another financial mess I'd gotten myself into. But this time, at least, I was sober and could see my way clear of it.

Discovering what a fine upstanding soldier you are and hearing about your brothers and sister made me proud. It's been years since I've had reason to feel like that about anything in my life. Your mother's the one who deserves the credit for raising you right, but I was there in the beginning. I had a little to do with it, too. The television reporter talked about you and said you were a hero. The buttons nearly burst off my shirt when he said that.

What I'm getting around to saying is that your letter gave me hope that I could come back to you all. I know your mother isn't going to welcome me into the family home with open arms, but Lindy said I could live with her for a while.

I've failed you in the past, David, but I intend to make it up to you now.

Your Father,
Buck Knowles

❖

David James Knowles
P.O. Box 984
Lubbock, TX 79460

You are hereby notified that you are in violation of your parole as stated in your court decree...Unless you contact your parole officer within the next five (5) days a warrant will be issued for your arrest.

Parole Board
State of Texas

❖

LESLEY KNOWLES

May 3, 1991

Dear Cole,

Our dinner was by far the most romantic of my life. You certainly know how to impress a girl! Champagne, candlelight and red roses. Thank you so much. I'm sorry you had to leave so soon, but I certainly understand.

In answer to your questions: Yes, I do want to see you again and yes, I think we just might have found something special.

Lesley

❖

Mr. and Mrs. Ronald Fullbright
Cordially invite you to the wedding of their daughter
Meagan Adele Fullbright
To
David Michael Knowles
Son of
Lesley Knowles
On Saturday, July 12, 1991
At three o'clock in the afternoon
First Baptist Church
Fullerton, California
Dinner and reception immediately following the ceremony

July 10, 1991

Lindy,

Sorry not to give you any notice, kid, but it became necessary for me to head out. I didn't have a lot of choice about this so don't be upset. The neighbor promised to feed your cat. I know you and your mother and your brothers will have a good time at David's wedding. He understands why I can't be there. Seeing that he chose not to mention my name on his wedding invitation, it seems he's not very anxious for me to come, anyway.

I'll be in touch.

Dad

Lesley's reading list for trip to Mexico with Jillian:

1. *Saint Maybe* by Anne Tyler
2. *The Firm* by John Grisham

❖

Book Jillian packed in her bag for Mexico:

1. *The Undeclared War Against American Women* by Susan Faludi

COLE GREENBERG
CNN CORRESPONDENT

August 8, 1991

Dear Lesley,

This note should be waiting for you when you and your friend return from Mexico. I'll be back in town September 7th. I hope you like Chinese food (and I'm not talking take-out chow mein, either).

Until the 7th . . .

Cole

A good man is hard to find
Lesley's fortune cookie

❖

JILLIAN LAWTON GORDON
331 WEST END AVENUE
APARTMENT 1020
NEW YORK, NY 10023

October 1, 1991

Dearest Lesley,

I haven't heard you sound this happy in years. I'm thrilled for you and Cole. You don't know how badly I wanted to shake some sense into you eleven years ago when you abruptly ended your relationship. I understood, but I wasn't sure I agreed.

Nothing you could tell me about Buck would surprise me. Why didn't Lindy mention earlier that he'd borrowed money from her neighbor? The poor kid must be mortified. It's bad enough that he left the way he did, but to place his own daughter in a financial bind is unforgivable. Lindy's always had her eyes closed when it came to her father. I hope she sees now why you wouldn't allow him to stay in your home. If you'd put out the welcome mat for Buck, I think I would've throttled you myself.

Thank goodness David and Doug weren't put in a position of having to defend him. And as for Christopher, I'm impressed (and relieved) that he was savvy enough to figure Buck out early on. One way and another, this whole year has been a bag of mixed blessings for you and your family.

I loved our time together in Mexico. Leni Jo informed me that she wants to go to camp every summer so I can travel anywhere I please and it won't upset her. Is my daughter telling me that she's a big girl and doesn't need her mother anymore? I wonder if she realizes that I still need her to need me. . . .

I'm having trouble slipping back into the routine of going to court every day. Dealing with everyone else's problems is fast losing its appeal. Who knows, I just might find a reason to retire early.

Mom's been feeling a little under the weather lately, but for 78 she's in remarkably good shape.

I know Cole is in and out of the country a lot, but as your fortune cookie says, a good man is hard to find. Cole is a good man.

Give everyone a hug from me.

Love,

Jillian

November 1, 1991

Mom,

Remember all I want for my birthday are Rollerblades.

Love,

Leni Jo

1993

Jillian's Journal

January 1, 1993

Happy New Year!

Happy is the way I feel, too. I'm content with my life. It's been just over six years since Monty's death, and it's taken me this long to feel comfortable with being a widow. Here's the surprising thing: now that I'm finally at peace with myself, I've met someone. Actually, I give my soon-to-be-eighty-year-old mother credit for introducing me to Gary Harmon. He lives in the building and he, ever the gentleman, introduced himself to her in the elevator. Next thing I know, Gary and I are having dinner together once a week. He's lonely, I'm lonely. He's a professional, I'm a professional. He's a widower and I'm a widow. What could be more perfect? Leni Jo thinks he's cool. That's a word she uses sparingly, so I know she's sincere.

I'm not the only one with a romance in my life. Lesley and Cole are still seeing each other. Cole's under contract to CNN and is constantly either on his way in or out of the country. How Lesley keeps track of his schedule is beyond me. The best part is that in between the numerous interruptions, they've managed to build a solid friendship. Cole is good for her. For the first time in her life, Lesley's experiencing a healthy, mature relationship with a man.

Well, Dad, brace yourself — another Democrat is about to be inaugurated into the White House. Are you rolling over in your grave? William Jefferson Clinton seems to have a number of refreshing ideas, and I can't help it, I like him and his wife. Hillary is going to rub a few people the wrong way. Strong women generally do. I'm willing to give them both a chance and even if we don't agree on everything politically, I feel the change will shake things up.

I can almost hear you arguing with me, Dad, but I'm suggesting you keep an open mind, let them prove themselves. Hillary's ready to take on the health-care issue and Lord knows, it's about time somebody did.

Leni Jo loves high school and continues to excel. She's a marvel, if I do say so myself. We're close and we can talk about anything. She's now starting to think about boys, but I have confidence in her good sense and her self-respect. I see girls her age in court every week who are already mothers. Babies having babies, as the social workers say. I feel such despair when I encounter these tragic girls with their often-hopeless lives — and even worse, their children. There seems so little I can do.

My term expires this year and there's pressure to run for reelection. I don't know yet. The thought of retiring is holding more appeal every day. I want to enjoy my daughter's teen years and give her the benefit of my time and attention. I sometimes wonder if all the problems Lesley has with Lindy might've been reduced if Lesley hadn't been forced to support the family, attend classes and divide her energy among four kids. No, I take that back. Lindy was a difficult child right from the start. Some people simply insist on learning their lessons the hard way. Unfortunately Lindy appears to be one of them.

Lesley had exciting news about David, though. He was hired by Microsoft, which is a wonderful opportunity for him. This is a company with a lot of promise. The only problem is the long hours he's putting in; in fact, Lesley said he often sleeps right there at the corporate offices. Meagan seems pretty understanding about it all, thankfully.

Doug's working construction for Nick's brother. Jim Murphy has owned his own company for the last ten years and is doing very well with it. No surprise there! When Doug's commitment to the Navy was finished, he returned to Pine Ridge. He needed a job, and I mentioned to Lesley that Jim was hiring and suggested Doug apply. Sure enough, Jim hired Doug and before long, he advanced to foreman for one of Jim's crews. Nick would be very proud of his brother's success. Angie sends me school pictures of the kids every year. Nickie Lynn will turn eleven in August. That child has a special place in my heart.

The year is getting off to a good start. I signed up for a new painting course and I love it. Painting relaxes me and I seem to be improving. I've even done a couple of portraits. There are plenty of flaws in my work, and to me they seem blatant, but no one else notices them as much as I do. I guess that's true of almost everything in life. In any event, I put forth my best effort, work hard and stare down the imperfections.

❖

January 10, 1993
Mom,

Can I borrow $300? You know I wouldn't ask if it wasn't important. I'll need it soon. I've enclosed a deposit slip for your convenience. I'll have it paid back on the first of the month. I promise.

Lindy

Surprise 80th Birthday Party for
Barbara Lawton
Helmsley Towers
331 West End Avenue
Apartment 1020
New York, NY
on
February 6th, 3 p.m.
Bring a balloon and be ready to laugh
Shh — remember it's a surprise!
Given by: Jillian Lawton Gordon
Leni Jo Gordon

Lesley's Journal

February 22, 1993

This hasn't been a good day. It started off with a crisis at work — we had a small fire in the building, one floor above us. Dr. Milton handled the situation beautifully. He was calm and in control, getting everyone out before the fire department arrived. I didn't take the alarm seriously at first and when I finally grasped that it was for real, was more concerned with transferring information onto a computer disk to take outside with me. Dr. Milton insisted I leave immediately; he firmly took my arm. Without any other choice, I walked out with him. We were the last two people to leave the building.

I went from one crisis to another. That afternoon, I had my annual appointment with my OB/GYN. Although I think the world of Dr. Milton, I feel uncomfortable about the idea of his giving me a pelvic exam. It's been easier to stay with the physician who delivered Christopher. However, after the fire this morning, I was in no mood for an exam, but it takes weeks to get an appointment with Dr. Nelson, so I went — and I'm grateful I did. There appears to be a problem. After the wretched periods I've had for the last five years, this didn't surprise me. He's scheduling tests for next month and we discussed the possibility of a hysterectomy. If that happens, I'll be looking at three to four weeks off work. After our disastrous morning, I didn't mention it to Dr. Milton. I'll wait until I know for sure and then tell him.

While I was at Dr. Nelson's office, the nurse asked about Lindy and the pregnancy. I could see that she instantly regretted saying anything when she saw my reaction. Lindy's pregnant? This was a huge shock! Then it hit me. She was desperate for $300 not long ago, and that's the cost of an abortion. I realized I'd given my daughter the money to abort my own grandchild. I've been sick at heart ever since. Sick to my stomach, too.

I called Lindy the minute I got home, and asked why she needed the loan, which I know better than to do. Early on, I learned that it's a mistake to give children the opportunity to lie. Wanting to correct myself, and before she could answer, I told her I knew about the abortion and asked about the baby's father. She immediately blew up at me and demanded to know if Christopher had told me. It's bad enough that she came to me for the money, but I consider it unforgivable that she involved her younger brother in this, too. Lindy ended up slamming the phone in my ear.

I should be accustomed to her outbursts by now, but I was upset. Still, I know it isn't me Lindy's angry with. It's herself. I called her again later that evening, and she tried to sound mature and sophisticated in an effort to assure me she knew what she was doing and why. She said that ridding herself of this pregnancy was best for all concerned. I asked her if it was best for the baby. That was when she started weeping. I longed to hold her. I longed to ask why she didn't discuss something so drastic with me first. I didn't, because I already knew the answer. My daughter was confident that this was what she wanted. She was afraid that if she sat down and talked this decision over with me, I might persuade her to change her mind. Now she's full of shame and regret.

Ever since we talked, I've been in a sad, weepy mood. I understand that I'm grieving for the loss of my first grandchild, and my failure as a mother. Poor Lindy. She assumed an abortion was an easy way out of her troubles, but there were consequences she didn't recognize or consider. I know she feels better that it's out in the open. It isn't my forgiveness she needs or even God's. Lindy has to learn to forgive herself.

❖

Lesley Knowles

From:	Cole Greenberg
To:	Lesley Knowles
Sent:	March 15, 1993
Subject:	Welcome to the World Wide Web!

March 15, 1993

Dear Lesley,

I'm glad you finally took my advice and came online. You'll find Prodigy a great way for us to keep in contact. I'm still in Waco, waiting out this David Koresh mess. The place is swarming with ATF officials. Talking to them, I get the feeling they don't know what the hell they're doing. This has the potential to blow up in everyone's faces if it isn't dealt with properly.

I can't say for sure when I'll be able to see you again. Soon, I hope. What's this about your needing surgery? It isn't serious, is it? Let me know when, and I'll work my schedule around it so I can be with you.

Don't worry, you don't need to spell out your problems with Lindy. You've been incredibly patient with her. Every kid makes mistakes. I certainly made my share.

I've got to go. Stay in touch. And thank David for me for setting you up with this computer system. It'll save us both a mint in long-distance calls.

Bye for now.

Cole

April 19, 1993

Mom,

Mr. Harmon phoned and wanted to know if you're interested in seeing *Kiss of the Spider Woman* with him. I told him you were. Give him a call otherwise, but he's getting really great seats. I was sure you'd want to go. Wake me up if you have any questions.

Oh, he got the tickets for next Friday night.

Love ya,

Leni Jo

April 20, 1993

Dear Dr. Milton,

Just a note to thank you for taking me to lunch for Secretaries' Day. This was an unexpected surprise, since I'm not your secretary! The lunch, in addition to the flowers, means a great deal to me. You've been a wonderful employer. I want you to know I appreciate my job and am grateful you took a chance by hiring me all those years ago. Your encouragement and belief in me saw me through the lean times. Without the flexible hours you willingly gave me, I might never have been able to obtain my degree.

Sincerely,
Lesley Knowles

Lesley Knowles

From: Cole Greenberg
To: Lesley Knowles
Sent: April 21, 1993
Subject: Please Forgive Me

Dear Lesley,

I'm sure you understand why I had to break our date. This whole Waco mess went crazy. If you caught my report, you saw what happened.

It was like being in the middle of a war zone. I've seen just about everything in my career, but this tops it. Heads are going to roll on account of this. Mark my words.

So I've got competition. The good doctor took you to lunch, did he? That's interesting. A fancy French restaurant, huh? You aren't even his secretary. What gives?

Cole

Cole Greenberg

From: Lesley Knowles
To: Cole Greenberg
Sent: April 22, 1993
Subject: You & Me

Dear Cole,

You're jealous! I love it. It's almost as if you and Jillian are comparing notes. She sent me a message and wanted to know if there was anything "romantic" developing between Dr. Milton and me. I want to reassure you both.

NO!

I'd never be able to look at him as anyone other than Dr. Milton. I couldn't even begin to think of him in any romantic way. He's my employer. So stop!

Lindy was over this evening and we talked again. Our relationship is on more solid ground now, although I ache for her and the poor choices she's made.

Let me know when you're able to visit again. It's been almost four months since I last saw you.

Love,

Lesley

BENCH AND BAR ASSOCIATION NEWSLETTER

NOTICE FROM

JUDGE JILLIAN LAWTON GORDON

Dear Members of the Bench and Bar:

I'd like to announce that after careful consideration I have decided not to seek reelection. I want to thank you for your continued support over the years. I eagerly anticipate traveling and spending time with my daughter.

Most sincerely,

Judge Jillian Lawton Gordon

From: Cole Greenberg
To: Lesley Knowles
Sent: July 1, 1993
Subject: I Miss You

Dear Lesley,

Are you sure you can't get away and join me here in Hong Kong? This is a wonderful kind of crazy. It's like a funky New Year's blast as Hong Kong reverts to Chinese rule. The hotels are swarming with British diplomats, Chinese officials and news crews.

I'll be landing in San Francisco on the fifth. Want to meet me there for one day? I'd stay longer, but I've got to get back to New York. I've booked an interview with Vince Foster for early in the week.

It seems I'm always having to apologize, doesn't it? Be patient with me, sweetheart. I was crazy about you nearly thirty years ago and nothing has changed.

Cole

❖

Dear Mrs. Gordon,

Thank you for the $25.00 for my birthday. I'm going to buy a Nirvana tape. I especially liked your letter. Mom told me that you used to date my Uncle Nick, but I didn't know he had a motorcycle and that he took you to the prom on the back of it (except you didn't really go to the prom). I think it's much more romantic that you danced under the stars at the football stadium. Is it the same stadium that's in Pine Ridge now?

Mom and Dad have a framed photograph of Uncle Nick in his Army uniform over the fireplace. I've always thought of that as just a picture of someone who died before I was born. Now he's a real person to me and it makes me wish he hadn't died in Vietnam. I wish I'd known him.

Thank you for the snapshot of you and my uncle Nick together. You looked different then, didn't you? I showed the picture to my best friend, Jennifer, and explained that I was named after the two of you. Nickie for my Uncle Nick and Lynn because it's your middle name.

Dad said you're going to retire this year. Jennifer told me her grandfather just retired and he's coming to visit her. When you retire, does that mean you'll be coming to Pine Ridge soon? I'd really like to see you. Dad said you're the only real family he has left and you aren't technically family. He says you are family, though, because you loved Uncle Nick and he loved you back.

Thanks again for the birthday money and for your letter.

Love,
Nickie Lynn Murphy

Lesley Knowles

From: Jillian Gordon
To: Lesley Knowles
Sent: August 10, 1993
Subject: My Visit

Dear Lesley,

My last day on the bench is October 1st so if you can schedule your surgery after that, I'll be available to come and spend time with you. I know Lindy will be there and the boys, too, but they're kids. And do you seriously think you can count on Cole to show up? Hasn't he broken the last five dates he's made with you? Okay, three, but you get the picture. (Actually I'm the one who's beginning to get the picture!) Let me know what you decide.

Jillian

September 1, 1993

HAPPY BIRTHDAY, MOM
Here's the news you've been waiting for!
Due March 17, 1994
YOUR FIRST GRANDCHILD
Sponsored by
DAVID AND MEAGAN KNOWLES

Sales Receipt

Linda's Knitting Needles
Pine Ridge, WA
6 50-gram balls @ $4.25
Baby Blanket Book $5.95
Tax 8.1%
Total $34.00
Check #1299 for $34.00

❖

Lesley Knowles

From: Cole Greenberg
To: Lesley Knowles
Sent: October 4, 1993
Subject: Michael Jordan

Dearest Lesley,

I've got an interview scheduled with Michael Jordan for October 6th. He's about to make one of the biggest announcements of his career and he's agreed to speak to me first. Are you curious? I'm going to make a stab at guessing what he's going to say. Let's see how close I am. He's planning to retire from basketball and try his hand at baseball. Mind you, this is pure speculation on my part, but we shall see.

I know, I know, I'm supposed to be in Pine Ridge right after that, and I will be. I'm flying in on October 7th and we'll spend three whole, glorious weeks together.

I'll see you again the following month. Thank you for understanding that I've got to be in D.C. to cover the November 2nd elections. But I know Jillian's arriving November 3rd and the surgery is scheduled for the 5th. I'll be at the hospital when you come out of the anesthesia.

Love,

Cole

P.S. If Michael Jordan commits suicide the day before I interview him the way Vince Foster did, I'm leaping off a bridge myself. As it is, I'll go to my grave wondering what Foster might have told me.

❖

November 1, 1993

Dear Jillian,

I know you're busy packing for your flight to Seattle, but I wanted to let you know that I'll miss you while you're gone. I understand Leni Jo is staying with your mother. I'll make a point of checking up on the two of them while you're away.

If there's anything you need, don't be afraid to ask.

Sincerely,

Gary Harmon

P.S. I'm on Prodigy if you want to get in touch via the computer

LESLEY KNOWLES

November 10, 1993

Dear Steven,

It's going to take me a while to think of you as Steven and not Dr. Milton, but in time it will be more natural for both of us. Thank you for the huge and very beautiful bouquet of flowers. I don't think I've ever seen a more gorgeous arrangement.

Having you there at my bedside when I came out of the anesthetic was one of the more pleasant elements of this ordeal. I appreciate your answering Jillian's middle-of-the-night questions, too. I suspected I'd developed a bladder infection following the surgery, but she wanted confirmation. You'll have to forgive my friend. She was convinced it might've been something serious. You were the one person she felt she could contact any time of the day or night. Jillian returns to New York the first of next week and I'll be back to work directly after Thanksgiving.

Thank you again for the flowers.

Sincerely,

Lesley

P.S. You're welcome to visit anytime. Also, if there's a question relating to matters at the office, I'm available.

❖

Gary Harmon

From: Jillian Gordon
To: Gary Harmon
Sent: November 11, 1993
Subject: I'm Coming Home

Dear Gary,

Thanks for keeping tabs on my mother and Leni Jo. I knew they'd be perfectly fine without me, but it helps knowing there was someone in the building they could call if they needed anything.

My friend is recuperating nicely. I'm flying home early Saturday morning. This has been a very satisfactory trip in a number of ways. As I explained earlier, I was born and raised in Pine Ridge. So, needless to say, this town has a lot of memories for me, most of them good. I saw several old friends and visited with people I hadn't seen in years. I have a special friend, a twelve-year-old who was named after me. We spent some time together and she's completely captured my heart. (I'll tell you more about her one day.)

Equally interesting is watching the action between the two men vying for Lesley's attention.

Cole is a longtime friend. Lesley and Cole renewed their acquaintance a couple of years ago. You've probably heard of him – CNN correspondent Cole Greenberg. He was scheduled to spend three weeks with Lesley. He managed to stay all of five days, left in a rush to cover some big story in Washington, D.C. and then came back the day of the surgery. His flight, however, got delayed and he didn't reach the hospital until Lesley was in recovery.

Act One, Scene Two. Enter Dr. Milton. Dr. Steven Milton, widower. Lesley has worked with him for years. He's all-around wonderful. Lesley has frequently told me what a good husband and father he is. Stable, secure, dedicated. He invited Lesley to lunch for Secretary's Day last April, and lo and behold, he was at the hospital during her surgery. In fact, he was holding her hand when she came out of the anesthesia. Cole wasn't there but Steven was. You get my point? So does Lesley. More importantly, so does Cole. He's sent her flowers every day since. Flowers, cards, candy. I wouldn't be surprised if – after leaving her dangling for the last two years – he finally found the courage to propose.

This visit to Pine Ridge has been wonderful, but I'll be happy to get home again. Don't you dare come to the airport. I'll grab a taxi.

Yes, let's definitely do dinner. I'll look forward to it.

See you very soon.

Jillian

From: Lesley Knowles
To: Cole Greenberg
Sent: November 28, 1993
Subject: You & Me

Dear Cole,

This isn't an easy message to send. It would probably be better if I wrote it as a letter, but I never know when you and the mail will connect. Besides, if I sent it through the news office, it could take weeks, and there's no telling how many other people would have an opportunity to read it. This isn't perfect, but it's the best I can do.

Your friendship over the last three years has meant a great deal to me. When I contacted you again in 1991, I was surprised to learn you weren't married. Now I understand why. Your career keeps you too busy for a wife or even a relationship.

During my recent surgery, I had the opportunity to spend time with someone I've known and worked with for many years. I've admired and respected him from the very beginning. His wife died almost three years ago and he deeply grieved her passing, but he's only 56, young enough to want love and companionship.

On Thanksgiving evening, Steven came to the house to talk about us. He was sincere and forthright and he asked if it was possible for us to date. He didn't want to intrude if you and I were serious.

Are we serious, Cole? I don't believe we are. We're each holding on to the other because of a fantasy we created nearly thirty years ago on a Hawaiian beach. If this relationship meant as much as it should, we would've found a way to be together. I'm not blaming you. I've been equally at fault. I was just as content to send e-mails as you were. We often went months without seeing each other.

I took a few days to think about Steven's question, and I'm ready to answer him now. I'm ready to tell him that you and I are the very best of friends, but that's all there is to the relationship. I'm fairly confident that once Steven and I start dating, we'll eventually get married. I might be taking a lot for granted, but I know him and I know how he thinks. He wouldn't ask to date me if he wasn't considering a long-term relationship. We both have grown children. We're comfortable with each other and we share the same values. In all honesty, I'm a little shocked by the strength of my feelings for him. I guess the foundation was always there and now the circumstances are appropriate — and right.

You've been a good friend to me, Cole.

Thank you for that and for your love, generosity and support. I wouldn't do anything in the world to hurt you. But I think you know as well as I do that while we made very good friends, we were never meant to be lovers.

Thank you for understanding.

Lesley

1997

Jillian's Journal

January 1, 1997

The nineties are speeding by so quickly. It seems I barely turned the calendar page to a new year and three more have slipped through my fingers. They've been eventful years, though, dealing with retirement, helping Leni Jo prepare for college, then losing Mom.

I still miss my mother. Her death caught both Leni Jo and me by surprise. It's almost two years since she died peacefully in her sleep. Leni Jo took it particularly hard. Mom's mental and physical health had started to deteriorate rapidly after her 80th birthday. I knew how desperately she wanted to remain in her own home; the decision to place her in a retirement center hung over my head and I'd delayed making it as long as possible. Even with her diminished capacity, Mom was well aware of her surroundings, and I simply couldn't take her away from everything that was familiar and comfortable to her. Not until there was no longer any choice did I move her to a nursing home. As it turned out, that was very near the end. I can't say her death was a blessing, but as always my mother's timing was impeccable. I miss her so very much.

Leni Jo loves Radcliffe. It's her first year away from home and I worry about her, but my daughter is certainly capable of forging her own path. She's let me know she isn't interested in practicing law, which doesn't hurt my feelings. She's talented and artistic — and has no idea what she wants to be or do with her life. At eighteen, she has plenty of time to figure it out.

I'm grateful we're so close. We talk either by phone or e-mail practically every day. I'm in frequent touch with Lesley, too. It almost feels as if we're back in high school, passing notes back and forth during class.

Gary Harmon and I continue to date, but not seriously. He'd like to make the relationship permanent but I'm not interested in remarrying, which has been a disappointment to him. I'm glad we can be honest with each other. Last year he explained that he didn't intend to live the rest of his life alone and then in June he started seeing another woman. To be honest, I was unsettled for a while but accepted that I was about to lose my dearest male friend. Apparently, the relationship didn't work out, and Gary and I are back together. We enjoy the same things, travel occasionally and are good companions. However, despite his preferences, this isn't a romantic relationship. Perhaps one day that'll change; I can't say for sure.

For now, I'm in a good place, emotionally and physically. With the Dow-Jones heading toward 7000, the investments Monty made for me have grown substantially. The ones I made for myself have done equally well. Whether credit should go to the Democrats or the Republicans is hard to judge. Dad, I know you have strong opinions on the subject, but I'm not up to arguing the point. Not on such a glorious day, the first of a new year.

If I were looking for an omen, I'd point to Hale-Bopp, which has proven to be a truly majestic comet visible to the naked eye. I was excited about the return of Haley's Comet back in 1991. All that news coverage and then what a disappointment. But Hale-Bopp is supposed to be incredible, and since it won't return until the year 4397, this is truly a once-in-a-lifetime event!

Lesley and Steven have been married nearly two years, and I can't recall any time in her life that she's been happier. I love Steven myself for being so wonderful to my dearest friend. They enjoy traveling and are constantly going here and there, especially now that he's taken on a partner and reduced his hours. No one seeing them together for the first time would guess that they're practically newlyweds. They know each other so well, it's as though they'd been married their entire lives.

Lesley took up golf and to her husband's delight, shows a real knack for it. Steven has been the father to her children that Buck was never capable of being. The boys idolize him, and he's managed to gain Lindy's respect simply because of the way he loves Lesley. At first I thought there might be a problem with his own daughters, but both have accepted Lesley and despite a few rough spots after they first started dating, everything's worked out on both sides.

Steven hopes to retire completely in the year 2000, and he and Lesley plan to spend a month in Central America treating the sick. They're going as part of a volunteer group, and I applaud their compassion and generosity. My own involvement will, however, be limited to a financial contribution.

David and Meagan are parents two times over, and Doug is married, too. I briefly met his wife at their wedding last October. Lesley thinks the world of Julie.

Thankfully, Lindy's had a turnaround. I don't know exactly what happened, but almost overnight, she went from being a rebellious, self-centered thorn in her mother's side to a responsible, well-adjusted adult. She's seriously dating a man any mother would love and, after much soul-searching, dropped out of school and accepted a position as a bookkeeper at Microsoft. David recommended her for the job but she was hired and promoted on her own merit.

Christopher surprised everyone and became

a teacher. He's working with Junior High kids who absolutely love him.

Our children are all settled and doing well. These have been the best years of Lesley's life. Mine, too, in some ways.

THIS DAY I WILL MARRY MY BEST FRIEND,
THE ONE I LAUGH WITH, LIVE FOR AND
DREAM WITH.
WE INVITE YOU TO BE WITH US AS WE BEGIN
OUR LIVES
TOGETHER.
LINDY KNOWLES
AND
JORDAN KEVIN PARKER
JUNE 7, 1997
2 P.M.
HIGHLINE CHRISTIAN CHURCH
2189 33RD AVENUE SOUTHEAST
PINE RIDGE, WASHINGTON
RECEPTION IMMEDIATELY FOLLOWING
RSVP

Lindy Knowles

February 10, 1997

Dear Dad,

I'm sending this to the last address I have for you, and that's care of your parole officer in Texas. No one's heard from you in a long time, two years at least. I want you to know I'm getting married in June to a truly wonderful man. We met last year, here at Microsoft, and started dating in September. I knew Jordan was the man I wanted to marry almost right away. Oh, Daddy, I'm so in love with him.

I took my time deciding on marriage, didn't I? Jordan's thirty-one, and has never been married, either. The funny part is I probably wouldn't have given him a second look a few years back. He's everything I was sure I didn't want. Successful, sane and sober!

Three years ago, I was dating losers. I attracted men more interested in drugs and alcohol than in me. Men I thought I could save from themselves. It wasn't until after I found out I was pregnant and had an abortion that I realized it wasn't *them* I was trying to save. I wanted to save *you.* I so wanted my father back that I was seeking out men just like you to redeem. Thankfully I woke up before I ruined my life.

I know this sounds critical of you. I don't mean to come across as harsh or judgmental. That's not my intention. The entire reason for this letter is to invite you to Jordan's and my wedding. I'd really like you to be there, Dad, and I'm giving you plenty of time to figure out a way to arrange it. If you need me to send you the money, then I'll do it. This is going to be a very important day for me, and I want you to witness the fact that I've grown up and chosen my life partner well. I'm eager for you to meet Jordan and get to know him.

As far as I am concerned, none of the past matters anymore. You've made mistakes and so have I. Everyone's always told me that I'm the Knowles kid most like you. Well, I want to show you that I'm capable of living a good life. If you see how happy I am, then maybe you can find that same serenity yourself. Here I go again, trying to save you, but that's all right because I took care of myself first this time.

I love you despite your problems and your weaknesses. Please let me hear from you either way. It would be good just to know you're all right.

Lindy

❖

East Side Imaging
30 East 60th Street
New York, NY 10021

February 17, 1997

Dear Mrs. Jillian Gordon,

Dr. Wilson has had the opportunity to review the x-ray from your mammogram. We request that you make an appointment with your gynecologist at your earliest convenience.

Sincerely,

Ruth Carey, R.N.

❖

Jillian Gordon

From: Leni Jo Gordon
To: Jillian Gordon
Sent: February 27, 1997
Subject: I'm Coming Home

Mom,

What do you mean, it looks like you need surgery? You can't just drop something like that on me!

This has to do with that lump in your breast, doesn't it? The one they found on your mammogram. I don't care what you say, I'm coming home for the surgery. Have you told Aunt Lesley yet? Let me know the day, and I'll make the arrangements immediately.

Oh, and Mom, I know now probably isn't the time to mention this, but I've met someone totally awesome. I'll give you more details later.

Love ya,

Leni Jo

March 20, 1997

The hospital released me this morning and it feels wonderful to be back in my own home. I'm very weak, and both Lesley and Leni Jo seemed to sense it. They put me to bed, ordering me to take a nap. Actually, I'm grateful and I relish these moments alone so I can record what happened while it's still fresh in my mind.

The surgery, which is so common among women, should have been routine. But for whatever reason, there were complications with the anaesthetic. In fact, Dr. Wilson, the surgeon, told Leni Jo and Lesley that I nearly died on the operating table. I think I must have, because I had the most incredible, lifelike dream.

The last thing I remember was looking at the anesthesiologist. She smiled at me and said calmly that everything would be over before I knew it. I closed my eyes – and that was when Nick came to me. I was so astonished to see him that I didn't know what to think. It was as though I was eighteen years old again. And Nick, with that cocky, sexy grin of his, looked just as he did thirty-one years ago. He took my hand and all the feelings I had when we first met came back, flooding me with a surge of unadulterated joy. Then he sat down, my hand in his, and started talking.

It was as if he'd been with me all these years. He talked to me about Monty, about the child I miscarried, about Leni Jo and her future. He told me he was pleased I'd made my peace with God. He reminded me that he had, too, in the worst of Vietnam.

I kept telling him this couldn't be happening. His response to that was a soft laugh. Then he raised my hand to his lips and kissed it. He told me he'd been waiting for me all this time, but that he was content to wait a while longer.

I've tried to remember as much of our conversation as I can, but I've already lost part of it. What I do recall is that Nick reminded me how much he loves me, even now. He's been dead nearly thirty-one years and he loves me as much as he did when we were teenagers. What's so astounding, he said, is that the power of love is stronger than any force known to man. Stronger than anyone has ever imagined. Love is strong enough to stretch from one world to the next, through all of time and through eternity. Stronger than life and stronger than death.

Nick assured me that when it was my turn to join him, he'd be waiting for me, along with my parents and Monty, and his dad, too. After that, he said he had to go. I protested and pleaded with him to stay, but he shook his head and told me not yet. Then he was gone.

The next thing I remember, I was awake in

the recovery room. Later, after I'd been moved to my room, I asked to speak to the anesthesiologist. When she arrived, I questioned her about people reporting lifelike dreams during surgery. She assured me it was a common thing and not to give it a second thought.

I can't do that. I refuse to dismiss this so lightly. That time with Nick was as real as . . . as my daughter and my best friend on the other side of this bedroom door. As real as my love for Nick.

I *want* to believe it was real. I've held the memory of that time close to my heart ever since the surgery, letting his words warm my spirit, and encourage me. Farfetched as this sounds, all my fears about death have faded away to nothing. Death no longer holds any dread for me.

Discovering I had cancer shook me. For Leni Jo's sake, I tried to hide how frightened I've been. I wasn't afraid for myself as much as her; I can't bear the thought of leaving my only child an orphan at eighteen. She still needs me!

I'm tired now. This is only part of the ordeal in confronting the cancer. Next I have chemotherapy and radiation treatments. I'm prepared to lose my hair and my dignity. They seem minor compared to the loss of my breast . . . and the possible loss of my life. It helps that I'm surrounded by those who love me — in this world and the next.

From: Lesley Milton
To: Steven Milton
Sent: March 23, 1997
Subject: Update on Jillian

My dearest Steven,

I thought I'd check in before I go to bed.

Jillian is doing well. Her chemotherapy starts almost immediately, and she assures me she's ready. She's been so calm through all this, so serene and peaceful. Her friend Gary has been wonderful and is completely devoted to her. It's obvious that he loves her. I know he'd like to marry her, but he didn't bring up the subject and neither did I. I was worried about her getting to and from the hospital for her treatments, but Gary plans to provide the transportation and stay with her. That's a great relief to both Leni Jo and me. Leni Jo heads back to school at the end of next week.

I'm grateful to have had this time with Jillian. We came so close to losing her during the surgery. I don't think she knows how very close it was.

I know you're curious and a bit uncomfortable about my seeing Cole, so I want to reassure you on that score, too.

Cole and I did have dinner and it was good to see him again. He looks well and happy. He's retiring June first, but I'll believe it when I see it. He's too much of a workaholic. As we chatted over a glass of wine, I realized we don't have much in common. We never really did. Part of what I saw in him — what attracted me most — was his insight into world events. I encouraged him, when he retires, to write about Vietnam and the changes since then. I told him he could be the Stephen Ambrose of our generation. He thanked me for that, and said it wasn't the first time he'd thought of becoming a writer. I hope he does.

One benefit of my stay is that I found the most beautiful pearl necklace for Lindy's wedding. What a thoughtful husband you are to think of such a lovely gift for my daughter on her wedding day.

I'll be home soon, my love. I miss you so much.

Lesley

❖

March 30, 1997

Dearest Aunt Jillian,

I hope you're home from the hospital and feeling better now. Will you still be visiting Pine Ridge for your friend's daughter's wedding in June? I hope so. It would be cool to see you again. It's always good to see you.

I'm taking driver's education and should have

my license by then, so if you need a ride anywhere just say the word. I'd love to be your chauffeur.

Your Niece,
Nickie Lynn Murphy

P.S. Mom and Dad send their love.

Peter Punch
Texas Parole Board
2190 Turtle Creek Road
Fort Worth, Texas 76105

April 5, 1997

Dear Lindy Knowles,

I'm writing in response to your query concerning the whereabouts of your father, David "Buck" Knowles. My last contact with him was in April 1996.

I regret to inform you that he died in a homeless shelter in November of last year. He was cremated by the city of Fort Worth.

Sincerely,
Peter Punch

Lesley Milton

From: Jillian Gordon
To: Lesley Milton
Sent: April 25, 1997
Subject: Re: Buck

Dearest Lesley,

I'm sorry to hear the news about Buck, but as you said, it's not really a shock. What a terrible way for Lindy to find out about her father's death. The boys might have reacted with more nonchalance, but I agree with you, it's bound to have an impact on them.

What about you, Lesley? You must've felt something, too. You were married to Buck for a lot of years and he is the father of your children. If you need to talk this out, give me a call.

Have you been watching the news from Grand Forks, ND? Those poor people! The town was half-underwater and everything that wasn't submerged was on fire. I happened to catch the CNN newscast, and you'll never guess who was reporting. Didn't you say Cole was retiring this year? Well, it appears he decided to hold off for a while. Same as you, I'll believe he's retired when I see it.

I'm feeling much better, thank you. Tell Lindy I wouldn't miss her wedding for the world. I sure as hell am not going to let a little thing like cancer keep me away!

I haven't met Leni Jo's male friend yet. Leave it to my levelheaded daughter to fall in love with an unemployed musician. I'm getting a taste of what my parents must have thought when I announced that I was in love with Nick and wanted to marry him. Nick, however, was employed! Paul Robbins isn't. I'll give you more details about this Bob Dylan wannabe when I hear them.I suppose it could be worse.

Love,
Jillian

Lesley's Journal

June 6, 1997

In a few hours, Steven will escort my daughter down the church aisle and Lindy will marry a good and wonderful man. I couldn't have found anyone better suited for her had I launched my own search! It's so clear to me that God's hand is on her and on this marriage.

Despite my certainty and happiness about the wedding, I'm a mass of nerves. I suppose every mother of the bride feels that way.

Lindy's wedding, the conviction of Timothy McVeigh for the horrible bombing in Oklahoma City a couple of years ago and the news of Buck's death are all keeping me awake. In light of all the bad news in this world, my ex-husband's death seems insignificant. Buck and I had been divorced more years than we were ever married, yet the news of his death hit me hard. It's understandable, I suppose. I loved Buck at one time, and he fathered all four of my children.

How I wish his life could have been different. I wanted better for him. Even after all the heartache and grief he brought me, I still had some feelings for Buck. I didn't believe it until Jillian asked me how I was taking the news. As I read her e-mail, the tears started to drip down my face. Once I started crying, I couldn't stop for the longest time.

What upset me so badly, I think, is that Buck had completely disassociated himself from the children and me. We didn't even know when he died. There was nothing on his person, nothing he carried with him, to link him to us. The letter stated that he lived in a homeless shelter. I find that difficult to accept.

The father of my children had sunk so low that he could no longer function in society. All I can say is I hope he found peace in death, because it was sadly missing from his life.

The boys accepted the news without any open display of emotion. Christopher was so young when we divorced that he barely remembers Buck. David and Doug and Lindy remember him, though. All her life Lindy's made excuses for her father. All her life she defended him to her brothers and me.

When she brought me the letter from

Buck's parole officer, her face was expressionless, as if she'd always known it would come to this, in spite of her hope that his life could be salvaged. I'm grateful Jordan was with her when she opened the envelope. She's going to be all right, I think, and so am I.

Within a few hours, my daughter will be Jordan's wife. Steven will fill in as her father. She was the one who made the request that he walk her down the aisle. I know that meant a great deal to him. For a long time, Lindy made it abundantly clear that she never wanted me to remarry. She still held out hope that Buck and I would reconcile. My little girl has done a lot of growing up in the last few years, and I'm very, very proud of her.

As a matter of interest, Cole Greenberg reported the news of the Timothy McVeigh trial. I don't think he'll ever retire. He's just not the type. I did notice something interesting, however. He's no longer with CNN. I saw him on the Fox News Channel. I wonder what that's all about.

❖

Paul Robbins

From: Leni Jo Gordon
To: Paul Robbins
Sent: June 8, 1997
Subject: Lindy's Wedding

Dearest Paul,

The wedding was so romantic. Lindy was a beautiful bride. My mom had tears in her eyes when Lindy walked down the aisle. I can only imagine Mom's reaction when she hears about you and me. No, I haven't told her that we plan to get married next year. Not yet. It'd freak her out.

This being apart is awful. I miss you, too, and I promise to e-mail you every day I'm in Washington State.

Love,
Leni Jo

❖

September 15, 1997

Dear Mom and Steven,

Julie and I want to invite you to dinner next week if you're available. We have a surprise for you both. Mom, it's time to bring out those knitting needles again. I hope you're planning on being around in February.

Love,
Doug and Julie

Jillian's Journal

November 20, 1997

Dearest Nick,

It's been years since I last wrote you. I gave it

up shortly after Monty died, but since my surgery and the dream, I feel closer to you than ever. Each night as I settle my head on the pillow and close my eyes, it's almost as if you're there with me. My mind is filled with thoughts of you. The dream keeps playing back in my mind: what you said, what you implied, what you promised. I've held on to as much of it as I could.

I used to be so impatient. That's been an unexpected benefit of having cancer — I've developed a whole new perspective on the meaning of time. Things that seemed terribly important a year ago have faded in significance — and vice versa. I've learned that small things matter — the moment of laughter, the beauty of autumn leaves, the sensation of wind on my face. You know what I mean, don't you?

I think a lot of people have felt that way since Princess Diana died. The news of her death touched everyone. There's been an almost unprecedented outpouring of grief, worldwide. It seems as though people needed that collective release of emotion, as though this was more than a response to one individual death.

The world is vastly different from the one you left behind. Everything happens at the speed of light. The Internet is capable of far more than relaying messages. People are online for every conceivable reason. There's even this site where people can auction items and you wouldn't believe what's being sold. War medals (which bothers me and would no doubt upset you, as well), Elvis albums, even Texaco signs from the 50s.

This year a sheep was cloned and just yesterday a 29-year-old woman gave birth to seven children. Our lives are being affected every day by scientific and technological change, and that is ever constant. Still, the one thing that remains steadfast through everything is love. That's the message you gave me, isn't it?

Leni Jo is head over heels in love and I'm biting my tongue to keep from saying things I shouldn't. I wanted someone a little more sensible, more stable, than this musician. Paul is very sweet and talented, but he isn't exactly brimming with ambition.

Just tonight, Leni Jo phoned to tell me they want to get married. I tried to remain calm, but I'm not sure how successful I was. Thankfully, she promised not to do anything until we've had a chance to talk. I'd be a whole lot more comfortable if Paul had a job!

Then I think about the two of us and how impossible we thought my parents were when we announced our feelings for each other. I told my dad in no uncertain terms how badly I wanted to marry you. Now history's repeating itself (well, sort of) in my daughter. Amazing, isn't it, how I've been given the opportunity to view this situation from the perspective of a parent? I wonder who said God didn't have a sense of humor.

2000

Jillian's Journal

January 1, 2000

For the first time in years, I stayed up past midnight to celebrate the New Year. Leni Jo insisted I should, and she was right. Like everyone else, I got caught up in all the hoopla surrounding the new millennium.

Fortunately, the dreaded Y2K bug didn't turn into the disaster the experts had predicted. If the world's computers had crashed, some of them would not have been missed – especially the ones having to do with government. I'm beginning to sound cynical, but it's hard not to, after the last year, during which the entire country was preoccupied with Clinton's affair. The impeachment process took months and millions of dollars, which could have been better spent. I blame Clinton for that waste. In fact, given his intellectual gifts, I consider much of his time in office a wasted opportunity. Good Republican that my father was, I imagine he's frothing at the mouth because of the corruption that's come out of the Clinton presidency. As for me, I've lost faith in both parties.

New Year's Eve was an incredible experience in New York! Gary, Leni Jo and I had a late dinner, then sheer madness overtook us and we joined the throng in Times Square. I couldn't believe I agreed to this, but I was just as excited as everyone else. Leni Jo said we'd regret it our entire lives if we didn't go. Years from now, she wants me to be able to tell my grandchildren I was there to celebrate the big moment, when New York ushered out one millennium and welcomed in the next. How grateful I am that I could spend this New Year's with my daughter and Gary.

I will admit that this is a wonderful time to be alive. When I think back over all I've seen in my 51 years, I stand amazed. I remember how thrilled my father was about the transistor radio. My great-aunt Jillian crossed the prairie in a covered wagon when she was just an infant, and before she died in the mid-60s, she flew in a jet plane. All of this in one lifetime!

When Leni Jo and I returned to the apartment, Gary wished us both a good night, and then my daughter and I sat up for another hour, talking. Time for just the two of us is a rarity these days and much to be valued.

My daughter is content and has been able to put the unhappy events of last year behind her. She loves her job as an assistant curator at Sotheby's. Leni Jo has always had a deep appreciation of antiques, especially china and porcelain. This position is the perfect blend of history and beauty, of art and business. She has a trip to London scheduled this spring and wants me to tag along. She'll be meeting an associate in the London office with whom she obviously has a good working relationship. Her job has been a source of strength and pleasure during the turmoil in her personal life this past year.

Paul broke her heart. It was inevitable. I saw how ill-suited they were early on in the relationship, but Leni Jo had to discover this for herself. Difficult as it is to sit back and watch one's child suffer, there are certain life lessons that can only be taught by experience. I grieved with her, although I suspected from the beginning that Paul wasn't the right man for her. Soon, and I believe this with all my heart, she'll rush home to tell me she's met someone utterly wonderful who shares her interests and appreciates the woman she is.

Leni Jo's relationship with Paul led me to do some soul-searching about my first love. If Nick hadn't been killed, what would have become of our relationship? I couldn't help wondering if we would've eventually parted, like Leni Jo and Paul. Somehow, I couldn't make myself believe it. Even now, all these years later, Nick remains with me, a part of me. I love him so intensely that I've been unable to visit the Vietnam War Memorial. I just can't do it. (But I've promised myself that one day, I will.)

I'll be fifty-two on the 15th. My health is good, with no sign that the cancer is recurring. I get a shock every now and then when I happen to catch my reflection in a mirror. After the chemo, my hair grew in completely gray. Still, I've purposely left it that color, as a reminder of everything I've experienced. (Actually I think it gives me a dignified appearance!) I'm well aware that I look very much the middle-aged woman I am. Gary likes it and compliments me often.

Art takes up a good portion of my free time. Despite Leni Jo's protestations to the contrary, I don't think I'm particularly talented, but I derive such pleasure from it that the question of my ability is irrelevant.

My life has fallen into a set pattern. I'm reluctant to call it a routine. I rise early, do my reading and journal-writing. Then Lesley and I exchange e-mails. I still think of this communication via computer as an updated version of passing notes in class! I've come to find this Internet thing completely fascinating and often spend one or two hours browsing Web sites.

Around ten o'clock, Gary and I take a walk through Central Park. We have our own route, and our own pace. This time is more an excuse to be together, but the exercise is beneficial nonetheless.

I do volunteer work most afternoons. I've been a docent at several museums and right now, I'm mentoring a teenage girl at risk. In the process I've learned about facets of this city I never knew.

Life in New York certainly isn't dull, but I shall enjoy my trip to London with Leni Jo.

❖

Jillian Gordon

From: LesleyMilton@friendsnetwrk.com
To: JillianGordon@friendsnetwrk.com
Sent: January 1, 2000
Subject: Happy New Year!!!!!!

Dearest Jillian,

Do you remember in high school when we talked about the year 2000? We tried to predict what we'd be like at the turn of the millennium. You thought we'd be wearing our hair in buns, walking with canes and wearing black nun shoes. (Remember those ugly heels that laced up?) At fifteen, that was our view of anyone over age thirty. Are you laughing yet? That isn't even close to describing either one of us. Without a doubt, this is the best time of my life.

I'm blissfully happy and madly in love with my husband. When I look back through the years with Buck and then as a single mother, I shake my head in wonderment. Everything I endured, every challenge and difficulty that brought me to this point was worth it. I didn't realize how miserable I was at the time because it took so much effort just to make it through the day. Everything has changed, and for the better.

Our New Year's party with all the kids, grandkids and everyone was hilarious fun. Between my four and Steven's two daughters we had a full house. At midnight David and the boys lit fireworks. After the show, we closed the evening with a huge catered buffet.

Frankly, I'm exhausted. I'll gladly wait another 1000 years for a repeat of this celebration!

I can't believe you were in the middle of all that madness in Times Square.

Today is low-key. Steven and I are both planning naps this afternoon.

I'll check in with you later.

Lesley

GORDON/LENI JO

Globe Trotters Travel
225 Fifth Avenue
New York, NY 10010
Phone: 212 178-4521
FAX 212-178-4522

PAGE 1 OF 3

CA 456-9071

INV-058497 **TKT-E01210457858**

AIR-348.00 **TAX 82.00** **TTL AIR 430.00**

ITINERARY RECEIPT * ELECTRONIC TICKET * POSITIVE IDENTIFICATION REQUIRED AT CHECK-IN
****REQUEST TERMS/CONDITIONS OF TRAVEL AND CARRIER LIABILITY NOTICES FROM TRAVEL AGENCY OR THE TRANSPORTING CARRIER****

RESTRICTIONS – BA ONLY/NON-REFUNDABLE-PNLTY FOR CHGS
ISSUED BY GLOBE TROTTERS TRAVEL, NEW YORK, NY

17 MAR 747 **BA 178** DEPART: NEW YORK **9:05 P.M.** NONSTOP **SEAT 32-C** (Class-Q)
FRIDAY

17 MAR ARRIVE: LONDON **9:00:00 A.M.** BAGS ALLOWED-3PIECE
SATURDAY ARRIVE TERMINAL H
NOT VALID FOR TRAVEL-BEFORE 17 MAR/AFTER 18 MAR

GORDON/JILLIAN

Globe Trotters Travel
225 Fifth Avenue
New York, NY 10010
Phone: 212 178-4521
FAX 212-178-4522

PAGE 1 OF 3

CA 456-9071
INV-058497 **TKT-E01210457858**
AIR-348.00 **TAX 82.00** **TTL AIR 430.00**

ITINERARY RECEIPT * ELECTRONIC TICKET * POSITIVE IDENTIFICATION REQUIRED AT CHECK-IN
****REQUEST TERMS/CONDITIONS OF TRAVEL AND CARRIER LIABILITY NOTICES FROM TRAVEL AGENCY OR THE TRANSPORTING CARRIER****

RESTRICTIONS – BA ONLY/NON-REFUNDABLE-PNLTY FOR CHGS
ISSUED BY GLOBE TROTTERS TRAVEL, NEW YORK, NY

17 MAR 747 **BA 178** DEPART: NEW YORK **9:05 P.M.** NONSTOP **SEAT 32-B** (Class-Q)
FRIDAY

17 MAR ARRIVE: LONDON **9:00:00 A.M.** BAGS ALLOWED-3PIECE
SATURDAY ARRIVE TERMINAL H
NOT VALID FOR TRAVEL-BEFORE 17 MAR/AFTER 18 MAR

JILLIAN LAWTON GORDON
331 WEST END AVENUE
APARTMENT 1020
NEW YORK, NY 10023

March 15, 2000

My dear Nickie Lynn,

I wanted to get this in the mail before I left for England. I'm joining my daughter there for three weeks of relaxation, fun and shopping.

Inside the box is a small medal. It's something very special that I've waited all these years to give you. This medallion has a long Murphy family history. It first belonged to your grandmother and she gave it to your Uncle Nick before she died. Years later, Nick gave it to me and I wore it around my neck as a reminder of his love. I'd recently left for the East Coast and college, and missed him terribly. He told me that whenever I got lonely I should hold on to it and remember how much he loved me. I didn't remove it until the Army assigned his tour of duty in Vietnam. That was when I mailed the medal back to him, and asked him to wear it. I prayed his mother's love and mine would protect him.

When I learned he'd been killed, my grief was so great that I completely forgot about his mother's medallion. When I did remember it, I assumed it'd been buried with him. Then in 1983, a friend of Nick's, a fellow soldier, contacted me. He had the medal. Apparently Nick had asked Brad to return it to me if anything happened to him. For one reason and another, it took Brad twenty-one years to keep his promise. I have worn this medal close to my heart from that day forward.

At twenty you're old enough to appreciate its history and its sentimental value. I'm convinced that the grandmother you never knew would want you to have it. I want it to be yours, too. Wear it with pride and my love.

Your parents gave me one of the greatest honors of my life when they named you after Nick and me. I've had the pleasure of watching you grow into an accomplished and beautiful young woman.

You have your whole life ahead of you. I know how proud your family is that you've chosen to become a teacher. Wherever life takes you and whatever you do, remember that you are deeply loved by your parents, by your Uncle Nick and by me.

Jillian Gordon

Lesley's Journal

April 15, 2000

I can't believe how much I miss Jillian. Three weeks has never seemed so long. It would help if we'd been able to e-mail the way we planned. I can't understand why anyone would be so heartless as to infect hundreds of thousands of computers with a virus, especially one that instantly aroused curiosity. Like lots of other people, Steven and I fell prey to the I LOVE YOU virus. Our whole computer system was destroyed, and we still aren't up and running.

Jillian will be back in New York tomorrow morning. Judging by the postcard she sent, she's had a wonderful time. Or so she'd have me believe. I've known Jillian nearly her entire life and something isn't right. I wish I could put my finger on what it is. (My fear, of course, is a return of the cancer, but I refuse to dwell on that possibility.)

Steven says I should fly out and see for myself, and I think I will. My friend might be able to fool others, even Leni Jo, but she can't pretend with me.

❖

Leni Jo's Journal

May 3, 2000

After three weeks away, it's marvelous to sleep in my own bed. Tired as I am from the flight out of Heathrow, my head is still buzzing. My heart, too. William Chadsworth is the reason. We've worked together for fourteen months via fax and computer.

The relationship was strictly business. For all I knew, he could have been a sixty-year-old curator. Thankfully he's not!

I don't know what he felt when we first met, but the strangest, most wonderful sensation came over me. This was meant to be a working vacation for Mom and me. I did plan to do some sightseeing and shopping with her, but Will and I ended up spending every spare moment together.

It's unsettling to think I could've fallen in love on such short acquaintance, but he's everything I've ever wanted in a man. I especially liked the way he treated my mother. I think she's half in love with him herself! He was so thoughtful and kind to both of us.

Mom didn't fool me. Most nights, she pleaded tiredness, so Will and I could spend time alone. Three weeks has never passed more quickly. He's ten years older, but that doesn't bother me. Dad was fifteen years older than Mom and they had a wonderful marriage.

I miss Will already, but if the five e-mails awaiting me once we reached home are any indication, he feels the same way. We both feel it's necessary to give this attraction a bit of time. Since he's in London and I'm in New York, that won't be a problem.

Our plan is to communicate via the Internet and by phone for the next six months, with the occasional visit when we can manage it, and then we'll see how we feel. That's the sane, sensible approach. I'm certainly in no rush to become involved again, especially after my break-up with Paul.

Will could meet someone else. For that matter, I

could too. Mother said there are advantages and disadvantages to long-distance relationships. Just now, I'm painfully aware of the disadvantages.

He's already suggested he visit New York in July; that would be perfect. This time the meeting won't be work-related. I'm counting the days already.

Mother liked Will immediately and she's an excellent judge of character. She knew after meeting Paul just once that he wasn't the man for me and she was so right.

I'm not the only one having company this year. Aunt Lesley's booked a flight for the first part of October. Apparently the trip's a birthday gift from Steven. It will be so good to see her again.

❖

Jillian Gordon

From: LesleyMilton@friendsnetwrk.com
To: JillianGordon@friendsnetwrk.com
Sent: July 25, 2000
Subject: My visit

Jillian,

I'm planning my itinerary. What do you think of visiting Washington, D.C.? I've always wanted to see the Smithsonian and the Washington Monument. Are you ready to visit the Vietnam Memorial?

Lesley

Lesley Milton

From: JillianGordon@friendsnetwrk.com
To: LesleyMilton@friendsnetwrk.com
Sent: July 26, 2000
Subject: Your visit

Dearest Lesley,

I'll be happy to visit Washington, D.C. if you want, but I'll skip the Vietnam Memorial this go-round.

We had quite a scare. Remember I told you that Leni Jo met a wonderful young man (a colleague in England)? He came over here to visit her. Originally he'd planned to catch the Concorde out of Paris. The very one that crashed and killed everyone onboard. Thank God he decided to book another flight!

This man is the one. I had that feeling the moment I first saw my daughter and William together. My guess is they'll be married within a year. I haven't seen Leni Jo this happy in a very long time.

She's so calm about it, so like Monty. William is well aware of what a joy she is. I hate the thought of her moving to London, but I suspect that's the way it'll have to be if they do get married.

Everything about this relationship feels right.

Jillian

Riverside Clinic
258 West 81st St.
New York, NY 10024
Dr. Louise Novack, Oncologist

August 11, 2000

Dear Jillian Gordon,

The blood work from your most recent check-up is in. Please make an appointment with Dr. Novack at your earliest convenience. We look forward to seeing you soon.

Sincerely,
Pat Terrney, R.N.

❖

Lesley Milton

From: JillianGordon@friendsnetwrk.com
To: LesleyMilton@friendsnetwrk.com
Sent: August 25, 2000
Subject: Your visit!!!!!

Lesley,

I've had a change of heart about visiting the Vietnam War Memorial. You're absolutely right (savor the moment!). It's time I faced the Wall.

I can't wait for you to get here. We're going to have a fabulous time.

See you the first week of October.

Love,
Jillian

September 19, 2000

Good Morning, Mom!

The coffee's on and I'm leaving for work early this morning. Did you hear Will and me on the phone last night? I couldn't believe he'd pay the big bucks to call when it's so easy to e-mail. But he had something to ask me and he didn't want to do it over the computer. I'll bet you can guess.

Mom, Will asked me to marry him and I told him yes. Then I got teary-eyed because I wished so badly that I could be with him. His visit in July seems like a lifetime ago. We want to be together and the sooner the better.

Neither Will nor I wants a long engagement, and we both prefer a small wedding. I hope that doesn't disappoint you. Now, here's the second part. We'd like to be married in London. Will's family is much larger than mine and it only makes sense that you and I travel to London instead of asking his parents, twin sister and brother to trek all the way to New York. We can have a reception here afterward, if you want. I didn't want to wake you to discuss it, so I made an executive decision and agreed. I didn't think you'd mind.

I was so happy and excited after we talked that I couldn't sleep. When Paul and I broke up I thought I'd never want anything more to do with men. You said I would and you were, of course, right. Oh, Mom, I'm so in love. Will is a wonderful, wonderful man and I'm crazy about him.

Call me once you're up. Shall we celebrate tonight

and have dinner out? I think we should.

Love,

Leni Jo

Jillian's Journal

October 15, 2000

I saw Lesley off early this morning and only now have time to reflect on her visit. With my dearest friend here and Leni Jo bustling about planning her wedding, I've barely had a moment to myself. Everything seemed to be happening at once. Leni Jo glows with happiness, and just being around her, I get caught up in her excitement and joy. Lesley is thrilled for her, too.

The highlight of her visit was our trip to Washington, D.C. I'd dreaded seeing the Vietnam War Memorial; I've avoided it for years. I was sure the emotion would be too much, that it would overwhelm me and break through all my hard-won contentment, my resignation. And the minute I found Nick's name engraved in the Wall, that's exactly what happened.

I'm thankful Lesley was with me. We hugged and wept together. When I found the strength, I placed my fingertips against Nick's name. At the same time, I saw my own reflection in the black marble. Actually and metaphorically, emotionally and spiritually, he was part of me. In all the years he's been dead, I've never felt his presence this profoundly — even more strongly than the day I had that near-death experience. I felt a sense of peace. I held my head high, proud to have loved Nicholas Patrick Murphy, proud of the sacrifice he made. The politics of the Vietnam War are forgotten, pondered only by historians, but the men and women who died there will continue to live in our hearts.

Visiting the Wall changed me. I wish now that I'd gone years ago. I remember Brad Lincoln's letter after his visit to the Vietnam Memorial; unfortunately I couldn't find it. As I recall, he'd had a very similar reaction. The Wall certainly focuses one's thoughts — on death and on life. The brave and honorable men who are commemorated here will remain forever young, forever loved and forever remembered.

Lesley knows. I've never been able to keep a secret from her. We weren't together a day and she asked me about the breast cancer. It's back, more virulent than ever. With her, I could reveal my fears. For Leni Jo and Gary, I've put on a brave front, but this is my second confrontation with the ravening beast and I'm feeling uncertain. Dr. Novack wants to do a second surgery, followed once again by chemotherapy and radiation. Just when I'd grown accustomed to my full head of gray hair, it appears I'm going to lose it.

I want to live, but if I should lose this battle, then so be it. At least I'll die knowing my daughter is happy and settled. I know my son-in-law will look after Leni Jo.

I've told no one else, certainly not my daughter or Gary. I insisted Lesley keep my secret. With the wedding less than a month away, the last thing Leni Jo needs to hear is this. We'll both be forced to face it soon enough. I'm certainly in no rush. I'm doing everything that's asked of me, taking the medication, dealing with the doctors and the almost constant appointments. I have faith that everything that can be done is being done.

My one complaint is how tired I've been lately. I wished I hadn't told Lesley so soon after her arrival. From that point on, she was worse than a mother, constantly monitoring me, asking how I felt and whether I needed anything. I'm afraid my patience has been in short supply these last few days.

I think Gary has guessed. He's suggested shorter walks and only three times a week. He insisted his knees were bothering him, but I don't believe it.

I didn't mean to be morbid, but I've chosen a headstone. Lesley was appalled. I've already paid for the plot next to Monty. It made sense to do so when we buried him. I knew then that I would never remarry. I've been blessed to love two wonderful men in my life and I wasn't about to press my luck.

William Chadsworth

December 1, 2000

Dear Mom,

I realize it's somewhat premature to call you Mom, since Leni Jo and I won't be married until next weekend, but I didn't think you'd object.

The purpose of this letter is to thank you for raising Leni Jo to become the woman she is. The woman I love. Although we'd worked together for a number of months, she was little more than a name at the bottom of a fax. I knew nothing about her personally, although I'd come to admire her integrity and spirit.

Before I met Leni Jo, I'd despaired of finding a wife. She was like a summer breeze that swept into my life, bringing laughter and wonder and joy. I fell instantly in love with her. To my everlasting gratitude, she feels the same way about me.

My family loves her and like me, is thankful that she's willing to become one of us.

All of this is a circuitous way of thanking you for Leni Jo. I love her more than I dared believe I could love anyone. When we say our vows, I want you to be assured that I will love and care for her the rest of my life. My commitment to her is complete.

Sincerely,
William Chadsworth

JUDGE JILLIAN L. GORDON, RETIRED
IS PLEASED TO ANNOUNCE THE MARRIAGE OF
HER DAUGHTER
LENI JO GORDON
TO
WILLIAM HENRY THOMAS CHADSWORTH III
ON
DECEMBER 9, 2000
A RECEPTION TO HONOR THE COUPLE IS
BEING HELD AT
THE WATER CLUB
500 EAST 30TH STREET
DECEMBER 30, 2000
AT 3 O'CLOCK
RSVP

2001

Jillian's Journal

January 1, 2001

I wish I knew what's happened to the last 12 months. I don't need a calendar as much as a stopwatch these days. The weeks just melt away. In part this is due to how busy I've been this past year. First the trip to London with Leni Jo, then this second bout with cancer, which seems to occupy my every moment, all my strength and all my resolve. Even after the first run-in with cancer, I treated my health almost casually. This has been a lesson well learned. If I'm cured — not if, WHEN — I will never again take my health for granted.

Leni Jo is blissfully happy. Will is a marvelous husband and I think nothing of hopping on a flight to visit her for a few days whenever my treatment schedule allows. It's exhausting but worth it.

I've seen more of Lesley this year than in the last five. She was here for my surgery and stayed both before and after. Gary and my dearest friend took turns watching over me. I'm feeling somewhat stronger now, and I'm very encouraged, especially with the new medications I'm on. The chemotherapy is rough and depletes me emotionally as well as physically, but Lesley and Gary have done their best to keep my spirits up.

Gary and I are closer than ever. After Lesley left for home, he took it upon himself to see to my care and comfort. He's been wonderful and I'm deeply indebted to him. I know he e-mails Leni Jo and Will with regular updates. We continue with our daily walks and have dinner together at least three times a week and sometimes more. He's my companion and dearest friend — after Lesley, of course. I know he'd like us to marry, but he hasn't broached the subject in some time and frankly, I'm grateful. I wish I knew why I'm so hesitant. Fear, I guess. I've already had two great loves in my life, Nick and then Monty, and lost them both. I don't think I could endure that kind of emotional agony again. Lesley thinks I'm cheating Gary and myself, and perhaps I am, but I have enough to cope with. I can't think about marriage right now. Especially now. I don't know what the future holds, not when I'm living with cancer.

Well, this election mess is finally over, thank God. Within days, George W. Bush will be sworn into the White House. Who would've believed this fiasco would drag on for weeks? I only hope this kind of confusion and craziness never occurs again.

I'm growing tired – a constant problem these days – so I'll cut this short. Gary is taking me for a walk in the Park later and then out to dinner.

❖

Jillian Gordon

From: LesleyMilton@friendsnetwrk.com
To: JillianGordon@friendsnetwrk.com
Sent: February 28, 2001
Subject: Earthquake!

Dearest Jillian,

A quick note to let you know that I'm fine and so are all the kids. The news said the Seattle-area earthquake registered 6.8 on the Richter scale. I can believe it — we were all badly shaken. No pun intended!

Several photographs and pictures fell off the walls and all the drawers in the kitchen opened and stuff spilled onto the floor, but that's minor compared to the damage in downtown Seattle. Now I know why so few people around here have brick houses. Thankfully, Steven was home and we were together when the quake hit.

I'll get back to you as soon as I can, but I didn't want you to worry.

Love,

Lesley

Lesley Milton

From: JillianGordon@friendsnetwrk.com
To: LesleyMilton@friendsnetwrk.com
Sent: September 11, 2001
Subject: The events of this morning

Dearest Lesley,

Dear God in heaven, how can this be happening? Terrorists, madness, death and destruction. I hardly know what to write other than to assure you that I'm fine. The phones are useless and there's no way I can call you and no way you can call me. By some twist of fate, Leni Jo and Will managed to reach me and I'm grateful to have spoken briefly to my daughter. We wept together and were cut off after only a few minutes.

My heart is screaming at the horror that is taking place so close to my home. I cannot believe anything this terrible would happen — not here in New York, not in my town, my neighborhood. Not to us as a nation. I am in shock, in pain and in mourning. I don't think any American will ever be the same again. How can we be? How will we ever recover from such evil? I have no answers, only questions. Everything that seemed so important only a few days ago is irrelevent now.

I can't donate blood, but I'll do whatever I can.

God bless America, the land of the free and the home of the brave.

Jillian

2002

Lesley Milton

From: JillianGordon@friendsnetwrk.com
To: LesleyMilton@friendsnetwrk.com
Sent: January 15, 2002
Subject: Sick To Death

Lesley,

I've put up as much of a fight as I could, but I'm sick to death of all this and want it to end. My medical team wants me to undergo a third series of treatments. I can't do it. These last sixteen months have been terrible. The cure is worse than the disease. What can cancer do to me that the physicians haven't already done? I've been poked, pinched, prodded. I've endured all I can. Don't bother to argue with me. It's too late. I told them "no more."

Do you remember when Monty asked the doctors to cease all treatment and let him die? I pleaded with him, begged him to change his mind and fight as long as he could. He so rarely denied me anything, but he did that time. He asked to die with dignity. I understand now. How very well I understand.

I can't do this any longer. I can't sit in another

waiting room, can't endure another day of this. I can't tolerate looking at myself emaciated and hairless. I can't stand the exhaustion or the nausea. I turn 54 today and I feel like 104.

After this last bout, I'm weary of the battle. The white flag is up. This soldier has laid down her weapon and surrender is imminent.

Don't be angry with me, Les, I'm just sick to death of being sick to death. As always, Gary has been wonderful, but I'm an emotional drain on him and I know it. It's been sixteen hellish months for both of us. I can't continue to put him through this — him or me. I want out!

Jillian Gordon

From: LesleyMilton@friendsnetwrk.com
To: JillianGordon@friendsnetwrk.com
Sent: January 15, 2002
Subject: Happy Birthday!!!!

Dearest Jillian,

No! I can't, I won't let you give up. You're my dearest and best friend and I refuse to let you die at 54. You of all people know how stubborn I can get.

I should've been there before now. I should've known. This does it, and Steven agrees. My bags are already packed and Steven is buying me a plane ticket as we speak. I'm flying out tomorrow to be with you and I'm not leaving until you kick me out the door.

Do you remember when we were in Latin class and I just couldn't seem to get the hang of those verbs? When it came to biology and chemistry, I was a whiz, but Latin was about to do me in. I wanted to give up and accept a C, but you refused to let me. For hours you drilled me, until I knew those verb conjugations as well as my own name. My dear, this is Latin class all over again, only this time I'm the one who's going to stand by you.

We're in this together. Cancer might have worn you down, but I'll be there by your side, my arm around you. This is one monster we're going to face together! Gary on one side and me on the other. As you said, you've been poked, pinched and prodded, and now you're about to be pampered.

I should've come sooner, should have realized you needed me, but I know it now and I'm on my way.

Mr. and Mrs. William Chadsworth
112 Waterbury Street
London, England

January 15, 2002

Dearest Mom,

Happy Birthday! Will and I have some wonderful news we've been saving for your birthday. We're going to make you a grandma. That's right, I'm pregnant. Oh Mom, you can't imagine how excited Will is. Was Daddy like this when you told him you were pregnant with me? The way Will's treating me, it's as though I'm the only woman in the world who's ever managed such a feat.

The baby is due the last week of August. You'll be able to come to England, won't you? I hate it that you've been so sick lately. You try to hide how dreadful this time has been, but I can read between the lines. Will and I hope that your first grandchild will give you something to look forward to.

We both love you very much. Oh Mom, I don't think I've ever been so happy or so in love.

Enjoy your gifts, book your ticket for August now and have a wonderful, wonderful birthday.

Will and Leni Jo

JILLIAN LAWTON GORDON
331 WEST END AVENUE
APARTMENT 1020
NEW YORK, NY 10023

Riverside Clinic
258 West 81st St.
New York, NY 10024

Attention: Dr. Louise Novack

Dear Louise,

A note to apologize for my behavior during my last appointment on December 30th. I hope you can forgive my negative attitude. You're right, cancer has its positive aspect in all the lessons it can teach us about ourselves.

In the past few weeks I've reconsidered and have decided to accept the next bout of treatments. It seems I'm to become a grandmother for the first time – and I have a very stubborn friend who insists on staying by my side. With this kind of incentive and support, I feel I must agree to these treatments.

Thank you for your patience with me.

Sincerely,

Jillian Lawton Gordon

March 1, 2002

Jillian,

A note on your pillow to tell you that you're the bravest person I know.

Lesley

March 2, 2002

Lesley,

A note on your pillow to let you know you're the craziest, funniest, most wonderful friend anyone has ever had. I can't believe you shaved your hair off for me so we could be twins! Are you nuts??! Yes — and I love it. Thank you for being my best friend.

Jillian

JILLIAN LAWTON GORDON
331 WEST END AVENUE
APARTMENT 1020
NEW YORK, NY 10023

July 3, 2002

Dearest Lesley,

I have wonderful news! The latest blood work

shows that my platelet count is back to normal – and that's the first time in almost two years. I won't officially be in remission for a while, but it looks encouraging. Just a few months ago, I was willing to suspend all treatment, and you wouldn't let me. I literally owe you my life.

I have another bit of news. Gary was by earlier this morning and he surprised me by announcing that he's purchased a condominium in Boca Raton, Florida. He has family there and plans to move within the next couple of months. He asked me to marry him, which he's done periodically over the years. He wants to teach me golf and take me sailing. He says the only reason he's stayed in New York is me and frankly, he's tired of waiting. It's now or never.

I already know what you're going to say. Marry him. I'd be a fool not to. Perhaps you're right, but I can't imagine leaving New York after all these years. Especially now, when the city needs support from the people who love it.

Gary loves me, I know he does, and here's the real surprise. I love him, too. I never thought that what we shared would extend beyond friendship. I was so crazy about Nick and then Monty, I didn't think it was in me to feel this intensely about another man.

I can already hear your next question. Why am I hesitating? Lesley, I don't know. Am I so settled in my ways that I can't deal with change? Am I a complete idiot? I just don't know. I can't bear the thought of losing Gary, and at the same time, I'm not sure another marriage is right for me, either.

If you have any pearls of wisdom to share, I'd greatly appreciate hearing them.

Love,
Jillian

Mr. and Mrs. William Chadsworth
112 Waterbury Street
London, England

July 15, 2002

Dearest Mom,

If you don't marry him, I swear I'll never speak to you again! All right, I will, but I'd forever think you a fool. Gary is the best thing to happen to you in years.

Enclosed is the latest ultrasound of your grandson. Isn't he perfect? Will is walking on air. Blue is such a lovely color, isn't it?

What do you think of the name Charles Leonard Chadsworth? It has a nice sound, don't you think? I can hardly wait to see you. It shouldn't be long now.

Love,
Will and Leni Jo

JILLIAN LAWTON GORDON
331 WEST END AVENUE
APARTMENT 1020
NEW YORK, NY 10023

July 29, 2002

Dear Gary,

It hasn't even been a month but I miss you so much. A dozen times I've started to call you – and then remembered you're not at that number anymore. You no longer live in New York.

I don't blame you for growing impatient with me. I can be a stubborn fool (as my daughter and my best friend have taken pains to point out). For the first two weeks, I waited for you to come to your senses and realize we belong together. It wasn't until this morning that I saw I was the one being unreasonable.

All right, Gary, I'll marry you, but I don't know if I can live in Boca Raton all year. Can we compromise? Can we divide our time between there and New York?

I feel I should warn you, my love, that there are no guarantees with regard to my cancer. It could return. It already has once, as you're well aware. But then you're not looking for guarantees, are you? You want a wife. We're both young enough to travel and for my part I intend to make frequent trips to London. Charles is going to know his grandma very well indeed.

I love you.

Jillian

Lesley Milton

From: JillianGordon@friendsnetwrk.com
To: LesleyMilton@friendsnetwrk.com
Sent: August 16, 2002
Subject: Cancer Walk

Dearest Lesley,

Now that Gary and I are married, I don't know why I held out for so long!

We delayed our trip to England until after the Cancer Walk this October; in fact, we've arranged our schedule around it. When I wrote you about the Walk, I was hoping you and Steven would be willing to sponsor me. I'm working hard at getting pledges from family and friends. What I didn't expect was your refusal. I have to tell you that took me aback, I quickly figured out what you're up to. You're flying out here and doing the Walk with me, aren't you? I love it! I couldn't be more excited or pleased. It's perfect. I'd never have survived this long journey without your love and friendship, and I'm not just talking about the cancer. You're the type of friend who divides my grief and doubles my joy. How I treasure you and all the years we've shared.

Come anytime — the welcome mat is out. Gary and Steven can play chess in Central Park while you and I join thousands of other women who are cancer survivors.

The fact is, we've survived so much more and are the stronger for it. This is the best time of my life. I'm happy, Les, really happy – despite the sorrows I've experienced, with Nick's death and Monty's, with the devastating attack on New York, with my own illness. Or maybe because of all that. Grief makes us understand what truly matters in life, doesn't it? Love, friendship, family. Being part of a community – and I've come to consider myself a New Yorker through and through. Memories . . . You and I have so many, and I hope we'll be granted the time to make lots more.

I can't wait to see you.

Love,

Jillian

The employees of Thorndike Press hope you have enjoyed this Large Print book. All our Thorndike and Wheeler Large Print titles are designed for easy reading, and all our books are made to last. Other Thorndike Press Large Print books are available at your library, through selected bookstores, or directly from us.

For information about titles, please call:

(800) 223-1244

or visit our Web site at:

www.gale.com/thorndike
www.gale.com/wheeler

To share your comments, please write:

Publisher
Thorndike Press
295 Kennedy Memorial Drive
Waterville, ME 04901